VELS

Dead Matter

"Strout's . . . great sense of humor, combined with vivid characters, a complex mystery, and plenty of danger, makes for a fantastic read. Urban fantasy fans should not miss this exciting series."

—SciFiChick.com

"Strout's good-hearted, bat-carrying hero is once again faced with extraordinary peril from both bureaucratic paperwork and things that go bump in the night. His skillful blending of the creepy and the wacky gives his series an original appeal. Don't miss out!"

—*RT Book Reviews* (top pick)

"Unusual urban fantasy . . . highly entertaining."

—*Romance Reviews Today*

Deader Still

"Such a fast-paced, engaging, entertaining book that the pages seemed to fly by far too quickly. Take the New York of *Men in Black* and *Ghostbusters*, inject the same pop-culture awareness and irreverence of *Buffy the Vampire Slayer* or *The Middleman*, toss in a little *Thomas Crown Affair*, shake and stir, and you've got something fairly close to this book." —*The Green Man Review*

"It has a *Men in Black* flavor mixed with *NYPD Blue*'s more gritty realism . . . if you think of the detectives as working the night shift in *The Twilight Zone*. It's a book (and a protagonist) that is going places, and those who enjoy something fresh in urban fantasy will enjoy what they find. Strongly recommended." —*SFRevu*

"A refreshing, exciting urban fantasy with elements of romance and horror that will appeal to fans of Jim Butcher."

—*The Best Reviews*

continued . . .

BOOK ONE OF
The Spellmason Chronicles

Alchemystic

ANTON STROUT

ACE BOOKS, NEW YORK

THE BERKLEY PUBLISHING GROUP
Published by the Penguin Group
Penguin Group (USA) Inc.
375 Hudson Street, New York, New York 10014, USA

Penguin Group (Canada), 90 Eglinton Avenue East, Suite 700, Toronto, Ontario M4P 2Y3, Canada (a division of Pearson Penguin Canada Inc.) • Penguin Books Ltd., 80 Strand, London WC2R 0RL, England • Penguin Group Ireland, 25 St. Stephen's Green, Dublin 2, Ireland (a division of Penguin Books Ltd.) • Penguin Group (Australia), 250 Camberwell Road, Camberwell, Victoria 3124, Australia (a division of Pearson Australia Group Pty. Ltd.) • Penguin Books India Pvt. Ltd., 11 Community Centre, Panchsheel Park, New Delhi—110 017, India • Penguin Group (NZ), 67 Apollo Drive, Rosedale, Auckland 0632, New Zealand (a division of Pearson New Zealand Ltd.) • Penguin Books (South Africa) (Pty.) Ltd., 24 Sturdee Avenue, Rosebank, Johannesburg 2196, South Africa

Penguin Books Ltd., Registered Offices: 80 Strand, London WC2R 0RL, England

This is a work of fiction. Names, characters, places, and incidents either are the product of the author's imagination or are used fictitiously, and any resemblance to actual persons, living or dead, business establishments, events, or locales is entirely coincidental. The publisher does not have any control over and does not assume any responsibility for author or third-party websites or their content.

ALCHEMYSTIC

An Ace Book / published by arrangement with the author

PUBLISHING HISTORY
Ace mass-market edition / October 2012

Copyright © 2012 by Anton Strout.
Cover art by Blake Morrow.
Cover design by Diana Kolsky.
Back cover and spine texture © Allgusak/Shutterstock.
Interior text design by Tiffany Estreicher.

ISBN: 978-1-937007-79-9

ACE
Ace Books are published by The Berkley Publishing Group,
a division of Penguin Group (USA) Inc.,
375 Hudson Street, New York, New York 10014.
ACE and the "A" design are trademarks of Penguin Group (USA) Inc.

PRINTED IN THE UNITED STATES OF AMERICA

10 9 8 7 6 5 4 3

ALWAYS LEARNING　　　　　　　　　　　　　　**PEARSON**

This one's for you, you greedy-eyed little reader, you

Acknowledgments

———— ☽ ————

Welcome, dear friends, to the first book of the Spellmason Chronicles. You don't know the strange, interesting people and creatures within this tome yet, but they've been dying (or undying) to meet you for quite some time. So come on in and let us enter the sacred communal weave of storyteller to storytellee.

Speaking (or writing, rather) of strange and interesting people and creatures . . . this series would not exist or be half as pretty as it is without the many fine people who have had a hand in bringing it from my brain meat to yours, including: everyone at Penguin Group, most notably the winged furies who inhabit the digital and paperback sales department; my editor, Jessica Wade, righter of writer wrongs (Don't she clean me up nice?); production editor Michelle Kasper, assistant production editor Jamie Snider, and copy editor Valle Hansen; Judith Murello, Diana Kolsky, and Blake Morrow for a gorgeously creepy cover; Erica Martirano and her crack team of ad/promo people; my publicist, Rosanne Romanello, and all of the publicity department, who parade me out from time to time to interact with the public; my agent, Kristine Dahl, and Laura Neely at ICM, who take care of all the nonwriting details that would drive me mad (well, madder, anyway); the League of Reluctant Adults for continued support and stocking of the bar; Lisa Trevethan for introducing me to the word *Alchemystic* thanks to her knowledge of the band with the same name; my family, near and far; and last but certainly not least, the ever-elusive Orlycorn, who puts up with long hours of me ignoring her while bringing these books to you. She has the patience of a saint and my undying love. Oh, and you, too, dear owner of this book. You didn't think I'd forget you now, did you?

Now, let's see what trouble we can get into this time, shall we?

As a means of contrast with the sublime, the grotesque is, in our view, the richest source that nature can offer art.

—VICTOR HUGO

One

☾

Stanis

Waking was easy. Something primal in the night sky called out to me like a banshee at the witching hour. When was the last time I had even encountered one of them? I wondered. I could not recall that . . . or much of anything. But that was always the way of waking, I remembered. The lingering disorientation of dreaming held its sway for a moment longer before slipping from my grasp like leaves on the wind. The haunting, faintly familiar face that had been the focus of the dreams faded. *Stanis,* the figure said, and nothing more. I fought to hold the image—that of a pale gentleman with wild black tangles of hair and kind blue eyes.

Had the hair always been black? I was not sure. Frozen fragments of my broken memories made me swear I recalled this exact same figure with a full head of gray as well, but already I could feel something in my mind pushing those thoughts aside as the routine of waking took over.

I stretched, every muscle in my form crying out with pure joy. As I relaxed my body, an intense itch flared down two long sections of my back. *My wings,* I remembered. *Of course.* I looked over my shoulder to find the giant stone wings like those of a bat curled close to my back. I worked the muscles along my shoulder blades, the heavy wings extending, flexing out for a moment to relieve the itch they had called forth upon my waking, both pleasure and pain in the gesture.

A hunger awoke in my chest, but I forced myself to ignore it for the moment. It would win—as it always did—but for now I fought it off as my hearing focused in on the sounds of the city rising up all around me. The occasional bleat of traffic down below sounded out, much like the sheep I remembered that used to roam the vast fields that had once occupied this island.

Manhattan, I recalled. Long ago, the whole island had looked more like the tiny park in front of the building where I had awoken, the one the humans called *Gramercy.*

A cool wind blew through the green leaves of the trees in it—had they not *just* been bare?

Was the word *Manhattan* even right, either? I was not sure and forced myself to concentrate through my still-lingering confusion of thoughts. I looked at the towers of glass and light rising up around me, hoping for familiarity and glad when I discerned a few that kept their long-standing forms, still unchanged in this modern world.

The tallest of the skyline's towers still stood off to the north of my rooftop, its lone spire illuminated in bright lights—this time red, blue, and white. Sometime in the near future the sky itself would light up in colorful explosive bursts, the humans celebrating, cheering . . . but surely it was not already that time of year again? I did not understand the ritual, but it was something I used to mark the passing of the years.

I turned from the building and its light, looking south now. In recent times, the skyline had changed a great deal that way. Two of its other great towers had stood there, once the highest and most majestic points on that horizon, but now there was nothing where I remembered those structures to have been, which only added to my sense of disorientation.

Before I could wonder too long whether I was mistaken in my thoughts, that gnawing hunger rose in my chest again, a burning need to *do*. What, though, I still was not quite sure. It picked away at me like a hammer at stone until I could ignore it no longer. The itching sensation between my shoulders rejoined it and I gave in to the pull of it all. Looking back over my shoulder, I watched my stone wings unfurl from against my body once more, stretching twice as wide as I stood tall. The itch died as I worked them, retracting the wings close to my body and then extending them to their fullest over and over.

My mind began to clear. All of the sensations rose to the center of my thoughts, a strong and unrecalled memory forcing itself forward—one of the rules.

Protect.

With wings extended, I leapt off my perch along the edge of the roof I called home, my body dropping into the night sky. As I tumbled down toward the park, my wings recalled memories of flight, lifting me before I struck the street full of traffic below. I set off, heading north, the red, blue, and white lights of the tallest tower a flaming beacon of orientation, all other thoughts leaving me as that one word once again consumed all other thoughts, burning them away.

Protect.

But just what I was meant to protect, I was unsure.

I flew.

Two

☾

Alexandra

Punching clay felt a *lot* more satisfying than any sexy-time *Ghost*-pottery-wheel-spinning nonsense ever could. Each strike released my anger, my balled-up fists sinking rewardingly into the unfinished statue's form, the clay still too soft to actually do any damage to my fingers or wrists. In my twenty-two years, I hadn't been violent by nature; nor had I ever spent my time punching much of anything, but in the moment, rage held its sway over me and I couldn't stop myself.

I pulled my hands free, flecks of clay flying and sticking into my long black hair. Normally I'd have already tied it up while working in our old unused Belarus family art studio on the seventh floor. But then again, normally, someone—namely my brother—wouldn't have dressed my latest attempt at a Gothic-inspired statue so it was wearing a basketball jersey and mirrored sunglasses, one of its now-deformed hands wrapped around a can of Pabst Blue Ribbon. As a final comment on my artistry, a half-smoked cigarette hung from its mouth, along with ten more discarded butts adorning the top of its head in an attempt at a Statue of Liberty–type crown.

A sound from somewhere up above the art studio, on the roof of the building itself, snapped me out of my red rage, making me step back from my now-even-worse-looking statue-in-progress. Whatever potential I had seen in it was now lost, its form pummeled and twisted like something Salvador Dalí would have envisioned. I let out a long sigh and wiped my now-gray hands down the front of the overalls I preferred to wear in the art space. They weren't exactly flattering, but function won out over fashion in my book, some of the clay getting on the straps of the black tank top I wore underneath them. My whole ensemble was coated in enough clay, it was most likely trash-bound anyway.

I walked across the large open floor of my family's building, out of my great-great-grandfather's art space with its dozens of historic pieces and hundreds of puzzle boxes, past his rows and rows of private library collection before sidestepping around one of the many mid-nineteenth century sofas there.

Having heard the sounds on the roof, which I was sure meant my brother, Devon, was up there, I threw open the door leading out to the small terrace just below it, walked out, and turned to face it as I stared up into the night sky.

"Hey, asshole!" I shouted. "Get the hell down here, right now!"

No response. Typical Devon. I stormed back in, leaving the July air to pour into the building, which was musty enough to need a good airing out every once in a while anyway. I went back over to the art studio, heading for the table I had left my shoulder bag on. I tore it open with such a fury I shocked myself, worried for a moment that I had ruined it. That thought riled me even more, to the point that by the time I found my phone, my hands were shaking.

I clicked on "Devon," then waited for it to dial through, my eyes panning the room as I stood there. Part of me was already secretly glad I had destroyed my work. Compared to everything else around the art studio—here thanks to the long-lost talents and skills of my great-great-grandfather Alexander Belarus—mine was a pale imitation.

"Yeah?" my brother's voice barked into the phone, causing me to jump. Short. Curt. So very Devon.

"Get down from the roof," I said. "Now!"

His usual heavy sigh came through the phone. "Lexi, what are you rambling on about now? I'm not even home. I'm waiting on a meeting."

I pulled my phone away from my face and checked the time. "At this time of night? It's nearly eleven!"

"Listen," he said. "Sometimes you're dealing with contractors, unions, architects, zoning, permits . . . and that shit waits for no man. Got it? You take the meetings when they come. C'mon, I realize you have no grasp of the family business—"

"Nor do I *have* to," I said. "That's what they have you for. I have zero interest in real estate development."

"Aww," my brother mocked. "I thought you were all about family and the Belarus legacy, Lex."

"Moving property and writing contracts are *not* the Belarus legacy," I said. "It's the actual art and architecture that our great-great-grandfather crafted for this city. You'd know that if you actually opened a book in our family library or just looked for once at one of his pieces of art here. Speaking of which . . ."

Devon chuckled. "Hey, you *just* said you wanted me to spend more time in the art studio, right?"

"Not *defacing* my art," I said. "I would appreciate it if you'd keep your hands off of my work."

"That's not work," he said. "Dressing up, learning the family business . . . *That's* work."

"Firstborn son gets all those perks," I said. "Not me." I had never even been on our father's radar for that type of stuff. Devon was the favored scion. Truthfully, I didn't care about all the construction and landlording . . . and Devon knew it, this not being the first time our differences on honoring the family's name had put us at odds. "Our true legacy, I have always and still believe, lies in the beauty of the buildings our great-great-grandfather designed, Devon. My work as a sculptor is the best way I know how to pay homage to that. You, *dear* brother, don't care about design or craftsmanship. You care about cold, hard cash."

"You should take an interest in the family business," he said, his voice dark now, his business tone.

I laughed into the phone. "Are we the mob now, Devon?"

"Carving pretty things isn't where the money is," he said. "That's why I did what I did to your precious statue—to prove my point. That stuff's not important for the Belarus name. It's land. It's property. Jesus, Lexi, do you have any idea how this company runs? This is about land in Manhattan, about who controls it, and who can earn off it. No one cares who designed the buildings."

"Half this city owes Alexander Belarus a debt of grati-tude!" I shouted.

"Fine, Lex, I'll build him a museum. We'll put all his stuff behind glass, charge admission. Then we might make some money. You'd be happy. I'd be happy. Everybody wins. Will that suffice?"

"Not really," I said, unable to let go of my anger, my short nails digging into the palm of my free hand. "You'd probably just screw up everything in the museum like you did here in the studio."

"Give me a break, will you?" he fired back. "There are bigger things out there than all that playing around you do."

"If history and art are playing around," I said, "then so be it."

"It wouldn't hurt you to learn the family business, Lexi," he said, short. "I have to go. Meeting time."

"And it wouldn't hurt you to be a better brother," I said. "Stay away from my stuff, Devon. We're not kids anymore. I feel stupid even having to say it." Tears of frustration began to pour, and before he could get in the last word as he always had to, I ended the call, slamming my phone down onto the soft leather of my bag. I ran into the library, opting for the comfort of one of the more shadowy sofas as far from the lights of the art studio as possible. The quiet darkness calmed me a little, but thinking about the ruined statue kept nagging at me.

I didn't know how long I had been sitting there—minutes, maybe a half hour—when another sound caught my attention, this time coming from the terrace outside the set of double doors off across the far end of the floor. Footsteps. I snapped out of my funk and wiped my tears away as best I could.

A small ray of happiness welled up in me as the sight of my favorite short-haired blonde appeared at the French doors, now sporting fresh bangs that sat just above her black horn-rimmed glasses. Her dancer's bag was thrown across her body from one shoulder to the opposite hip, and she twirled around in perfect form once through the doors.

"You going to air-condition all of Manhattan now?" Aurora Torres asked, pulling the doors shut.

"Maybe, Rory," I said. "I thought your apartment all the way down in the Village could use it, what with your thermostat issues."

Rory started across the room toward me. "Appreciate it. Our air conditioner *still* isn't working. Marshall dropped it off to get fixed, but the guy is giving us the runaround. If it doesn't get fixed by the Fourth, I'll leave it to Marshall to set off his own fireworks. He's used to battle, after all, what with running Roll for Initiative."

I laughed. "See? Something good came from looking for a roommate on Craigslist."

She nodded. "It's amazing how Marshall spending all his college savings on his tabletop-and-role-playing-game hobby-turned-business can keep him going," Rory said. "Plus it gives me endless things to tease him about. But conflict seems to be part of his day-to-day. They do a lot of 'war gaming,' or so he tells me. I don't get any of it."

"Let your roommate fight the battles," I said. "Nice."

She stopped in front of my sofa, pulling her evidently heavy bag off her shoulder and shaking it at me. "Like I've got time between my course load and dance rehearsals for my MFA program."

"Your program is already one of the toughest in the city," I said. "Which normally has you a little frantic anyway. I thought summers were for lightening all that."

"Not when you take a summer intensive," she said. "And it is intensive, overachiever that I am. Then there's the workout of climbing up your fire escape to avoid the rest of the Belarus clan. My body *hurts*." She put the bag down, bending with it, and that was when she noticed my face. "What's wrong?"

I wiped the tears from my eyes with the back of my clay-flecked forearm, avoiding the bits of it stuck there. "Three guesses," I said.

"Douglas Belarus," she said, then tapped the side of her head like she was thinking. "He's worried that his daughter doesn't spend enough time getting holy and taking to the knee at Our Sister of Perpetual Bowing and Scraping."

I laughed despite my tears at the truth of it, snorting through my now-running nose. "Wrong, although I'm sure he'd love it if I did join him more often. Love the parental dad unit, but not really looking to get my church on that many times a week."

"Okay, then," she said. "Juliana Belarus, then, caring mother but also a quiet mouse when it comes to who wears the pants in the family."

I shook my head. "Strike two."

"Ah," Rory said, dropping onto the sofa next to me. She threw her arm around my shoulder and squeezed, her deceptively thin frame still well muscled enough to make it hurt a little. "Big brother strikes again. What did he do *this* time, as we continue on into the third decade of the Sibling Cold War?"

I pointed over to the art studio side of the floor. Rory's eyes caught sight of my former masterpiece and let out a low, slow whistle.

"Wow," she said. "Made your art his own personal punching bag, I see."

My face went flush with embarrassment, but I couldn't help but let a small laugh escape my lips. "Actually . . . that part was me."

"Really, now?" Rory stood and walked over to the area, circling the table the tall slab of half-molded clay sat on. "I'm impressed, Lexi. You been working out? Maybe I can make a dancer out of you yet. You did some serious damage here."

"The punches are mine. All the rest is Devon, though."

"It's good you got out some of your aggression there, Lexi," she said, and I gave her a wary sidelong look. "I mean it! Look, I know he's family and all, but some people are just born mean-spirited. He's a natural-born asshole, my dear. Your reaction to his bullshit is *normal*."

I stood up, walking back toward the art studio. "I knew I picked cubby partners well back in third grade," I said. "Thanks."

Rory gave an elaborate flourish and a bow, each motion fluid and graceful.

My phone vibrated on my bag at the table next to her. Rory snatched it up and waved it for me to see. "Speak of the devil," she said.

"Give it," I said, but Rory held it away from me while it kept on ringing.

"No," she said. "I know you, Lexi. You're just going to be the one to be all apologetic and try to make nice, as usual. And it's not okay. The way he treats you borders on abuse. You have every right to be pissed. Say it."

"This is stupid," I said. "Just give me the phone."

"Say it," she repeated, unwavering. There was almost a pixieish glee in her eyes.

"Fine," I said, just wanting the phone at this point. "I have every right to be pissed."

Rory rolled her eyes. "*Mean* it."

Whether I was exasperated with her game or the fact that I just wanted my damn phone, I wasn't sure. I only know that it triggered something deep inside me that snapped. "I have every right to be pissed!" I shouted.

Rory jumped in surprise, then handed the phone over to me. "Excellent," she said. "Now have at him!"

I swiped my finger across the screen, lifted the phone to my head, and screamed into it. "Go screw yourself, Devon," I said. "Next time you see me, you'd better walk off in the opposite direction. For real."

A pronounced silence filled the line.

"Hey there, ass!" Rory shouted with a bit of a suppressed giggle to it, apparently loving the fury I was throwing at him.

A man's voice came on the line but it was not my brother. "Is this Lexi? Lexi Belarus?"

"Only my friends call me Lexi," I snapped, ignoring the stranger's butchering of my last name. It came out *Bell La Roose*, reminding me of the childhood jibes of *Bella Moose*, not at all sounding like *Bell Air Us*. That didn't bother me so much. I was more upset at him using the familiar version of my first name. "Which one of Devon's friends is this? You can go screw yourself, too."

"Sorry," the man said. "That's the only name that the phone shows."

"Who the hell *is* this?"

"This is Officer Michael Lawrence of the NYPD. May I ask how you are related to Devon?"

"I'm his *sister*," I said, my anger mixing with growing curiosity.

"We found this phone lying on the street, and you're the last incoming call listed. I think you should know that there's a distinct possibility your brother may be in trouble."

"Trouble *how*, exactly?"

"Do you have any association with a building on St. Mark's Place?"

I had to stop and think for a moment. "I think so," I said, my blood running cold. "That's one of my family's properties. We're in real estate."

"I regret to inform you that there's been an accident."

"What . . . kind of accident?" I went to lean back against one of the drafting tables in the studio, but missed it completely. Rory caught me and didn't let go, especially since I had just said the word *accident*.

"A building collapse, miss," the officer said. "Your family's building."

"That can't be true," I said, feeling all the emotions of the past few minutes drain away, a little more every second. "I just spoke to him . . . maybe half an hour ago . . . ? You're mistaken."

"I wish I were, miss," the man said. "But it is unlikely."

"Maybe he wasn't there," I said, panic filling my chest, the beat of my heart rising up into my throat. "Maybe he got out. That's why you were able to find his phone."

"Was he wearing a ring with a dark green stone in it on his left hand?"

"Yes," I said, clutching at the similar one hanging around

my own neck from an old silver chain. "It's a family thing. There should be a crest of sorts carved into it, a sigil. Kind of looks like bat wings surrounded by an octagon, stylized *B* on it."

"Yes, miss, I see it," he said. "Since you were the last person he talked to, we're going to need you to come down to the Ninth Precinct and identify his hand."

"Just his hand?" I asked, a nervous, hysterical laugh overtaking me.

"Holy hell," Rory whispered, then clamped her hands over her mouth.

"Jesus Christ," a man somewhere in the background on the other end of the line said. "Give me that goddamn thing. Hello?"

An older voice this time.

"Yes? What's going on?"

"I'm sorry about that, miss. My partner shouldn't have said that."

"Just tell me what is going on!" I said, shaking now. *"Why was he asking me about my brother's hand?"*

"Because," the older man said. "It's all we found. It was still holding the phone."

Three

Alexandra

When you have your own catacombs—in the basement of your family's building, no less—having a funeral is a relatively quick and painless affair. Painless, I suppose, except for grief caused by the tons of bricks that had crushed my brother. Still, as I stood down there on the upper of the two levels among family and friends to bury Devon, I found just being in the space comforting, a welcome escape from the last few weeks. Ornately carved Gothic pillars rose up high above, the aisles full of stone tombs and markers where our ancestors had lain buried for well over a century, all of it dimly lit by the addition of subtle modern lighting that set a somber subterranean tone for the catacombs, keeping the solemn nature of the space intact.

Before the place had filled I had taken a moment alone to thread my brother's ring with the family sigil on it onto a chain and left it hanging off the top of his tomb, but with the crowd down here now, I could barely see the raised stone walls of it, let alone the ring itself. The space was packed, mostly with men who smelled a bit too much like cigars and cologne. Despite the fact that everyone around me was dressed up, I still felt like I hadn't so much come dressed for the occasion, but had instead stepped out of a Tim Burton movie in a long black dress covered in antique lace. It was courtesy of a short-lived period Rory and I spent in our youthful Goth phase, and I had my inability to get rid of anything to thank for it. I had been happy to find a single item other than overalls covered in clay and paint, anyway.

"You okay?" Rory asked in a whisper.

My best friend stood at my right shoulder, Marshall Blackmoore at my left. Both of them were dressed to the nines. Rory's hair was mostly hidden by the hat and short black veil she wore over her face, and I was surprised to see Marshall in a suit and tie. I hadn't known he owned something dressier than shirts with clever sayings, superheroes, or gaming references I didn't get on them. He put a hand awkwardly around my shoulder, but it was a welcome gesture. His kind brown eyes peeked out from under a mess of unkempt black hair, full of sincerity, so much so I wanted to cry, although at the moment I surprised myself by realizing I was slowly filling up with a building anger.

"Look at all these people," I said, keeping my voice low. We were standing far enough away from my mother and father, who were right up by the tomb itself, that they wouldn't hear, but I didn't want to draw any attention from the gathered crowd, either. "Did any of these vultures even *know* my brother?"

"Maybe," Rory said. "Your family has its fingers in a lot of pies. Delicious, real estate pies. And let's face it . . . you don't really know the business side of things all that well, Lexi, so of course they're all strangers to you."

"Why do I feel like *that's* all about to change?" I said, pushing down a sudden panic that rose in my throat just picturing myself faking my way through the family business. "God, I look horrible in pantsuits." I was trying to keep things light. Devon had been a first-degree asshole, but I was still stricken by his death, what it meant for our family. Quips helped me cope.

"Alexandra," Rory said, "I hardly think your clothing is what you should be fixating on right now."

I didn't like my emotions running the show and concentrated on my breathing instead. It was hard to have a panic attack if you could control your breathing. "Fine, then," I said as my heartbeat began to calm. "I'll fixate instead on being angry at all these strangers being here. Happy?"

"That's healthy," Marshall added in a whisper, giving her a thumbs-up. "Good work, Rory."

"It's not her fault," I said. "It's all me. Hell, I don't even have the right to be angry at them for their lack of sincerity. Who am I to judge *them*? I'm the person who wanted to kill him myself the night he actually passed away. I was *so* furious at him for messing up my stupid art project . . . which just sounds petty now."

"Hold on," Rory said. "Never forget. Your brother was an asshole, Lexi. Not to piss on the dead."

My heart hurt, but Rory was right. Still . . . "He was *my* asshole," I said, as if claiming some sort of ownership of him could somehow fix the conflicting feelings I was having over his passing.

The service going on closer to the tomb itself ended and the crowd began to break up. Men and women in expensive suits and dresses whom I didn't know started offering me their condolences, and all I could do was shake their hands and nod politely as I offered them a solemn thank-you. Eventually, my mother, my father, and the spiritual leader of his church would make their way over to me and my friends, but I didn't plan on being around for that. I wasn't sure I could take the churchier side of things an occasion like this was sure to bring out of my father.

"Let's go lower," I said to my friends after shaking hands with a particularly mothbally-smelling woman. I spun and headed off into the rest of the crypt far away from the ocean of businessmen and -women. "If I have to shake another hand, I'm going to start crying again."

I led Rory and Marshall back through the catacombs, the sound of the funeral fading off into the distance until it was no more than a faraway echo. Toward the rear of the upper floor of the catacombs a long, sloping staircase came into view and I brought us down it into an older section.

"I've never been to a funeral like this," Marshall said, looking around the space. "Like, ever. Then again, most of my friends don't have their own family crypt."

Rory laughed, but there was hesitance in it. "How come the older we get, the creepier this place gets? We used to tear through here playing. Then we got all teen and moody and started listening to the Cure down here. Now I just wish it were a regular basement."

"I miss my basement," Marshall added. "You don't really get them here in the city much."

I gave him a weak smile. "You miss it? Why? What was in *your* basement?"

"Most of my old gaming stuff," he said. "Rule books, miniatures, maps . . ."

"Wow," Rory said, slapping a hand over Marshall's mouth as we continued walking. "Just . . . wow."

"Yep," Marshall said with a mix of pride and shame once he pried her hand away. "I'm a poster child for alpha geeks everywhere."

"Alpha?" Rory asked. "Really? You're ranking yourself that high, are you, now?"

"I have to," he said, nodding. "Otherwise, I was just an only child playing Dungeons and Dragons alone down there, and that's just sad."

Rory went to speak, but then she stopped herself and the crypt went quiet once again. I really wished she had continued on, though. Their lightness made my heart less heavy.

"Not to be morose," Marshall said, turning to me, "but doesn't this place creep you out a little?"

"Why?" I said. "Sometimes I come down here for a little inspiration in my art."

"What's so inspirational?" Marshall asked, looking around with nervous eyes. "All it inspires in me is a healthy fear of zombies and bloodsuckers. No offense to Clan Belarus."

I waved it off. "None taken.

"Strange as it may sound," I said, "this place is comforting to me. This crypt is original to the building. Which means my great-great-grandfather planned this place out at the same time. It makes me feel very connected to it. With all his artistry and architecture sprinkled throughout Manhattan, it's just amazing to have some that's—I don't know—just ours."

"*He's* buried here, too?" Marshall asked.

Rory gave him a look of disapproval through her veil.

"What?" he asked. "I've never been down here. We always hang out up in the art studio and library."

"*His* library," Rory said. "Everything about this place is his, so yeah, he's buried here."

"Generations of us are," I said, moving off into the dim lights farther back among the older tombs. I came upon the marker farthest back on this lower level, that of Alexander Belarus, my namesake. The carving of the figure on top of the sarcophagus was exquisite, a likeness I could only imagine was close to the way he actually looked when alive, covered in carved stonework with adornments all over it. Seeing the gemstone sigil set into the stone at the center of the figure had my fingers going to the similar one I wore around my neck.

"Uncanny," Marshall said, looking from the figure carved on the tomb to me. "I see the resemblance. Although, truth be told, I like *your* hair more. The black, wavy shoulder length looks better on you."

"Less stony, too," Rory added.

I laughed out loud, finding the sound refreshing in the empty echoes down here in the family crypt.

"Thanks, guys," I said, leaning against one of the pillars, wrapping my arms around myself. "You somehow made this all a bit more bearable."

"Absolutely," Rory said, coming over and hugging me close. "It's the least a best friend could do."

Marshall came over and hugged me as awkwardly as only he could. "I know I'm relatively new to your guys' life and all, but I'm glad to be here, too."

After the hug lingered on for a bit, Rory finally put a hand on both our shoulders, pushing the three of us apart. "No hitting on the grieving," she said. "Got it?"

Marshall's face went beet red. "I—I wasn't. I mean . . . I'd never—"

"There you are," my father's voice called out from somewhere farther forward in the crypt, the hint of his Slavic accent in his words, even though he was third generation and born here. "I thought I might find you down here." He approached us, his balding head sweating. He dabbed it with a handkerchief held in one of his meaty hands, then gave a nod to Marshall and a firm smile to Rory. "Aurora, thank you for coming. God bless and keep you."

Despite the solemn occasion, Marshall couldn't help but snicker at the use of her proper name.

"Marsh!" Rory snipped. "What are the rules?"

He fought back his smile by coughing into his hand. "No laughing at your full name," he said. "*Aurora*. Sorry. Rory." Composed once again, he turned to my father. "Sorry, Mr. Belarus. I don't mean any disrespect. I just get nervous laughter when it's most inappropriate."

There was a sadness in my father's eyes, but he managed a kind smile. "Dark times could use a little lightness," he said, then turned to Rory. "Aurora is a fine name." He clapped her on both shoulders. "Your boyfriend should call you that more often."

Rory's face went pale. "Marshall's *not* my boyfriend."

My father turned to me, his eyes narrowing. "Hey! He's not my boyfriend, either," I said, quick as I could. "I've only known him as long as Rory's been going to the Manhattan Conservatory of Dance!"

"No, no," Marshall said, feigning disinterest. "Please don't all jump at a chance to date me at once, ladies. My dance card is pretty full."

This seemed good enough to satisfy my father that Marshall was no threat, and he turned back to Rory. "Again, thank you so very much for coming," he said, softer once again, "but I must steal my daughter away from you."

I stiffened. "You need me *now*?" I asked. "Don't you have, like, a million people up there who want to talk to you?"

"Yes," he said, all pleasantries falling from his voice as he turned to me, somber. "That is why I need you, Alexandra. There are people you *must* come meet."

My stomach clenched up at the underlying implications of it all—that now that Devon was gone, I would have to take his place. "Dad, I'm really not feeling it. You know I'd do anything for you. But are you sure it's the best time for a meet-and-greet right now?"

"Alexandra," he snapped, his voice raised. Marshall jumped. My name echoed over and over through the silence of the lower catacombs. "It is *not* a request. Come."

His words struck my soul. I looked to my friends, but they were too stunned. My father turned and walked off without another word, not bothering to excuse himself from Rory and Marshall's presence.

A chill ran down my spine. I thought it must have been my father's words and his tone, but it felt like more than just that. The catacombs seemed alive despite the heavy air of death that permeated it. The carved faces on the tombs seemed to follow me with their stares, as well as those of the blank-eyed gargoyles lining the tops of the support columns. The occasion itself and my father's sudden harshness put such a creeped-out mood over me that I found myself startled, swearing I saw a movement among the gargoyles. Not wanting to come off crazy to my friends, I told myself it was all an illusion caused by the stress of the day.

Despite rationalizing it to myself, I stopped looking up or around and fell in behind my father, trading my creepy-crawly sensation for hating the idea of what was coming instead. He wanted me to meet his suits, his businesspeople. I had thought burying my brother would be the worst of it today, but between being dragged before my father's colleagues and my guilt over the last words Devon and I had exchanged, I didn't think there was much of a chance of any part of my day improving. At least my father hadn't brought his spiritual adviser down here with him. That was a small comfort in an otherwise uncomfortable day.

Four

Alexandra

"Rules, Miss Belarus," the Tribeca Y's artist-in-residence said from behind his oversized and over-cluttered desk at the front of the large, open art space. "You must learn to use rules if you are ever going to pretend to create art here. Others would have gladly paid for the privilege of attending this series of events. Do you realize this?"

My ears burned at his words. Even though it had been four months since I had done a damn thing artistic—since Devon's death, really—I wasn't new to art, either, even if the shitty sketch on my easel suggested otherwise. It was a mystery how this supposedly legendary sixties artiste had already reached the same level of persistent annoyance of me that had taken the dearly departed Devon Belarus decades to cultivate, but there it was all the same.

I stared at my charcoal sketch on the easel before me. Lines, squiggles, nothing coherent yet, but after four months of not a lick of artwork produced by me, it was something, wasn't it? Before Devon died, I was working as a part-time barista at this creepy-cool coffee shop in the East Village called the Lovecraft Café, planning to save enough self-earned money to move to my own apartment. Now that he was gone, my mother was so fragile, I felt I couldn't leave . . . and my father was insistent that I learn the real estate business. My creativity had dried up, and Rory had sweetly signed me up for this art night class to try to get it flowing again.

The fact I was being called out on "not doing art right" only filled me with a growing frustration. I tossed my half of a charcoal stick down into the easel's tray with some force. "But," I countered. "I'm experimenting, going free-form, letting my heart go with it. Isn't art about expression of emotions, playing off the heart? Doesn't the concept of rules fight directly against the very soul of that?"

"No." He sighed, not even looking up from his art portfolio, which he was packing up. "It does not. Rules are the manacle by which art stretches on its chain to greatness."

I wasn't sure I bought that line of bull. I looked around the art space, where the mix of artsy devotees and bored Real Housewives looking for a hobby were all focusing on our discussion. "But—"

"The argument is pointless, Miss Belarus," he said with some bite to it, closing his portfolio and picking it up. "Art is not folly. Art is commitment, and that means establishing boundaries, meaning *rules*. I trust that is why you paid good money for this series of seminars. To learn something, yes?"

"I *didn't* pay for them," I said. "They were a gift."

"Then perhaps you should at least do the gifter the courtesy of showing up on time for them instead of fifteen minutes late," he said, and walked out of the studio, leaving the handful of students finishing up their own work with only me to stare at. I turned back to my easel. The disdain in his words cut deep and to the quick, but the artist in me—the one who wanted to commit the time—couldn't argue with him. I *had* been late, though I had worked very hard during the rest of the class. I hated the fact that yet another meeting to check over one of our family's renovation sites had been the cause of me rushing into the art seminar late tonight.

I couldn't let my anger go. Whether it was with myself or the professor, I really wasn't sure. Well, that wasn't true, now, was it? I was both tired and pissed at being dressed down by

him. I wanted to kick him in the teeth with my purple Docs—
my only remaining nod to my own fashion style—but I worried too much about the possibility of ruining the expensive
dark gray suit I wore with them. I let my mind wander off onto
that dark, gory tangent. Maybe the long white smock covering
most of my jacket and skirt would catch the blood—

Jesus. Perhaps Rory had been right in giving me this gift.
Maybe the real estate-ing day job *was* stressing me out more
than just a little bit.

I pushed the artist-in-residence out of my thoughts and
stared at my sketch on the easel before me. The rest of the
Y's art studio faded into the distance as I concentrated on the
mismatch of charcoal lines before me. I stared at them, hoping
they would resolve into something meaningful, but the longer
I stared, the less sense there seemed to be in them. I swore
under my breath, running my hands through my long, dark
curls of hair, not caring about the charcoal that coated the
tips of my fingers. They had left gray smudges all over the
Y-logoed smock, but I wasn't worried about my hair so much
as I was my sketch.

Fighting against my own artistic instincts, I gave up,
relaxed, and tried to focus on applying his damned rules.
Letting creativity be harnessed felt so counterintuitive to me
when my heart screamed that it *had* to be free-form, but for
now I forced myself to let go of that mentality.

I snatched up another stick of charcoal in my hand and
began adding strokes, focusing on the rules of perspective,
all lines leading off into one distant point on the horizon. My
mind opened as pieces of the world within the sketch began
to form. I smiled when I recognized what was unfolding—a
picture I must have remembered from one of my great-great-
grandfather's architectural sketchbooks up in the family
library.

Over time, the image resolved in front of me, the arch of
a church rooftop fading into the background as I continued.
In the foreground, I added a figure, the new lines forming a
twisted face and muscular body, all in stone, terrifying bat
wings rising up behind it. A gargoyle, like the one on top of

our very building, just one of many of the architectural details Alexander had been known for. My heart raced as the elements of it all came together, becoming clearer with each stroke. It was all starting to make some kind of sense, even though I was loath to admit that perhaps a little application of rules had been the right call. I was so lost in the drawing that I hadn't realized class was officially over.

"Hey, Lexi!" a familiar voice called out. I jumped, losing my concentration on my work and looking over to find Rory standing at the art studio's door, her short sometimes-blond hair now dyed Cookie Monster blue. Her striking eyes of a lighter version of that color were partly hidden behind her black-rimmed cat's-eye glasses, but they showed concern. At her side stood Marshall in all his tallness and sporting an *Avengers* T-shirt, black scruffy hair and a similar look of concern in his brown, gentle eyes.

"Hey, guys," I said.

Rory started over, her five-inch Frankenstein boots clopping loudly across the art studio floor, before stopping and looking me up and down.

"Nice suit," she said. "The white coat makes you look a bit Muppet Labs, though, and I'd peg you as Beaker, judging by your twitchiness." Her eyes met mine. "You okay, doll?"

"Yeah," I said with a slim smile, and pointed to the easel. "Was having a little bit of a breakthrough, actually. Well, first a fight with the teacher, then everyone staring at me, but *then* a bit of a breakthrough."

Rory looked around the art space. To my delight, the other remaining students were all busy working on their own stuff, and thankfully no one seemed to be taking any notice of me. "Glad to see that my birthday gift to you is really helping you make friends," Rory said, giving me a thumbs-up. "No fighting, though, okay? The idea was to help you *relax* from the day job, remember? Now, let's get you out of that lab coat and jet."

"It's a smock," I corrected. "It's for the doing of the art, and the saving of the grown-up clothes. Duh."

Marshall clapped me on the shoulder with a light touch. "Your bosses would be so proud," he said, mock sniffling.

"Parents," I reminded him. "Humping real estate on behalf of my family from one group of people to another is not my idea of my dream job, okay?" I turned to Rory. "And while I appreciate the gift, Ror, *nothing* is going to help me relax from the day job. I know I decided not to abandon them, and I don't think my mom could take it right now. But it doesn't mean I have to like it. "

"I don't get it," she said. "HGTV makes real estate look so easy."

"It probably is," I countered, "but most people probably don't answer to their parents as their bosses in that profession, do they?"

"Fair point," she said.

"They grow up so fast," Marshall said, continuing with his melodramatic crying. He put his hand on my back and started rubbing between my shoulders.

I squirmed away from his touch, agitated. "Hands off, Marsh," I said, and he pulled away like I was on fire, just the reaction I was hoping for. I let out a long sigh, letting go of the mounting tension I didn't know I was even carrying until that moment.

"You're a good daughter," Rory said, without a bit of snark to it whatsoever. "You turned out well, despite the fact that your parents always thought I got you into Goth in our teens because I wanted you to worship Satan."

"I wish!" I said, raising my hand like I was Dracula trying to mesmerize someone. "At least then I could hex some of the contractors I'm dealing with, get them to fall in line. Under budget and on time. Maybe give them boils, make their hair fall out . . ." I trailed off. Two of the Real Housewives were staring and rolling their eyes at me, one whispering to the other behind her hand.

"That's great, Lexi," Marshall said, disappointment in his voice. "I'm pretty sure that's how the Donald got ahead, too."

"One problem, though," Rory added, holding up a finger.

I kept my eyes on the women as they sat chatting at their respective easels off across the art space. "Which is . . . ?"

"We aren't fifteen anymore, dressing Goth, or sneaking

into the Harry Potter movies hoping that magic might actually be a real thing."

My face sank and I turned my powerless hand toward me, looking at it. There was no fantastical magic there, only chipped nails and torn cuticles. "Crap." I grabbed up one of the thicker paintbrushes at my station and waved it like a wand. "Still, I bet it would be pretty 'magical' to see how far I could shove this up their—"

"Lex!" Rory shouted, grabbing the paintbrush away from me.

I spun back around to my easel, staring at the gargoyle on the page. "Sorry," I said. "At least I was on my way toward getting a little sketch therapy out. It's just so frustrating to work so hard and feel like I'm failing. I mean, the Belarus family tree has at least one great artist in it, so it's got to be somewhere in my blood, right? I *should* be able to do this!"

Rory gave me a condescending pat on the back. "I'm not sure art's really a genetic thing, doll."

"I wish it was. My great-great-grandfather built huge swaths of this city when he came over from Lithuania. He laid stone back when it was still an art craft, not just bricklaying. The sketchbooks, the statues . . . All right, I'm letting it go," I said, forcing myself to relax. "Besides, this really *was* a thoughtful gift, and I don't want to waste it lamenting my life as artist—crowded out by my new life as a real estate tycoon—even if I do blow at the job. My bosses/parents have been stressing me out with all the running around to appointments. This time in this art class is *supposed* to help me get to my happy place, right?"

Rory put her hand on my shoulder and gave it a squeeze. "Well, we're here now, your portable happy place. Feel the love?"

I smiled at that. "Yeah, thanks," I said. I leaned over and grabbed my thick plastic art tube—complete with straps—sitting on the floor next to me and popped off one end of it. "Let me just pack up my stuff so I can get the hell out of here." I rolled up the sketch from my easel, first placing a thin sheet of vellum over it to keep it from smudging, then slid it into the tube, capping it. When I looked back up at my friends, Marshall looked a bit like he might pass out.

"Marshall . . . ?" I asked, worried.

"Can I have a minute here before we leave?" he asked. I followed his eyes across the room to the two blond ladies-who-lunch who had been talking about me.

"Oh, no, sweetie," Rory said, like she was his mom and not his roommate. "You don't want to crash and burn on something like that."

He nodded, not taking his eyes off of them. "Yeah, I do. Older women might just be my thing. I mean, women my age certainly don't seem to be my thing."

"Maybe Marshall just likes fine leather," I said, half-catty and half-joking.

"Shush," he said, his breathing rapid now as he worked up his courage.

"Trust me. Nothing good will come of talking to them. Give up while you're ahead, Marsh."

"They might be nice," he countered, sounding like he was trying to convince himself more than either of us.

"What are you talking about?" I said. "Bravo TV dedicates ninety percent of their whole network to programs about women who look like them. Nice doesn't even enter their vocabulary."

"We shall see," he said, and started off across the room before I could talk him out of it.

"It's so cute when he tries so hard," Rory said. "Bless his little heart!"

I hopped down off my stool, starting after him.

"Don't," Rory said, grabbing me by the arm. "Let him go."

"Why?"

"He can't help himself," she said. "That man needs to learn some of life's harsh lessons. He's too nice. He's got the strictest moral compass of anyone I've ever known. You should have seen him handing out fliers for Roll for Initiative over near the Manhattan Conservatory—"

I winced at the mention of the school, unable to stop my knee-jerk reaction. *"Alexandra,"* Rory said, scolding.

"I can't help it," I said, hating how whiny I sounded to myself. "I'm jealous, okay? You get to hang out with the graduate school crowd. Look at me. I'm dressed up in a fancy pantsuit and talk square footage and utilities with people all day."

Rory rolled her eyes. "Poor you," she said. "Heiress apparent to the Belarus family real estate holdings . . ."

"All because of a building collapse that *killed* Devon," I reminded her. "As wonderful as you think *heiress* sounds, the price paid for it was too high, if you ask me. God rest Devon's soul. This is not the life I planned on. These classes are the first time in *months* that I've remotely felt alive. So screw your whole 'Lexi's princess of the real estate kingdom' thing, okay? Everything has its own special way of sucking, believe me."

"Anyway," Rory said, ignoring me and jerking a thumb across the room toward Marshall before turning back to me by my now-empty easel. "His funeral."

She looked at the plastic art tube in my hands. "About that picture," she said. "Totally hideous. But in a good way."

"Thanks," I said. "I think. I remembered these sketches that my great-great-grandfather did. There's a whole volume of them. They should be in an actual museum, but my parents—hoarders that they are—won't let them leave their building. I think he called them his *grotesques*. They're an architectural detail that he used—something to do with re-directing rainwater to keep his buildings from collapsing. They're haunting but I love them."

"You're creepy like that," Rory said.

"I'll take that as a compliment."

"As you should," she said.

"My sketch tonight," I said with a little frustration in my tone. "It's at least something more than what I've been doing lately, but there's no life to them. They're copies of his works from my memory, but that's all they are—copies, not *real* art."

"Don't say that, Lex."

"Did you ever hear about Van Gogh and his doctor?" I asked.

Rory shook her head.

"Van Gogh struck an agreement with his doctor that he

would pay him with art, which the doctor accepted. For the rest of their lives after that, the doctor and his children labored at re-creating those works. They even showed them at the Met here in the city a few years back. I went to see them. Those Van Gogh reproductions were the same quality as what I'm doing here. *Lousy.* They vaguely *looked* like Van Gogh's work, but they lacked . . . I don't know . . . I guess soul. Maybe at heart I'm just a copycat, too."

"Alexandra . . ." Rory said, exasperation in her voice. She would have gone on, but Marshall had just about made his way back to us. "Well? How did it go?"

His eyes held a little bit of sad puppy dog in them and he gave Rory and me a halfhearted smile. "I thought it was going good," he said.

"Yeah?" I said, hopeful.

"It was," he insisted, "until they filled my hood with paint." He turned around slowly. The hood hanging out over the back of his jacket was wet from the inside, a hint of red seeping through it, running down the back of his jacket.

Rory clapped him on the shoulder. "Glad you got that out of your system?"

Marshall nodded, then smiled, mustering as much pride as he could for a nerd who had just been shot down. "The end result didn't matter, ladies. The important thing was the trying."

"Tell that to your dry cleaner," I said, packing up my materials.

"We're headed to that new bar that opened up over on First Avenue, the one around Eighth," Rory said. "You in?"

I checked my watch. "I don't think so," I said. "I need to get home to deal with the bosses. Update them about the meeting I cut short to get here and the closings I didn't get set up today, all before hurrying down here for the art sessions. I have to at least put in an appearance as the dutiful future of their empire. Hopefully, they don't fire me."

Marshall laughed. "As their daughter? Can they do that?"

"That's not the point, Marsh," I said, wanting to slug him.

"Excuse me," he said, still laughing, "but what is the point, then?"

Rory slapped me on the back. "The girl doesn't really have much choice, does she? It's very adult of her. Missing hanging out with us is just a bonus."

"Fine, then," he said, hurt, the laughter dying. "While we're out making memories, she can go about making nice at home."

I sighed. "All right, all right," I said. "Why don't you guys swing by my building after you hit the bar? I'm sure I'll be done dealing with the lord and lady of the manor by then."

Rory looked over at the other two women still standing across the far side of the room. Both of them were laughing. She looked up at Marshall. "You sure you don't want me to beat them up for you?" she asked, then flexed her arms. "Dancer's muscles. Hella strong."

Marshall shook his head.

I slapped him on the back, my hand making a squelching sound. I pulled it away, my palm now red with paint, and I went for one of the rags hanging at my art station to wipe it off. "Better luck next time."

Marshall gave a weak smile and shoved his hands into his coat pocket.

"You think things will be okay with the bosses?" Rory asked me.

I shrugged. "Who knows?" I said. "At least at home I won't have to deal with any artistic commentary." I slapped the plastic casing of the art tube.

Rory smiled. "That's no reflection on what you produce," she said. "Art is not their thing. Doug and Julie have just always been practical people."

"Practically perfect in every way," I said in my best Julie Andrews voice.

"Not bad," Marshall said. "Have you been practicing?"

"Not really," I said, heading for the door out of the art studio. "Sometimes it's just more pleasant living in my head with dancing cartoon penguins and singing chimney sweeps than it is dealing with life at the decrepit Belarus Manor."

"You could move out," Marshall said.

"Not until my mom is more stable. And plus I'd have to give up my three a.m. access to my great-great-grandfather's library and art studio," I said, with a small smile back over my shoulder. "I'll manage. Besides, bitching is just my way of dealing with all the life changes. It'll pass, I'm sure."

"Good luck!" Rory called after me, raising an invisible glass into the air. "Tell Doug and Julie I say hi! We'll toast to them!"

"I hate you, you know," I reminded her, but Rory only shrugged.

"It's okay," she said, chipper as always. "You hate everybody these days."

I didn't even stop to argue. Sometimes it was better to keep your mouth shut, especially when what Rory was saying was oh, so close to the truth.

Five

Alexandra

Deep in thought, I discovered far too late that I had walked way east before correcting myself and turning left onto Second Avenue, heading uptown through the East Village on my way toward Gramercy Park. The walk did much to clear my head of all the annoyance that had gone down during the art session. Now if I could avoid a wave of crap on the home front, I could sneak up to my namesake's deserted art studio in our building along the west side of the park and hopefully get back to work on the sketch rolled up in my art tube. I was excited by the breakthrough I had felt earlier tonight, my eyes becoming attuned to following some of the rules that governed the art world, and while I hated conforming to much of anything, I had to admit it really did help with producing the work I wanted to achieve.

My mind wandered off once again as I walked along East Sixteenth Street, crossing into Stuyvesant Plaza Park in front of Beth Israel, meandering along the oval stretch of walkway within. The trees there always made me feel like I was deep in the woods, despite the lights and sounds of the city all around. It reminded me of the times Rory and I would gather there as part of our own private would-be teenage coven, just to hang and talk about love-potioning various guys from high school. I was so lost in the pleasant memory that I barely heard the quickened footsteps of someone approaching from behind me until it was too late.

Strong arms grabbed for me, one of them catching the family pendant around my neck, choking me as I dashed forward. The heavy chain snapped and I was free, but before I could take off, fingers wrapped themselves in my hair with a pained jerk while an arm wrapped hard around my waist. A man's arm. The art tube lay pressed between us as he tugged me close, and judging from the breath on the back of my head, he had to be at least half a foot taller than me. I contorted my body to break free, but it was no use. The stranger's grip was solid, and my body went cold in pure fear.

"At last!" the man's voice hissed, quiet yet intimidating. He held my necklace up in front of me. "You're oh, so weak, aren't you?"

I pulled my pendant out of his hand, which I noticed was tattooed with an ornate symbol looking like some kind of stylized but blocky demon. I filed it away for a future police report—that was, if I ever got to make one. He pulled his hand away, tugging my hair as he settled the other around my waist.

"Where is it?" the voice hissed hot in my ear. "We've been looking so very long."

The man was talking crazy. *Looking so long?* Was it someone I knew? Had someone followed me all the way from the Y in Tribeca? My mind barely had a moment to process it, adrenaline and fear taking over. My whole body shook, a combination of that fear mixed with anger and rage. "My wallet is in my purse," I managed to stammer out. "Just take it and go. *Please.*"

"I'm not interested in your money," he said, pulling me closer.

Panic rose in my chest, my blood pumping hard. There was only one thing someone like this guy wanted when money wasn't the answer. I fought against his hold on my hair, even if it meant I had to lose a painful chunk of it to get free, but his grip was too strong to break. His other arm moved out of sight, and when it came back an ornate knife with a carved white hilt was in his hand. He pressed it to my throat.

"I don't want *that*, either," he said, just as quiet as before. "Just tell me where it is."

I gave up struggling. "I—I don't know what it is you're talking about," I said.

"Wrong answer," the man said. His body tensed, the knife pressing against my throat harder. How long before it would break the skin?

A quick look around the park told me there was no hope of rescue in sight, but thankfully, I rarely counted on others when it came to taking care of myself. Whatever this crazed lunatic had in mind, I had to get out of there. His increasing menace caused something to snap deep inside me, and all I knew was that I was determined not to be the victim here.

I brought the heel of my Doc Martens back up behind my body, finding its mark right between the man's legs. A half cry, half whimper escaped his lips, his hand dropping the knife as he doubled over in pain, letting go of my hair. I ran forward, not even considering going for the knife. That was the kind of thing that got people killed in the movies. Instead, I tore across the small park toward the opening in the gate, and out onto Fifteenth Street.

I sped off, thanking my lucky stars that I wasn't wearing typical girly-girl impractical fashionista shoes, always opting for a combat boot, occasionally going for something a bit more dressy-sexy but always comfy and low-heeled. Tonight, my Docs were fine for putting some distance between my attacker and me. Fifteenth Street was deserted this time of night, but the grid of Manhattan was too much for me to traverse if I thought I'd make it to safety without taking a short-cut to get up Irving Plaza to Gramercy Park. I glanced back over my shoulder, surprised to see the lone figure closing in much faster than I expected. Turning right, I ran up an alley in the middle of the block, dodging past recycling bins and an oversized Dumpster.

I turned left down an even tighter section of the alley.

I heard my attacker close behind, causing my skin to go cold. Rounding the next corner, my heart sank. The wire mesh of an upcoming fence blocked my way, and panic took full hold of me. There was no way I could scale the fence before my attacker caught up. Still, there was no way in hell I was just going to wait there like a helpless victim, either. Without breaking stride, I pumped my legs harder and leapt at the fence in a full-on run.

I grabbed on lower than I would have liked to, but started climbing as fast as my body could go, the wire of the fence digging cold into my palms and fingers. The sounds of my attacker farther back in the alley grew louder, although thankfully it sounded like he was still around the corner. Higher and higher I went, until I looked up at the top of the fence, stopping as my heart beat into a full panic.

"Razor wire," I said, my toes slipping out of the holes in the fence, letting my legs dangle, the strain in my arms burning. "Shit."

Six

Stanis

In the midst of the freedom of flying, a panicked sensation overwhelmed me like lightning coursing through my stone form, catching me so off guard that my body curled in on itself, my wings folding in around me. Stunned, I fell through the clouds toward the ground far below before something deep inside kicked in once more. I extended my body fully, arms and legs stretched out to the very tips of my claws until my wings extended, catching the air and carrying me aloft as I twisted and turned to avoid the buildings I had just been plummeting toward.

The alarming buzz of the sensation stayed with me, settling into a slow burn at my center. The initial shock of it gave way to a forgotten but familiar calling, and I was struck with a memory—this was the sole purpose of what drew me to the night sky in the first place, this call to action. Without hesitation, I flew off, banking away from the glass wall of the nearest building, trying to ascertain where the pull of the sensation was strongest. A few aerial swoops in each direction told my body where the calling came from, and I followed the pull though the night sky, darting lower and lower between the buildings as I went. Even after so many years, speed still exhilarated me, more so with a direct purpose at hand behind it.

My eyes searched the streets below, taking in the lone figure of a woman hanging at the top of a fence within the close quarters of an alley. Another figure, this one hooded, came down another section of the alley, moving toward her, the gleam of a blade in his hand. Everything about this woman called out to me, and although I did not understand why, I desperately wanted to help her, whatever the source of her distress was. The one rule screamed out all-consuming in my head.

Protect.

I pressed myself lower in flight, twenty feet off the ground now, before swooping into the tight confines of the alley. Maneuvering was difficult here, but centuries of experience were on my side. I came down in front of the blade-wielding figure, landing on my feet as the man, still running, slammed into my chest, and I sent him flying into a large metal cube along the side of the alley that stank of rotting food.

The figure stood, disoriented, until he noticed me there. He ran at me, stabbing with a shimmering blade in his hand. I did not think to move as the man lunged, sparks flying off my stone skin as the knife dragged down my chest. The gesture was futile, but it awoke something dark and furious inside me. I lashed out with my left arm, knocking the blade out of the attacker's hand as something solid underneath the man's skin gave way. He roared in pain, pulling his arm to his body, part of it sticking out at an odd angle from the rest of it. *How fragile these creatures are,* I thought. I had forgotten.

The sound was almost inhuman and it would no doubt draw attention, which concerned me. That would violate the second of the rules, one of many rules that came as instinct to me more than anything. *Remain hidden from humanity.* I should leave, but the first rule held a stronger sway over me, and I simply could not leave this man here for fear of harm coming to the woman.

The cries of my attacker faded, giving over to a pained whimper. I grabbed him by both his shoulders, digging my claws in, then leapt into the sky as he screamed. His added weight forced me to correct my flight, lengthening the strokes of my wings, but it took only a second to adjust before I compensated, shooting straight up into the night sky. The pained man craned his head to look down. His whimper turned back into a fear-filled scream of panic as he wrapped his good arm around mine.

I rose higher, ignoring his cries until we cleared the clouds and entered the quiet moonlit space above them. When I looked at the man again, his sounds of distress had ceased and the human stared at me with a mix of shock and wonder on his face. He examined me, my mix of carved beauty and horror no doubt puzzling him.

"You," he managed to say. "It *is* you."

"You—you know of me?" I asked, faltering in my flight for a moment, rocking unsteadily.

"My people had given up hope of ever finding you," he said, grim. "You are the whisper of legend. *Stanis.*"

"Stanis," I repeated, letting the name roll through my mouth as if it were new to me. I had thought the word before, but long had it been since I had uttered it. When it left my lips, I felt the power in it. Why this man should know my name was unclear, but my mind awoke to that mystery, demanding answers. "How do you know of me? Why were you chasing that woman?"

His face went dark, his eyes narrowing. "Because that woman must die for what they did to you," the man snarled, still clutching to my solid arms. "Her and her kind. If not by my hand, then by another's."

My other questions fell to the back of my mind as the first rule rose up once more, all-consuming. The protection—the protection of *the family*, I remembered—overrode all other things. "That cannot be," I said. "I cannot allow that. For you, this ends here. Now."

The man struggled in vain to free himself, not that it would matter this high up. "More will come, Stanis," the man said. "You have been missed and you *will* be found."

"Then let them come," I said, no longer able to resist the rise of the rule. *Protect.* "I am Stanis. I am death."

I shifted my hands to the sides of the man's head, holding him by it as I slowed my flight. He grabbed at my arms, holding on for support as his legs fought to find some form of purchase, but it did him little good.

Such frail creatures, I thought once more before pressing my hands together on either side of the man's skull until they met. Screams gave way to silence, and the burning at my center faded and was no more.

Seven

☾

Alexandra

The sound of chaos somewhere off in the alley behind me had died down minutes ago, but the pounding of my heart hadn't and I remained where I was, stunned, my fingers locked through the loops of the fence, holding myself up there as long as possible. I lasted until I could no longer feel the wire digging into my hands, and when one of my boots slipped loose from one of the loops, I let go, landing hard on the pavement below. I pulled the art tube off my back and held it out in front of me like a sword, the simple length of plastic giving me the courage to race back to the last corner before giving a tentative look around it, my heart still beating in my throat.

It was quiet now that the sounds of chaos had died down completely. Fighting, a cracking and popping—had that been bone? A pained cry from a man's voice; then the signs of struggle in the alley had fallen away in less than a heart-beat, followed by the strangest sound of all. The man's cry of pain, still going on, faded like the quickly passing siren of a high-speed police chase. Only it wasn't going away from me uptown or crosstown. Irrational as it was, in just seconds the voice had disappeared . . . straight up into the sky, followed by silence.

I moved forward with a slow caution, rounding the corner I had turned down before the fence had dead-ended me. There was no one in the alley now, which, in a way, caused me to panic more. Having heard what I had just minutes ago, I looked up into the night sky, feeling foolish when the only thing I saw were the dark clouds high overhead. I turned my gaze back to the alley all around me, my brain unable to process the mystery of what the hell had happened to my attacker. Had I missed whoever it was? Had he snuck down the alley behind me, waiting to spring? I spun around, expecting to see him, but there was no one there. A glint of light on the ground caught my eye—the knife the man had pressed against my throat. I knelt down as I continued to watch for movement in the alley, and took the knife by the handle. I stood, the power of the blade giving my courage a boost, but not by much. The idea of stabbing someone held no appeal, but if we were in a me-or-them situation, I'd do what I had to if it came down to it. Or so I imagined.

"Hello?" I called out, my voice tiny and weak despite the power I now felt holding the blade, but there was no answer.

Nerves got the better of me and a creepy sensation washed over my body. I began to shake as my pumping blood slowed and the chill of the fall night air finally caught back up with me. I slid the strap of my art tube back around my shoulder and fished my cell phone out of my bag, hand at the ready to dial the police, but my fingers wouldn't move. Instead my head turned back toward the sky. What the hell was I going to tell the authorities? That the voice of my attacker had gone straight up into the night sky? Telling someone that seemed patently absurd. I stood there, unsure, until the crick developing in my neck took over and I turned my eyes back down to my surroundings.

Still clutching my phone in one hand and the strange knife in the other, I made my way back down the alley to the street, still fearing a rush from the shadows of the alley that were big enough to hide someone. When no one attacked, I ran out onto Fifteenth and hurried up Irving Plaza, wondering how much worse my evening could really get. Then I remembered the talk I expected with my boss-parents, and suddenly the idea of getting knifed in an alley didn't seem all that bad a way to go.

I must have checked behind myself a thousand times as I ran all the way home to Gramercy Park, and by the time I reached my family home on the west side of it, I felt fairly certain that I hadn't been followed. I ran into the main doorway of stately Belarus Manor, keyed into the building, and started off across the lower floor, which comprised the offices for the family's real estate dealings. Just being inside behind a locked door within my family's half-a-block-wide, seven-story building was enough to calm me, if only just a little. It was home; it was safe, a refreshing oasis away from the harsh desert of the messed-up outside world.

By the time I hit the elevator up to my family's main living quarters on the second floor, my breathing was almost normal. As the doors slid open on the dimly lit main family living area on the second floor, I looked down at my hand, still holding my attacker's knife. I slipped it into my shoulder bag, careful not to slice up any of its contents. I stepped out onto the floor, picking a path through months of neglected accumulation lining the main hall—newspapers, mail, and assorted bric-a-brac. I made my way to the spacious living room, where my parents sat zombie-eyed in front of a tiny, old-school television watching the evening's financial reports. A slight nod of both their heads gave an indication that they at least acknowledged I was in the room, which was better than some days these past four months since Devon's death, I supposed. My father had been the one who convinced me to stay, and pointed out that leaving would be damaging to my mother, but now it seemed that as long as I was doing what they wanted, they didn't have much to say to me.

My mother looked away from the television to me. Despite only being in her early fifties, Devon's death had aged her considerably these few short months. Her hair, thanks to chemical treatment, remained as black as mine, but her face had grown pale as of late, thin to the point of skeletal. Her mouth gave a twisted, one-sided smile, the only kind she seemed capable of these days. My father, who always seemed to vacillate between stoic man of business and peaceful man of God, didn't react at all beyond his initial nod.

I thought about not telling them about my attacker, letting the strange silence settle between us. They already had enough grief weighing on them still, without me worrying them more by adding to it with the tale of my impossible disappearing assailant. Dark and brooding was the new black in the Belarus family. I kept my mouth shut and headed for the back hall that led off to the stairs to the other floors. Maybe I could salvage my evening if I could just leave them to their creepy little viewing party, obsessing over the latest financial stories on the news. I hoped so, anyway, backing myself into the hallway slowly so as not to draw attention.

The tiniest hint of interest awoke on my father's face. He scratched at the little semicircle that remained of his black hair.

"How was your day?" he asked, shifting his focus to me, his words coming out pointed beyond his hint of an accent. His blue-green eyes, my own eyes, stared back at me.

I stopped where I was halfway down the hall. "Oh, fine," I said, words rushing out of me, breaking the strange wall of silence. "You know, the usual . . . showed some apartments, met up with some contractors . . ." I backed myself slowly down the hall as my words trailed off, but my father lowered the volume on the television with his remote.

"I heard from Randy Rosenzweig," he said, all business tone, "at the Hell's Kitchen project. You skipped out early on an appointment with him today, yes? Would you care to explain that?"

Something about his tone, switching from melancholy to business on a dime, hit me the wrong way. I stopped in the hall again, then hurried back into the main room. "Do I get a choice? Any chance I can convince you not to be concerned . . . ?"

"What I am concerned with," he said, stern this time, "are your growing issues in timeliness when it comes to our business, what you're doing to sabotage our family's name in certain real estate circles. This is a family business, Alexandra. It will be *your* business. Do you understand that?"

My mother *tsk-tsk*ed behind closed teeth. "Alexandra, tell me . . . what is so important that you have to keep shuffling appointments around?"

I sighed and spoke. "Remember that envelope Rory gave me for my birthday back in August?"

My mother's face winced at the mention of my oldest friend, but I let it slide. Like most mothers, she blamed my oldest friend for every bad idea I'd ever gotten mixed up with. I was pretty sure she'd be doing the same thing when I was fifty.

"She's seen how ragged learning this business is running me, so she just thought I might relax a little if I spent a little more time with my passion, so . . . she enrolled me at the Tribeca Y for one of the artist-in-residence series they offer as part of their art studio programming."

"*Art* again?" my father asked, treating the word like I had just said I was entering the drug trade. "Alexandra, we have been through this. I fail to see how *that* will remotely help your future. We want you to be prepared to fully take over the family affairs if—*when*—the time comes."

"You had Devon all polished up for all that, didn't you?" I asked. I tried to bite back my words, but I couldn't. "I didn't ask for all this. I never wanted it."

My father sighed, his voice going dark. "We're talking about you right now, Alexandra, *not* your dead brother, God rest his soul. You did not ask for this choice, but it is a better one than your brother faced."

"I nearly faced death, too, you know," I said, snapping. I reached into my purse with caution and pulled out the knife. So much for not saying anything. "Tonight. I almost got accosted in an alley on the way home. *This* is what my attacker had at my throat."

My mother was up like a shot, running over, but stopped short of where I held the ornate knife. My father got up a bit more slowly, his eyes full of concern, and walked over to me.

He took the knife from my hand, inspecting the carvings along the white of its handle. Something that looked like a black serpent with four heads wrapped up and down it. "This is something ungodly," he said, meeting my eyes with all seriousness.

My mother stepped closer, giving me an awkward hug. "Are you okay?" she asked.

"I'm fine," I said, but the way her body was shaking against me told me she wasn't convinced. Nor, as it was becoming apparent, was my father.

"I don't want you leaving the building until further notice. Understand?" he said.

"I'm okay," I said, feeling all of sixteen again as I pulled back from my mother. "I . . . lost my mugger in an alley farther downtown." Given how wide my mother's eyes were, *lost* sounded better than *disappeared*, which would probably explode her head. "But not leaving the building? With my workload, how am I supposed to get to meetings, showings, and closings, then? Look. I'm fine. This is New York. I'm a little shaken up, but frankly I'm surprised I haven't been mugged sooner. This isn't some weird evil churchy thing, okay? Just wanted a little sympathy here. I'll be fine going out and about. I'm a grown-up now."

My father's eyes met mine, unamused. "I'm sorry, but you will stay at home for now, Alexandra," he said. "Never mind visiting job sights or showing places."

I bit my tongue, incredulous and angry. Was I getting grounded? At twenty-two? I went to speak, but the look of terrified panic on my mother's face stopped me, killing any of the fire left in me. "Fine," I said, giving in.

My father nodded, a lighter look in his eyes now that I had acquiesced. "Besides, there's plenty of work you can do here," he said, handing me a stack of folders. "Since you love your great-great-grandfather's old studio on the top floor so much, why don't you work on these there for the time being?"

"Till when?" I asked. "Not that I mind the break from appointments. I'm just . . . surprised, is all. How long are we talking?"

"I'm not sure," my father said, pulling the knife closer to his face, lifting his glasses to examine it more closely. "I will consult with the reverend in the morning."

He handed the knife back to me before he and my slowly calming mother headed back to the couch. Once they were settled in, he raised the volume of the television once again, both of them falling silent.

The reverend? Why hadn't he suggested the cops? I could have argued with him about how ridiculous going the religious route sounded, but there was no way I was going to enable all his churchiness. I knew better than to try to sway him from anything religious. There was really no point in arguing with him, anyway.

At least they hadn't fired me from the family business, or the family, for that matter. Even though it was for the benefit of my mother mostly, feeling sorta grounded at twenty-two sucked majorly. I headed toward the back hall of the building, mounting the stairs farther up as a newly found sympathy for Rapunzel settled over me. Despite the enormous size of the Belarus building, it hadn't ever felt so claustrophobic.

Eight

🌙

Alexandra

I dumped the stack of folders on a huge desk in my great-great-grandfather's studio. I pulled off my boots and threw my shoulder bag over by my favorite couch; then, despite my adult "grounding," I tried to be the dutiful daughter by grabbing a handful of the folders and settling in.

Despite my best effort, I found myself too wound up from my earlier encounter to concentrate on the work. Who could pay attention to kitchen renovation costs, contractor billing disputes, and square footage when there were strange knives and disappearing attackers to concern my brain with?

I closed the folders, pulled out one of my notebooks from my bag, and fell to sketching instead. I drew the events of my evening—the shadowy figure in the streets, the strange tattoo on his hand, the knife he had held at my throat. The occasional tear fell on the page as waves of processing emotions ebbed and flowed, but I continued on, lost in the process of it. I started one sketch of what I thought the results of the evening *could* have been, but stopped myself, my mind unwilling to go there.

Instead, I pulled out my laptop and went searching for bits

of inspiration in the designs and architecture of all the buildings I knew Alexander Belarus had built across the city.

My mind must have wandered, because time passed—how much, I didn't know—but I snapped to when a sound rose up to catch my attention above the clamor of the city seeping in through the French doors I had cracked open across the room to let in a little of the crisp late-September air. A *close* sound, one of footsteps on the metal grates on the fire escape rising up the far side of the terrace.

I leapt up from the couch and quickly padded across the room. I swept up one of my great-great-grandfather's works as I went—a great stone book, one of the heavier ones I had the strength to lift. It would work for braining anyone stupid enough to try coming in through my window, if I could raise the damn thing over my head.

My heart pounded hard in my throat. *Stupid,* I thought. Had I been careless enough to have been followed home by my attacker? I didn't think so, but at least I was ready this time. I pressed myself to the side of my window and hefted the book up, my arms already aching. Suddenly I realized the knife in my bag would have been a better choice, but it was too late for that now.

The doors flew open and a single shadowy figure dashed into the room before I could even bring the book down on top of it, which was fortunate for me. A certain blue-haired girl twisted around when she saw me standing there with the massive stone book. She tripped over her own feet, going down with none of her dancer's grace to help her, landing with a heavy *thud* on the floor.

"Rory . . . ?" I said, relieved. I lowered the stone book. "You know, normal people use the stairs."

She stood up from where she had landed on the floor, brushing herself off, her breathing a little labored. "When you make some normal friends, let me know."

I thought about it for a moment. "Fair enough . . ."

She pushed her messed-up blue bangs out of her eyes.

"Jesus, Lexi," she said, eyeing the stone book in my hands. "Who were you expecting? Charles Manson?"

I relaxed, lowering the book until it hung at the ends of my arms. "Sorry," I said. "It's been a night."

"I bet," she said, smoothing down her shirt. "Glad to see you didn't end it with the murder of your best friend."

Another sound rose up on the terrace and I spun around. Well, as quick as someone carrying a stone book half her weight could, anyway. I had the book almost over my head when Rory put her hands on mine, easing it back down.

"Easy," she said. "It's just Marshall."

Marshall's lanky body came into view climbing up the stairs of the fire escape. He crossed over to us at the French doors, his eyes fixed on me, full of terror.

"Relax," I said. "I'm not going to hit you."

The terror stayed on his face as he fumbled his way in through the doors, slamming them shut behind him. "That's not it," he said, fighting harder for each breath than Rory had. "Heights . . . Don't . . . like them."

Rory patted him on the shoulder. "Funny for a guy who stands so tall."

"That fire escape terrifies me," Marshall said. "It's just bolts holding it into brick. Don't trust it. And as to your point, dear Rory, the difference is that if I slip while just standing around, I don't plummet several stories down, now, do I?"

Rory shook her head and looked at me.

I shrugged. "It's a fair point," I said.

Marshall looked at the stone book in my hands, nervous now. "Is that . . . Were you going to . . . ?"

"Crush our heads in . . . ?" Rory offered. "Yeah. What gives, Lexi? What's got you so jacked up?"

"Promise me you'll be less freak-outish to my story than my parents were," I said, going for my shoulder bag. I fished out the knife with the white carved handle and held it up. "Almost got accosted, raped, and/or stabbed tonight. So there's that."

Just saying it out loud had me shaking, rage and fear rising up together as I thought about my close call.

"Holy shit," Rory said, coming over to me at the couch.

Avoiding the knife in my hand, she came in close and hugged me tight, and with my free arm I hugged her back just as hard.

"Are you okay?" Marshall asked. "Did you call the cops?"

"No," I said. "I ran until I got here; then my parents were, well . . . my parents. I've been up here the rest of the time. Just trying to process it. Besides, my attacker sort of . . . disappeared."

Rory pulled back from me, hands on my shoulders. "Um, what, now?"

I sat down on the couch, put the knife away, and told them the story from beginning to end, showing them the few sketches I had produced—the symbol on the man's hand, his face, the alley where he should have caught up with me but instead disappeared. Well, flew away was what it had sounded like, but I didn't share that.

"This is my fault," Rory said. "If I didn't get you these classes for your birthday, just trying to get you out of your work head space, you wouldn't have been out there in this asshole's path."

I shook my head. "Rory, are you kidding me? Outside of this whole encounter, these classes are what have kept me from falling into a full-on depression. That whole weirdness is just random, you know? You can't live all your life in New York City without having at least one criminal act happen to you."

"True," Marshall said. "Although, technically I've already been mugged, like, three times, which is way above the norm. I guess I look nerdy enough to have a high-paying job or something. I make a great victim." He put his arms halfheartedly in the air. "Go me!"

Rory laughed, but it was cut short by a cacophony of sound rising up from somewhere in Gramercy Park on the east side of the building—tree branches rustling and snapping, followed by a heavy *slap-thud.* All three of us jumped, turning to face the terrace.

"What the *hell* was that?" Marshall asked.

"The city that never sleeps," I said, grabbing my boots and heading out the French doors.

We came down the fire escape and hit the bottom of the alley at a run, lights coming on in all the buildings along the edges of Gramercy Park. I stepped out onto the sidewalk, a small crowd of passersby already gathering along the north side of it.

"What is it?" Marshall asked, as we headed up the west side of my block.

"I'm not sure," I said, stopping once we hit the corner. The gathering crowd stood at the gate peering into the darkness of the park itself. "I think they see something, but they can't get in."

I started toward them with Marshall, but Rory grabbed my arm and pulled me back around the corner. It took Marshall a second to notice I wasn't next to him anymore, and he spun awkwardly in his tracks and ran back to join us, jumpy. "We don't want to go with the crowd?"

Rory shook her head.

Marshall peeked back around the corner of the black wrought-iron fence. "Do you think they saw me?" he asked, nervous. "That looked normal, right? I mean, people turn around and walk away all the time, right?"

Rory hit him in the arm. "Relax, crazy pants," she said. "You acting normal would actually *draw* attention."

"Why'd you stop us?" I asked.

Rory gave a dark smile, then nodded down the block to the south corner before taking off at a slow jog. "I hate crowds. Come on, Lex. You still have your key?"

"Yeah," I said, breaking into a run after her.

"Good," she called back over her shoulder.

"What key?" Marshall called out behind me.

I spun, grabbed his arm, and pulled him after me. He stumbled forward but managed to fall in next to me as the two of us watched Rory turn the corner heading around to the south side of the park.

"Gramercy's a private park," I said. "One of two left in the New York area, actually. Only the tenants living on the park itself get keys. They charge an arm and two legs if you lose them, but my family's been here forever, so . . ."

Rory was waiting for us at the southern gate, which was

unoccupied, straining in the darkness to see into the park.
"I can't see anything," she said. Her arm flashed out toward
me, fingers wiggling. "The key. Give it."

"We're not going in there, are we?" Marshall asked.

"Well, I don't know about *you*, Marsh," she said, turning
to the two of us, "but I am."

I hesitated, and Rory rolled her eyes at me.

"I want to see what's going on," she said, lifting the chain
from around my neck where I wore the key. I didn't resist.
"Besides, you *are* a key-carrying member of the privileged.
That means you have every right to be in there if you want to."

"What if my psycho's in there?" I asked as she slid the key
into the modern lock of the ancient-looking gate. "I think I've
had about all the crazy I can take tonight."

Rory flipped her blue hair back out of her eyes and gave a
toothy grin, adjusting her glasses. "There's a good chance
someone called the cops about whatever made that sound, so
I'd say we're pretty safe."

The sigh Marshall let out indicated his flustered displea-
sure with her choice, but before he could actually form words,
Rory cracked the gate open ever so slightly and slid her skinny
body into the opening, entering the park.

I shook my head, gave him a smile, and slid in following
Rory. I heard the sounds of Marshall finally coming after us
seconds later, but I had already moved on to searching through
the shadows for my best friend. The ample lights outside the
park barely penetrated through the trees within it, the swaying
shadows in the light fall breeze making it hard to pick out
Rory's figure anywhere. The cobblestones beneath my feet
were uneven and had me moving slowly or risk twisting an
ankle on the ancient surface that covered most of the paths
through the park.

"Where's Rory?" Marshall whispered as he caught up to
me, grabbing onto my arm.

"Not sure," I said. "And let go of my arm. This isn't a date."

"Sorry," he said, pulling away. "Just nerves. I'm sure the
place is lovely in the daylight, but right now it's super creepy.
Don't worry. I'll protect you."

I gave a small laugh. "That's comforting."

He laughed, too. "Fine. You protect me, then."

"Chivalry is dead," I said with a shake of my head. "Come on."

I moved with caution toward the far side of the park, continuing my snail's pace. After a few moments, Marshall grabbed my arm again.

"Is that the sound of a river?" he asked.

"Yep," I said, not stopping. "And I don't want to fall in it. That's why we're going slow."

He cocked his head. "I can hear it, but I have no idea where it *is*."

I grabbed Marshall's hand. It was clammier than I had imagined they'd be. "Stay close," I said, moving to the left of the path, closer to the tree line there. The sounds of the small river increased with each step we took, so much so that I didn't even hear the lone shadowy figure as it crashed out of the trees directly in front of me. I went to scream, but a hand clamped down over my mouth. The metallic taste of several rings filled it instantly.

Rory.

One of her hands was over my face and the other was raised up to cover Marshall's mouth. Even with Rory's speed at silencing us, a muffled cry came from him behind her fingers.

"Shh!" Rory hissed, then whispered, "There's someone else in the park."

I pulled her hand away from my face, then spat to get the taste of metal off my tongue. "Who is it? One of my neighbors?"

Rory shook her head, looking off toward the center of the park. "I don't think so," she said. "I mean, I'm not sure, but he or she is hiding by the statue at the center. That doesn't exactly sound like resident behavior, now, does it? Come on."

She turned, walking off with her hand still firmly planted over Marshall's mouth, her fingers clutching his cheeks. He didn't even bother to put up a fight. Dazed, he simply followed after her.

Rory didn't seem to have any trouble seeing in the dark, stepping sure-footed over the thin stream of water that I caught myself avoiding at just the last second. The center of the park was an open space surrounded by iron benches, and a lone statue sitting at the middle of it.

Marshall pried Rory's hand from his face. "Who is that?"

"We don't know yet," I said. "Didn't you hear Rory?"

"I meant the statue," he said in a hushed tone. "I doubt it's like Superman or something."

"Oh," I said. "Sorry. It's Edwin Booth—some old-time actor—dressed as Hamlet."

That seemed to satisfy him and he returned to peering at the base of the statue. "So where's this other person?" he asked Rory. "I don't see anyone."

Rory pointed low. "Down there," she said. "Hunched down by the base."

I couldn't see anything abnormal about the base of the statue. It was a large rectangular block of shadow from here, but there might have been the hint of a shape just on the other side of it. Marshall moved forward first, with Rory and me falling into step right behind. The closer we got, the more obvious it became that the hidden shape was that of a man, and that he was no longer living. The shapes of a body were familiar—an arm along the left side of the base and the bend of a leg beneath it, twisted, broken. The clothes were familiar, too, as was the symbol tattooed on its left hand—the stylized but blocky demon. Thick tree branches lay scattered and torn apart all around the figure.

My eyes rose up to what should have been the person's head, only what was there could no longer be called one. What remained reminded me of the teen Halloween years when Rory and I used to hang with the badass boys who went around smashing pumpkins. The arrival of flashing red and blue lights drove away the shadows for a second, revealing a spill all around the body that definitely wasn't pumpkin guts or seeds.

"What the hell happened to his head?" I asked, but as soon as the words were out I felt my stomach rise in my throat and I turned away from the sight of it. I stumbled away as the contents of my stomach pushed their way up. It burned as I threw up and unfortunately there was no quiet way to do such a thing. Flashlight beams from outside the gates turned on me just in time to catch my dinner from hours ago splash into some of the shrubbery in front of me.

"Hey!" a man's voice shouted, full of authority. Cops. "Stop where you are."

I stood to respond, but my stomach coiled up on me once more and I doubled over, still hacking.

"Shit," one officer said to another, his light finally training in on me. "A bunch of drunk kids in the park. Looks like one is passed out."

"We're not drunk!" Rory shouted out.

"Shut up and *don't move*!" the officer called out. "One of you get over here right the hell now and open this gate."

"Hold on! Hold on!" Rory called out as she came over to me, rubbing my back as she did best-friend duty pulling my hair out of the way. "My friend is throwing up."

"Stupid underage kids don't know their tolerance," the other officer said.

"We're not underage," Rory called out. "And we're not drunk. It's worse than that . . . We think someone's . . . dead."

"Son of a bitch," the officer swore. Uncertainty crept into his voice. "Think the kid's telling the truth?"

"Only one way to find out," the other one said. He shouted, "Get your ass over here. Now!"

Rory gave an angered sigh. Marshall stumbled over to us. "Shut your mouth, Ror," he said, holding his hands up like he was being robbed. "This is no time to drop attitude on anyone, *especially* an officer of the law."

"But—"

Marshall pointed toward the bright light shining on us. "He's got *a gun*," he said. "Will that convince you?"

"He does . . . ?" The wind went out of her words as she spoke them.

"Get the hell over here right *now*!" the officer repeated.

Without brooking further argument, Marshall stepped carefully off in the direction of the flashing lights, raising his hands even higher. "We're coming," he called out, his voice wavering with obedient fear.

Rory helped me up. I wiped the back of my coat's sleeve across my face and allowed her to lead me toward the gates as well. My arms and legs felt like jelly, twitching and shaking as I tried to walk.

"Easy," Rory said, noting my weakness.

"Open the gate, slowly," the officer said. Up close, I could finally make them out, one younger, taller, with a short blond crew cut, and the other shorter, stockier, older. They didn't scare me as much as the short, rectangular end of the gun Tall and Blond had pointed at the three of us.

Rory saw it, too, and didn't argue as she fished my key out of her front pocket and slid it into the gate, unlocking it from the inside. The blond officer pushed the gate open toward us using his foot.

"What's this about someone being dead?" he asked.

I nodded, and raised my arm, pointing into the park. "There is," I said. "At the base of the statue."

"Back to the center of the park," Short and Stocky said, already driving us back as he walked forward with caution. "Now."

I shook my head, my legs shaking. "I don't think I can," I said.

"You can," he insisted, grabbing one of my shoulders hard, "and you will. You'll do as we say until I see what's going on there."

It's amazing the strength you can find when someone is pointing a gun in your general direction. Although I had no desire to go anywhere near what I had just seen, I found myself doing as I was told. When we were close enough to the statue for Tall and Blond, he turned his light on the base of it. In regular light the body was more broken and tangled than the shadows had told. A crimson-brown spatter of blood radiated out from the body, and it was all I could do to turn away before my stomach retched again.

"Jesus Christ," he said. He flicked off the light and turned away from it as his partner focused his on it instead. Tall and

Blond's voice went from dark wonder to something colder, more formal. "Would you care to explain what you were doing in here?"

"That man," I stammered, unable to shake the surreal, dreamlike state that was slowly washing over me. "His head . . ."

The officer's eyes fixed on mine, unmoving.

"I need you to explain what you three were doing in here. Now."

I couldn't speak. The image filled my mind, threatening to take it over. When I felt someone touch my arm, I just about screamed before I realized it was Rory.

"Relax," she said. "Does it look like any of us could have done *that*?"

He considered this, then sighed and went for the thick black book sitting in the oversized pocket on his uniform. "You live here, then?"

I nodded. "Not in the park . . ." I corrected, then felt my face flush.

Rory squeezed my arm and stepped forward. "She's just flustered, but yeah. She does." She pointed to the west side of the park. "Over there. The Belarus building."

I could have hugged her just then. Even though she had been the one to rush into the park, Rory was busy talking while I simply couldn't.

The officer scribbled in his book. "And the three of you are each other's alibi, I suppose?"

"Alibi?" Marshall said, nerves filling every word. "What do we need an alibi for?"

"We were walking along the south side of the park and saw the cop car lights flashing," Rory said. "From the *other* side of the park, so I used her key so we could cut across and see what all the fuss was."

"Did you see anything?"

"Other than the body?" I said, finally able to speak, but still in shock over the deformed shape of the dead man's head. "No. We didn't even know it *was* a body until we got close to the statue . . . Are we in trouble here?"

The officer shrugged. "That depends on how cooperative you are, miss."

I shook off my shock as best I could. He was right. I needed to tell him everything. The symbol on the man's hand, my encounter with him earlier—

"If you want her cooperation," my father's voice boomed out from somewhere back toward the direction of the police lights, "you will have to talk to me first."

Both officers turned. "And you are . . . ?" the short and stocky one asked.

"Douglas Belarus," he said, moving close enough that I could see his face. "Her father." His eyes were locked onto the two officers. "Is there a problem here, gentlemen? I'm a trustee of the park. My family has been for several generations."

"Hello, Mr. B," Rory said, giving him a grim half smile.

He looked at her as if he was noticing her for the first time, giving her a curt nod.

He turned to me, his face cold, but his eyes concerned. His heavy hands rose and came to rest on both my shoulders, squeezing. "Are you all right, Alexandra? What is going on?"

"I asked you a question, Mr. Belarus," the officer continued, his voice full of indignation at being ignored.

"I'm fine, Father," I said. "We're all fine . . . just a little unnerved."

He relaxed a little, his grip easing. "Good. I thought I told you not to leave the building."

I didn't want to get into that here, now, and flicked my eyes over toward the cops. *They're waiting.*

My father looked over his shoulder at the officers, but made no attempt to turn to them, which seemed only to piss them off.

"So tell me, Mr. Belarus," the blond officer said, looking down at the shadow-covered body over by the base of the statue. "How do *you* think this body got here?"

"Body?" he repeated, raising an eyebrow.

The second officer waggled his flashlight back to the base of the statue, drawing my father's attention to the broken body lying there.

I started to speak, wanting to tell the police what I knew

of the man, but my father silenced me with a firm squeeze of my arm and spoke instead.

"I am certain I have no idea," my father said. "I have no idea who would have done something so heinous. Why someone should leave a body with a caved-in head here in our park is simply beyond me."

"No one just left him here," Marshall added.

My father gave a grim chuckle. "Oh, really? He certainly didn't climb over the gate and walk in here of his own accord with a crushed-in skull like that."

"That's not what I mean," Marshall said.

The blond officer turned to him. "Well, what *do* you mean?"

Marshall pointed at the ground beneath the body. "See that spatter? That's from impact. Whoever he was, he fell from at least ten stories."

I stared at him.

"What?" he asked.

"How does your brain even come up with that?"

He shrugged, then looked away. "I had a cruel Dungeon Master in my D and D group. He made us work hard for every experience point. Lots of puzzle solving in our games. I can't help but think critically in a time like this."

"So what we have is a jumper," the blond officer said to the other.

Marshall shook his head. "The buildings aren't that tall around here," he said, looking up. "And we're in the *middle* of the park. He couldn't have jumped this far in from one of the buildings. It's impossible."

"You sure you didn't have something to do with this?" the dark-haired officer asked, shining his light in Marshall's face.

What little color there was in Marshall's face went away. "N-no, sir."

The officer turned back to my father. "Well, then, any thoughts, Mr. Belarus?" he asked.

"Maybe he jumped from a plane," Marshall offered.

My father's eyes turned on him, on the verge of burning like lasers straight through my friend.

"Marshall," I warned. "Shut it."

"You explain it, then," Marshall said, getting defensive.

I gave my father an apologetic look, going for the most disarming expression I could muster under the circumstances, but he turned his glare to me and it was withering.

"Go home, Alexandra," he said.

"But—"

His withering look that meant there was no arguing with him. "Go home. Now. I will deal with these officers."

I didn't even bother trying to respond when he had his business voice on. I simply turned from him and headed toward the north gate, Rory and Marshall falling in behind me. My father must have bigger contacts out there than I thought because the officers didn't make any move to stop or detain us. Sometimes I forgot how hard-core a leader of industry he could still be despite his flakier moments.

"I expect you to be alone when I get home," he called out, causing Rory to swear under her breath.

The three of us pushed through the crowd standing outside the gate and walked down the block back toward my home. None of the other arriving officers tried to stop us.

"Did you see the way your dad just took over?" Marshall asked once we cleared the gathered crowd, still walking.

"And they just let us go!" Rory added.

"You sure you're not some sort of Mafia princess?" Marshall asked.

I shook my head. "Not Italian, remember?"

"You going to be okay?" Rory asked when we stopped in front of my home. "We can wait with you if you want."

I shook my head. "I'll be fine," I said. "I'm just creeped out. Did you see the mark on his hand?"

Rory and Marshall both shook their heads.

"I'm pretty sure that was the guy who attacked me earlier tonight," I said. "He disappeared in that alley . . . and now he turns up here. Dead."

"A shocking coincidence, I'm sure," Marshall said.

"That's an understatement."

"On the plus side, guy's dead," Rory reminded me.

"Rory," I said, tweaked. "Show some respect."

"Respect?" Rory laughed. "Lexi, the guy pulled a knife on you."

"I know, but—"

"But nothing," she continued, her voice getting serious. "Maybe you need to get out of your family's building a bit more, but this city is jacked up, Lexi." She pointed off to the park. "Case in point. You might not see it every day, but it's out there. So when someone who tried to take a swipe at my best friend turns up dead, I'm sorry, but I really don't mourn their loss."

"That's cold," Marshall added.

"It's *not*," Rory insisted. "I just think if it's us or them, I prefer that we're the survivors."

"Go," I said, feeling my nerves get all jangled up again. "Now. This is all getting to be a bit too much and I already need to steel myself for a talk with my father when he's done . . . bribing them, or whatever the hell it is he's doing in there."

Rory nodded and grabbed Marshall by the arm, dragging him down the block with her as she left. "Good luck with all that," she said. "Come on, Marsh. Let me give you pointers on how not to impress the ladies by bringing up your 'Dungeon Master.' "

"I wouldn't *want* to be with a woman who didn't appreciate it, you know," he countered.

"You may never be with a woman *ever* at this rate," she said, continuing on, but her voice fell out of earshot as they rounded the corner, heading west. I hated to see them go. They may have been annoying the way they picked on each other, but at least they were a welcome distraction compared to whatever stern dressing-down my father had in store for me later.

On the plus side, I was still better off than the dead man in the park, rest his unfortunate soul.

Nine

Alexandra

When my father caught up with me later that evening, I was sketching at one of the old drafting tables my great-great-grandfather had once used.

"Alexandra," he said, sounding just as pissed off as he had in the park, only now I was ready for it, having had some time for the shock of seeing the dead body to wear off and to regain my composure.

"This is not my fault, so please don't take that tone," I said, hearing it reflected in my own words. "Before you say anything else, I need to know something. *Have* to know."

He paused, his face a mask of frustration, and gave a reluctant nod. "Yes?"

I let out a long breath, the shaking of my nerves returning from earlier. "I may regret even asking this, but here it goes. Are you . . . connected?"

His eyebrows creased, his vast expanse of forehead wrinkling as his eyes narrowed in puzzlement. "Connected . . . ?" he repeated, his voice unsure.

My stomach tightened. "You know," I said. "Like to the mob? Like in *The Godfather*. Only a more Slavic version, I guess."

My father's eyes widened with dawning comprehension. A smile rose up on his lips and he did something he rarely did. He laughed. I couldn't remember the last time I had heard that sound out of him. Certainly not since before Devon's death, at least.

"What's so funny?" I asked.

"Tell me, Alexandra, where did you come up with such an idea?"

I wasn't about to tell him the whole truth on the matter, that Marshall had put the thought in my brain. It would probably get him—and Rory by association—banned for life from my home. "You're a well-respected man of business, but I don't know many businessmen who can talk the police out of pursuing a case. You just told them you'd deal with them and they let me and my friends go without further question. Plus there was an actual body left outside our building . . ."

My father shrugged. "It is true that I am a powerful man," he conceded, "but such is true of anyone who owns real estate in Manhattan."

I wasn't convinced. "And the body out in the park? That's not some kind of horse-head-in-the-bed kind of warning?"

He gave me a dark smile. "Do you forget we live in Manhattan?" he asked. "There is crime. New York is an amazing city, but let us be honest here—people are murdered every day."

"Since we are being honest," I said, "I just thought you should know . . . that person in the park . . . wasn't some random person. That was the man who attacked me earlier this evening."

His face went stone serious. "I see," he said, and walked over to one of the couches in the library section of the floor, groaning a little as he sat. He patted the seat next to him for me to join.

I got up from my desk, walked over, and sat down. My father looked me in the eyes.

"You have been through much tonight, my darling daughter," he said. "But trust me when I tell you that God is watching over you."

"I'd be lying if I said I understood your unquestionable faith in God or the universe or whatever," I said. "But I'm sorry, Father. I have a hard time buying into it. After all, God didn't seem too keen on watching out for Devon."

I waited for him to react—sadness, anger, something—but he stayed calm and fixed me with a peaceful smile. "Even the blessed must suffer to know at times how truly blessed they are. The same applies to our family."

"How can you be so sure, so . . . full of faith?"

"I have lost one child," he said. "I have faith my family will not lose another."

"'The family,'" I repeated. "You sure we aren't mobbed up?"

He smiled and patted my leg. "We are not, but I think perhaps that would make more sense to your way of thinking than what I'm about to tell you, oh, daughter of little faith."

I settled back on the couch, turning to him.

"Our family has been very fortunate over the years," he said. "Lady Luck, she has smiled on us, for several generations."

"Maybe our luck is running out," I said. "It didn't help Devon."

A pained smile crossed my father's face. "No," he said, "but nothing—not even our luck—is perfect, rest his soul. Besides, who is to say Devon is not in a better place? All of God's plans are not meant for us to know."

I could have argued with him. The odds didn't really seem in the favor of Devon ever reaching the pearly gates, unless being cruel had been added to the terms of admission there. Then there was the deeper philosophical argument of whether there even *was* an afterlife, but that was something I *definitely* wasn't ready to get into with him, so instead I nodded and waited. The pain slowly faded from his face as he began talking once more.

"It started with your namesake, Alexander, whose first luck came when fleeing to this country from Kobryn, along what was then the Lithuanian side of the border with Poland. He was fortunate as a stonemason to escape a life of servitude under the quite mad reign of the local lord Kejetan Ruthenia. Kejetan *the Accursed*, he was called."

I pointed at one of the statues on the far side of the studio space, one depicting a Slavic-looking man with an enormous jaw and heavy brow. "That's him," I said. "Although my great-great-grandfather labeled the base of the statue 'The Bloody Lord.'"

"My own father, your grandfather, talked about that when I was growing up," my father said, a faraway look in his eyes, lost in his own memories. "He said Alexander never spoke of why he fled the old country, only that he came to the Americas to start a new life with your great-great-grandmother and his two surviving children. My guess is that, yes, the lord of the land earned the name on that statue, but Alexander escaping tyranny under his rule was the first bit of blessed Belarus luck. He came to America and settled in New York City, helping to build it as it rose higher and higher into the sky. Your great-great-grandfather's dealings in the construction of this city only grew, making a name for him that ensured the well-being of his family for generations. We have benefited greatly from that, living well."

Enrapt as I was in this bit of family history I had heard only in bits and pieces, I still fought the urge to contradict the "living well" comment. After all, Devon certainly wasn't.

"But there have been times of misfortune, too," he said, a little of the sparkle slipping from his eyes. "When I was a young boy, no more than fifteen, my friends and I used to sneak out and hang where we weren't supposed to. We loved to go out on the ice up at the reservoir in Central Park. Only one night, I go to meet my friends, and, stickler for time that I am, I was early, but that also meant I was alone when some men in the park came after me. Hoping to escape them, I was forced to run out onto the ice, something I would never do alone. My friends and I knew the dangers of not having someone with you, but what choice did I have?"

"No offense," I said, "but I'd like to state for the record Rory and I have never done anything half that dangerous."

My father eyed me as if he didn't believe me, but continued on. "I fell through the ice. I pray you never know such a horrid feeling as this in your lifetime, Alexandra. The chill, the shock, the confusion of it all. I fought to get back to the surface, following what little light I could make out above me, but every time I came up, I was under the full sheet of ice. I could not find the spot where I had fallen through, and, panicked as I was, I could not break through. That night, I was going to die and, what was worse, I knew it and could do nothing."

His breathing was rapid now, as if he were somehow reliving the moment. He paused to catch his breath, and when he spoke again, he was calmer, quieter.

"That was when I saw it—the angel. Long wings extended, coming down hard on the ice, sending a ripple of cracks all throughout the space right above me. He drove back the men, smiting them with the power of the Lord, sending them flying across the ice. Its fist came down through the ice and I felt it lifting me. Cold, barely breathing, I felt it carrying me off through the sky, and I gave myself over to the sensation, expecting to wake in Heaven. When I instead woke in my own room, I knew I had witnessed a miracle." He crossed himself. "We are blessed. We are watched over. That must have been a good forty years ago."

"Dad, you had a traumatic childhood experience," I said. "That's all. You probably fell through the ice, got rescued by someone, and blocked the rest out. You were in shock."

Then the worst thing in the world happened: My father looked hurt. For just a moment his face was filled with a look of sadness and pain; then he simply shook his head and looked into my eyes.

"I know what I saw," he said. "I know what I believe."

This conversation was going a little too into the deep end of the baptismal font for my liking, so I checked the time on my phone. It was nearly two a.m. "I should probably get to bed," I said, standing up.

He grabbed my wrist with considerable force, startling me. The second I jumped, however, he loosened his grip and sat me back down on the couch with him.

"This isn't about my faith," he said. "This isn't even about how blessed we are. This is about something I noticed in the park on that man's hand."

"You saw the mark?" I asked, my eyes flying wide. "That demon-looking thing?"

My father nodded. "That's the real reason I tried to 'ground' you. You see, Alexandra, I have seen that before, back when I was a boy. My attackers on the ice, they bore the same mark."

"What does it mean?" I asked.

My father took my hands in his and squeezed them tight, something I still found reassuring even as a grown-up. "I do not know," he said, "but please believe me, whatever your own beliefs are, my daughter, I need you to exercise caution. God is watching over us, but he helps those who help themselves."

I tried to laugh. His words bordered on ridiculous, melodramatic, but the sheer sincerity in his eyes drove any humor out of me. I didn't have to be a believer in much of any kind of religion to understand the concern my father had for me. I hoped he was right about our family's luck.

But I was afraid it was running out.

Ten

Alexandra

I had done all the work I could on the files my father had given me to take up to the studio while I remained inside. I seriously doubted anything would happen during broad daylight. The streets would be crowded, full of commuters on their way to work, and in the light of day, it almost seemed ridiculous to cower inside. Hoping to get a jump on the day and that maybe my family had gotten over this idea of grounding me, I grabbed up the file folders from last night and headed downstairs relatively early. If I could get out of the house before anyone could stop me, I was sure my initiative would pay off. It beat sitting around the building wondering about the deeper religious question of last night—whether angels were real or not. The jury was still way out on that one in my mind.

Except I never made it past the large dine-in kitchen down on the main living floor. Not only was my mother already in there; she was making breakfast for Rory, and not just oatmeal. There was bacon, eggs, fresh-cut fruit, hashed potatoes, and toast.

I stopped in my tracks, dropping my shoulder bag full of file folders onto the granite island where Rory was helping herself to a slice of toast, sprinkling sugared cinnamon over it. "Oh, hello," I said. "What's all this?"

My mother looked up from the stove where she was folding an omelet over itself, a slight smile on her face, looking over to Rory. "Do I know my daughter or what?"

Rory snickered. "That you do, Mrs. B."

"Do you mind letting me in on it, then?" I asked, feeling a bit territorial over their in-joke or whatever it was. I certainly didn't get the full breakfast treatment all that often, and here was my bestie chowing down.

My mother plated part of the omelet and slid the plates over to Rory and me. "*I* knew once your father and I forbid you from leaving the building, that would be the one thing that would motivate you to actually get out of it."

"So you're not going to stop me?" I asked, going for the fruit.

She put the pan back on the stovetop and held her hand out toward Rory. "I'm still shaken by what you told me, Alexandra, but . . . well, why do you think I called her? This way you'll have someone with you as you head off on your appointments."

I raised an eyebrow. "And this is okay with the boss man?"

My mother smiled at me like I was a child of ten again. "I will handle your father," she said. "I'm sure he'll relent once he knows at least Aurora is with you. I know it's daytime and all, but still . . . be careful."

"You're okay with this?" I asked Rory. "Don't you have graduate school things to do?"

She nodded as she enthusiastically devoured her piece of cinnamon toast. "I don't mind skipping out of class," she said. "I'm on one of my nondance days, anyway."

I'd already had the white-handled knife in my shoulder bag for protection, but having Rory around would be an added bonus. I told my mother I'd call after each appointment, and then Rory and I were off. Surprisingly, we hit all five boroughs in one day and knocked out most of my appointments with Rory waiting outside them for me, and I was glad to have her. Having her in tow passed the time all the quicker and actually

kept me motivated. Even so, the sun had set about half an
hour earlier when we arrived at the last appointment of the
day, putting us straight in the heart of the Bowery at one of
my great-great-grandfather's worn-down locations.

Rory stretched on the edge of the sidewalk. "I'm beat," she
said. "I think I'd be less beat if it *had* been a dance day for
me. You want me to come in?"

Rory had really thrown herself into the role of bodyguard
all day, but I had resisted all her offers. Bringing a pretty
blue-haired girl into my appointments wasn't going to get any
of the brokers, contractors, or work crews to take me seriously.
"I'm good," I said, sliding all but the last of my folders into
my shoulder bag. "Stay out here."

"You sure?" she asked, arms extended high overhead like
she was being pulled on an invisible rack.

I nodded.

"I should be fine, Rory," I said, examining the folder for some
of the base specs on the building. "Really. It might get ugly in
there, but only because I may have to flip my bitch switch to
make sure they stay on schedule with the renovation."

Rory gave a quick golf clap. "Look at you," she said. "Get
down with your badass business self."

I curtsied once before heading into the building and was
off. The lobby and lower floors looked in good shape as I rode
up the elevator, poking my head out on each floor. I wasn't
worried about them anyway. According to the file our biggest
problems lay at the top floor and reinforcement of the roof.

The doors opened onto a half-finished hallway. Exposed
wiring hung running from light to light along the skeleton
structure of the open ceiling and continued on down the hall.
I consulted the notes in the folder and worked my way down
to the door that led into the largest, unfinished part of the
floor. It opened up onto a large open space full of construction
debris—broken plaster, torn-out wood, stacks of uninstalled
flooring and Sheetrock. I checked for a light switch, but the
area had yet to be wired; thankfully enough, light from the
hallway spilled into the room so I could check things over for
the progress report I needed to file back at the offices. Where

the effing contractors were was anyone's guess, but that was only the first bad mark on a report that already looked ripe with potential problems in the space.

The plaster of the ceiling was still coming down as marked on the last progress report, but it didn't look like much had been done to it since then. In the interest of being thorough, however, I wanted to inspect it more closely.

A stack of Sheetrock sat piled in one section of the room under one of the problem areas, which seemed to be my best chance of getting close enough for a better look. I shoved the file folder into my shoulder bag and crawled my way to the top of the Sheetrock pile. Standing, I found I still had trouble assessing the true state of the ceiling, not that I really knew what I was looking for. Frustrated at my lack of knowledge and inspecting abilities, I looked down and found the contractors I had been looking for—piled behind the Sheetrock, unmoving and with pools of blood slowly radiating out from under their forms.

My stomach sank and I swayed with vertigo on top of the Sheetrock, falling to my knees as my legs gave out. As I crawled my way off it, the light in the room changed. The door behind me was closing, and when I turned, it was shut, the only light now coming dimly into the room through the windows along the far wall.

A man stepped out of the shadows, partially hidden by the hood he wore under his jacket, but what I could see of the face was unkind, menacing. I backed away from him, startled but surprisingly not as scared as I had been the night before, despite having just seen several more dead bodies. My fear then had made me feel small, weak, diminished me, and I refused to let that rule over me now. Even my father's speech about our luck and our being blessed had given me some of that back. As I pulled the white-handled knife from my shoulder bag, it strengthened my resolve even further.

The man's eyes went to it, and he laughed, the sound echoing through the large open space. He raised his own hand, holding a similar knife in it. The tattoo on the back of his hand was also familiar—again, the stylized demon.

"You had better know how to use that," the man said, his voice thick with the accent of our people from the old country. "Although the very fact you are in possession of one of our sacred blades means that you must have some prowess to have claimed it."

"I didn't do anything!" I shouted in growing anger and frustration. "Leave me and my family alone. We didn't do anything to you."

"You have wronged those whom I serve," he said. "That is enough. And once I bleed the location of your entire family out of you, they will reward me with the Life Eternal."

"Wow," I said, a bit of fear creeping back into me as I caught the madness on his face. "You know what, mister? I didn't kill your friend, but if you're threatening my whole family, I wish I had." I lifted my knife, ignoring how it shook in my hand. Whether I could use it was another story, but I'd be damned if I was going to play the victim again. Something dark was rising up in me.

The man moved in fast, coming at me from my left. Slashing to my side, my blade flew completely past the man, leaving him unharmed. I may have pulled up short, my body still unwilling to stab at someone, and I shrunk back from him as my false bravado dropped away. His blade caught the strap on my shoulder bag, slicing it and slipping the bag to the floor, its contents spreading out everywhere. I went to run, but I slipped on one of the damn folders and the attacker had me by the wrist, prying the knife from my hand.

Disarmed and caught in the man's viselike grip, I allowed myself to give in to my growing fear, heading straight into full-blown panic.

Eleven

———— ☾ ————

Stanis

I stood as a silent rooftop sentinel in one of the older city sections called the Bowery, waiting for the woman within the building while her blue-haired friend lingered on the street below. After last night's attack in that alley, I found my mind focused solely on her. I could not remember the last time I had done anything more than just fill myself with the joy of flight, but something about last night's attack set my thoughts ablaze. The mark on the back of the attacker's hand as he clung to my arms high above the city last night before I ended his life, the horns and fangs . . . there was a familiarity to it . . .

So lost in my own thoughts was I that when a sudden wave of panic flared out from the woman somewhere nearby, my chest knotted like a fist balling up, catching me off my guard and driving me to my knees.

The surface of the roof beneath me cracked from the impact, and I did not bother trying to stand back up. The woman's panic radiated with intensity directly from somewhere on the floor below. I lifted my fists high over my head and brought them down hard on the rooftop, over and over.

I did not know what I would find below. One of the rules screamed out to me—*Conceal myself from humanity*—but

Protect the family was the master rule, and if it meant revealing myself in that endeavor, then so be it. Her primal call for help was a compulsion like no other I had ever felt. Cracks spread out beneath me as the old tar, stone, wood, and plaster finally gave way from each passing blow. The roof shifted beneath me, caved, and I dropped into the dark room below, my wings spreading to slow my fall. Time slowed as I took in the situation. A lone male figure stood directly behind the woman, his arms wrapped around her as she struggled to break free. I arced my wings, aiming for the man, then narrowed my wingspan to speed up.

With perfect accuracy, my stone form hit the man *hard*— as I had intended—driving his body away from the woman, the sound of cracking running through him. *So fragile, these creatures.*

The man shuddered in shock on the floor as the lifeblood left his body and he went still. The woman watched him, her own body shaking, but she did not move, the two of us standing there as he jerked and fell silent. As she was distracted and had her back to me, there was still a chance I could keep to the rules if I left quick enough. I turned, seeking out the hole I had left in the roof. I stepped across the broken wood and crumbled stone debris I had created from my entrance to better position myself, but that effort alone had it crunching underneath my feet, breaking the brief silence.

"Wait," the woman said, her voice shaky. Despite my desire to leave, I found I could not, held in place by a force unseen. "Let me see you."

I turned to her, getting my first look at the girl's face up close. There was something familiar to her features, but I was not sure what it was. The dark eyes, wide with wonder now, the sharp angle of her chin, the slow and steady slope of her nose . . .

"Th-thank you," she managed to get out, quiet and barely able to speak while she stared at me standing there in the darkened room. A mix of fear and calm emanated from her, its blast washing over me in confusion.

"You are . . . welcome," I said.

She stepped toward me. "You helped me the other night, didn't you?" she asked. "In that alley in the Village . . . ?"

I nodded.

She looked down at the remains of her attacker, shock and the hint of fear filling her eyes. "You . . . *killed* that other man and this one. Why?"

"They would have done the same to you," I said without hesitation.

She leaned over the man, staring into his wide, unmoving eyes. "Would they?"

"Yes," I said. "That is what I believe."

"Why me?" she asked. "Why are they trying to hurt my family?"

I stepped forward into the light that came down from the hole I had left in the ceiling. The woman seemed to notice the wings rising up behind me for the first time and gasped. I pulled them close against my body, leaning down to lift up one of the attacker's arms. I turned it back and forth in my hands until I found what I was looking for.

"There," I said, pointing one of my clawed fingers to the closed fist at the end of the man's arm. The demon sigil that marked the skin on the back of his hand trailed up the rest of his arm.

Hesitant, the woman stepped toward me to look it over. "The man who attacked me the other night had similar markings," she said. "What do they mean?"

"It is an ancient mark," I said, finally recalling it. "The more sections, blocks, the longer it is, the higher up their place is in the order."

"*What* order?"

"The Servants of Ruthenia," I recalled, but nothing more.

The woman shuddered as she looked at the arm, then turned her eyes to me. "What *are* you?" she asked. "How do you know that?"

"I was created to *protect*, both you and your family," I said. I paused, trying to recall something more about the Servants. I lowered the dead man's arm and stood. "As to how I know this order, I am not sure. My thoughts are not what they once were; long has my mind been dormant." I pointed at the mark on the hand again. "It has been a long time since I have seen such things."

The woman's eyes narrowed. "How long are we talking here?" she asked.

"I am unsure of that as well," I said, noting the disappointment on her face at my words. "I am sorry. To my recollection, I do not think I have talked to anyone in many a year. At least, no one I did not then kill."

A sudden spike of fear radiated off of her and she stepped back. "You're not going to . . . you know . . . ?"

When she did not finish her words, I cocked my head. "Explain."

She let out a long breath, then spoke in a rush. "You're not going to kill *me* . . . are you?"

I shook my head. "I am sworn to protect," I said.

The woman visibly relaxed, looking around the chaos of the room, her eyes passing quickly over the bloody body of her attacker lying between us.

"You should go," I said.

She nodded absently. "What about you?"

"I will take care of the body of this man who attacked you," I said.

"There are others . . ." she said, walking with a great hesitation over to a stack of thin gray slabs. "Other men here who that man killed."

"I can take care of them as well."

She looked up at the hole in the ceiling. "Can you make it look like the roof caved in on them? Like the building was structurally weak? I'm going to need to explain some of this insanity to other people."

I nodded. "I can do that," I said. "Once I dispose of your attacker."

The woman, eyes still wide and locked on mine, gave a small, pained smile, then averted her gaze and started for the door. She was almost to the hallway when she spun around, still shaken.

"Wait," she said, looking down at the crumpled body of

her attacker. "You're not going to leave . . . *him* in the park like the other one, are you?"

"You do not wish this?"

She gave a nervous, grim laugh, looking as if she might be violently ill any moment. "No," she said. "I do not wish that."

"As you wish," I said, then added, "but you should tell no one of this."

She nodded, her eyes glazed, uncertain.

"You should go," I said. "I will first remove this man from here, then come back to finishing damaging this roof."

"What *are* you going to do with him?"

"The ocean is deep," I said, looking down at the body. "This man will be another mystery lost to it."

The woman moved closer, wonder on her face. "Why *did* you leave that other man in the park outside my family's building?" she asked.

"As a warning."

"A warning?" she repeated. "To who?"

I moved closer to her as well, looking down into her face and those hauntingly familiar eyes. "To anyone who would wish to harm you or your family."

She shook her head and gave a short, nervous laugh. "Why the hell would anyone want to do that in first place?"

"I am not sure," I said, moving to gather the man's body up in my arms and walking over to the hole in the ceiling. I looked up through it, gauging how much clearance I had.

The woman ran over to me. "Will I see you again?" she asked.

"Hopefully not," I said, my heart heavy with the admission.

"Hopefully not?" Was that disappointment on her face? It was hard to read these humans. "Why not?"

"If you have seen me, then I have broken one of the rules I am meant to follow. Tonight, for instance. I have failed."

"Failed?" she said, the pitch of her voice rising, incredulous. "You saved my life!"

I considered this for a moment. "There was little choice in doing that," I said, "but nonetheless, I failed to follow one of the other rules set upon me. I must assess what this all means." The necklace around the woman's neck caught my eye, something familiar to it. Still cradling the dead man, I reached one of my hands out toward it. The woman recoiled first, but let me catch it with the tip of one of my claws, and I lifted it away from her. A small stone disc hung from a metal chain, the stone itself giving off the same form of energy I felt when I was at the Belarus building.

"There is a power in this talisman," I said. "But it is fading. It is with this as it is with your home. You must heal these things."

"Heal things?" she said. "Heal things how? I don't understand."

"Heal the stone; heal the house," I said. "The stone was once strong. Now it is not."

"Says who?" she asked, anger creeping into her confusion.

"My maker." I tensed my legs and leapt up through the opening in the ceiling, knocking free some of the surrounding debris as I took flight.

"And who is your maker?" she shouted up after me.

"The one who swore me to protecting your family," I said, looking back at her frail form down in the room. "The Spellmason Alexander Belarus."

I took to the sky, heading out to sea, the feeling of confusion coming off the woman fading the farther away I went, but the familiarity of the woman's face hit me. I knew those features, I realized. I had been seeing them for a long time, always upon waking. They belonged to the face of the man who haunted my recurring dreams, the man whose name I had just invoked. The woman was not just the maker's kin; she looked the image of him.

Twelve

C

Alexandra

Rory paced back and forth like a panther and turned to me as I came out of the front door of the old building clutching my broken-strapped shoulder bag and file folders. She ran over to me, eyes wide.

"Are you okay?" she asked. "I heard something like a car accident up on the roof. Jesus, Lexi, you're covered in white dust. What the hell happened up there?"

I barely remembered leaving the apartment upstairs or how I had gotten back to the lobby, walking in a bit of shell-shocked haze. *I'm cracking up,* I thought. For the first time, I looked down at my body. Bits of plaster dust, ceiling fragments, and splinters of wood were covering just about every inch of my clothes. I looked back up to Rory, my brain having trouble processing the events of the last half hour. If what I had just witnessed was actually real and not some imagined figment due to work- and mugging-related stress, I wasn't sure how to even articulate it. The small ball of sanity I was struggling to hold on to had me wondering whether I should even try to right now.

I fought for the most basic yet honest of answers I could use. "Roof collapse," I said after a moment. "I'm fine. Structural integrity issues. It's why we were working on the place. Bad build."

"Jesus," Rory said, still looking me over. "You sure you're okay?"

I nodded.

"Were your workers up there?"

The mere mention of them brought a flood of images—the pile of bloody corpses—and tears formed at the corners of my eyes, but I held my tongue. Hadn't my mysterious savior told me to tell no one? He said he would take care of the situation. I nodded.

"Shouldn't we call the police or something?"

"No," I said, trying to restrain the sudden panic in my chest. "Listen, Rory, it's a real mess up there. You saw my dad and how he handled the police the other night. I'll let him figure out how to handle this whole job site fiasco." I didn't know if or when I was going to ever get into that with him, but that didn't matter much. Right now I just wanted to get as far away from this place as possible. "Can we get out of here? I'm a little bit on edge after all this."

I didn't have to lie or fake being shaken. It was just the *why* of it all that I was keeping from Rory. Part of me hated lying to my best friend, but I sat silent on our cab ride back up to Gramercy Park, wondering not only how I would tell her but *if* I would tell her.

The surreal nature of my evening had me wondering whether I wasn't just flat cracking up.

Once at my front door, I convinced Rory that all I needed was some sleep to center myself again, and although reluctant to do so, she left once she saw that I was safely in my family's building. Alone in our lobby, my mind wandered back through the night's events, already seeming like a distant, strange, and unpleasant nightmare. So deep in thought, I found myself up in the art studio with no memory of how I got there. With two lapses in time tonight, I worried that I'd blink and end up somewhere completely different or, worse, back outside the comfort of my home, so I settled down onto my favorite comfy couch up there, half-terrified, half–in shock, one hundred percent determined not to move.

My hand snaked up to the family sigil hanging around my neck. *Heal the stone; heal the house,* the creature had said. What did that even mean? And what the hell was a Spell-mason? Was this my mind trying to tell me in some effed-up way that real estate was the cause I was meant to embrace? Was all this mental drama its way of telling me to accept it?

My thoughts wove in and out of one another, looping around and around, getting nowhere until I was finally shaken out of them many hours later by noticing the sun rising over the city. I went to stand and stretch, and when I did, something slid off of my lap with a dull *thud* onto the old worn area rug at my feet. My heart caught in my throat. It was one of my great-great-grandfather's statues. I didn't remember picking it up from its pedestal off in the art section up here, but I must have. That caused a chill down my spine, but the greater one came when I actually recognized the figure—a much smaller version of last night's creature—convinced now that I had imagined it.

I grabbed it up off the rug, and, armed by the false bravado of daylight, I ran to the back of the art studio and took the stairs up to the proper roof. The light was blinding compared to the long dark night I had just stayed up through, and the streets were still relatively quiet for this time of early morning in New York City. I walked among the scattering of uncarved and half-finished blocks of stone up there until I reached the edge of the building that overlooked Gramercy Park, where the larger version of the statuette in my hand stood.

It looked like him. The creature who had saved me.

By the light of day it was still an imposing bit of work, but I felt the fool for thinking it anything more than a well-carved chunk of stone depicting an impressively striking man with long hair and batlike wings, a bit of Gothic artwork done by my great-great-grandfather. Compared to the statuette, which was perfect due to being kept inside all these centuries, the stone figure was pockmarked from the wear of age and rain, and it had even been tagged at some point along one of its legs by a street artist. My rational mind settled itself back in place as the flaws in the stone and the sheer inert quality of the piece reassured me. The bit of graffiti—the defacing of the art—made me almost sad for it, but it also brought me back to reality.

Thanks, Brain. I'll take a hint. Overwork plus a near mugging are taking their toll.

My father wanted me to stay around the building and I had succeeded in finding a way out yesterday with Rory as my escort, but not today. I was already planning how to spend my day relaxing when I stopped, my eyes catching something. The claws on the creature's hands. They were coated in a drying reddish-brown liquid, and although I was no medical expert, I knew blood when I saw it.

Whatever relaxation I had started to allow myself evaporated. I clutched the statuette of the creature as I backed away from the large stone version of it. I looked down at the figure, noticing for the first time a name for the piece of art etched into the bottom of the piece.

Stanis.

It wasn't much to go on, but with a wealth of handwritten information to sift through in my great-great-grandfather's personal library, it was a start.

Thirteen

Alexandra

There was little shame in falling asleep in my great-great-grandfather's studio library. The shame came from waking up only a few hours later, sun high in the early-afternoon sky, lying sprawled out in one of the aisles with my head pressed into several books, drooling on the shelf as my phone went off in my pocket.

I pulled it out. *Rory.*

"Hey," I said, simultaneously wiping the drool away and attempting to sound awake, but failing completely on that last count.

"Were you *sleeping*? It's, like, one thirty in the afternoon."

"Let's just call it post-traumatic stress after the cave-in last night," I said. "My body really needed it."

I didn't necessarily feel rested, but then it struck me what I had been looking for before I fell asleep. I pulled myself together, stood, stretched out my pains, and stared at the massive aisle of books towering before me.

"Fair enough," she said. "You working today? Or are you up for hanging? Marshall said he could bring over some of the new games that came in over at Roll for Initiative. I won't play but I'll watch you guys and provide snarky commentary."

I usually welcomed the distraction offered from the types of games Marshall sometimes brought over, even if I didn't get the references or why he would be practically bouncing in his seat with nerdiness, but not today. I was on a mission to prove that I wasn't losing my mind.

"Can't," I said. "Not so much a workday here, but I have some . . . family business I need to look into."

"Well, okay," she said, disappointment in her voice. "But the invitation still stands. I don't want to get trapped too long in his store. Despite the nerd renaissance the world seems to be having, I still draw stares just for being a girl in there when I stop by. So if you ch—"

"Yeah, sure," I said, killing the call as the enormity of my task reclaimed my brain. I tried to begin last night's search in earnest once again, but instead just found myself standing there, staring at all the books before me. And there were more aisles beyond the one that was already intimidating me.

Thing was, I had crashed out because trying to do a general search through my grandfather's countless notebooks was proving fruitless without knowing *where* to start. Much like his collection of puzzle boxes, these books were a puzzle unto themselves. Thousands of notations jumped from one book to another, but the subject matter was so cryptic and vague that unless you knew and *found* the starting point subject, you were kinda screwed.

So my real question was: Where to effing start?

This wasn't my first bout of frustration with my great-great-grandfather and his organization skills. I respected the cleverness and design that went into his statues and architecture, and especially the intricate puzzle boxes that filled the shelves of his art space, but he was crap on organization.

Unless, of course, that was what he *meant* others to think. I mean, maybe there was a method to his madness. If I had the secrets of being a "Spellmason" to hide, would I leave them in plain sight? No, I'd hide them carefully.

The question was: Where?

The puzzle boxes . . . Maybe there was a connection between everything Alexander did. Despite my not understanding whatever system he had put in place, nothing he created was without purpose, so I set to thinking about what connections could be made between them all, starting with the most basic piece of the puzzle: the one thing that I knew so far.

I knew Stanis existed, and, as far as I could tell, was his most impressive creation ever, easily outdoing any piece of architecture around Manhattan. I started there by going and grabbing the statuette of him off the art studio table I had left it on. If I was looking for information on Stanis, how would this possibly relate? Looking it over, I wasn't sure. Other than the name *Stanis* carved into the base of it, there were no other markings.

Unless you counted the base itself as a sort of marking. Which, I decided, was just want I wanted to do. The stone base's shape was different from that of every other statue, roughly the shape of an octagon but with two flared-out sections on either side that mirrored where the wings of the creature hovered over them.

I had grown up knowing there were several octagon-shaped puzzle boxes scattered along the art studio's shelves, but never really paying *that* much attention. Resolved, I set off to find them, running into the studio section and pulling down puzzle box after puzzle box, until I found one that held the corresponding shape. It was twice the size of my head and the stone of it was heavy, set in blocked-out areas that reminded me of a strange Slavonic script–covered Rubik's Cube. I set to twisting and turning it, searching for some rhyme or reason to the markings on it. My knowledge of the old country's written language was shaky, but several of the letters were more familiar than others on the moving pieces, and, keeping with my plan to simplify my approach to puzzle solving, I set about making them spell out the one word I thought might fit.

Stanis.

The box sighed with a soft *click* as the bottom of it popped free, a small but thick Moleskine-like notebook set into the hidden space. Age had been kind to it, perhaps from years of being perfectly preserved in the box itself, and with excitement I carefully removed it from the slot, falling into the task of unraveling my great-great-grandfather's most hidden secrets.

The notebook, however, proved to be just as puzzling as any other book in the library. Parts of his cursive scratching were in English, other parts in a broken Slavonic and Lithuanian that Devon and I used to use as kids when playing, but *none* of it organized in a linear fashion. In order to make some sense of it, I ran over to the regular stock of paper and notebooks I kept in the studio's supply cage and grabbed a fresh Moleskine of my own. I settled in at one of the art tables, laying out my blank book next to my ancestor's one, and set about trying to trace my way though his notes.

The going was slow thanks to the cryptic order of his words and the arduous task of deciphering it, but after countless hours cramped and hunched over his notes, I had assembled some notes of my own:

A reminder from Great-great-grandfather Alex, inscribed: "A book is meant to be well red" (his typo, not mine!)

—Stanis—Alexander's most ambitious creation as a Spellmason

—Which begs me to ask: What the hell is a Spellmason? Does not come up on Wikipedia!

—Alexander studied and discovered a prowess for folk magic back in Kobryn (Belarus, Lithuanian border town), led to exploring greater power, which in turn led to joining a (secret? Since it's not on the internetz anyway) order. ARE THERE OTHERS? Or more importantly, where did they all disappear to?

—My G-G-GF mentions that part of Spellmasonry is alchemy, using arcane chemical processes to imbue materials with different properties than they would normally have, i.e. living stone, Stanis

—A few notes on the alchemical process in Spellmasonry: "The magic practitioner must be ever mindful. Transmutation to living stone is wrought with perils, he warns of trickster and malevolent spirits that seek out, crave, vessels to occupy. Controlling the stone is an issue. Your Will will be your guide.

—But how to transmute? No reference points or how-to manual on doing something like that other than the word Kimiya . . . hidden elsewhere? He references there is a master book of his arcane knowledge, but I can NOT find the damned thing in the family library . . . so where the eff is it?

—Stanis said, "heal the stone, heal the house" . . . yeah, right, getting right on that great-great-gramps . . . Is there a power that's weakening?

Alexander mentions protection over and over in his notes:
First, our sigils
Second, as his knowledge grew, the house
Third, setting Stanis to his "rules" . . . list
    somewhere?

—worried about how powerful Stanis can truly be. In order to exact control over the creature, he "drew forth" parts of his energy, trapping them in "soul stones," for what he says was both for his protection and ours.

—"I pray there is never any need to restore him. The Revelation of the Soul is something I do not wish on the creature."

—"His is to serve and protect the name Belarus. The names of the dead haunt me already, but I pray his watchfulness will prove some penance for my failings in life."

Not the most cohesive note taking I'd ever done, but considering the web I had been sorting through all day until the sun had gone down, it was a start. As a bonus, I felt a little less like I was cracking up now that I had something tangible in hand, something concrete that told me I wasn't crazy. Unless I was imagining all this as well.

No. I pushed that thought aside. Red pilling, blue pilling it was a road to madness. Still, I had little belief in magic or matters arcane, save my experiences from last night, but seeing the words in my great-great-grandfather's script made starting to accept its existence easier to swallow. Yet my mind held fast to its nervous reluctance. I needed to prove something to myself.

Alexander's notebook held a map, one I recognized, of this very studio, which I knew oh, so well, but not, apparently, as well as I thought. I scooped up the book and took it with me to the metal-barred supply cage near the back right corner of the studio, entering it. Tools, paint, clay, and a host of my modern art supplies filled the old area, but I was looking for something more. The map showed an area sequestered behind one section of ancient tooled shelves built into the wall, and after several minutes of examination, I came across two different pressure plates both the size of the tips of my fingers. They clicked in, locked; then the entire shelving unit slid in and rolled behind the one next to it.

I stepped forward into the space, the light of the studio allowing me to see the racks and shelves full of metal flasks, glass tubes, and jars, all stoppered one way or another, some still filled with their contents.

What a lovely little alchemist's kitchen.

I grabbed a small tin flask marked with the one familiar name mentioned in my great-great-grandfather's book, *Kim-iya*, and stepped out of the space, my heart starting to race in my chest. I ran to one of the clear art tables, laid out Alexander's notebook, then pulled the chain from around my neck, placing the stone sigil of it flat on the surface. The "recipe" listed in his book didn't include measurements. Hell, it barely contained a phrase to go with them, and *that* was in Slavonic. Erring on the side that my will wasn't necessarily all that willing a guide, I unscrewed the top of the flask and coated my small stone with the slow-pouring crimson liquid that came out of it. I set it aside, then placed my hands to either side of the stone, reading the phrase in its native tongue, although the phrase filled my head in English.

My words, my bond.

Not sure what I was doing—trying to perform magic?—I stared at it hard, wanting it to do something, but as the moments passed, I was basically looking at a wet, reddish stone on a length of fine silver chain just sitting there. So much for my will being my guide . . .

Although, if I was honest, had I really expected it to move? Who knew what the shelf life was on tin-flasked alchemical substances, anyway? No, I hadn't given it my all, because if I was being honest with myself, I felt foolish.

Which, maybe, was part of my problem, wasn't it? If I felt a little ridiculous, I wasn't really giving all my will over to the attempt, now, was I? I looked down at the stone, still sitting there, doing jack.

Screw it, I thought, and settled my hands back down on the table, one to either side of the sigil. If Rory and I played at having magical powers like Hermione Granger ten years ago, I could certainly go all in and give this a bit more of my all.

"My words, my bond," I said, and I let my desire to control the stone of my necklace take over, imagining my will rolling off me like a wave toward the necklace.

It *twitched*. It not only twitched; it began to rock, the motion in it increasing until the rocking became a gentle spin that coiled the chain around it as it went.

I stepped back, my hands coming away from it, and the stone was already slowing, but for a brief second I had felt the connection. I was practically beside myself, giddy with a fresh rush of excitement. It felt like I had passed my O.W.L.S.! I thought of Rory, who would have pooped herself had she seen it, which caused me to laugh out loud. It was strange to hear the sound, but I welcomed it and the return of hope that came with it.

Yes, there might be men trying to kill us, but with Stanis we had a powerful ally. Or at least I thought we did. What I really needed to do was try to communicate with the creature some more. Excited and—dare I think it—hopeful, I grabbed up my necklace, Alexander's book, and my own Moleskine, heading for the stairs at the back of the house, hurrying my way up to the roof.

The chill in the air was a bit more pronounced this early-October night as I stepped with care among the blocks of unfinished statues. I didn't know what I was going to say to the creature, rolling a myriad of questions through my head as I went to the edge of our building that faced Gramercy Park,

but I needn't have worried. The winged creature was gone
from where I had stood yesterday, back when I was wondering
whether my mind was playing tricks on me. This was no trick.
The statue had gone somewhere, presumably under its own
power, confirming that everything I was reading had some
merit to it.

My excitement died down a little, but I had to admit it was
probably all for the best that it wasn't there tonight. Given my
lack of sleep and hours of bleary-eyed research, the odds of
me even being capable of asking anything coherent were slim.
Besides, tomorrow was another night, and if I hoped to get
anything accomplished, I should probably catch up on sleep
before then.

Wouldn't do to try to make nice with a gargoyle with bags
under my eyes.

Fourteen

Stanis

The first thing I noticed upon waking perched on top of the Belarus building—other than the fading memories of my maker's face—was a cool wetness against part of my stone skin. It was nothing like the falling rain, which had worn away some of the finer details on my body's carvings over the centuries now, but rather something . . . bubbly.

Without moving from the ledge of the building, I cast my eyes toward what was causing the unique prickling sensation along the curve of my right calf. The maker's kin was there, her dark hair down to her shoulders, frantically scrubbing away at my stone muscle with a bristly brush that she kept dipping into a pail of soapy water every few seconds. She was dressed in a black T-shirt and what I would have normally thought of as a men's work coveralls, but who knew whether that was the right term for it anymore. The world was constantly changing around me.

Not sure of what to do, I returned my eyes to the sight that had greeted me tens of thousands of times—the fleeting, soft orange glow of a sun that was once again vanishing beyond the horizon. Much of my view had altered over the years as newer buildings rose with the world's progress, but bits of the horizon were still available. As the dregs of daylight slowly gave way to the blue-black of the nighttime sky, the stiffness in my body left me, which made holding my position even more difficult while the maker's kin continued to scrub away.

"You can move if you like," she said with a smile. "It's all right. I know you're awake now . . . or alive, or whatever it is."

"Forgive me," I said. "Being talked to is still . . . an unfamiliar thing for me. Until the other night, no one has spoken directly to me for countless years." The maker's kin went back to her work on my leg. I stretched myself up to my full height and stepped off of the ledge and onto the roof proper. The woman gasped and the smile faltered on her face.

I cocked my head at her.

"I'm sorry," she said. "I wasn't really prepared after the other night, in all the chaos . . . You must be at least seven feet tall . . . and those wings!"

I expanded my stone wings to their full ten-foot span. "I understand," I said. "Your kind looks incredibly frail to me in comparison."

The maker's kin shuddered. "Like the attacker you left in the park for us."

"Yes," I said. "Like him."

She looked off across the empty expanse of roof, dotted only by the occasional unfinished blocks of carving stone. "I guess you don't get many of us up here . . ."

"I have known one or two of you in my time," I said, sadness in how long it had been since I had seen any of her kin.

I paused, looking down at her tiny, fragile frame.

"What were you doing to me?" I asked, flexing my neck as I bent to examine my wet leg. The stone there was covered in markings I could not identify. Had I always had them? I could not recall, but the large colorful letters were half–scrubbed off now.

"Trying to clean you up," she said, holding up the brush she had been using and waving it at me. "Looks like you've been the victim of vandalism at some time. Someone tagged you."

"Tagged?"

"You know, spray-painted with graffiti . . . ?" she said. I stared with blank eyes back at her. "On second thought, no, I guess it's quite possible you *don't* know what I'm talking about, huh? I don't imagine you're familiar with modern customs, then?"

I shook my head slowly.

"Graffiti," I repeated after a moment. "That word I am familiar with. *Tagged*, however, I am not. But I shall add this colloquialism to my knowledge."

I bent my still-wet leg and placed it back up onto the ledge where the woman could reach it again.

"You may continue," I said. "And thank you."

"Not a problem," she said. The woman stepped back to me, this time with more caution than before, and started scrubbing again. "It's the least I could do after you saved me. I've been coming up here for years just to get away from the family and whatnot, and I always had an appreciation for your sculpted figure, but I guess I never noticed you had been vandalized at some point. I couldn't stand to see you marked up like this. It offends my artistic sensibility."

I cocked my head at her again. She looked up.

"I'm an artist," she said by way of explanation. "At least, when I'm not playing dress-up as a tiny female Donald Trump." She resumed scrubbing away at my leg, harder this time. "Does that hurt at all?"

"Hurt?" I repeated, then laughed at the mere thought of it, the bass of my own voice surprising me as it boomed out. "No. It does not hurt. I am afraid it would take far more than that."

The woman stopped scrubbing, dipped the brush back into the bucket, and, when she started up again, scrubbed even harder. The tag was almost gone now, a mere ghost of the vandalism.

"By the way," she said after several more moments, "I'm Alexandra."

I watched her fragile arms working their way back and forth against my stone skin.

"Of course you are," I said. "After Alexander, yes?"

She seemed surprised I should know that. "Yes. We're related."

"I am . . . Stanis," I said. It sounded strange, as it had the night I'd told her assailant.

The woman looked up and smiled.

"I know," she said, dropping the brush. She reached down and picked something up off of the roof. It was a leather-covered notebook. She brandished it like a weapon, then placed it gently on the ledge before she retrieved her brush and fell back to scrubbing. "I looked you up, albeit in a very puzzling way, in the family library. So tell me about my great-great-grandfather."

I had not remembered much about the man in centuries, but at her command my mind opened up to me.

"You may wish to write this down," I said, but I need not have told the girl, who was already producing another notebook from the leather bag she had with her as she settled down on the rooftop. "I do not recall when or how I was made, but this is one of the earliest encounters that I can remember of my maker, Alexander Belarus. I remember his words with perfect recall."

The woman's eyes flickered up at me. "Tell me what he told you."

I thought for a moment of one of the most important encounters with the man, one in the little changed art studio of the building. "I remember one evening in the studio with him. 'There is much for you to learn,' he said to me, his voice thick with an accent I did not and do not know, 'but before there is learning, there are rules, no? And for such a learned occasion, I thought it best to dress properly, Stanis.'

"Having only recently been taught that my name *was* Stanis, I gave a simple nod to the man. There had been times the dark-haired fellow with the kind eyes had shown up to meet with me in workman's coveralls spattered with mortar and bits of stone, but that day the dim light cast from the lanterns within the studio showed a different Alexander, one dressed in a three-button frock coat and pin-striped dress pants. The highest fashion of his time, if I am remembering correctly. For once, his hair was combed and free of the rock dust that stonemasons of his time usually sported.

" 'Now, then,' he said, making an arcane gesture with his hand, *always protect the family.* That is the first of all rules. Do you understand?'

"A tingling sensation washed over me and I nodded. 'I understand.'

" 'I know the very concept of family is new to you,' the man said, patting me on one of my solid stone shoulders, 'but I've shown you the photographs of those closest to me—my kin. And there will also be the kin to come, yes?'

"He turned from me and moved farther along the edge of the roof to my right until he stood in front of one of the massive blocks of solid stone sitting along the roof's ledge.

" 'Do not worry,' he continued. 'You will not be alone in this task, but before I fashion another, first we must continue your education.'

"He had me repeat the first rule. 'Always protect the family,' I said.

"He was pleased and he moved back to a chair he had set up across from me. A black journal—much like the one you're using now—lay on the chair and he grabbed it, flipping it open.

" 'Secondly,' he said with another gesture, 'always return here before sunrise. Trust your instincts. You will feel the pull of the building calling to you, and you must always return here before the light of day transforms you.'

"I nodded again as the tingling sensation hit once more. I had already experienced the phenomenon the man was describing on one of the few flights I had taken while first testing the limits of my new body. There had of course been nights in my first few weeks of my creation when the man Alexander had not come to me, so as random thoughts began to form in my fledgling mind, I had begun to explore the world . . . as I suppose a child would have.

" 'Always return before the light of day,' I repeated.

"Alexander smiled at me then and said, 'Lastly, do your best to keep yourself hidden from humanity.'

"I stood quietly for a moment, going over the rules in what little mind I had developed already.

" 'What is it, Stanis? What's wrong?'

"When I could finally find the words to speak, I asked, 'Why?'

" 'Why?' the man asked with a laugh. 'Why what?'

"Something unsettling stirred in the rock of my chest. 'Why must I hide away from you, from those like you, and why does your family need protecting?'

"His eyes lit up. 'Excellent!' he said, 'Excellent questions, both of them! You're learning, as I hoped you would. Your natural curiosity drives you!'

"He walked toward the other side of the art studio and gestured for me to follow. He led me up the back stairs of the building and onto the roof proper. I strode after him, the roof shaking under my feet as I walked, still unaccustomed to any form of movement other than flight. The man waited for me at the far northern edge of the building. When I arrived, he reached up and put his hand on my shoulder.

" 'Our ever-growing Manhattan!' Alexander said to me. 'Every day a new invention of some kind comes into being, like parts of this very building we're standing on top of. Look out at the horizon . . . Nothing stands taller than we do! And why? Because of the creative minds of the Otis Elevator Company. After just a few short years, the landscape of this island has already started to take on a whole new look.'

"Alexander laughed and said, 'Everyone thought Brooklyn was going to be the big city around here, what with all its room to grow and expand outward. "Manhattan's only an island," they said! Well, now that Manhattan can build upward, I suspect all that's changed . . .' "

Alexandra was still watching me, rapt with attention.

"We stood there in silence watching the city with all its tiny lights burning in the windows of other, lesser buildings until Alexander turned away and headed back inside and down to his art studio. He sat back down in his chair and resumed flipping through his notebook.

" 'Everything in this city is happening so fast . . .' Alexander said, weariness in his voice. 'I can barely keep up with all the orders for more and more unique stonework coming in, let alone look after my family. God only knows what the future holds for them. The higher we build toward the heavens, the more I worry about the dangers that still roam the ground. Who knows what lies ahead? The past, no matter how far you run from it, has a funny way of catching up, and I do not wish my family to pay the price.'

" 'Price for what?' I asked, but my maker would not answer. He fell silent for a time as he read through his notebook.

" 'You, my friend,' Alexander said when he looked up, 'are my legacy. *You* can stand sentinel for the ages, keeping my kin from harm as long as they reside here. Family . . . Respect . . . These are the things I need to instill in you.'

" 'I understand,' I said.

"Alexander looked up, a kindness flickering in his eyes.

" 'No,' he said, 'I don't think you do . . . but you will. Stay hidden. Keep yourself safe. Keep *them* safe.' "

Alexandra dropped the book she was writing in and stared up at me. She stood, switching the notebook in her hand for an older one.

"So my great-great-grandfather sculpted you, breathed life into you, and you're really a gargoyle," Alexandra said with wonder in her voice. She pushed her hair over her ear and went back to flipping through the second, newer notebook. "There was this cartoon on the television about them I watched in reruns, but I didn't think they actually, you know . . . existed."

"Gargoyle," I repeated with a shudder. "Such a crass name. I prefer the term *grotesque.*"

"That sounds a lot worse, actually," she said with a frown.

"Really?"

The girl nodded. "By modern standards, yeah, but it's the word I use, too. I learned it years ago in the family library."

"The Spellmason hated the term," I said. *"Gargoyle* was the layperson's term for what I was. He preferred to call me his *chimera* or his *grotesque.*"

"Well, a hundred years later, it doesn't sound so great." She reached out her hand and ran it down the worn, pock-marked stone of my arm. "Looks like you've had your fair share of acid rain or something. You've got a little bit of erosion going on there."

I pulled away. I had little familiarity with humans touching me. I reached up and felt along the same area where a few of the spots on my arm were worn down. I sighed. "I am not sure my maker could have predicted how swiftly the modern world would wear on a grotesque such as I."

"Still," she said, sensing my sadness, "the underlying carving is exquisite. The wings, the claws, the, ummm . . . demon face."

I smiled. "Thank you," I said. "A love of stonework runs in the family, I see."

"Not really," the woman said. "I'm the first to even take an interest in the art of it all. My brother, when he was alive, anyway, only seemed to like defacing it. I wouldn't be surprised if that graffiti were his doing. But when our parents told me about our past, the history of our family, something about that time period and my great-great-grandfather's craftsmanship just spoke to me. How well did you know him?"

"As well as any piece of stone can know its maker, I suppose," I said.

She laughed. "You've got quite the sense of humor," she said. "You know, all things considered."

"Your great-great-grandfather built me with the capacity to learn all things," I said. "I do not know if he ever knew I would come to feel and joke, though. I wonder often about that."

I stood lost in quiet contemplation of that until the woman spoke again.

"You said there were three rules? Always protect the family, always return to the building before daylight, and always keep hidden from humanity?"

I nodded.

"Well, two out of three ain't bad," she said, holding up two fingers.

"There were more of us to come, but . . ." I looked to a large block of half-carved stone that sat farther along the ledge next to me, one I had not looked over at in quite some time.

Alexandra put the notebook down gently and walked over to the block and examined it.

"It's broken," she said.

I shook my head. "Not broken. Never finished."

"Too bad," she said, sadness in her tone. "I would have loved to have seen whatever my great-great-grandfather saw when he started carving it. He never got around to finishing it . . . ?"

I shrugged, causing my wings to flap.

"What happened?" she asked.

"One night your great-great-grandfather simply did not show up."

"I'm sorry," she said with a nod, then turned away from the block. "He died later the summer he carved you, from what I've been able to read." She held up the notebook. "It's slow going. Half these books are in a mix of Slavonic and Lithuanian."

"Your kind die so quick," I said.

"I guess we do," she said. She stood up and started walking to the far end of the roof.

"Those wings," she said as she crossed. "You flew away the other night, after saving me. So they're more than just ornamental, aren't they?"

I cocked my head. "What do you mean?"

"I saw them work a little when you left. You can fly well, then?"

I nodded.

Alexandra stopped at the edge of the roof and stepped up onto the ledge.

"Good," she said, and jumped.

Before she could even fall out of sight, I heard the words of my maker in my head as if he were alive today, screaming one of the rules at me. *Always protect the family.*

With my inhuman speed, I ran across the roof and dove over the side. The girl was dropping fast, but I flapped my wings and closed the distance as quickly as I could. The wind rushed over me and I pressed myself to close with her.

I reached out, remembering how fragile these humans were, and carefully grabbed for her.

I caught her by one wrist, and before I could begin flying back to the top of the roof, she pulled herself around me, clutching both arms around my neck, the drumming of her heart hard against my chest.

As I flew straight up into the nighttime sky, Alexandra stopped shaking, settling herself against me. I should have landed back on the roof, but something else compelled me and I kept flying upward instead.

This human closeness was strange, but not unpleasant, and the woman stayed there a long while before lifting her head off my chest, looking back over my shoulders. "Your wings," she said, eyes widening, "they're so quiet but . . . but they're *stone*. I thought they'd make some kind of noise or something, but you're flying effortlessly."

I said nothing but continued to fly higher, feeling the great-great-grandchild of my maker tightening her grip even more. Once we were higher than any of the surrounding buildings, I swooped back down through the concrete and metal canyons, angling back and forth through the gaps in the buildings until the Belarus building came back into sight. I landed, setting Alexandra down, and stepped away from her.

Anger flushed through my body. "I do not engage in games, child . . ."

"I just had to see it for myself," she said, still breathless and stumbling around as she got used to standing on the solid rooftop again. "If everything my great-great-grandfather wrote in his book and what you say is true. You told me about the rules to always protect, and you did!"

I stood there, unmoving.

"Relax," she said, and I felt myself do just that. "Art's not the only thing about Alexander Belarus I found interesting. His library is full of books and notebooks, a lifetime of learning. I think, perhaps, there's a bit of truth to some of the magic and alchemy of which he wrote, though it is hard to figure out. You're living proof. What was it you told me the other night about healing?"

"To heal the stone, to heal the house."

"Yes!" she said, clutching the talisman once more that I had felt the faded power in. "And I'll do that just as soon as I figure out where all that information is in the library. So much of his work is partial references that then refer to other partial references in *another* book. But I am fascinated to learn what it took to breathe life into stone."

"Only the maker could do that," I said with a shake of my head.

"Yeah, well, I'm going to start small," she said, placing the notebook to the side and grabbing up her scrub brush from the bucket again. "Getting this paint off you is just the beginning. Most of these blocks up here look unfinished. I don't think my great-great-grandfather meant for you to be alone. Maybe I can do something about that someday."

The woman set to work and I joined her as she handed me a second brush, although in truth I had no knowledge of the task at hand. I followed what she did, scrubbing at myself, and soon I found I was fully immersed in the task. The longer I worked, focused as I was, a distracting sorrow built in my chest, but it was not my own, forcing me to look around. The woman stood there, her brush lying at her feet, her eyes wet with tears.

"This pain of yours," I said. "I feel it. What is the matter, Alexandra?"

Her shoulders heaved up and down in a rapid motion as she cried. She raised the back of her hand to her eyes and wiped.

"You said you were created to protect my family," she said. "Right?"

"Your great-great-grandfather set me to that task, yes. As I have told you."

The girl took in a deep breath and let it out slowly. "So . . . why didn't you protect my brother?"

"I do not understand," I said.

"My brother," she said in a low, even tone as her eyes filled with sadness. "Devon. He died in a building collapse. Why didn't you try to save him?"

I cocked my head at her. "I was unaware of this," I said.

Her eyes widened. "How can you have been unaware? He was *family*."

I felt around inside for some sense of connection, but there was none to be found. "I do not know what to say. I have had a sympathetic bond with all of your blood over the centuries, but I did not feel any such distress from him."

"How is that possible?" she said, her voice cracking. "He was crushed to death when one of my great-great-grandfather's buildings collapsed on him. He's *dead*—do you understand that?"

"I understand what death is," I said. "I have seen many of your kind grow old and pass on. But that does not change what has happened. I did not feel the danger to your brother . . . but you say one of Alexander's buildings fell in on him. Where?"

"The Lower East Side," she said. "On St. Mark's."

"I remember such a place," I said. "The stone was strong there. It was one of the first buildings Alexander ever put up."

The girl gave a pained laugh. "Well, he should have built it stronger, then . . ."

"It *was* strong," I insisted. "I know that stone. If that structure fell, it was by no accident."

"Someone would do that *on purpose*?"

"I cannot say. I only know your great-great-grandfather's craftsmanship."

I did not know what more I could say. Pain radiated from the girl, but I was not lessening it, and that shortcoming in me, the inability to calm it, burned like fire. I wondered what I could say to help, but I did not have to wonder long. Before I could figure out what might ease her pain, she was running for the doors leading back down into the Belarus building.

Fifteen

Alexandra

I came down the stairs fast, taking two at a time with the old, worn notebook clutched in my shaking hands. I flew past Alexander's library, down past mine and Devon's floor, and found my parents sitting together at opposite ends of the large couch directly across from the television. My father worked at an elaborate lap desk with ledgers and printouts weighing it down, my mother staring blankly at some graying talking head on the screen. When she saw my face, her hand darted for the remote, lowering the sound on whatever financial program they were watching.

"Honey," my mother started in that quiet voice of hers. "What's wrong?"

"Leave the girl alone," my father said, stern, not looking up. "She has been through much these past few days. She will rally."

"I'm not going to rally, dad," I spat out. My tone drew his attention. Despite my anger, tears escaped from the corners of my eyes and I hated that I couldn't help it. Still, everything the creature had said . . .

My father closed the ledger he was working in and set the desk on the floor next to him. "Alexandra," he said, softening. "What is it?"

"Anything you want to tell me about my brother's death?"

He glanced at my mother, then back to me. "What do you mean?"

"Like maybe it wasn't an accident . . . ?" I asked, but there was little reaction except confusion on their faces.

"Alexandra," my mother said, confusion filling her eyes. "What are you going on about?"

"Come, sit," my father said, patting the couch, and I went to him like I was four, sitting down. He put his heavy arm around me and squeezed my shoulder. "Miss Alexandra, you should know, there are no accidents in this world."

I looked up at him. "No?"

My father gave me a soft smile. "Of course not," he said, pointing to the ceiling. "All of this is according to His plan."

I doubted he meant the gargoyle sitting on our roof, and I stiffened. I didn't love the idea that whatever Power there Might Be went around planning how to kill people like some twisted game of *The Sims*. Still, Stanis had been sure the building collapse hadn't been an accident, and I wasn't ready to go down the road of blaming the Almighty for carrying out some elaborate scheme just yet.

I wasn't looking for a lecture on theology, realizing I could investigate the nature of the accident on my own. And now knowing my father's story about falling through the ice as a boy, I also didn't want to have the "Your guardian angel is actually a magical gargoyle" talk with him *just* yet. That wasn't the real reason I had rushed down here so suddenly, anyway. That had been because of Stanis's reaction to the death of my brother . . . For someone sworn to protect the family, he had seemed relatively uninterested in Devon's death. Whatever the arcana was that ran Stanis, it was messed up. If not, there was only one other alternative that made logical sense to me.

"Was Devon really my brother?" I asked.

My father laughed out loud, but not before hesitating. "Of course he was your brother," he said, waving a dismissive hand.

I searched his eyes, watching as he quickly shifted them away from me. "I mean, biologically. By blood."

My words were met with silence from both my parents, but it was my mother who finally spoke up after a long moment.

"Tell her," she said.

My father gave a heavy sigh and nodded. "It is true. Devon was not your biological brother."

"Why haven't you told me before?" I asked, my heart hurting.

"Please do not take this the wrong way," my father said, "but when you were born, while we were very happy to bring you into this world, I was a little bit in shock."

"Why?"

"We Belarus have always been very strong about our family, about our kin. For generations, the firstborn child was always a male. We held our strength in the belief that a patriarchy was part of what assured our continued success, our continued luck. Call it superstitious, if you like—"

"Your father loves you very much," my mother impressed on me, putting her hand to rest on my knee.

"Please hear me out," he said, turning his eyes down from me. "When you were born, I was . . . disappointed." After a moment he looked back up with a weak smile on his lips. "I was young and foolish and determined that there must be a male to continue the family's success. Someone who could grow into a man of business. So before you were old enough to remember, we . . . adopted a boy. He was meant to take on the burden of business in this family."

"And you never told me," I said, anger rising up in my chest.

"I'm so sorry," my mother said, her hand squeezing my knee again. "The timing was never right, and we kept meaning to, but the more time passed, the easier it got to not bring it up."

"Since when has Dad ever shied away from anything? He's got the Lord on his side!"

My father's eyes turned to me, a mix of fear and anger. "You leave God out of this."

"Gladly," I said, standing up to face them. "My point is that I should have known."

My father turned away from me, staring at the silent television. "I lost a son," he said, simple and cold, but I wasn't going to let him shut down on me like that.

"And I lost a brother," I fired back just as cold and with real anger building. "Or at least I thought he was my brother. And now I'm stuck with his job that I've been *busting my ass* on, by the way. Do you think this is what I want for myself? I've been doing it to please you."

"Oh, honey," my mother said. "Devon was *always* your brother. Even when you two were fighting like cats and dogs, he was always your brother."

"You haven't had a bad life, have you?" my father asked, dead serious with a little venom in his words. "You've been able to follow your own pursuits . . . That is, until the accident."

"I don't want to come off as a spoiled brat, but yes, and I'm very thankful for that. I've been able to mostly pursue what I want, as long as I stayed close to home."

"The Belarus family keeps close," my mother said from behind me, but I was still concentrating on my father.

"Everything I've studied of our family's cultural legacy, everything you've ever encouraged me to do, every bit of my being wants to be connected to history and art . . . Now you're taking that all away from me. And the worst of it is, you didn't ask me. You just *told* me."

"Running the family business *is* part of your legacy now," my father said.

I held up my great-great-grandfather's notebook. "So is the art and design and . . . other things. *That's* the only legacy I care about."

"We won't have anywhere to keep any of that legacy if we lose our business," my father said, his voice turning agitated. "Think of *that*. Don't be such a selfish girl. You *will* learn the family business. *Think of your mother.*"

The veins in his neck were pressed out so far I thought his head might explode. His tone was so vehement I knew there was no arguing him, and right now I had better things to think about than the family business.

"Well, for the sake of the empire, I hope you'll be more forthcoming about the family business than you were about Devon," I said, standing up. I stormed off, beyond crying anymore. Fury and bitter resolution had replaced my tears. My mother called after me, but I didn't bother turning back. What good would it do? It wouldn't change the fact about what they expected of me, and right now the family business wasn't foremost in my thoughts.

The past few hours had been a roller-coaster whirl of fantastically awesome to painfully shocking. The last thing I wanted to think about was real estate law and zoning codes or whatever it all involved. I headed back upstairs to the library, book still in hand. There were dozens of references in this notebook about Alexander Belarus and his gargoyle, all of them leading to dozens of other texts hidden somewhere around the room. It was going to take hours to make sense of it all, and in the face of being forced daily into a business suit, I welcomed the distraction from that new aspect of my life.

I went about the busy work of gathering reference book after reference book, my mind turning back to some of the darker thoughts at hand, thanks to my talk with the creature. My brother's death hadn't been an accident, I was fairly certain. Then someone in a secret order had tried to kill me—twice—and if not for that creature on the top of our building, who knows if I'd even be alive now. Someone wanted us dead, for whatever reason, but I wasn't going to go quietly—that was for sure. I had a freaking gargoyle on my side. Even with that surreal bonus, though, I was going to need help, but first I had a lot of reading to get started on.

◖

Sixteen

Stanis

I awoke with my eyes still closed, the image of the maker in my head and his voice still ringing in my ears. The rules, he reminded me, always the rules. They were a part of me—this I knew—but saving the woman the other night by break-ing through the roof of the building had brought one of them in conflict with another, and my mind could not quite remedy how to process it, except being haunted by the reproach and disappointment in my maker's voice, even though he was long gonc.

Ready to stretch my hunched form out, I paused. The words I thought were only in my head were not, but instead came from directly in front of me on the roof. They belonged to the maker's kin, the woman Alexandra. Her voice had the same even rhythm and cadence as his, making it hard to tell her words apart from the ones in my mind's ear.

When I opened my eyes, she was not alone, a problem for me. Minding the rules, I held myself in place. The blue-haired female and the tall male I often saw her with were there. The three of them stood around mid-conversation by the single door that led down into the building.

"You sure you can't just tell us your surprise inside?" the

man said, shifting from one foot to the other. He rubbed his hands up and down his bare arms. "I didn't bring a jacket tonight. I wasn't really ready for the cold snap yet."

The maker's kin shook her head. "What I have to show and tell you can't be done inside," she said. "I can't help it if you haven't switched your calendar over to October yet."

"Suck it up, buttercup," the blue-haired one said to the male. "I like show-and-tell!"

"Can we at least make this a speed round, then?" the male said, hugging his arms around his body now, the wind whipping through his scruff of black hair. "I get sick at the drop of a hat. It's my fragile gamer physique."

"All right," the maker's kin said, holding up several tattered notebooks. "Well, I've been doing some research and I figured out what happened to that man—my attacker—in the park. Why it looked like he jumped."

"You did?" the blue-haired one asked, stepping closer.

She nodded. "Yes, but I need you two to promise me that you're not going to freak out."

"Oh man," the male said, rocking back and forth on his feet. "You asking that only freaks me out *more*."

The blue-haired one reached out, grabbed him by the shoulder, and stilled him. "Cut it out," she said. "You're making me more nervous than whatever Lexi's trying to tell us about." She placed her other hand over her heart. "I solemnly swear not to freak out. I can't vouch for Marshmallow here, but I'll try to keep him in line if he does."

The maker's kin let out a long, slow breath. "I suppose that's the best I can get out of you, but, Rory . . . I *really* need you to keep it cool. What I'm about to show you, you can't tell anyone, okay? This can't be like the time we drove up to Montreal when we were eighteen and you caved to my parents when they saw a Canadian leaf sewn onto your jacket."

"Fine," the blue-haired female said, her voice testy.

The maker's kin turned to the male. "Swear on something you hold sacred, Marshall."

He thought for a moment before answering. "Okay," he

said. "I swear that I won't freak out. I swear on my limited-edition original Dungeons and Dragons Red Box set."

"Okay," Alexandra said, unsure. "I'm going to assume that's something really 'special' to you."

"Just tell us, already," the blue-haired one said in agitation.

"Screw telling," the maker's kin said. "I'm skipping straight to the showing." She turned to face me and walked over to where I stood crouched at the building's edge. Her mouth turned up in a half smile. "I'm nervous, like I'm introducing a new boyfriend to them."

"Lex . . . ?" the blue-haired one said. "Who are you talking to?"

The maker's kin spun around to them. "Arise," she said.

One rule told me not to reveal myself to others, as it had done so for centuries, yet despite it, I rose up from my crouch to the full extent of my height, wings spread out behind me. The blue-haired one and the male both stepped back from me toward the door, reaching out to grab onto each other in support.

"I'm a big fat liar," the male said, fumbling to grab the blue-haired woman's hand. "I need to freak out. You can have my Red Box D and D set."

She took his hand and stumbled toward me, pulling the man along behind her. "Sweet mother of *what the hell is that*?"

"That," the maker's kin said, "is Stanis. My great-great-grandfather crafted him. Stanis, this is my oldest friend, Aurora. Rory, for short. The man cowering behind her is Marshall."

"It's a living effing *gargoyle*," the male said from behind the blue-haired woman. "Jesus, Lexi, step away from it! We fight these things all the time in my weekly campaign. That thing will *kill* us . . . won't it?"

"I don't know," the maker's kin said, holding a hand out toward me. "Why don't you ask him that for yourselves?"

The man gave a sickly smile. "For real?"

She nodded.

He stepped out from behind the other girl, turning to

address me. "What *are* you?" the male asked, then added, "Sir."

"I am Stanis," I said, meeting his eyes, "and as you say, I am an effing gargoyle."

The maker's kin laughed and I cocked my head at her.

"You don't need to use the word *effing*," the maker's kin said. "Marshall said that as a statement of surprise more than anything. It's shorthand for a worse one, actually."

"So noted," I said. "I believe I know what one you mean. I have heard that word much these many years, but have not had any opportunity yet to use it myself. It has been a long time since I have conversed, since my maker, Alexander, went away."

The man took a step toward me, then stopped, looking up into my face, serious. "So to be clear . . . you do not intend us any harm?"

I thought for a moment. "I cannot say," I said. "That would depend."

He narrowed his eyes, one foot sliding away from me in retreat. "On?"

"Do you mean any harm to the Belarus family?" I asked.

"Nope," he said with no hesitation, and I saw there was pure truth in the word.

"Then I do not intend you any harm."

The blue-haired one approached me and pressed her hands to my chest, her flesh cool against the stone of my skin. There was no fear in this one, only wonder. "Holy hell," she said. "This thing killed that man? The one who attacked you?"

The maker's kin nodded. "Apparently, it was built to protect us," she said.

"From what?"

"There are those who would harm your family," I said to her, then turned to her friends. "I have seen to their protection."

The blue-haired one patted my chest. "Thanks for that," she said, and stepped back from me.

"I need no thank-you," I said. "I am merely functioning as I was meant to."

"Whatever," she said. "Nonetheless, anyone who keeps my oldest friend from being stabbed to death in an alley has my thanks."

"Very well," I said.

The blue-haired woman let go of the man's hand and crossed her arms. "So what do Doug and Julie think about all this?"

"I haven't told them. I don't think they know and I'm not sure I'm up for that conversation quite yet. Nor was I up for my last conversation with them, either, where I told them that we don't think my brother's death was an accident."

"You don't?" the male asked.

Rory held up a hand. "Wait. 'We' who?"

"Stanis and I," the maker's kin said.

"How can you say it wasn't an accident?" the male asked.

The maker's kin turned to me. "Tell them about the building on St. Mark's that collapsed and killed Devon."

"I have known of that building for a long time," I said. "I know most of the buildings fashioned by my maker. The stone was sound in that one. It was strong. That building did not come down by accident, I assure you."

"Someone wanted Devon dead," the maker's kin said. "Not sure why, considering I found out today that he's not even really part of the family."

"What?" the blue-haired woman said. "I'm sorry, Lexi. Maybe I'm a bit overwhelmed with sensory input right now, but what are you talking about?"

"Some regrettable patriarchal choices on my father's behalf years ago," she said. "Male heir to the throne BS and all that. He was adopted. It's been a rough forty-eight hours, between learning that, that my brother was probably murdered, and the two attempts on my life."

"Jesus, no kidding," the blue-haired one said, and hugged her tight, the maker's kin returning the embrace.

Marshall came toward me, but stopped about five feet away. "So why are people attacking Lexi and her family again?" he asked.

"I do not know," I said. "I am unsure of a great many things. My past, for one."

"Which," Alexandra said, "is why I asked you two here. I've been reading most of last night and most of today, when I could find the time." She held up another notebook, similar to the others but unravaged by time. "I've compiled notes from a bunch of sources in Alexander's library. The man might have been a sculptural genius, but he wasn't much on organization. There are references to material and other books all over the place. A lot of it seems to reference a master book of arcane knowledge I can't even *find* in there, but here's what I've pieced out so far."

"Wait, wait," the male said. "What are you trying to do here exactly?"

"My grandfather created him to watch over the family," she said, then pointed to the half-carved block next to me on the edge of the building. "He meant to carve more. A companion, at the very least. And with people getting all stabby around me lately, I'm all for reinforcements."

"So you're just going to make a gargoyle?" he asked.

The maker's kin looked down at her notebook. "Eventually," she said. "I'm translating Slavonic and Lithuanian here, so it's slow going. He talks a lot about willpower at the heart of art, the heart of creation. There are gestures, kind of like a karate kata, but in trying to just get an idea of *how* any of this is even possible, I decided I needed to understand how he works before I go trying to create something similar."

"Wow," the blue-haired woman said. "You're really embracing this, aren't you?"

The maker's kin shrugged. "Are you kidding me? This sure as hell beats reading building code violations."

"So what's the first step?" the man added. "I could run down to our apartment and pick up my Player's Handbook."

"Thanks, but no," the woman said with a forced smile. "He doesn't seem to remember much of his past, other than having always watched over my family, so I searched through the books for something that might help restore his memory and I pieced together something my great-great-grandfather called the Revelation of the Soul. The more he remembers about how Alexander made him and the psychos who are trying to kill me, the better."

The blue-haired woman gave her a strange look I could not interpret. "And you needed us because . . . ?"

"I have no idea what I'm doing here," she said. "You're here to . . . umm, spot me."

"Awesome," the blue-haired girl said with a slow breath and mock enthusiasm.

"We're here for you," the male said. His enthusiasm for this seemed to shock the maker's kin.

"Really?"

He nodded. "I've been faking this stuff for years with pencils and paper and dice and the public mocking, so if there's a chance I'm not just having some vivid hallucination and imagining all this, I say go for it."

She looked satisfied with his answer. "All righty," the maker's kin said, handing the book to the other woman. "Can you hold this open for me? I think I'm going to need both hands free."

"Sure," she said, taking the book and positioning herself in front of the woman. "Try not to get us killed, okay?"

"Will do!"

The maker's kin took a moment to compose herself, focused, then set herself into a series of motions with her arms and hands as words in a language I did not understand came from her. The other two humans watched in silence as she continued through them, a familiar poetry in her movement, all of us no doubt waiting for whatever was going to happen. After several minutes, the maker's kin came to a rest and the four of us stood there in silence.

"Well?" the male asked after another long moment passed. "Did it happen? Is our large stone friend here healed?"

The three of them were looking at me. "I do not think so," I said.

"I don't get it," the maker's kin said. "I mean, I felt a little ridiculous going through it, but I really tried to focus here, push my will into it. I went through the series of somatic motions. It's like learning a whole new world of sign language. I spoke the words, breathing life into them, committing my very self to the art of it. If belief was a definite component here, I was believing the shit out of it. I wasn't sure what to expect, but I was definitely expecting something more than nothing."

"Some cinematic pyrotechnics, at least," the blue-haired female said.

The maker's kin stared up into my face, looking me over. "You sure you don't you feel any different?"

I took a moment to assess myself. "I do not think so."

"Crap," she said. "I thought for sure I was doing it right. The words, the feelings, the gestures . . ."

"If I may," the blue-haired female said. "Let me take a page from the Book of Dance. There is dance—" She pressed herself up on her toes and spread out her arms like the wings of a bird. She then lunged from side to side before spinning herself around over and over. The motion was fluid, functional.

"And there is *dance*," she continued, and did the same moves over again. This time there was a perfect elegance to each of the moves that made her first attempt at them look clumsy in comparison. "Extension, line, poise. It's not enough to just do the steps. You have to commit to each of them. There is a difference between dancing and *being* a dancer. If there is also an art to what you're trying to do here, Lexi, those might be the kinds of things that matter. Try again."

"See?" Marshall said, giving the maker's kin a look. "You're just doing it wrong."

"I get it," the maker's kin said. "First to believe in magic, first to disparage my ability at it."

The male held up his hands, defensive. "Are you kidding me? As a gamer, I'm eating this shit up. But truth be told, the results are a bit underwhelming."

The maker's kin sighed. "I can go to just about anyplace in this city for lessons in dance, singing, any instrument I like. Hell, I can take up erotic massage, but what I'm attempting here isn't something I can go take a class in, you know? Learning something as unique as this?" She tapped the open book before her. "This is it. Notes from my family's scattered history. I have no idea if any part of what I am doing is actually right or if any of this even really works."

The man went silent.

"*I* can tell you," I said. "It does work for real. I am proof incarnate. You are of the maker's kin, Alexandra. Do as your blue-haired friend suggested and try again. Her way."

She nodded, the frustration in her eyes leaving as she drew her focus. Once more she went through the words and motions of her spell. This time there was commitment in every gesture, in every sound, and the build of energy that washed over me told me that something was going right.

The power reminded me of my maker, a sweet sadness flooding me as the long-lost sensation took me, driving me to my knees. His kin continued on, a shooting pain rising up in the center of my being. I fell to my hands as the stone of my chest twisted, shifting its shape, my very landscape altering.

The maker's kin finished the last of her gestures and dropped to her knees in front of me, her eyes full of concern. "Are you all right?"

"Jesus Christ," the male said. "You killed a gargoyle."

"I am fine," I said, rising to my knees. "I was not prepared for such a sensation. It has been a long time since I have felt . . . well, anything."

"His chest," the blue-haired one said, pointing. "It's different."

All of my pain was gone, replaced by a warm sensation. I looked down, the once-smooth carving now covered with a twisted inset pattern like vines on a wall wrapping in on themselves.

"Did it work?" the maker's kin asked me, a nervous smile on her human lips. "Did I restore your memory?"

I concentrated my thoughts before answering. "I do not think so," I said. "I do not recall anything new that I am aware of."

"Dammit," she said, slamming the book shut and rising to her feet.

"What is that?" the blue-haired one asked, pointing at my chest.

I ran my fingers over the carvings. "I do not know."

The maker's kin threw her book of notes down onto the rooftop at our feet.

"Easy," the blue-haired one said. "You may not have restored his memory, but you did make *something* happen here." She stepped right in front of me, no fear, her fingers tracing over the design.

"Alexander's books called the whole thing Revelation of the Soul," the maker's kin said. "Talks about controlling his power, protecting all of us from it. We could use that power to deal with these mad men. Shouldn't there be some soul revealing going on?"

"Maybe that's what you did," the male offered. The two women looked over at him, waiting. He walked over to me, pointing at areas of my chest without touching it. "What if that's exactly what you've done here? There are depressions in this carving . . . here, here, here, and *here*. They look to me like missing pieces."

Alexandra ran over to her discarded notebook, scooped it up, and flipped it open once more. "I noted something about gems in here when I was researching earlier," she said, rushing through the pages. "There are sketches everywhere in my great-great-grandfather's books. None of the writing alongside any of them made much sense, but I've started sketching some of them myself. There's a reference here . . ."

She kept the book open in one hand and scooped up one of Alexander's older books, flipping through it with some excitement.

"*Soul stones,*" she read. "I made a note about them, that they were taken from him for his protection . . . and ours."

"They must be powerful, then," Marshall said.

"And we could use as much power as we can get if we want to get at the bottom of who's after my family," she said. "I wrote them down because they reminded me of some hippie-dippie healing thing my dad might get into with his spiritual leader. And later on down the page is the Slavonic word for *binding*, which I've already come across at least a dozen times in searching through all the books in the library trying to unlock his memories."

"You sure we want to even be doing that?" the male said, stepping back from my form. "Your great-great-grandfather went through a lot to keep this creature's soul from him. You sure we should even be *trying* returning it so fast?"

"The notes I've compiled so far say there's a greater power to be unleashed by the Revelation of the Soul. We're going to need that to stop these men who are trying to kill me and my family."

"So then where are these stones?" the blue-haired one asked.

Alexandra continued searching through the pages of the book. "That I don't know," she said. "There are several notations referring to specific books here, some I can't seem to find, and a master book of sorts, but I don't think I've ever come across it in his library. Not yet, anyway."

"Maybe we shouldn't be messing with this, ladies," the male added.

"Don't be ridic, Marshall," the maker's kin said. "People are trying to kill my family. Restoring Stanis to the full power my great-great-grandfather hints at is going to stop that from happening."

"You don't know what type of power you're dealing with, Lexi," the male said, anger in his words now.

The blue-haired girl looked up at me. "Surely you have an opinion on the matter, right, big fella?"

Foreign though the idea was to me, my mind turned the blue-haired girl's words over and over in my head until they settled down into one desire. "My maker had created me to think, to learn," I said. "Yet I am unsure of any instruction he meant for me to have on pursuing my own past. However, I think I should like to know more."

The blue-haired one slapped me on the shoulder, pulling her hand away, rubbing it. "There you go, sport," she said. "You need to start doing things for yourself there. Start spending a little 'me' time."

" 'Me' time?"

"Never mind," she said, then looked at the maker's kin. "We can work on idioms later. Much later."

I did not know what an *idiom* was, but now was not the time to learn, apparently, which was fine by me. I had been standing here conversing with these creatures for too long after waking, and my body cried out for the sky. "I must fly," I said, stepping toward the maker's kin. "If you want to protect yourself, heal your talisman, heal the home. The power in them makes those who wish ill for your family blind to discovering you. The talismans have rendered you invisible to those with dark thoughts against you. The stone of the house keeps it hidden to them, but all are fading. It is how these men have been finding you. I do not know for how much longer the house will remain concealed from them, but for your safety, you must fix this. Your great-great-grandfather always had this master tome you spoke of, one that he kept his most sacred of words in. It is there that you will most likely find your answers." Without waiting for a response, I leapt up into the air, wings extended and working hard to lift me higher and higher.

There had been a discomfort tonight, in revealing myself to so many, in conversing, but the strangest part, the one that got me airborne, was being asked what I desired. More so, I had been surprised to hear that I did have an answer for that. Still, I had not the will to wait while they discussed it. Their talk was of restoring my memory to better help find a motivation behind those who wished the Belarus family harm. I knew nothing of those matters, so I set myself to what I knew best how to do. I did as the master rule bid me, trying to protect, the only way I knew how—seeking out any threat to the Belarus family.

I patrolled.

Seventeen

C

Alexandra

After the gargoyle had taken to the sky, we headed back into my great-great-grandfather's studio and library and threw ourselves down across several of the couches laid out in the reading area.

"That didn't go as planned," I said, disappointed.

"If it were easy, everyone would be doing it, right?" Rory asked.

I sighed. "True," I said. "I had just hoped the more complete that creature is, the better off it would be at protecting us. I thought restoring his memories and such might provide us more answers."

"Like who's trying to kill you?" Marshall asked.

I nodded. "Or how to heal my sigil talisman and the house," I said. "They both seem to offer protection so we're not directly on the radar of these knife-wielding, hand-tattooed freaks, but the gargoyle seemed to sense it is fading, which would explain how they've been able to find me when I've been out and about at night."

"Not for nothing, but I'm impressed there even exists a magic that can last as long as it has before starting to fade,"

Marshall said. "We need to find that master tome the big guy mentioned."

I looked around our massive private library. "*That's* going to be easy," I said. "That creature told me that my family has always been secretive. My father and my grandfather always thought Alexander meant to write the family history down, but he must have passed away before he even got a chance."

"What if he didn't put it off, though?" Marshall asked. "Think about it. Look around the room. The man loved puzzles. Maybe he wrote down everything he wanted to pass along, but was worried about other people finding it. He would have hid it, right? You say all those notebooks cross-reference dozens of other sources here, but if there's a master tome at the center of all of it, that's going to be the most secret one of all."

I had been through most of the objects in the studio the night before, and had not seen a huge book lying around. Then I realized . . .

"Alexander Belarus was a clever man," I thought out loud to myself. "He would have hidden it well." I walked back over to the display shelves, pulling down the stone sculpture of a book I had almost brained them both with the other night when they came up the fire escape after the attack on me in the alley. "Where better to hide a book than out in the open?"

Marshall laughed, grabbing it from me, attempting to heft the ornate stone book up with his own hands, his gangly arms barely able to lift it. "Good luck reading *that*. Got a chisel?"

"Just drop it on the floor," Rory called out. "Maybe it's a stone piñata and a real book falls out."

"No, don't," I cried out, pulling the book back from him.

"I wasn't going to drop it," he said, hurt. "I don't do everything Rory tells me to, you know."

I laid the book down on a stand in the center of the room and spread my hands over the cold surface of it.

"That's some heavy reading," Rory said.

"Shush," I said, shooting her a stern look. "Think of it this way. That creature is fantastical, stone that is animated. Rock and stone don't normally act that way, last I checked. Something changed it from its true physical nature . . ."

"Alchemy," Marshall said.

Rory and I turned to him, staring.

"And you thought my years of Dungeons and Dragons wouldn't be useful for anything," he said.

"Isn't that, like, turning base metals to gold or something?" Rory asked.

"It's not just that," he said. "It's really the transformation of any matter to another form, explained away by the use of chemistry and magic."

"Well, then," I said. "Much like the gargoyle itself, something alchemically changed that book from its natural form to stone." I examined the knot work design along the cover. "There are words here."

Rory squinted at it. "Where?"

"Written along the actual knot work itself. It's Slavonic or Lithuanian, but I think I can make a little of it out. 'A book is meant to be well red,' although English was not his first language and he's spelled *read* wrong. It's the same as the dedication page in his Spellmason primer that I discovered."

"Maybe you hold a real book up to it," Rory suggested. "You know, something actually readable."

I went to the shelves and pulled down a book, one with a red binding. "Let's go with 'read' and 'red' as a combo," I said, and pressed the book against the stone one, and read the sentence on the knot work out loud using the little old-country language I could muster.

A moment passed. Then two. Then three.

"Anything?" Rory asked.

I shook my head. "Maybe it doesn't like that book, though," I said.

"That's not the only thing that's red," Marshall said, looking over to Rory. "Give me one of the hoop earrings you're wearing."

Rory's eyes narrowed, her face uncertain. "I don't think the pirate look is going to work on you. Unless you're heading down to the Village . . ."

He held his hand out to her, flexing it open and closed like an impatient child. "Yeah, yeah, yeah. Come on, now."

Rory pushed back the hair on the left side of her head and removed the large golden hoop there, handing it to him. Marshall bent it so the exposed post no longer lined up with the circle of the hoop.

"I think I see where this is going," I said, "and you can stop right now, Marsh. I don't need you getting your blood all over one of my precious family heirlooms."

"I'm not going to," he said.

"Good," I answered, relieved.

"*You* are."

I backed away. "Not too keen on the sight of my own blood, either. Why me?"

"Because it's *your* family heirloom; therefore it should be *your* blood."

"Can't we try yours first?" I asked, the bones in my legs feeling weak as I fought off thoughts of my blood running. "Or how about Rory?"

"The man has some sound reasoning, Lexi, even if it's Dungeon Master logic. That . . . gargoyle's drawn to you, as are its enemies. If anyone's blood stands a chance of opening this book, it's got to be Belarus blood."

I shut my eyes and held my hand out to Marshall. "Make it quick," I said, and before I had finished my words, his hand clamped down around my wrist and I felt a stinging prick at the end of my right index finger. "Yeouch!"

"Sorry," he said.

I opened my eyes. A good trickle of blood was running down my finger. Marshall moved my hand over the center of the design on the cover of my book, squeezing. The blood hit the cover and disappeared into the dark cracks of the carving. Marshall shoved my hand down over it. "Say the words on the knot work again."

I repeated them as I had the first time. The crack of power was instant, like when you accidentally shock yourself. Underneath my palm the stone shifted, the knot work uncoiling as the feel of leather replaced it, the cover turning to a dark brown. The rest of the tome turned to paper and I pulled my hand away from it, sucking the blood off my finger.

"Voila!" Marshall said, smiling with pride.

I grabbed the book and flipped it open on the floor. There were hundreds of pages in it, all of them crammed with Alexander's handwriting and drawings on every last inch of it. "Maybe I can get this in audio," I said.

"You don't need to figure it all out in one sitting," Rory said, patting me on the head.

"Well, let me see if I can find something I've been trying to follow the threads through the library on—this *heal the stone* stuff," I said, pulling off my necklace and laying it down next to the book so I could see the Belarus sigil there. I scanned the book, looking at the drawings as I went until about three-quarters of the way through I came across the symbol. "Excellent!"

I looked up at Marshall. "Can you go out on the terrace for a moment?" I asked.

"Why?" he asked, wary.

"I want to try something," I said.

"Okay," he said, standing up with suspicion in his voice, "but if I miss out on you two exploring the ways of lady love, I'm going to cry."

Rory shook her head at him.

"Just wait out there until Rory calls you back in here," I said, ignoring him.

Marshall went across the room, opened the French doors, and stepped out.

"Okay," Rory said, turning back to me and the book. "What's up?"

"I want to see if something works," I said, reading over the words on the page. "When I first met Stanis, he looked at my necklace and told me to *heal the stone; heal the house*. I found mention of it in Alexander's primer notebook, but I wasn't sure what it fully meant. But I've been tracing the *how* of it back through the rest of his library and his master book, and now I think I might be able to do it. Heal the stone, anyway. Who knows if I'll ever figure out how to *heal the house*, but at least I'm going to try to 'heal' the talisman. Then I want to see if it can affect Marshall."

Rory nodded, and fell silent as I went over the words and gestures listed there. Keeping in mind what she had said about commitment to each part of it, I cleared my mind, scooping up the talisman and pressing it between my hands. I pressed my will into it as I spoke, moving it through a series of deliberate ritual poses, twisting my arms this way and that to get it right. The warmth in my hands told me it was working, boosting my confidence, which seemed only to increase the heat in my hands until it became unbearable to hold and I dropped it to the floor.

Rory picked it up by its chain, and tested the stone with her finger. "It's cool," she said, handing it back to me.

The stone was cool, but I now felt the energy of it. I slipped it around my neck. "Send Marshall in, but don't talk to me, okay? Just start talking about—I don't know—your dating life."

"*What* dating life?" she asked, but she smiled, loving the game of it all, and ran to the doors to get Marshall while I stood and focused my mind on one thought. Marshall was an enemy. Marshall was someone I wanted to avoid. The idea was at its heart ludicrous, but I pushed that away from my thoughts.

Rory walked Marshall back across the room to where the book lay at my feet, the two of them already in conversation.

"I'm not terribly interested in dating," Rory said, stopping when she was about a foot from me, staring into my eyes even though she was talking to him.

Marshall stopped next to her. "Where's Lexi?"

Rory gave him a sidelong glance. "Seriously?"

"Yeah," he said, giving up trying to find me although I was only a foot away from him. "Never mind. Let's get back to you. How can you not be terribly interested in dating? Everyone's terribly interested in dating."

"Not me," she said, looking from him to me, then back again. "I've got enough on my mind to think about without worrying about someone else and how they're taking it. I've dated; I just don't care for it."

I moved my head to try to make eye contact with Marshall,

but when I moved, his eyes seemed to find something else nearby to focus on instead of me.

"That's very monastic of you," he said. "So, what? You're a monk now?"

Rory thought about it for a moment, then grinned. "Yeah, I suppose I am. Maybe I should move up to the Cloisters . . ."

"Maybe its not that you don't like dating," he offered. "Maybe it's that you just don't like dating *men*."

"Marshall!" I scolded, but he didn't hear me. Rory laughed, shaking her head.

"Oh, I've tried that, too," she said, which got a smile out of him. "I mean, you love who you're going to love, and that hasn't always been guys, but at the moment, I'm not taking applicants from chromosome columns X or Y."

Marshall looked around the room once more, again not seeing me right in front of him, and lowered his voice to a whisper. "When I first met you guys, I thought maybe you and Lexi were . . . you know."

"Marshall," I chided, louder this time.

Rory laughed, and my face went red. "Lexi and me? No, that would be . . . weird. We're besties."

"Marshall!" I screamed as loud as I could, which drew his attention, but just barely. His eyes flickered toward my voice, and he did a double take when he saw me standing there. I let my thought of Marshall as an enemy go.

"Oh, hey, Lexi," he said. "I thought maybe you went downstairs for something." His face turned beet red. "We were just . . . talking."

"So I heard," I said. The stone's energy was all but gone now, but I turned my thoughts back to Marshall as an enemy. Much to my disappointment he just kept looking at me.

"You okay, Lexi?" he asked.

"Yeah," I said, taking my necklace off, the stone no longer giving off a lick of energy. "Was just experimenting. Thought I might have fixed something, but it was only temporary. Going to have to work on that." I leaned down to pick up Alexander's secret tome. "I hope I don't have to bleed out every time I want to open this damned thing."

"But still, it worked for a little bit, right?" Rory asked. "That's promising."

I nodded, giving Marshall a pitying shake of my head.

"What worked?" he asked.

"Nothing," I said, flipping deeper into the newfound master book. "There's more in here about those soul stones the gargoyle mentioned. Cross-referenced to half the library, naturally: book threads to follow listed as the Crown of the Titans, the Eye of God, the Ruler's Chest, and the Heart of the Home. That's going to take some serious heavy reading." I flipped to the earlier sections of the tome. "There do seem to be a few things here I wouldn't mind experimenting with—that is, if our gargoyle friend comes back anytime soon. And I'm going to get to the bottom of something."

"What's that?" Rory asked.

"Devon's murder," I said, and shut the book.

Eighteen

Alexandra

Although the building collapse that had killed my brother had happened more than four months ago, not much had changed at the site on St. Mark's Place. The only noticeable difference now in the debris-filled lot was the construction walls put up around it that bore the Belarus business logo—an octagon with a stylized *B*, like the marking on my necklace sans wings. Traffic, both the pedestrian and vehicular kind, came and went along the cross street in small packs, which probably made Rory, Marshall, and me look like just another group of NYU students returning home from a late-night bender. The October weather was just cool enough tonight that I welcomed the extra padding of my puffy North Face jacket, as it kept the stone book in my backpack from digging into my spinal column too badly.

"Love what you've done with the place," Marshall said, peering into one of the gaps where the hinged board door met with the rest of the surrounding wall. "So glad I left my Magic: The Gathering tournament to come out at midnight to meet you for this."

"What can I say?" I asked, not expecting an answer. I stepped to the padlocked chain that ran through the center of the closed-off entrance. "I warned my family I'm really bad at the family business, even before Devon was crushed here. There are higher priorities among all the properties they have me working on right now. In my defense, I at least had them close it off with this pretty blue plywood. Not that you can see any of it beneath all the posters for the Roseland and other concert venues."

Rory took the chain from me once I pulled it clear, and after a pack of NYU kids passed by, I slipped inside the lot with the two of them following quickly behind me. Neither of them was as mindful of the ground as I was, and both slipped on chunks of brick lying loose on what remained of the sidewalk. Rory danced across them with grace, swinging the chain in her hands as if performing some strange dance, handing the length of it back to me at the end. Marshall, however, twisted his ankle and went down hard onto a nearby pile of stone and wood. He recovered as I rechained the gate from the inside and slipped the padlock back onto it.

I turned to see Rory already marveling at the large pile that rose several stories to a peak at the center of the open lot. "This looks like the most dangerous game of King of the Hill ever," she said.

"Wow," I said, intimidated by the sheer amount of it all. "Finding anything regarding Devon's death will actually be *worse* than finding a needle in a haystack. I doubt hay is as painful as brick."

"How the hell are we supposed to examine this?" Marshall asked, dusting himself off and kicking at the crumble of bricks all around our feet. "We'd need a backhoe or something."

I gave him a smile. "I brought my own," I said.

"What?" Marshall asked, still looking down at his feet.

Rory's eyes darted to the skies. "Incoming!" she shouted and lunged at Marshall, driving him back, stumbling across the outer rise of the pile. Stanis slammed down onto the ground, his approach silent up until that moment, only the crunch of rubble under his feet rising up from the impact.

Rory's arms were still around Marshall, who had gone

wide-eyed, shaking. He flailed his arms for his freedom, eventually causing Rory to let go and back off. "You could have killed me!" he shouted.

Stanis straightened up. "I would not have landed on you," the gargoyle said, folding his expansive wings in close to his body.

Marshall looked down at the ground where Stanis stood. "I'm pretty sure that's *exactly* where I was standing, in fact."

Rory leaned in close to him. "Let me get this straight," she said, draping an arm over his shoulder. "Are you picking a fight with a gargoyle?"

A sickly sheepish grin crossed his face, all bluster leaving him.

"Maybe you should apologize for calling him a hoe," she said, clapping Marshall on the shoulder.

"I *didn't*," he said, backing away. "I said we'd need a *back*-hoe to get through any of this."

"Voila!" I said, gesturing to the gargoyle. "One backhoe." I turned to face him. "Good evening, Stanis." As far as large, magically enchanted stone men went, he wasn't bad-looking, and I couldn't help the small smile curling up at the corner of my mouth.

He turned from Marshall and Rory, rising to his full height, almost a foot taller than me. "And to you, Alexandra."

"Lexi," I corrected.

The gargoyle paused as if in thought.

"What's wrong?" I asked.

"I am sorry," he said, his words curt. "That does not sound . . . proper to me. My maker was Alexander and you are of his kin. If you do not mind, I would prefer to call you Alexandra."

"No big," I said, shrugging it off, but deep down, if I was being honest with myself, it stung, his unwillingness to be familiar. I turned my attention back to the collapsed building, gesturing toward it. "If you would . . ."

"As you wish," the gargoyle said, and stepped past all of us, heading straight to the edge of the pile, setting to the task of clearing a way to and through the heart of the lot. The sound of his efforts echoed across the lot and off the walls of the surrounding buildings, and I wondered what kind of attention we might be drawing. I ran to the gate and peered out between the cracks at the joints, but no one was currently passing by and for the moment I breathed out a sigh of relief, pressing my back against the wall.

When I opened my eyes, Rory was giving me a look.

"What?" I asked.

"Shouldn't we help?" she said.

"Why? It's not like we're going to be able to move much of this."

"That's not the point," she said, giving an uncertain look over at the gargoyle. "It's rude, isn't it? To just watch?"

"Rude? How is it rude? It's magic and stone we're talking about here."

Marshall remained silent, watching the work.

"It's what he wants, guys," I told them, but after hearing them, it was hard not to notice that I sounded like I was trying to convince myself. "He was designed to aid our family, so that's what he's doing. It's what makes him happy. His only purpose."

"Whatevs," Rory said. "You're the sorceress supreme."

Marshall unfolded his arms and pointed to the creature. "I don't mean to criticize, but at this rate, I don't think we're going to get anywhere, even by dawn."

It was true. The gargoyle worked like a machine, hefting huge chunks and piles of broken brick aside as he cleared a path, but for every pile he shifted, more slid down into place for him to move.

"I'd help," Rory said, holding up her hands and wiggling them, "but this would run havoc on my nails, and I'm already fighting an almost losing battle with them on my dance days."

I glanced over at Marshall, who held his hands up defensively. "I'm more of an idea man myself," he said. "Not too keen on my arms falling off trying to deadlift bricks and all."

"So how about some ideas, then?" Rory asked, but I was already working my backpack off my shoulders.

"I needed to spend more time in this spell book, anyway," I said. "I don't think I'm *quite* up to building him a companion yet to help him dig, but maybe there's something I can use here . . ."

The book was heavy, even in paper form, so I sat down where I thought the light was best and tried to read the book. Part of a streetlamp leaked behind the wall, and the book was legible enough here, despite the fact that much of the language *within* the books was still indecipherable to me.

I don't know how long I had been studying, but by the time I found something promising, Rory was busy stretching herself out and Marshall was sitting on the ground next to me.

"Well?" Marshall asked when he saw me looking up.

"I *think* I have something," I said. Rory stopped what she was doing and came over to us. "It seems a small thing, really, that I've been toying with since picking through my great-great-grandfather's notes. Part of what binds Stanis into what he does has to do with what Alexander called 'speaking to stone.' I don't think it accounts for what makes up his higher functions, but I was thinking of experimenting with it on a small scale." I opened my notes, breathed out the words written on the page, only partially understanding them, then pressed my will into one of the bricks Marshall had slipped on. I willed it to move, and like a shot it flew across the lot and into the side of the building off to our left.

"Wow," Marshall said, then looked at the pile at the center of the lot, his face falling. "You only have to do that a billion more times now."

"I was thinking of taking a shovel approach," I said. "This is about will and determination, and believe me, I'm more than determined to find out what really happened to my brother. Hey, Stanis!"

The gargoyle had worked through the start of a path into the mountain of debris, stopping when I called to him. The three of us walked over to him.

"We're going to try something new," I said, "but I need you as backup in case it . . . you know, doesn't work."

Rory clapped me on the shoulder. "She means in case she crushes us."

He nodded. "Very well."

We moved past him to the front of his path.

"Stay close, everyone," I said, adjusting the book in my hands. "I don't know how large an area I can cover with this."

"Comforting," Marshall said from a few feet back, his voice catching in his throat.

"Cuddle up," Rory said, pulling him closer. "At least we'll be together if all this collapses down on us."

"That will not happen," Stanis said, coming up behind us. "I will go last, and if need be shield you with my wings."

I wasn't too sure that would help but I wasn't about to get into it, not with the look on Marshall's face, anyway. The boy looked like he was about to throw up. Any further delay, and he just might. "Come on," I said. "I'm not sure how strong this spell is and I want to get moving before I lose my nerve, determination or no."

I consulted the book once more before closing it and pressing forward. It was my will against that of the stone, bound to it, but mixing with it at the same time. I stepped forward tentatively and the bricks before me tumbled away like I was pushing them aside with an invisible plow. There was resistance, thick in the air, but not enough to stop me. Not yet, anyway. I'd have to see how it went once I went deeper into the giant pile of rubble.

Without any further hesitation, I moved forward, the stones yielding to my passage. The safe space around me spread out like a ball radiating from my body, its shape becoming clearer the deeper I pushed us.

When we were shoulder-height deep into the rubble, Marshall grabbed my arm.

"Hold on a sec," he said. I heard him fishing through his backpack, but didn't turn for fear of losing my concentration. A moment later, there was light shooting forward over my shoulder.

"Thanks, Boy Scout," I said, and started forward. Stone

caved in on top of the bubble around us, but none of it hindered my progress, although with each step deeper my body felt more and more like it was sludging through knee-high snow.

"You okay?" Rory asked after bumping into me when my progress slowed.

"Yep," I managed to squeak out, only then realizing how clenched my jaw was from exerting my will over the brick and stone.

"Maybe we should turn back," Marshall said. "You look like you're about to burst a vein."

"Just . . . taking a lot of . . . effort, is all," I said through my teeth.

"He may have a point," Rory added. "You don't want to overdo it."

"Not leaving," I grunted under the increasing effort. "Until I find something of my brother."

"Well, let's hurry on, then," Marshall said, swinging the light in a searching arc back and forth in front of us. The stone continued parting out of the way, despite our depth, my own grim determination keeping it from crushing down on us.

I stopped, a strange sensation rising in my awareness. "Marshall, flash your light off to my left."

A different type of stone jutted out from the debris, darker and, more important, seemingly one piece. Intricate scrollwork decorated it, reminding me of the knot work design I had uncovered on the gargoyle.

"What is that?" Rory asked from over my other shoulder.

"I'm not sure," I said, pressing the bubble of my will toward it. My teeth ground together so hard it took a conscious effort on my part to relax my jaw without causing an avalanche on top of us. "However, I can't seem to move it."

"Great," Marshall said with nervous enthusiasm. "Time to go, then. Let's back it out of here."

"No, wait," I said, realizing it was a stupid thing to stay buried this far under the collapsed wreckage. "I need to check it out."

I headed off toward the exposed piece of stone, watching the broken bricks tumble away as I closed in on it, but the polished stone still wouldn't budge. In fact, the closer I got, the more debris fell away from in front of it, a familiar shape forming before me.

"A door," Marshall said.

"Ya think?" Rory asked, only partly giving him grief. Her eyes were transfixed on the door, too, and she brushed passed me, pressing all of her hundred and twenty pounds against the ornate knot work twists along the front of it. "Awesome. Won't budge."

"I told you that," I said.

"You want me to try?" Marshall asked, and I held back the urge to laugh at him.

"Don't strain yourself," Rory said. "Lexi, magic it some more, will ya?"

"If I can," I said, far less sure than Rory had sounded. I looked up at the mountain of rock pressing down against my spell. "I don't think I can keep us in this bubble and push this thing open at the same time. I might kill us all."

Rory and Marshall both fell silent as I stood there staring at the formidable stone door before me.

"I can keep the stones off us," Stanis offered, and spread his wings. At their fullest width, he twisted them ever so slightly so they rose above us like a massive umbrella.

"You sure you can keep all that up while I concentrate on the door?" I asked. I couldn't hide the skepticism on my face or in my voice.

Marshall snorted. "I trust his physical presence holding all that up more than I trust the invisible ball surrounding us right now," he said. "No offense."

Rory grabbed him by the shoulder and whispered in his ear, "Please don't piss off the person generating said invisible ball," she said, and Marshall fell silent.

"All right," I said, relaxing my concentration a little. "I'm letting go."

I eased my mind off thoughts of keeping the bubble active, the tension in my jaw letting go. A cloud of red-brown dust came down on us while I listened to the scraping of stone on stone settling onto Stanis and his wings. The veins in his stone neck bulged out from the effort, his lips pulling back to reveal the fangs within his mouth. It was hard not to stare; I found I could not turn away.

"I have it," he said, "but I would urge you to hurry."

I opened up my book of notes and held it at the center of Marshall's light, flipping like mad through it. The stone of this door wasn't going to yield to conventional pushing and shoving, not if I understood his love of puzzles. This was going to take more than just brute force, but what? From my all-too-limited understanding of my great-great-grandfather's arcane art, driving crumbled bricks was fairly mundane, even though it was clearly taking a heavy toll on my body pushing the spell too far tonight. Something this well carved and able to resist an entire building falling on it was going to need something with more *oomph* to it, and I wasn't sure whether I could muster any more of it at this point.

Still, whether I was moving rubble or rocks or trying to affect this door, some of the magic principles should be the same. I could make this move. I just needed to sort out the *how* of it.

Marshall coughed from somewhere behind me, then sneezed. The light source bounced away from the page for a second. I prayed he wouldn't drop it, and with haste I kept looking through my notes on binding the stone, blowing fallen brick dust off of the pages as I continued my reading.

"Got it!" I said, thrilling as I found the passages. Most of it, thankfully, was familiar to me, similar to the power that I had used in holding back the avalanche, only with minor variations and adjustments in both the language and somatics of it. I incanted the spell, focusing my concentration and will on it as I rushed the words out. I spoke the final one and gestured, then felt the power leave my body, but something didn't quite feel right with it, the bond lost.

More bits of brick and dust came raining down from up above, finding their way around the gargoyle's wings. A sizable chunk of brick hit my head, and I swore, feeling a warm trickle of blood running down the left side of my face.

"It's not working," I shouted, my frustration with myself rising.

"Relax," Rory said, although her voice cracked when she said it. She pressed her back against mine.

"You relax!" I shouted back at her. "I can feel your heart pounding away like the drilling of a jackhammer."

She pushed herself away from me. "Sorry," she said, turning to face me and grabbing my arms, "but for reals. You need to relax. When you rush things, you screw them up. Keep it committed, extended, just like in dance. Take your time and get it right . . . once."

The cloud of brick dust growing all around us filled my nostrils, forcing a sneeze out of me as it had Marshall, but I fought off the urge to sneeze again. If I couldn't get the incantation out properly this time, it would be only a matter of time before Stanis's strength gave out.

I did as Rory instructed, relaxing myself as much as one could under several tons of stone held up by an enchanted stone statue. This time I went through every motion and every word as if it were the most important thing in the world. Given that we were about to die, it definitely was, but I tried my best not to think about that and held my concentration on what mattered most.

The downpour of dust and debris grew, more like a constant curtain now, but I took my time. I finished, the buildup of power once again leaving my body, only this time a connection snapped to and joined me with the stone of the door. I pressed against the door with my mind, but it was still unmoving. Rather than get worked up, I kept my concentration and continued pushing at it with my will.

The heavy stone door gave a slight shift, and once I noticed it was hinged along its right-hand side, I slid as far to the left of it as I could with my body as well as my mind now, using the leverage to my advantage until I stumbled forward, falling into the darkness behind it as it gave way, opening. Rory, then Marshall, tumbled in after me, both landing on top of my already prone body. Barely visible through the falling rock,

Stanis's figure struggled in through the frame of the doorway, then darted forward, folding his wings in as he dove into the room.

The three of us scattered, rolling left and right to avoid being crushed under his weight, but we needn't have bothered. Once through the doorframe, his wings shot out and the gargoyle flew over us and into the center of the room behind us. I rolled over to follow his path, taking the room in. Marshall's flashlight barely lit up the enormous space, but the hint of its height and width were evident in the traces I could see of the gargoyle arcing up high into the room. The three of us scrabbled to our feet. I snatched the light from Marshall and shone it around the room as the gargoyle swept down behind us from out of the air.

A circular room carved of the same polished stone on the outside of the door sat within. Stone tables and chairs sat around the outer edge of the space, the same octagon with bat wings from my necklace notable in several decorative elements within the stonework of the walls.

"Is this an ornate clubhouse?" Marshall asked. "Or, like, the Belarus Cave? Please tell me there is a Belarusmobile."

"I have no idea," I said, stepping farther into the room. "This looks like a meeting facility of some kind, but as far as I know, my great-great-grandfather didn't keep a large circle of friends. Runaway exile from the old country. Go figure."

"Stop!" Marshall shouted when he finished marveling at the details of the room and noticed me, but it was too late. Then a stone under my foot sank into the floor, a series of quick clicks sounding off like bones breaking. I pulled my foot off of it a second too late as a barrage of large stones tore free from their place among the decorations on the walls and flew toward me at the center of the room.

Stanis dashed forward but he was too far away. My stomach dropped as I closed my eyes and curled myself into as small a ball as I could, hoping to avoid their crushing blows as panic filled my mind, awaiting the impact.

Oddly, there was none, only the gritty, shifting sound of

stone. I opened one eye, sneaking a peek. The floor around me now stood in a haphazard protective globe all around me, the only opening in it a small hole the size of my fist at the very top. The sounds of the flying rocks outside echoed loudly as they smashed into the outer side of the barrier.

"Thanks, Stanis," I shouted up through the opening as I choked on the swirling cloud of dust filling the confined space.

"I did nothing," the creature said, his voice calm and even.

"Well, I know Rory and Marshall didn't do it."

I heard scrabbling on the outside of the walls, and Marshall's face appeared at the opening at the very top of the stone prison. "I tried to stop you," he said. "One of the cardinal rules of a dungeon crawl: Always check for traps."

"This isn't one of your games," I reminded him.

"I think my point still stands," he said, and disappeared from the opening, sliding back down.

"Lexi, I think you might have done this yourself," Rory called out.

"How?!" I shouted out. "I didn't even have my damned notebook open!"

"I don't know," she said, "but from out here, it looked pretty much like a knee-jerk reflex action."

"Great," I said, giving a thumbs-up through the opening. "Now get me out of here."

"Can't you get yourself out?" Rory asked.

I pressed my will into the surrounding stone all around me, the way I had outside this room, but met nothing but resistance.

"I don't think so," I said. "This isn't like pushing away broken rubble or opening a door." I slapped my hands against the sphere, running my hands over its cold, jagged contours. "This shit is fused together. Solid."

A lone claw set itself into the opening at the top, curling in along the edge. "I will free you," Stanis said, and pulled at the first of the stones. It held for a second, but soon cracked under the pressure of the creature's strength, pulling it away to widen the opening. After several minutes of this a space opened wide enough for me to wiggle my way out, leaving the rest of the sphere there like some creepy alien egg.

I slid down the side of the sphere, Marshall catching me.

"You need to be more careful," he said. His eyes were narrowed at me, pissed. "Think, Lexi, won't you? The man who made your stone Batman here, the same one who built this indestructible room—don't you think it's possible he may have put traps in place as a preventative measure?"

"I thought this place might be safe, actually," I countered, but he just shook his head at me. I pointed around the room. "Look. It's got my family's sigil everywhere mixed in with all the other markings; why wouldn't I be safe here? I'm part of Alexander's blood!"

"Sure, there's magic in play here," he said, "but I doubt the magic *itself* is anything sentient. How is this place supposed to know you're his great-great-granddaughter?"

Marshall had a point. The fact that this place even existed in the first place was a minor miracle. Why was I getting so demanding of it like I knew anything about what was really going on here? Just simply being a Belarus didn't ensure my safety, despite the large shift in protection that came from having your very own gargoyle watching over you. During the day, for instance, I was as vulnerable as the next person, and realizing that made me feel incredibly fragile, but I fought the insecurity I found mounting.

"Okay, then," I said, shaking it off. "Everyone step careful. *Don't* do as I do."

I moved at a snail's pace around the room this time, checking the floor before every step, shining the flashlight up onto the walls as I went. Marshall walked up to one of them and pointed at the markings carved there.

"These symbols are everywhere," he said.

"It's in most of his books back in our library, too," I said.

"Recognizing the symbols is great," Rory said, "but unless you can read Aramaic or whatever this language is, we're not going to get anywhere. Specially with all that debris now caved in at the door leading out of here like that."

"It's not Aramaic," I said. "And I recognize it."

"Really?" Rory asked, sounding impressed.

I nodded. "It's the language he wrote a great deal of his notes in, kind of a bastardized old-country Slavonic-Lithuanian hybrid. My brother and I actually used it back when we were little, you know, when we actually got along. Much of my family's older accounting records were written with it, but we didn't know that when we were kids, obviously. We just thought it was a cool secret code we could write letters in." I studied the panels on the wall. "Some of this makes sense to me, but it's been a while. My ancient Belarus is a bit rusty so you'll have to forgive me."

"What does it say?" Rory asked.

I went silent as I sorted it out, trying to make sense of it all and fill in the blanks of what was implied in what I could not make out.

"I don't suppose this makes any sense to you?" I asked Stanis, who turned to look where my eyes were fixed.

The gargoyle stared at it for a long while before finally answering. "I am afraid not," he said. "Alexander spoke of his language, his language of secrets, but I believe he already had a hard enough task in impressing your American English on me."

Marshall walked over to my side, looking over the elaborately carved wall himself as he took his flashlight back. "Usually I'm a fiend for puzzles," he said, "but I don't think I can break down and decode a whole language right now. What can you make out of it?"

"Well," I started, "I don't think my great-great-grandfather was just the simple solo magic practitioner some of his books make him out to be."

Marshall did a full circle, swinging his light around the ornate room. "One man does not build something as monumental as this just for himself."

"Exactly!" I said, pointing up at the wall. "This section here talks about a 'closed' society, but I think the translation is a little lost here. I think he meant a secret one . . ."

"Like the Shriners?" Marshall asked.

"More like the Freemasons," I corrected, then jabbed

my finger up at another spot along the wall. "He even invokes a similar name, that this space was to welcome the Spellmasons."

"And this was like a guild hall," Marshall offered. "A safe place where he could meet with others of his kind."

"So there are others of these Spellmasons?" Rory asked.

"I have no idea," I said, walking off toward the darkness of another wall, drawn by the glimmer of something along its surface. I reached out, my fingers brushing the cold, smooth surface of it. "Glass. Hey, Marsh, shine that over here."

Light revealed a large glass case with hinged doors that hung open, the contents behind them containing more than a dozen shelves filled with beakers, bottles, and vials, much more full than the secret area in Alexander's studio.

"Looks like the Spellmasons were going to have a hell of a pharmacy," Rory said. "What is all this?"

I picked up a brown jar the size of my hand, liquid still held within it after all this time. The handwritten label, the same script as in Alexander's notebooks, read "antimony trichloride." "I'm not sure," I said.

"I am," Marshall said, joining us. "It's for alchemy."

Rory ignored him and looked around the space. "Do you think your brother knew anything about this?" she asked.

I took the light back from Marshall and flashed it around the room, searching. Something scattered across one of the long stone tables on the far side of the room caught my eye, and I went to it. "Pretty sure," I said, picking up a thick manila folder from the table. "I'm pretty sure they didn't have modern-day office supplies back in Alexander's day."

"So, what?" Rory asked. "Your brother brought this place down on himself playing Harry Potter?"

I flipped through the folder, full of the type of papers and schematics I dealt with now. "I don't know," I said, frustrated. "He was always good at making poor life choices, so it's possible he crushed himself to death screwing around with this." Not like I'd been so far away from it myself.

I closed the folder, the back side of it showing now. A billing invoice from a slip at a Brooklyn shipyard sat clipped to the back of it. A date and time written on it in my brother's handwriting. "This is from the night he died."

"What is it?" Marshall asked.

"A bill of lading."

"Lading . . . ?" Rory asked.

"It's a legal agreement between shippers and carriers," I said. "We deal with a lot of suppliers in renovation and construction. Devon must have had it with him, for his meeting."

"Then we should check it out," Rory said.

"*I* can check it out," I said. "Back at the office. We should have all our dealings with them on file somewhere."

Marshall sneezed.

"We should go," I said, stuffing the folder into my backpack and flipping my own notebook back open, readying the incantation once more since there didn't seem to be any other way out. The four of us gathered at the door. My jaw still ached slightly, but I'd have to endure it again. What other choice was there? If I had better command of this power, I probably wouldn't be hurting myself so much attempting it . . .

"Just give me a second," I said. "I swear I've been spending all my non–day job time reading up on all this, but it references so much else in my great-great-grandfather's library. I need more time. But first, I'm going to sleep for a thousand years."

"You will be dead by then," Stanis reminded me from somewhere behind us, and I couldn't help but smile. "That was one of your 'idioms,' was it not?"

"You're learning," I said. "I knew you were good for something other than heavy lifting."

He smiled. And as he did, I immediately felt unbelievably guilty about what I'd said about his only purpose being to serve me.

"And flying," Rory added.

"And that eternal-living thing," Marshall offered.

I sighed and pressed my will against the stone spilling into the room from outside the door. I just wanted to be out of there, despite how architecturally interesting the space was.

The only thing I really cared about right now was the bliss of my bed. The spells, alchemy, the Spellmasons, searching out the documents we found . . . All that could wait.

If sleep was for the weak, then I was the weakest person alive right now, and I was okay with that.

Nineteen

———— ☾ ————

Alexandra

I slept in and I slept late, my family's business schedule be damned. It wasn't like contractors weren't used to keeping people waiting, anyway, and my body had been craving rest by the time I'd gotten in last night. When I woke around noon, my jaw still ached and my very soul felt made of lead, but I forced myself out of bed. Within a half hour I pulled myself together—showered, ate, rescheduled the meetings I had missed before hitting the offices down on the public street level.

If there was an order to our current filing system, I didn't possess a high enough education degree to figure it out, which meant it took most of my afternoon to check the bill of lading against our records.

Numb from the search, I snuck away around three and headed to the studio upstairs to get back to what was really on my mind—deciphering more of Alexander's magic ways. By the time Rory stepped out of the elevator a few hours later, I had switched to overalls, already covered in flecks of clay that also coated both my hands like gray gloves.

Rory walked over to me and grabbed me by my forearm,

raising my hand up to look it over. "New look for you," she said. "I like how it hides your chipped, broken nails."

I pulled my hand away, going back to the clay I was working with a piece of brick on the table. "You took the elevator up," I said, ignoring her comment.

"It was a dance day," she said, throwing herself down onto the nearest couch as her bag hit the floor. "Just a little too sore to haul myself up the fire escape, which means of course I ran into your father."

"Sorry," I said.

"Don't be," she said. "I caught him in a good mood. He only blessed me three times."

"Only three?" I asked. "Wow. That is a good day. I think he's happy as a clam because he saw me working in the office earlier. Of course, he thought I was actually getting work done, but most of it was investigating that appointment my brother had the night he died."

Rory stuffed one of the pillows under her head, slid her glasses off, and looked over to me, squinting now. "Anything?"

I shook my head, nodding toward the folder at the end of the worktable I was at. "I couldn't find record of them as one of our shipping vendors," I said, "but the address on it points to a slip at a shipping yard belonging to Varangian Freight. Strangely, it's from the old country and arrived back at the top of July."

"Where is this slip?"

"Out in Brooklyn."

"Should we head out there? Do a little recon? Maybe after a little nap . . . ?"

I laughed. "Not quite yet," I said smoothing down the last of the clay to the project I was working on. "I have something to show you. Come here."

Rory let out a miserable-sounding groan, but got up and shuffled over to me at the worktable I was set up at. Bits of brick, stone, statue pieces, wire, and half-packed clay blocks were strewn across my work area, my great-great-grandfather's secret tome laid open off to the side. I wrapped my hands around my project and stood it up. A crude statue formed from brick stood there on two clay legs reinforced by wire within, the entire thing still reeking of chemicals I found among the contents of the art supply cage in the studio. It wasn't pretty, but it was a functional human form, if a bit stocky, reminding me of a tiny, no-necked football player.

"You ready?" I asked.

"For what?" she asked back, slipping her glasses back on.

"Watch," I said, and turned to my crudely carved clay figure. I pressed my thoughts into it. My *will*. I stared at it, wanting it to move, the minutes passing. After several had passed, Rory cleared her throat. I broke my focus on my failed statue and looked at her.

"I appreciate your attempt at modern art there, but I have to say maybe you should stick to those art-class sketches you were working on."

"Shush," I said, and turned back to it. I blocked her out completely and threw my concentration into the clay, trying to wrap my mind around it. Unfortunately, all it was doing was giving me a headache right between my eyes across the bridge of my nose, but I refused to give up. If I had read my great-great-grandfather's book correctly, half of it was belief, and I felt halfway to believing, even though each passing moment let a little bit more doubt settle in.

Then it happened. The clay wasn't just something I was staring at. It was something I felt pressing against me, resisting me. I pushed it back and felt the space beneath it give way. Wobbling like an unstable toddler, the block of clay and brick took a step back. It teetered on the brink of falling over but I was too far away to make a grab for it. I lashed out with my mind as my body tensed to reach forward anyway, my thoughts wrapping around it, steadying it. The figure righted itself, and Rory laughed in surprise at my side.

"Are you doing that?" she asked. "For real?"

I didn't answer. I didn't dare for fear of losing control. Instead, I forced the clay-and-brick figure to nod.

Rory ran over to it, leaning close to it, but not *too* close,

I noticed. "Holy crap," she said, marveling at it. She bounced in place, clapping her hands together. "What else can you do?"

I paused before answering, still fearful of speaking. "I'm not sure," I said. The creature stayed in its place, a little uncertain on its legs still, but in no danger of falling over. "Let's see what I can do."

I danced the figure around in an awkward circle, my teeny Frankenstein obeying my will.

"How are you doing that?" she asked.

I laughed despite the building headache that continued to grow, piercing behind my eyes. "I'm not entirely sure," I said. "It's all very new to me."

Rory gave me a sidelong glance, full of doubt. "You sure that's wise? Isn't your next move to make the big fella a companion . . . ? Didn't you say you were going to? No offense, but I don't think this little thing here is going to provide much in the way of protection."

Part of me held my tongue because a surprising and sudden jealous twinge rose up in me—I *didn't* really want to make Stanis a companion, did I? Maybe I was being selfish, but I didn't love the idea of sharing my protector with anyone, let alone someone made for him, but I wasn't about to tell Rory, who would no doubt immediately start teasing me about sexual incompatibilities with creatures that could only chafe you. "Baby steps," I said, avoiding the question.

"If some crazies dropped a building on *my* brother and tried to kill me . . ." she said. "Don't you think two gargoyles—*grotesques*; sorry—would be better protection than one? Stanis could have a pal, and we need strength in numbers, especially since there's a stream of tattooed psychos looking for you, whatever their reasoning is."

"Baby steps," I repeated, sticking to my misdirection, despite the fact she had a point. "Have to learn how the little things work before going full scale." I wasn't sure I was prepared to argue about my newfound jealousy of this potential stone companion for Stanis, and fell silent as I concentrated on my little living brick-and-clay man.

Rory's face fell a little, but she stopped talking for a while as she watched my creation until she spoke with concern in her voice. "It's living, yes?"

"I don't think so," I said. "I'm controlling it."

"Maybe you should stop," she offered.

"Stop? Why?"

"Until you have a better idea what exactly is going on there . . ."

"I know it's not a gargoyle," I said, becoming defensive now, "but it's a start! Frankly, I'm a little hurt that you're not more enthusiastic."

"I'll grant you that it's fantastic," she said, "but I'd rather know exactly what's bringing it to life."

"*I* am," I said, unable to hide the harsh tone in my voice.

She walked over to me and got right in my face, meeting me with as much attitude as I was giving. "Are you sure?" she asked. "Because I'm not."

"Why not?" My clay figure continued walking in little circles on top of my art station as I pulled my focus more to dealing with Rory.

"Why not?" Rory repeated. "Because Alexander warned you in his books of trickster or malevolent spirits! Consider that *grotesque* that watches over your family. That creature isn't just reacting to your control, your pushing and prodding of it. It acts on its own. There's life to it. Giving something life doesn't just happen in a vacuum. Until you figure that out, you need to stop this. Now." She grabbed both my arms hard, as if she were trying to restrain me, which set me off.

She wasn't wrong. There was certainly more to Stanis than stone. But I was frustrated with what felt like an interrogation. I shrugged her off and stepped back, raising my voice.

"Did you just see what I did here, Ror?" I shouted. "Did you?"

She nodded but didn't move, only meeting me with silence.

"Jesus, can't you just be excited for me?" I said. "I find one thing that breaks me out of the monotony of learning the real estate market in New York City, and you can't just join in the fun for a single moment—"

"Lex," Rory said, looking over her shoulder. Her voice was stern, but I was having none of it or her attitude.

"Let me finish!" I shouted.

Rory waved me over without turning to even look at me. "Can't," she said. "Too important."

"Tough," I said. "What I have to say is important to me."

She grabbed my arm and pulled me to her. "You need to calm down," she said.

"Why?"

She pointed at my art station. "*That's* why."

My tiny figure shook on the table, looking like a junkie going through withdrawal, the bulk of its body falling over as the brick dragged around the tabletop, and it wasn't alone.

Every other piece of stone or clay on the table was also in motion. Bricks, lumps of clay still in the package, and even fragments of discarded stone twitched and slid around the surface, many of them threatening to tear apart the pages of my great-great-grandfather's secret book.

The pulse of the chaos beat in time to the anger I was feeling from my argument. I tried to calm myself, but everything continued to stay in motion, a jagged chunk of broken brick dragging across the book now. I ran over to it, laid my hand on the book, and breathed out the words of power to transmute it back into its stone form. The page under my hand went cold, turning thick and heavy in seconds. I grabbed the piece of animated brick off the page and stepped back.

Calm, I thought, fighting to follow that in my mind.

Everything on the desk slowed until they came to a stop, several of the pieces toppling over.

I let out a sigh. "Jesus, that was—"

Rory pointed behind me toward the floor. "Not over," she said.

I spun around. My little brick-and-clay monster fiend was tottering off across the floor at a remarkable pace, my feelings on it a mix of horror and pride. "Shit," I hissed out. "Stupid teeny rampage." I wasn't sure how much damage the little guy could do, but I didn't want to wait to find out, especially with so many of Alexander's precious books and works of art all around the space.

"Do something!" Rory shouted. "Stop it, Puppet Master!"

I reached out for it with my mind to disarm the little bastard, but it continued on, knocking one of my boots across the room and through a pane of glass on the French doors leading out to the terrace.

"I can't control it," I said, unable to exert my will over it, the connection lost. I reached for my large stone book on the table, picked it up, and ran after my creation.

I dropped the book on top of the figure, its legs flying off the body, shattering as they went lifeless. Signs of struggle from beneath the stone book continued until it slowed, then stopped altogether.

"You want to take back what you said earlier?" Rory asked after a moment of silence. "About you being in control of it?"

"Okay, fine," I said, vexed that she had been wary and, worst of all, right. "I was controlling it at first, but I don't know . . . I'll concede, as you so astutely pointed out, that there might be some merit in my great-great-grandfather's warnings about trickster spirits and the like, that spirits seek out a vessel to occupy. I guess any vessel will do. In some small way, that's a positive, right?"

Rory went over to the stone book on the floor and hefted it up with her well-muscled but still petite arms. "*That* I might believe was some form of malevolent spirit, yes. But Stanis? He's something completely different, far more complex, Lexi. I want you to learn how to build more of them for your family's protection, but until you figure that part out, I wouldn't play around too much with this part of the process."

She handed me the book, and I laid it on one of the empty worktables nearby. "I need to get out of here," I said, "before I destroy the place."

Rory went to the folder off to the side of the worktable and picked up the bill of lading from the shipyard. "Brooklyn, then?"

I nodded, grabbing up my shoulder bag and single boot

before stepping carefully past the broken glass and out onto the terrace to fetch my other boot. "Let me change first," I said, heading for the stairs at the back of the space that led down to my living area. "Hitting Brooklyn in overalls might make me blend in a little *too* much."

Twenty

Alexandra

The strangest thing about Brooklyn was figuring out where the hip, habitable areas ended and the closed, run-down areas began. Only when the crowds on the street thinned out did I find us heading in what looked to be the right direction. Some of the waterfront had been taken over by developers, all of the buildings fresh and new, but the address on the bill of lading took us well away from those to a land of shipping cargo containers stacked several stories high on top of one another, large freighters docked all along the water. We watched from a distance for about half an hour. The cargo area was patrolled by the occasional slow roll of a security van with Port Authority markings, but the ships themselves were comparatively unattended. A dockworker running a forklift pointed us down the long strip of pavement along the waterfront, and we set off counting down the slip numbers until we found the one on the paperwork.

"These people have been docked here for more than four months," I said as we walked. "I want to know why, or at the very least if any one of them met with my brother that night."

"What if they were the ones who dropped a building on him?"

"I guess we'll see what I can drop on them, then."

Rory and I stopped, looking up at the ship docked there. It was like the other freighters, more rust than paint on it, and it was massive, rising several stories higher than the tallest stack of cargo crates onshore.

"Well, now what?" she asked, shoving her hands deep into the pockets of her coat.

The gangplank leading from the ship met with a closed-in tower on the land, a door at street level leading into what I presumed were stairs within.

"We go up," I said, and headed for the tower.

Rory grabbed my arm. "We do?"

"It's broad daylight and there are security vans patrolling nearby," I said. "Nothing's going to happen. We go up on deck, check it out, and if things look too sketchy, we bolt for safety."

"All right," she said, letting go of my arm but still sounding unsure. "But I think we've already hit sketchy just by being down at the waterfront."

We headed into the tower, metal stairs taking us up to the gangplank. We snuck off across it to the ship, my hands gripping onto both railings as we went, when a man appeared on the deck of the ship in a brisk walk toward the dock.

"Hey, Blue Hair!" he shouted in a gruff voice.

I touched the talisman around my neck, feeling only a remaining hint of its charge left. He apparently had noticed only Rory, but now that he was staring straight at my blue-haired friend, his eyes also turned to me. "You two . . . Did a couple of the crew order up some . . . entertainment?"

"Yes," I said without thinking, running with the impromptu bluff. A wicked smile crossed his face and I dropped my hand away from my necklace. Unfortunately his eyes went straight to my talisman with recognition, and his face went from wicked and amused to dead cold.

"Holy shit," he said, and, reaching into his coat pocket, pulled out a now-familiar sight to me, although I wished it wasn't—a white-handled knife, held in his tattooed hand.

"Does this count as sketchy?" Rory asked.

"Totally," I said. "Full retreat."

I spun around with Rory, headed back toward the tower,

but before we got more than ten feet a man with a short brown crew cut and hard features came into view, blocking our way, a knife in hand also.

"Shit," I said. The two of us started back out the center of the gangplank, men now closing in from both ends. I struggled to get my backpack off while holding on to the railing, and pulled Alexander's tome free from it.

"Please tell me you have something," Rory said.

"Not really sure what I can do on a metal walkway fifty feet off the ground," I said, flipping through the pages, "but I'm looking." Between the heights, the pressure, not having near enough time studying the book, and the men closing in, it didn't look promising. "Don't think I've got anything."

The men were maybe ten feet away on either side of us, knives in hand. Rory turned to me, taking off her horn-rimmed glasses. "Hold these," she said.

"What are you doing?" I asked, but it was too late to answer. Rory had already turned to face the man coming for me, running at him. At the last second she planted her hands on the railing, stepped up onto it, and, with an open-legged lunge, went over him. She landed with that dancer's grace of hers, and brought her right leg around like a ballerina going into a turn, catching him behind the knee. He dropped, falling forward, and she planted the heel of her boot in the center of his back, driving him under the rail and off the gangplank, down into the water gap between the ship and shore.

Her eyes were wide, her face flush with anger. I had never seen her this way before. She tore past me toward the man still blocking our escape. As she ran, she planted her hands again on the railing, and, anticipating her, the man raised his knife high, unwilling to fall for the same thing his fellow toady had fallen for. I didn't bother to tell him that the last thing you should do is try to anticipate Aurora Torres.

She wrapped her hands tight to the railing, and threw herself into a spin around the railing itself, coming in under it just as fast. The momentum slid her like a shot across the gangplank, again, perfect grace and form as she compacted herself down, shooting between his legs. Rory came up hard into his crotch with both hands, using her accumulated speed to drive her bunched fists into him. He fell to the gangplank, the knife falling over the edge of it, and his hands flew to grab himself.

Rory rolled into a standing position, then came at the prone man, pummeling him with a barrage of kicks, her powerful legs lifting him each time she connected. The first few he reacted to in pain beyond that of her initial blow, but after the blood started flowing, he didn't seem capable of reacting anymore and his eyes rolled back into his head.

"Whoa, whoa," I said, pulling her back from the figure on the gangplank. "He's down, he's down."

Rory's eyes were wide, her breath coming in heavy rasps. Her muscles were tensed in my grip on her, reminding me of a feral cat I had once tried to rescue in an abandoned lot down in Alphabet City. I only hoped that Rory wasn't about to leave me with a set of scars the same way the cat had.

The man at our feet still breathed, but I didn't think he'd be getting up anytime too soon. Rory lashed her foot out in his direction to strike again, but I tugged her back from him even farther.

"Where the hell did you learn *that*?" I asked. Her wild eyes relaxed a little, but she stared through me. I shook her hard, her body loose in my hands like a rag doll.

"I don't know," she said, her words dull on her lips. "Years of dance training?"

"That's wasn't dance," I said. "Dance isn't brutal like that."

Her eyes finally shifted to me, a hint of panic in them. "It's pretty brutal, actually. You train your body hours on end and then something like this happens . . . I couldn't help myself." She looked down at her bloody boots, then over at him. "Crap . . . I didn't kill him, did I?"

I let go of her and stepped toward the body, but not too close. If horror movies had taught me anything, it was to never get close to the lifeless body. I wasn't going anywhere near enough for him to leap up and grab at me.

"I think he's alive," I said, looking him over. My eyes stopped on his face, which was covered in red. "There's blood everywhere. You could have killed him, Aurora!"

Rory glared at me. "Very compassionate of you, Lexi, but he and his friend were both going to eviscerate us, if you remember thirty seconds ago. If you've got a problem with me keeping us alive, by all means, please let me know."

I sighed. The familiarity of bickering with my old friend was oddly comforting in all this chaos. The sound of commotion rose up on the deck of the ship as a group of men started to form.

"We need to go," I said, dragging a still-stunned Rory along with me. "Now."

She didn't answer, but I was glad to see she put up no resistance. After that display, I think I feared more for those men's safety than ours.

Twenty-one

Alexandra

Rory's brutality on the docks must have messed my head up more than I thought, and I spent another restless night tossing and turning as various gruesome combat scenarios played out in my head, almost all of them ending with our grisly deaths.

I didn't want her doing the fighting for us, not if it brought out her inner cage fighter. Yes, I could learn to eventually—hopefully—build an army of gargoyles, but if yesterday's early experiment with my little brick-and-clay friend was any indicator, that was a *long* way off.

The next logical step was to first restore the animated friend I already had—Stanis—as soon as I could, which meant hunting out more information about the missing soul stones and restoring them to the four slots hidden beneath the gargoyle's chest. The strange and mixed language of my great-great-grandfather's master tome was becoming clearer to me, but what I really needed time for was deciphering his myriad of notebooks and clues about the stones—the Crown of the Titan, the Eye of God, the Ruler's Chest, and the Heart of the Home.

So after *another* quick morning of rescheduling real estate showings for later, I spent my time searching through my great-great-grandfather's library for notebooks that tied to the main book or references to the gemstones in question. A barrel or two of coffee helped to stave off my restless night, and after hours of following handwritten notes and book references down a variety of rabbit holes, one passage struck me about the Crown of the Titans, talking about the jeweled crown of the Titans down in Tartarus.

Tartarus? I was pretty sure it wasn't a name for an old section of town like Tribeca or Hell's Kitchen. According to the Internet, the Greeks called it a place where souls were sent to be punished, an abyssal pit set beneath the underworld. I could think of only one soul-draining punishment beneath New York City—riding the subway. But where exactly? There were miles and miles of tracks connecting out to almost all the boroughs. My great-great-grandfather could have worked on dozens of them. I looked back at the rest of the clue. The Crown of the Titans. How many stations were likely to have Greek statues, I wondered. Not many.

I checked through several of the library's more historical records, and I had what I was looking for, although the name of it—Herald/Pennsylvania—sounded totally unfamiliar. There were currently Herald Square and Penn Station stops, but it looked like there had once been a previous station that now sat unused from when other subway lines grew around it. Checking it against my smartphone caused my heart to sink. It was an actual station, deep under the heart of the city, but it was long abandoned. Looking up the name in another of Alexander's notebooks, I lucked upon an old map of the city, full of street names I weren't sure even existed anymore. Still, the lead was promising, on at least one of the stones, anyway. Thanks to the map, I had a vague idea of *how* I might find my way to the old abandoned subway station, but I wasn't going to go it alone. I needed help.

I rallied the troops via text message (MEET @2, U.S.-N& R), then switched to an older pair of jeans, a worn tank top, and an old beater of a fall jacket before heading out into the city with my great-great-grandfather's tome strapped across my back in my last-season poppy patent flap backpack.

By the time I made my way down to the Union Square subway station, I was surprised to see Marshall already waiting for me at the uptown end of the N and R platform, wearing a Miskatonic University T-shirt and a good-sized backpack of his own.

Three or four trains passed us by while we waited before Rory finally stepped off of one, her massive dancer's bag draped across her body as usual. Her short blue hair was a mess, and she ran her hands through it to fix and shag it out as she came quick down the platform to join us. I was glad to see she looked far less riled up today.

"So what's on the agenda?" she asked.

"Oh, I don't know," I said with a dismissive shrug. "I thought we'd take a day off from beating people to death."

"Oh, good," she said. "Sorry I look like shit. I came straight down from dance class, as quick as I could. If I need to dress up or something, you're buying me clothes."

"You're fine as is," I said. "You're dressed for adventure and I'll need you nimble."

Rory gave me a suspicious look, then took notice of Marshall. "How'd you beat me here?"

"I texted Marshall first," I said.

Her suspicion turned to full-on wariness, her eyes narrowing behind her glasses. "You did? Why?"

I felt my face going red a little bit. "He's got experience with this."

"With what?"

"Dungeon crawling," Marshall said with a proud wide grin.

"Sorta," I said. "We're going under the city."

"Really, now?" Rory asked, her expression changing as her face dropped. "Gee, I'm so glad I flew all the way downtown here so fast. I've always wanted to meet the mole people and all." She looked at Marshall and his backpack. "Are we going camping afterward?"

"No," I said. "I just thought it best to be prepared. That's why I texted Marshall. Not that he has real-life experience in these things, as such, but I figured that those 'dungeon crawls' he always talks about give him some sort of strange experience in this."

"If you were going into a dungeon in a game, you'd bring equipment, right?" Marshall asked her.

Rory shrugged. "Would I? How would I know? You know I refuse to play."

"Yes, and I've been meaning to talk to you about that—"

Rory cut him off before he could finish, patting his backpack. "So whatcha got, Sir Nerdsalot?"

He looked a little hurt at first, but got excited as he opened up his backpack. "Just some basics," he said. "PowerBars in case we get hungry, flashlights, compass, a tack hammer, a Leatherman's tool, fifty feet of rope—"

Rory held up a finger. "Fifty feet of rope?"

"What?" he said, defensive. "It's an adventuring staple! Always have it in D and D. In *The Lord of the Rings*, Samwise laments forgetting to bring some. Rope is important to have!"

Rory gave him a look like he was crazed, started to speak, but thought better of it and turned back to me. "And just why are we going under the city?"

"Because that's where my great-great-grandfather put one of the soul stones," I said.

"Of *course* he did," Rory said, rolling her eyes. "Why make it easy on us, right?"

"Now, now," I said. "Where's your sense of adventure?"

"I think I left it on the docks yesterday."

"What docks?" Marshall asked.

"Long story," I said, then pulled from my jacket pocket one of the worn leather notebooks I had taken and opened it to Alexander's hand-drawn map of the city. "It says the Crown of the Titan in Tartarus is jeweled."

"Tartarus," Marshall said without hesitation. "The Grecian underworld. Well, technically that's Hades, but I suppose this is the best we have to go on." He peered down the tunnel leading out of the station, looking a little green at the gills.

I turned to the gated narrow path that led alongside the entrance to the tunnel, staring into the darkness. "Let's go."

Marshall didn't move, uncertainty filling his face. "So we're really going down the tracks," he said. "Down the tunnels. In search of Tartarus."

"Yup," I said, mustering what false confidence I could despite my beating heart. Maybe I was wrong about what my great-great-grandfather had written?

"Live tracks," Marshall said, his voice growing smaller. "Third rail all brimming with *zap bam*!"

I reached over and gave his arm a reassuring squeeze. "We're only going to be on the active track line for a little bit," I said. "This is the N and R line, the Never and Rarely. We'll be fine. Promise."

"Maybe we should wait until nightfall and let our big stone friend do this," Marshall offered.

"Scared?" Rory asked with a little more vocal sting to her ribbing, no doubt hiding her own nerves as she adjusted her bag.

"I'm not scared," he said, annoyed. "Just being practical."

She shook her head at him. "Should have taken me up on those dance lessons when I offered them," she said, twirling on point, her bag floating out from her body in a perfect arc. "Then you wouldn't have to worry about stumbling on the tracks. *Zap!*" She grabbed at him as she said the last word, causing Marshall to jump.

"Guys!" I shouted before it could escalate further, stopping them both. "Focus. I thought about that, Marsh, but whether it's night or day, there's no subtle way to just march a gargoyle down onto the platform here. Don't worry, though. We don't need brute force for this. Hardest part is going to be getting off the main tracks, which I just told you is going to be cake."

I wasn't wholly sure I believed it myself, but it seemed to shut Marshall up. I turned back to the open track next to me and waited.

Movies and television made it look so easy, but timing an inconspicuous entrance into the subway tunnel off the platform was harder than it looked. As trains approached, then left, there was always too much of a crowd exiting from them to make our way surreptitiously, but finally after about ten minutes, the timing worked out and we found ourselves on a near-empty platform as an R train pulled away.

"Let's go," I said, and, without waiting, pushed past the short metal gate that blocked the path leading down into the tunnel.

I wasn't too thrilled at the idea of electrocuting myself, either, and stayed close to the outer wall as I went. Between the distant lights uptown at the Twenty-third Street station and my eyes adjusting to the darkness, my vision wasn't too bad. The markings running down the steel struts of the tunnel's structure were faint, but the occasional bare bulb hanging about the path on industrial-grade wiring helped me make the writing out, also allowing me to check the notebook.

"Oh, ladies!" Marshall said a short time later, panicked. "Train!"

I looked up from my book and peered down the tunnel. The rising glare of lights grew at the far-off Twenty-third Street station as a train pulled into view there.

"Everyone stay calm," I said, stopping under one of the bulbs to get my bearings. We were somewhere near the path that led off of the main tracks, I was sure, but I double-checked my notes. The sound of skittering rats somewhere nearby and the stench of rotting garbage did little to help me concentrate, but I studied the map as quickly as I could. "Two markers down. Step lively. Carefully, but lively."

All three of us picked up our pace, Marshall pushing past us and taking the lead. I prayed his gangly form didn't stumble because if he went down we *all* were going down with him. The train roared back into motion up ahead as it pulled out of the station, its lights growing ever closer to us.

"This one?" Marshall asked, slapping his hand frantically on one of the supports.

I double-checked my book. "That's the one," I said.

The honk of the approaching horn rose up, making my ears feel like they were going to burst.

"Now what?" Rory asked as she slammed into me from behind.

I studied the spot, but it didn't make sense to me. "Son of a bitch," I said, and flipped through the book some more. "There should be a doorway here, but there isn't!"

Marshall went wild examining the space. It was easier to see the area now, what with all the light pouring down on us from the approaching train. "There's just this whole cluster of cross beams," he said, "but I think there's an opening I can squeeze into."

"Get through there, then," I shouted, a bit of panic seizing me, and shoved him forward. Marshall squirmed between two of the beams about waist high, disappearing into the darkness on the other side. I grabbed Rory by the strap of her bag and pushed her through, shoving her bag after her. I dove through, catching my backpack with the book in it on a beam, my legs still hanging out onto the tracks. I sucked my stomach in, curled myself forward, and pulled on the steel beam beneath me. The bag slipped free and I sprawled into a flailing pile of limbs.

The wind generated by the passing train washed over us as we untangled ourselves, and I'd be lying if I didn't say my heart was beating in time with the wheels on the track.

"Anyone else's heart about to explode?" Marshall asked, clutching his chest.

Rory and I both raised our hands.

Marshall checked his bag for damage, then reached in and handed me a flashlight, standing. "I want to get away from here, like, now," he said. "So lead on."

We regrouped, and by the time the train had fully passed, we were already heading into a world of older tracks that hadn't been used in decades, maybe even longer. The dark became far more impenetrable the farther away we got from the main working lines of the subway system, but the added bonus was the change in smells. The rot of garbage gave way to something older, stale, and while not pleasant, either, it was a marked improvement as we made our way deeper under the city. We went on for about twenty minutes with me consulting my great-great-grandfather's notebook and correcting our course on the fly before anyone spoke again.

"Not that I'm getting freaked-out or anything," Marshall said in a quiet voice. "I'm not, really. Just . . . how much farther is this place?"

I checked the map, then the ancient rails beneath my feet. "Not much farther," I said, continuing down the tracks. "We should be coming up on the old station soon. I'm dying to see it."

"Why?" Rory asked from farther back.

"Are you kidding?" I said. "Have you ever seen early pictures of the old city stations? They're like . . . cathedrals to transit. They're gorgeous. Then just imagine my great-great-grandfather's hand adding to all of its grandeur."

Rory stopped and I looked back at her. She angled her flashlight past me and up. "I don't have to imagine," she said. "Look."

"Whoa," Marshall added, already seeing it.

I turned back around and looked for myself. "Whoa is right," I said. "Holy . . ."

I couldn't finish my words. The tracks opened up into a large stone dome made from thousands of tightly fit blocks, rising high over our heads. I wasn't sure whether it was a trick of the light, or rather the sheer absence of it, but the magnitude of the space felt like I was standing in an underground football stadium. Two sets of tracks skirted a large central area that was covered with bits of old tumbled columns and long-broken statues. Dozens of carved figures lined the walls, Grecian soldiers easily towering three or four times our height, the grand scale of the place both haunting and awesome at the same time.

The three of us hoisted ourselves up onto the actual main platform, rolling in the dust of years upon years as we did so.

Marshall coughed. "This is intense," he said. "It's like *Raiders of the Lost Ark*."

Rory dusted herself off, then headed farther down the platform. "Impressive," she said, "but also daunting. There's a lot of ground to cover here. A lot of carving to look over just to find a single stone."

"Let me consult the Book of Alexander," I said, checking

over his old hand-drawn maps. "Remember, we're not looking for the soldiers. We're looking for the crown of one of the Titans. Let's check the far end of the platform." I shone my flashlight in that direction, but the range of it didn't stretch far enough to light more than thirty feet ahead through the fallen debris.

We made our way down the platform, working through the rubble along it until we came into view of a series of large, decorative sculptures where the platform ended. My great-great-grandfather's depiction of ancient carvings. They rose up much higher than the rest, a tangle of ancient figures, Greco-Roman in their carving for sure, but no doubt made by my great-great-grandfather's hand.

"There," I said, pointing my flashlight to one of the central figures. The highest head among them was that of Medusa, her tangled hair of snakes weaving out in all directions, the tip of each adorned with a now-dust-covered gemstone. "Our Titans."

"Technically speaking," Marshall offered, "Medusa wasn't a Titan. They were deities. She's a Gorgon."

"And that's not really a crown," Rory added.

"You tell Medusa that," I said. "Alexander's a puzzler. You think he's just going to be that obvious in his clue giving?" I stared up at the giant mythological creature. "Jesus, she's tall."

Marshall swung his bag around to the front of his body and rifled through it. "I brought rope, but I don't think I brought actual rigging or climbing gear."

I turned to him. "Can you improvise?"

He shrugged. "Maybe," he said, searching up above with his own flashlight. "I just need to figure out how to secure the rope best."

"Screw rigging," Rory said, climbing over the stone barrier originally meant to keep commuters back from it, no doubt. "I can get them."

Marshall reached into his backpack and pulled out a leather case that fit into the palm of one hand, handing it to her. "Take this."

"What is it?" she said, unsnapping one end of it open. She

pulled free what looked like a set of metal pinchers with a thick-channeled handle.

"It's my Leatherman tool," he said with a bit of pride.

"Leatherman?" she asked. "Are you one of the Village People?"

Marshall sighed and shook his head. "It's like a Swiss Army knife, a multi-tool. Should help you with the stones."

She shortened the strap on her dancer's bag, bringing it in close to her body, then slid the tool into her pocket and smiled. "Thanks, Marsh," she said, and spun back around to the mammoth piece of art.

"You sure—" I started to ask, but she was off like a shot, already swinging herself up into one of the crooks where a few of the figures' knees came together.

"Jesus," Marshall said with a low whistle. "She's like a spider monkey."

"She's . . . Well, she's something," I said, watching her progress slow the higher she got. "Be careful! I don't know where there's a hospital near here."

"Where *is* here, anyway?" Marshall asked, looking around.

"I think we're somewhere by Penn Station," I said. "I think. They called the station Herald/Pennsylvania, before the lines expanded, but it was closed and built around forever ago."

We watched in silence as Rory climbed, both of us steadying our light on her figure and any handholds around her that we could make out from the ground.

"This is very Indiana Jones," Marshall said. "It's like we're defiling a temple. Ten to one these statues come alive and attack us. Can you cast 'Detect Magic' or something?"

"If that means what I think it means, I don't sense things like that," I said, "but then again, I'm not entirely sure what I *would* be able to sense. I don't think what my great-great-grandfather dabbled in quite works that way."

"That's comforting," Rory said from halfway up the statue now. "The only statue I'm currently concentrating on is the one I'm climbing, and I'm concentrating on not falling off it."

I pulled off my backpack, opened it, and tapped my fingers happily against the back of the book. "Give me a sec," I said.

"Maybe there's something in here to make the stone more . . . *cushiony* when you fall."

Rory grunted as she tightened her climbing grip. "Or I could just, you know, *not* fall."

Marshall let out a quiet, nervous laugh. "Let's try for that one," he said. "My money's still on the statues coming to life."

Rory hugged her way up the torso before grabbing onto one of the statue's outstretched arms, swinging herself up onto its shoulder, her arms among the tangle of snake hair. She looked down at us, smiling and triumphant. "I'd be more worried about 'defiling the temple,' Marsh, if we weren't somewhere underneath Macy's."

"Even so," I said, "Marshall has a point. Stay sharp."

"Will do," she said, and began working on the cluster of gemstones on the statue's "crown" of snaky hair using Marshall's Leatherman tool. The scraping of metal on stone echoed out into the darkness surrounding us, drowning out the nearby chittering of rats. One by one the stones came free and she lowered them into the shoulder bag hanging around her waist. She gave a quick anticipatory look around the room. Marshall and I did the same, waiting for something to happen, but nothing did.

Rory started back down the statue, but my flashlight remained fixed where it was on the Medusa's head. The stone snakes were *moving*.

"You might want to hurry, Ror," I said. "And don't look up."

She looked down at me, then naturally did what I told her not to do and followed the beam of my flashlight back up to the head, where the snakes were in full swirl now. Her feet slipped as the statue came alive, the dust shaking off it and all the others around them as they did the same. Rory's arms were around the forearm of a soldier on Medusa's right, and as it swung away, her grip broke and she fell to the floor in front of Marshall, landing hard on her ass.

Marshall absently offered his hand to her, his eyes still fixed on the Medusa, which was making its way toward the low barrier between us. Rory took it, dusting herself off with her free hand as she stood, then gave the Medusa a quick glance before starting toward me.

"We need to run," she said, letting go of Marshall's hand, checking to see whether her bag was still intact.

"No argument from me," I said, slamming my book shut. I turned and started off, Rory following.

"Awesome," Marshall said, still fixed in place.

Rory grabbed his arm and forcefully dragged him into a run with the two of us. "Awesome?" she repeated, punching him with her free hand. "How can you say that?"

"Well, I *told* you that would happen," he said. "It's not often that I'm right."

She shook her head wearily at him. "Feels great, don't it?"

"Yeah," he said. "Except the possibly dying part that might come from it."

Two of the soldiers had worked their way past the barrier and were starting after us now. Out in the surrounding darkness, the sounds of others coming to life came from all around us.

It was hard enough running with only three bouncing flashlights to light the way through the treacherous, debris-filled platform. If I didn't come up with something, those things would catch us in no time. We were a little faster than them, but they had numbers. "We need to split up," I said.

"Why?" Rory asked.

"We need to sort through those stones, and now," I said. "We need to figure out which one of them is the true stone, which is a part of Stanis."

"Good enough reason for me," Rory said, already reaching down into her bag for the gems, counting them as we continued running. "I count a dozen or so. Hard to tell, being on the run and all."

I grabbed her bag and Marshall's arm, stopping for just a second. More movement came from down the platform as more and more statues fell in behind us for the chase. "Both of you grab a handful," I said. "Then pick a direction and run."

"How is *that* going to help?" Marshall asked, hesitant.

"Just do it!" I shouted, and shoved my own hand into the bag, drawing out a fistful of gems.

Marshall didn't pause, scooping out a handful of his own. "Now run!"

I took off, my boots sliding on the grime and rubble under my feet as I made a sharp left turn in the main area of the station, not waiting to see which direction the others would choose. When I thought I had enough of a lead, I stopped and spun around, both to catch my breath and assess the situation developing behind me.

To my surprise, I had more than just a lead. None of the pack had followed after me. Neither had they followed Rory, who had kept going straight down the far end of the station and was not slowing and turning. We both watched the pack of stone soldiers, a dozen or so, chase off after Marshall, every last one of them.

"I didn't defile your temple," he shouted, looking back over his shoulder. "It was the blue-haired girl!"

"Nice," Rory shouted out as she slowed her own run, shaking her head. "Asshat."

"Rory!" I called out to her. "Drop your stones!"

I threw mine on the ground, letting them roll off into the darkness of the station, sounding like tiny claws scrabbling away from me, and Rory did the same, but looked confused.

"Now what?" she asked from several hundred yards away across the massive platform.

"We chase down Marshall," I said, starting off toward his small circle of distant light on the other side of the station.

"We do?" Rory asked as she caught up with me. "With those things on his tail right behind him?"

"We do," I nodded, still winded and hating the fact that Rory seemed to be breathing just fine. "This is the fastest solution I could come up with."

"For what?"

"For the process of elimination."

"If you're looking to eliminate Marshall, good job," she said.

Marshall was backed against a wall next to a collapsed entrance that might have led him off to safety had it been otherwise.

"Eliminating the gems," I said. "Those things are not protecting all those stones. They're protecting *the* stone. This was just a quick way for me to figure out which stones are which and eliminate the rest. We keep narrowing it down until we find the proper one."

Rory smiled. "Smart. Dangerous, but smart."

I laughed through my gasping for breath. "This whole damn endeavor is dangerous," I said, then shouted to Marshall, "How many do you have left?"

Marshall looked into his cupped hands while still keeping an eye on his foes. "Seven!" A spear slammed into the wall next to his head and he stumbled to his right.

"Divide them into two handfuls," I shouted. "We're coming!"

Rory sighed, then stopped running. "We are? I like the guy, good roommate and all, but I'm not sure I want to take a spear to the head for him."

I stopped, too, as much to talk as to rest my legs. "They won't pay you any attention," I said. "These soldiers, these centurions or whatever they are, are not as complex as Stanis. They're single-minded of purpose, focused just on the stone. I need you to grab one of Marshall's handfuls and run with it."

"So there's only a fifty-fifty chance they'll spear me now?" she asked.

"You're not going to get better odds than that around here right now—I'll tell you that," I said. I ended my debate and ran for Marshall, going straight through the crowd of stone creatures rather than around them. As I had hoped, they ignored me. I grabbed Marshall's right hand, surprised that I couldn't pry it open. I looked up at his face, and it was petrified with pure fear. Rory appeared on my left, working on his other hand.

"Open up, buttercup," she said, singsong sweet, and slapped him across the face hard. His hand opened in mine and the stones fell into it.

Marshall came to and stared at Rory, her handprint on his face already turning a bright red.

"Sorry," she said, then shoved him off to the right. "Now run!"

The three of us each shot off in a different direction, but this time it was Rory the statues chased after.

"Toward me!" I shouted. "Come to me!"

I ran toward her as she sprinted toward me, her voice growing closer. "I hate you so much right now," she said.

"Hand me half!"

Rory looked down into her fist. "I can't hand you half!" she screamed, perplexed and near hysterical. "I have three!"

"Give me one or two, then," I said and held my hand out.

She slowed long enough to clasp her shaking hand in mine, released, and then ran off again. I looked down into my hand. *One*. I didn't bother to wait and see if it was *the* one, not with the statues bearing down on me. I dashed off, then gave a look back over my shoulder. The statues were still with Rory, who was finally showing signs of fatigue.

"One more time!" I called out, and started back to the center of the station.

"Really, really, really hate you now," Rory said as she closed the distance and we met once more, and she handed me one of her two stones. "Did I mention how much I hate you?"

I ran off, shouting behind me as I went. "Best friends forever! Even in the afterlife!"

This time the statues changed their course and started off after me for a change.

"Now what?" Rory asked, coming to a stop and doubling over as she gulped in deep breaths of air. One of the stone statues bowled into her shoulder as it headed after me, and I winced as she went flying through the air and skidding across the station's floor.

"I have the stone," I shouted, "and I have the book, but now I need the time to actually read the damn incantations to stop them."

"This way!" Marshall shouted from somewhere off to my right. I followed his voice, heading toward a pile of debris about as tall as I was. I rounded it to find him crouched there on the ground, his backpack off and its contents spilled out all around him.

"This," he said, holding up a piece of rope that trailed off around the edge of the pile, "is why you should always carry fifty feet of rope." He tugged the line. I peeked my head above the pile of debris to see the line spring up taut across the path I had just run, acting as a trip line. The statues hit it, toppling forward and pulling at the line with their massive weight. Marshall went sliding face-first across the dirty platform, but didn't let go of the rope. I grabbed his feet and held on, stopping his slide.

The remaining rope tangled among all the feet of the oncoming statues, causing them to crash down on top of one another in a mess of twisted, broken limbs. Marshall picked himself up, his face and front covered in slime, dirt, and bits of . . . *something*.

"Thanks," I said.

"You might want to hurry up," Rory called out from where she stood far off across the station.

The sound of the statues struggling to right themselves got me focused again. I laid the book out on the floor and flipped through it in haste, searching out the right words. Out of the corner of my eye, giant stone hands clawed at the top of the pile of debris, but I ignored them, intent on what I was looking for. I found the page and clasped the stone in both my hands as I invoked power over it, reclaiming the stone in the Belarus family name. It burned warm in my hands and I looked up to see the faces and arms of five of the remaining statues staring down at me, weapons raised and coming down fast. It took everything in my power not to stumble over the last of the words of binding.

I spoke the last of them and dropped to the floor, waiting to see if my power would ward them off, but the sound of the statues continued to grow louder as more joined the pack on the other side of the debris pile. "Shit," I said. "I tried."

Rory came running around the side of the pile of debris, skidded out, and fell down next to me and Marshall.

"Great," she said, breathless. "Looks like more running, then."

"Ladies—"

"I don't think I can," I said, my legs seizing up when I tried to force myself out of my crouch.

"Me, either," Rory said. "Just wanted to get a little sarcasm in before they crush us."

"Ladies—"

"Fair enough," I said, grabbing my oldest friend's hand.

"Guys!" Marshall shouted, stopping both Rory and me. "Do you hear that?"

"Hear what?" I asked, listening hard. "I don't hear anything."

"Exactly," he said, and scurried to stand up.

Rory and I joined him, albeit a bit more slowly, and looked back over the pile of debris. All of the statues were simply standing there in a uniform line, motionless.

"It worked," I said, allowing myself a small smile in all this.

"What are they doing?" Rory asked.

"Awaiting orders from their master, I would guess," Marshall said. "Alexandra."

"You think?" I asked, taking a tentative step out from behind the pile of debris.

"Try," Rory whispered, but I didn't notice her making any effort to step out with me. "Before they take a swing at you."

"Okay," I said, then turned to face the statues full-on. "Good work, men. Excellent job. This was just a test of our security here, and, ummm . . . you passed! Congratulations."

The statues remained stone still, and I looked over at Rory, who was rolling her eyes at me. "Do you think they want praise or smoke blown up their ass?" she asked. "You said yourself that they're far less complicated than Stanis."

I shrugged. "So what do I do?"

"Give them an order," she said.

I looked back at the statues again. "Back to where your maker intended you to stand," I said, then added, "Please."

Without hesitation the statues turned on their heels and returned to their original spots all along the walls of the old subway station, settling back into their places.

"'Please'?" Rory repeated, raising her eyebrows at me.

"It doesn't hurt to be polite," I said, staring down at the green stone resting in the palm of my hand.

"Can we get out of here, *please*?" Marshall asked, brushing the grime and muck away from his face. "I think I may have swallowed something living."

"Yes, let's get," Rory said, leaning down to pick up the sprawled contents of his bag for him, slipping the Leatherman into his bag among them all.

I didn't argue. I wanted out just as much, especially since I was dying to see what effect the return of the gemstone would have on Stanis.

"Next time, we bring the gargoyle," Rory said, rubbing her shoulder.

"Agreed."

Twenty-two

Stanis

A strange pulling sensation of the maker's kin called to me in a slow, subtle rhythm, and I dropped down off the roof to the terrace below, my extended wings slowing my descent. The double doors leading into my maker's study were wide-open, and I pulled my wings into my body to fit through them, entering.

Alexandra stood with her friends on the far side of my maker's studio, the three of them holding glasses, clinking them together. They turned as one as the sound of my stone feet on the wood floors carried over to them.

"What sort of ritual is this?" I asked. "Is this alchemy?"

Alexandra gave a laugh. "Sort of," she said. "We're toasting."

I cocked my head at her. "Toasting?"

"We're celebrating," the blue-haired one explained.

"Celebrating what?" I asked.

"Living," the man said, and shot a closed fist up into the air.

Alexandra offered me her glass, but I had no need for such things and waved it away. "When I awoke, I felt something pulling at me, as if I missed something, something that had passed."

"That would be from how we spent our afternoon," she said. "I have a little surprise for you, Stanis."

Alexandra pressed her other hand out toward me and opened her closed fist. A pale green stone sat in the center of her palm.

I took the stone using just the tips of my claws to grab it and examined it. There were many facets and the inside of it seemed to swirl in a pale green cloud of mist. "Is this a part of me?" I asked.

She nodded, then set her glass aside. "I think I've even worked out how to implant it."

"Stanis is getting implants," Marshall said with a snicker, which I did not understand, and now did not seem the proper time to ask.

Alexandra grabbed me by the wrist and walked me over to the workbench off to her right, away from the bottles and glasses. One of the maker's books lay open there, and much like she had the night she introduced me to her friends, she laid her hands on the smooth stone of my chest and incanted the words written on the page. I still did not understand the language, but I felt the effects of her words as they washed over me. The stone deep in the center of my chest twisted with sharp jags of pain and unwound as it had done the time before. The sensation was strange, but my growing familiarity with it brought back memories of the way her great-great-grandfather had worked his arcane knowledge over me so many years ago. There was comfort in her efforts and I found I welcomed it despite the pain involved.

She pulled her hand away, revealing the knot work symbols carved there with its four indentations marking the slots for the stones.

"Is this like Operation?" Rory asked. "Maybe this stone restores his funny bone . . ."

"Each piece has its own shape," Alexandra said, raising her hand with the gem in it, spinning it around and trying it in each of the slots. When it finally settled in the one on my left side, she stopped. "There." She looked up into my eyes. "You ready?"

I nodded.

She pressed her right hand over her left and turned back to the book. When she spoke this time, a calming warmth spread through me, radiating quickly from her hand throughout my whole body. I welcomed it, basking in the sensation . . . until it kept growing, burning. Every piece of me, even the tips of my wings, felt as if it were on fire and I could only imagine this was what true and total pain felt like. I held my place while she worked her arcane words on me, the claws on my feet involuntarily digging into the wood of the floor beneath me, tearing great strips of it away. The gem gave way to the stone of the intricate knot work, bonding to me.

A flash of new memories washed through my head, driving like a spike into the center of my being. Walls of stone rose up all around me, but I did not get long to assess where I was. All of it was lost as the core of the memory took hold of me. The sensation of crushing weight filled my body, every part of me screaming out until the world went dark and silent as I stumbled forward, once more in the study with the maker's kin's hand still against me. At the center of my body the stone and the setting were becoming one as the pattern coiled in on itself once again, closing up, my chest restored to its smoothed-over state.

Alexandra's hand felt warm against my chest, and strangely I did not want her to pull it away from me, but her arm dropped, exhausted, as she stared at the spot.

"How do you feel?" she asked with trepidation in her voice. Her face was flushed.

The unbearable heat ebbed away from me, dying down in my chest, leaving me with a strange connection to Alexandra as if her hand were still against me. I sensed she felt it, too.

I uncurled my claws. "I think I am fine," I said. "Although there was a memory of great pain, weight crushing down on me."

"Are you all right now?" Aurora asked.

I nodded.

"Other than that, do you feel any different?" Marshall asked.

I turned to him. "Not that I am aware of, no."

I was not sure what I was prepared for, but other than the flash of pain from the past, I had not expected nothing. I pressed my hand against my own chest, half thinking the stone would be where I could feel it, but the stone there was smooth now.

Rory raised her glass to me. "Glad we almost died for nothing," she said, then tipped the glass to her lips, emptying the half-full vessel.

I looked to her, then back at Alexandra. "Died? Where exactly did you find this piece?" I asked.

Alexandra laughed, then crossed back to her glass and a small leather notebook sitting by it. "I've been doing my homework while you were busy being petrified by daylight," she said, raising her glass as well. "My great-great-grandfather wrote about where the four stones are hidden, but he does *not* make it easy to find them. After running through several of his resource books here, I pieced together some notes of my own. We found this first stone as part of one of the statues Alexander did for the early subway system lines."

I pointed at the blue-haired one. "To be clear, what does she mean when she says you almost died?"

"It means we went through some serious shit," Marshall said, bravado mixed with nervousness in his words. By his gentle sway back and forth, I believed he was what humans referred to as *drunk*. "Crawling down the train tracks, almost getting run over, fighting a metric ton of large stone statuary that came to life."

"That would explain why I awoke feeling that lingering sensation of alert," I said. "Without being able to deal with the incident during daylight, my body still somehow felt the connection, experiencing some of it." I felt the sensation returning, then realized, no, this was different. Something unfamiliar began to fill me, and I could not help but react to it—I was angered.

"I do not appreciate when you needlessly put yourself in harm's way," I said, my voice rising to a low growl. "You make it very hard for me to do what I was *made* to do."

"Hey!" the male one said. He stepped with a stagger between Alexandra and me. The young man looked like he might be ill, but his words came out strong nonetheless. "It sounds like pretty poor planning to make a protector who can only do his job fifty percent of the time, in darkness. Most of that Lexi spends asleep!"

"I have watched over this family for centuries," I said, moving close to him, staring down to meet his eyes with mine. My hands closed into fists, my own claws digging into the palms of my hands. "I will not be lectured by one who is not the maker's kin."

"But seriously, Lexi," he continued on, turning to her, unfazed by the threat of me. "Did he think your family would just be peachy-keen fine during the day?"

This, to my surprise, seemed only to fill me with a deeper anger, my voice coming out in low, measured tones. "Alexander was a great man. I will not stand by and hear anything less than that. Do you understand my words? It was always his intent to make my kind able to function during the daylight hours, but he passed away far too soon for that. Do not speak ill of him."

"I'd just like some answers," he said, an earnest and angry quality to his words. "It seems pretty ridiculous to me. I mean, how much protection do we really need while *sleeping*?"

"Maybe you should take a break," the blue-haired one said, lifting his glass out of his hand.

I could not control this long-dormant but growing feeling of anger. I lashed out, grabbing the man by the front of his jacket, my claws tearing though the heavy cloth of it with ease. I stormed across the room and out onto the terrace, one of my wings catching on one of the doors, pulling it from its hinges as I passed. "Trust me," I said, throwing him into the open air up above the balcony. He flew several stories upward, his arms and legs flailing like he might somehow gain the power of flight, his mouth locked in a silent scream. I leapt into the air, wings spreading as I rose to meet him on his descent. I let him drop past me, then grabbed him by one leg. I landed on the edge of the balcony, dangling the fragile human over the edge. "Your kind does need protecting."

"Let me go!" he shouted, his voice coming out much higher than normal, panic in his words. He reached for the ledge, but it was not close enough. "No! Wait!"

I stood there on the ledge, unmoving, leaving him struggling and failing to catch hold of the side of the building. There was . . . satisfaction in that, I discovered. I rocked my arm back and forth, swaying him away from the side of the building.

"Stanis!" the maker's kin shouted. "Stop it!"

I froze in my actions, the power in her words binding me in place.

"Easy, now," the blue-haired one said.

"Put him *down*," Alexandra said, concern rolling off her with a nervous smile on her face, then added, "on the *terrace*."

Part of me resisted, a part I had never felt before. The sensation was so unfamiliar that I snapped to, finding a comfortable familiarity in doing what she said. I pulled my arm back over to the terrace side. The man grabbed hold of the carved ledge and held on to it until I lowered my arm. He pulled away from me, rolling onto the open area of the terrace before scrambling to his feet and clutching the edge of the remaining door.

He pulled up his pant leg, revealing broken skin. "I'm bleeding!" he said. I recognized the look in his eyes. I had come to know fear when I saw it in these creatures.

I looked down to examine the tiny breaks in his skin, blood running from them like tiny red rivers. I raised my hand, examining my claws, the tips of them coated in the same red.

"Stanis!" Alexandra scolded, eyes wide, fear and anger in them. "What was that all about?"

My initial sensation of newfound anger faded, changing to one I was more familiar with—curiosity.

"I am not certain," I said, unable to look away from the innocent man's blood on my claws.

The blue-haired one went over to Marshall, who was

already hobbling toward the metal stairs leading down the outside of the building.

"You are *not* taking the fire escape," the blue-haired one said. She slid her arm under his and turned him to face the doors leading into the building. "We're taking the elevator, even though we risk running into her family."

Marshall gave me a brief look before shifting his glance quickly to Alexandra. "Learn to control that . . . *thing*," he said, but my maker's kin was already shaking her head.

"He won't hurt you again," Alexandra said, her anger dropping away. "Our bond together is growing. We're just working out the kinks." She turned her pleading eyes toward me. "Right, Stan? Tell them it's safe. Tell them *you* are safe."

I thought for a long moment before answering with a shake of my head. "That I cannot do," I said. "That gem awoke something inside me, something I have not felt in . . . I do not know how long."

The blue-haired one backed the man through the French doors and into the building. "Learn to control that thing, Lexi," she said, shaking her head.

"*Thing* is right," Marshall added.

"Stanis is *not* a thing!" Alexandra called after them, but they kept on walking. "Don't go! This is all new to us. There's going to be tough times with this. He's not dangerous to us!"

The dark red of my claws contradicted that, only clouding what little understanding I had of the feelings that had awakened in me tonight. "Perhaps they have the right idea," I said, spreading my wings wide behind me. "I must go."

Confusion filled her face, and her eyes darted back and forth from them to me. "No," she said, her voice on the hard edge of panic. "Don't! I . . . I forbid it."

"You can not forbid such a thing," I said, resolve in my voice. "My primary function is to protect you and it is clear right now that I pose a greater threat than the protection I provide. This I cannot abide. Mine is to protect. Therefore, for your safety, I must go for now. I need time to consider all of this and what it truly means."

Alexandra went to protest, but I saw little point in allowing it to continue on any further. I pressed off into the night sky above, rising higher and farther away with each flap of my wings. Despite my rapid ascent, I was shocked to feel a hint of pain growing in my chest. It was even more of a surprise when I realized it was not just my own I was feeling.

Twenty-three

———— ☾ ————

Alexandra

I crashed hard that night, what with Stanis gone and neither Rory nor Marshall returning my calls. Images of large stone statues chasing me through endless subway tunnels filled my dreams that night. I dared to call them dreams because they varied from the *actual* events of yesterday afternoon. In them, Stanis flew to my rescue underground on the old disused subway platform each and every time, although my heart still wanted to explode with panic every moment leading up to it, filled with mind-numbing peril.

I awoke to find his solid stone form perched motionless outside on the terrace of my great-great-grandfather's studio, where I had fallen asleep with his master tome still open on my lap. Had the panic in my dreams been enough for him to sense it, calling him back to watch over me after flying off so abruptly? Surely that kind of emotional response to come and watch over me meant that Stanis was more than I had previously taken him for, far more capable of humanity than my friends right now. Was such a thing even possible? I wasn't sure, but seeing him there instilled in me some kind of hope that he was much more than I originally gave him credit for.

There he stood watching over me nonetheless, and there

he was still standing when I got back from a day of real estate pimping. Compared to the chaos of the past few says, doing normal business things was a nice break. But still, by late afternoon, I had resolved myself to get back to solving some of the mysteries surrounding my great-great-grandfather's secret life's work.

When Rory showed up I had already changed back into a tank top and overalls, committing myself once again to research and building mode in the family library. She came up the fire escape, stopping to check out the inert gargoyle on the terrace before coming in through the newly rehung French doors. Rory crossed the room to the far end of the art studio where I was studying the stone book of arcane knowledge, a noticeable limp to her gait. I hid my sheepishness by pointing to her leg.

"You okay?" I asked, holding my place in the book with my finger.

Rory nodded. "Between yesterday's antics, hobbling Marshall out of here, and the five-hour contemporary dance workshop today, my body's a bit worse for the wear and tear," she said, flexing herself up on point. "I'm too young to be complaining like this, I know, but life's been a bit busy lately." She looked back over her shoulder at the gargoyle out on the terrace, then back at me. "How're you?"

"I slept like the dead," I said. "I don't know when Tall, Gray, and Stony set up camp out there, but I have a feeling my night terrors over those statues attacking us down in that abandoned subway station might have something to do with that. I also had a horrible dream that I worked in real estate, but then I woke up and realized it was no dream and had to go to work."

Rory laughed at that, shattering the discomfort from last night, and I knew we were good. Or at least we would be.

She nodded at the book. "What's going on?" Her eyes glanced over to a cloth I had draped over my latest project, the fabric twitching a little. Rory took a step back from the art studio toward the library. "You haven't been animating things again, have you?"

I nodded. Rory took another, warier step back.

"Forget everything that happened with the little clay man," I said. "Promise?"

Rory eyed me with growing suspicion. "Why? What did you do?"

"Relax. I think I've found a way to keep any sort of trickster spirit from inhabiting my new project. I think you'll be happy, but promise me that you won't do anything crazy."

She let out a long and wary breath. "Fine," she said.

"Good." I pulled the cloth away, revealing the surprise on my worktable.

Standing no higher than a person's knee was a tiny figure. Its "body" consisted of a full red brick with a toothy, smiling face and wide cartoon eyes I had painted on it. Thin arms and legs of metal wiring covered in clay stuck out of it, giving it a crude Mr. Potato Head sort of look. It swayed back and forth, a little unsteady on its blocky wooden feet.

"Is this one homicidal, too?" Rory asked. She stepped back from it, grabbing ahold of one of the heavy stone statuettes on the shelf next to her.

"Easy," I said, my face beaming with pride. "I think this little guy is harmless."

Rory paused, then bent forward to give it a closer look. "You sure? What did you do this time?"

"Well, Jewish mystics would probably call this version a *golem*, which it *kind* of is. When I tried this before, I was attempting to press my will into the clay, which left it open for other spirits to gain control of it. But I've been reading up. In this spirited little guy here, what I did was animate the stone alchemically."

"Spirited?" Rory asked, moving farther back from it again. "Is this thing truly living?"

"Yes and no," I said. "Not like you and me, but all things in this world are living by nature. The trick is how to invoke it, to transmute the material. I don't think it explains how something as complex as Stanis is constructed, but it's definitely an improvement over last time."

Rory laughed. "He still looks potentially dangerous, Lexi."

"He does?"

"Sure," she said. "It's a brick, Lexi. Clearly you've never been menaced by someone holding a brick before."

"It's okay," I said. "Bricksley's mostly harmless."

"Bricksley?"

I looked down at my new little friend. "Not the most original, I know, but doesn't he just look like a Bricksley?" Rory looked at me like I was crazy, and my face went flush. "The naming of things holds a power, too. To name something—like the wind or this little figure here—binds it to you. It's how I control him. Besides, with a name like that, he sounds like a little butler, doesn't he?"

Rory looked down at the little figure. "Bricksley!" she shouted out like a drill sergeant. "Bring me a book."

The tiny golem stayed where he was. I stepped closer to the little figure and did my best to sound authoritative.

"Bricksley! Fetch me that book on the table by the couch."

The little brick figure jumped down off the table, turned like a toddler, and stumbled off to the coffee table across the room. When it got there, it hit the edge of the table, scooped up the book in both of its tiny hands, and started back across the room toward us. With the giant book in his hands, I couldn't help but laugh.

"I don't know how to socialize something like him yet," I said. "He follows my commands, but he barely does that. I have to speak very plainly. Just trying to get Bricksley here to follow orders gives me a real sense of the complexity that my great-great-grandfather must have put into a creature like Stanis."

"Great," Rory said. "Now all we need to do is whip up a thousand or so of these little guys, and you should be safe the next time someone attacks you."

"I don't think so."

"No?"

"Watch," I said. I walked over to one of the windows and pulled open its closed curtain. A patch of blinding white sunlight fell across the floor. Bricksley continued on his path across the room, but the second he stepped into the light from outside, his body froze and he teetered forward with the book clenched in his tiny doll hands. The weight overbalanced him, and his lifeless body rolled onto its side as the book fell to the floor. "Poor little guy. Just like Stanis. Doesn't work in daylight."

"So I guess you don't go out during the day at all, then," Rory said. "Problem solved! Unless you've got your necklace on."

I shoved at her with one hand, and felt the stone of my necklace with the other. I found its touch reassuring despite its waning power. "Shush!"

Rory went over and poked the fallen figure, but there was no hint of life to it. "Why *does* that happen, anyway?"

"I haven't gotten to that chapter yet with all the reading I've been doing," I said, yawning and scooping up the book Bricksley had been carrying from the floor. "You're asking me to explain magic out as if it were science, and I can't. At least, not yet. The alchemical parts of treating the stone are a bit easier, like following a recipe, but even that is going to take its own branch of study, much of which I suspect is in that Spellmason hall Alexander had been building."

Rory got that mother-hen look over the top of her black horn-rims, which seemed a bit strange to me, what with her blue hair and all. "You need more sleep."

"Sleep?" I asked, giving a weary smile. "What's that? I seem to remember that magical word . . ."

Rory nudged the figure on the floor. "Afraid Bricksley here might smash your head in while you're out?"

"Not quite," I said. "Brix is a good little guy." I closed the curtain once more and picked him up as he squirmed to life. I cradled him in my arms like a baby. "You wouldn't harm your maker, now, would you?"

As if in response, my creation nuzzled the top of his head against the bottom of my chin, the rough texture of the brick scraping me.

"Ouchie," I said, moving him away and rubbing the spot.

Rory clutched her hand to her heart. "Oh, my God, I am dying of the cute here!"

I held Bricksley up at arm's length in both of my hands. "Who's a bad little reanimated brick? You are!"

My eyes were on the squirming creation in my hands, but I sensed Rory's eyes watching me, waiting.

"Lexi, listen," she said once I turned to look at her. Her voice had changed, taking a serious tone, which was never a good sign. "Marsh and I have been talking and . . . well, he's a bit skeptical. After last night and now after seeing your second attempt at this, so am I. Marshall might not mention it directly to you because he hasn't really known you all that long, but I will. Are you sure you can trust this gargoyle, this *grotesque*?"

I set Bricksley down on his feet, and he teetered off across the room like a windup toy. "How do you mean?"

"Controlling a brick is one thing," Rory said. "Not to belittle your accomplishment there, but that gargoyle is a different matter altogether. You saw what it did out in Gramercy Park to that man's head."

I felt my defenses rising up, unexpectedly and quicker than I had imagined they even might have. "He did it in the name of protecting the family. He did it protecting *me*!"

"And what about tossing Marshall around last night and cutting his leg?" she asked. "You said it yourself. You couldn't imagine what it would take to socialize something simple like Bricksley there. Stanis is far more complex. You sure that gargoyle is clear on what right and wrong is around here? He's potentially a killing machine and I don't want any of us to become . . . accidental casualties or anything."

"You didn't seem to have any trouble nearly kicking that guy to death down at the docks," I snapped back. "Maybe I should be worried about you as well."

"This isn't about morality here," Rory said. "You and I know how each other think and work. We're human. We've been friends for years. As for what I did down on the docks, how dare you even question that. If someone comes after us in that violent a fashion, I have no qualms about defending us and I would expect the same from you. I did it out of loyalty, friendship, Lexi. I do it so you don't have to."

This was turning into a lecture. "What's your point?" I asked, sharpness in my voice.

"Why does Stanis do it? How does he know right and wrong when a stupid walking brick needs things expressly pointed out to him? There's more to Stanis than this spirit of the stone you talk about calling forward. There's something more to him, and I don't want to find out the hard way what it is if he suddenly decides to crush our heads because in his mind he perceives us as a threat, by whatever standard is built into him."

"It's not like I can just go and take a course on Spellmasonry, you know," I said. "I'm winging it here. I've got to research every little choice I make. Some of this is part innate family blood talent at work, but the rest is study and ritual. Much of it doesn't even make sense, but who am I going to ask about this? My parents? They've got religion explaining their guardian angel theory for them. I can't even begin to go there with them over this."

Rory came over to me, fast. I wasn't sure what to expect, flinching, but was surprised when she hugged me.

"I'm not attacking you," she said, calmness and love in her words. "I swear. I'm just worried about everything that's going on. It's part of having your back. And you know Marshall. He's used to his gaming group torturing him. He's always looking for the cloud of doom hanging overhead. I just want to make sure your head is clear while you're doing all this magic stuff, and I'm not sure it is."

"Why wouldn't it be?" I asked, calming a little myself.

Rory let go and stepped back from me.

"I wonder where your head is at, concerning Stanis. You dodged me the other night, when I asked how building a companion for Stanis was going. We need allies, right? But, I don't know . . . You seemed like maybe your heart isn't into keeping that promise anymore. Other than building little play toy creatures."

I turned away from her, focusing myself once more on the book in front of me, spreading it out on the table. "Well, I *have* been busy with the family business, figuring out what happened to my brother, and just keeping alive."

"So that's all it was?" she asked, and I could hear the skepticism in her voice. "You were just too busy to get to it?"

"Yes," I said, eyes down in my book, avoiding the real issue again. "This stuff is incredibly detailed. Bricksley here is my new high-water mark of achievement and it's all I can do to keep *him* on point. Carving that half-finished block of stone up on the roof into something living is going to be quite the feat, but I'm on it, I swear."

"I see," Rory said, hopping up onto the table next to where I was reading, sliding her butt back. "Thing is, I saw the way you couldn't meet my eyes just a second ago, Lexi. There's more going on here."

I kept my eyes on the books in front of me, not liking where this was going. "I'm busy here."

"You know what I think?" Rory asked.

I shook my head. "Enlighten me," I said, against my better judgment.

"I think you don't want to really get started on that particular project," she said. "Even though I have zero idea how much work must go into something like that, I think you're stalling."

My stomach clenched and I gave a nervous, dismissive laugh. "Why would I do that?"

"Honestly?" she said. "I don't think you want to share. I mean, you've got a big, strong protector in Stanis, don't you? Must be nice to feel so safe and secure, huh?"

"We're in the twenty-first century now," I said. "Women don't need protectors. Besides, I'm so a Hermione, not a Bella." I felt a twinge in my heart. Sometimes I hated that Rory knew me so well. She was right, of course, though it was hard to admit it to myself. I *had* been stalling, for selfish reasons, but let's face it—saving him for myself was ridiculous, wasn't it? If I had any consideration for him, wasn't Stanis entitled to some happiness? Wouldn't creating a companion bring him that? I secretly vowed to refocus my efforts, but gave Rory a flush-faced smile. "Are you saying I have a thing for the man of stone, Aurora Torres?"

She smiled and raised her eyebrows. "You only use my proper name when I'm really getting to you, *Alexandra*," she said, crossing her arms. "Well, do you?"

I closed the book in front of me, shaking my head, laughing into my hands. "Well, realistically, Stanis is *not* human. I can't have a thing for him . . . can I?"

"Why not?" she asked, insistent. "You've dated guys with less personality than him. At least you know this one is a faithful and loyal protector."

"Don't you think me needing a protector is a bit chauvinistic these days? We're post–women's liberation movement and all . . ."

"When a creepy mystical order is out to kill you, I don't care who you are . . . You don't just want protecting; you *need* it. You want proof? Look at the collection of broken or crushed body parts running through your recent past!"

"I—" I stopped. I couldn't argue that. "Okay, fine. You have a point. There is a comfort in that, I'll admit. But as far as you calling me out on it, I don't think you're being all noble here. I think that *you're jealous*."

Rory laughed. "Me? Jealous how?"

"You've *always* had my back growing up. Now someone else is kicking ass on my behalf, and it's *not* you. You're feeling replaced."

"This isn't about someone cutting in on my ass-kicking quota," she insisted. "I'm happy not to have to babysit you every waking moment, darlin'. The difference here is that I kick ass because I care for you, *not* because I've been programmed to."

"Look," I said. "I'll admit that I *like* having Stanis watching over me. It's nice to feel that security, no matter how artificial that may be. But . . . he's a magical construct."

"I'm not saying any of this to hurt you," Rory said, putting an arm around me, her head on my shoulder. "I want you happy. I just want to keep you focused on what needs to be done here. Put aside whatever feelings you have and keep working on this because we *need* allies. We need to find the rest of Stanis's gems to help him remember his past so we stand a chance of figuring out why so many people want you dead."

"How about we discuss this tomorrow?" I asked, pleading, my brain overloaded with the tasks ahead but also a little relieved for being called out on the surprising fact that I cared so much. "My mind is about to melt."

"Fine," Rory said, heading back toward the terrace, stopping to put her arm around the stone-still gargoyle out there. "But if you think Stanis is just your cuddly protector, you're fooling yourself. There's something human to him and I hope for your sake it's a good thing . . . but it might also be bad." She spun around, curtsied, and jumped up on the ledge of the terrace. "Good luck!"

Rory left via the fire escape, sliding out of sight. I turned in time to catch Bricksley once again carrying a book but stuck up against the wall like a broken Roomba.

I went to retrieve my book and righted my little brick of a creature, picking him up and looking into his drawn-on face. "What do *you* think, little buddy? You think Stanis has any human in him? You think I can Spellmason it out of him?"

As if in response, Bricksley shuddered as the magic left him, and fell to the ground, his component parts scattering as any control I had over him went away completely.

"Then again," I continued, looking down at the still-smiling brick and feeling somehow terribly sad for it, "maybe I have no business playing with powers I don't fully understand yet. I certainly have no business standing here talking to inanimate brick men about gargoyles—that's for sure."

I scooped up the pieces and brought them back to one of the worktables on the other side of the studio, the book tucked under my arm. I laid out the pieces and began going over how I had joined them together in the first place. If I couldn't keep something as simple as Bricksley in one piece, what chance did I ever hope to have working on the block of stone up on the roof? Did I even want to?

I should build his companion, I told myself. Not only would it help protect my family better; it would bring Stanis happiness.

But couldn't *I* make him happy myself? I needed to investigate more of Stanis's human tendencies if I was ever going to get to the bottom of this.

Either way, I was in for a long night.

Twenty-four

C

Alexandra

Now that I was alone and my latest creation was toast, I read what I could about Spellmasons—the ability to transmute stone into a living thing, establishing connections through alchemical processes, and trying to figure out just where I had gone wrong with my mini-Frankenstein monster. My frustration with almost getting my friends killed kept rising to the surface so by the time Stanis awoke, I was ready for a bit of kick-ass vengeance mixed with some fact finding about being dead-ended out in Brooklyn at that shipping freighter.

"I must apologize," Stanis said, once we were airborne, me cradled in his arms.

"For what?" I asked, trying not to shiver as the wind of a higher elevation rolled over me in our flight.

"For leaving in such haste the other evening," he said. "I am afraid I am not quite myself these nights. Or rather, perhaps I am more like myself than ever as I regain pieces of me. I am just not accustomed to the new sensations. I did not mean to strike out in anger."

"This is new to both of us," I said. "No harm."

"But there was harm," he said. "The more I am restored,

the more I must contend with emotions. I am unprepared for such a thing."

"I know the feeling," I said with a smile. "Emotions are hard to sort out, whether you're made of stone or flesh."

"Yes," he said. "The strongest seem to be the ones deepening in me toward you."

I wasn't ready for this, but I couldn't help feeling an excitement hearing it, no matter where his human tendencies came from. "I feel it as well," I said, finally being honest with myself, then fell silent as we flew on.

"How is the male?" Stanis asked a short while later.

As we dropped down through the clouds, the East River came into sight along with the long row of ships docked along the Brooklyn waterfront. I thought of the way Marshall had limped away with Rory the other night. "Marshall will be fine," I said, pointing off toward the boat I was looking for. "He was just shaken more than anything."

"I regret my actions," he said. "Please let him know that."

"You can let him know that yourself, next time you see him. That's how we humans roll. We apologize."

"As you wish," he said.

I realized I probably had some apologizing of my own to do with certain people, but as we came down onto the deck of the ship, landing in shadows, I tried to focus on the mission at hand instead. Stanis released me and I started off across the empty deck, looking for an entrance. "Stay close," I said. "And step lightly."

We worked our way down into the ship, the corridors large enough for Stanis and me to fit through easily side by side. At the sign of our first tattoo-handed thug, I pulled Stanis into the shadows just as he was raising his claws to strike. I chose to go with subtlety over conflict. The fewer alarms we raised, the better.

"Please tell me you are keeping track of where we've been," I said after a few more minutes of wandering into large, open cargo holds and more corridors than I could count. "Because I'm a bit lost."

He nodded. "I may still not have recovered all my past memories, but my retention of the here and now is intact."

I breathed a sigh of relief, then narrowed in on the sound of a commotion down one of the corridors off the large cargo hold we were currently in and started off in its direction. I moved down it, sticking to the shadows as best I could as I approached the next room, stopping dead as it came into sight.

Ornate European throne rooms didn't normally appear on large shipping freighters, but here one was nonetheless. Every chair around a massive oak table at the center of the room was elaborately carved, but the wood of them was worn and chipped, and I could see why. The creatures sitting in them were made of large, jagged clumps of rock and stone. Marshall owned a T-shirt for the Fantastic Four that had something that looked like them on it, a man made of orange rock, but these creatures were far less human-looking. The rest of the room was filled with old-world furniture and piles of books laid out everywhere on a long line of tables.

"Please tell me I am imagining this," I said.

"You are imagining this," Stanis said.

I turned to look at him. "Am I really?"

"No, but you instructed me to tell you."

"That's another idiom," I said, smiling and turning back to look at the room. Whatever they were, they were in deep conversation around the table, but it was difficult to hear. I dared to move closer, abandoning the shadows, pressing myself close to the wall as I went, clutching my talisman.

Even closer it was hard to make out anything. The size of the room and its echo were not helping. One of the creatures turned from the conversation, appearing to look in my direction, but I wasn't sure. I pulled my head back around the corner out of sight, but the scraping of a massive chair suggested I had been seen. "Shit," I swore under my breath. "Let's go."

We took off through the maze of corridors, each one looking like the last as far as I was concerned, but Stanis led the way and seemed to be moving with a sense of purpose. The sound of pursuit faded, thankfully, and my panic calmed a bit as we moved toward an empty cargo hold dead ahead. Stanis entered with me close behind, and that was when a thick, malformed stone arm struck out hard, from our left, at the gargoyle. He tumbled end over end through the air like he had been shot from a cannon, trying to get his wings open, but it wasn't happening. He crashed into the heavy steel of one of the walls and slid down it, dazed. I started into the hold after him, going right to avoid his attacker, but the large creature spotted me and grabbed me by my shoulders, lifting me. Stanis was busy struggling to get back up and started back across the room, but he would be too late to help.

I awaited my fate, expecting pain. I did not expect the creature to pat me on the head, the rough stone scratching through my hair to the scalp beneath it. The gesture was patronizing, and worse, I recognized it, having been at the receiving end of it all my life. Up until four months ago, that was.

I stared into the dark hollow sockets of stone where the creature's eyes should be, the moment surreal, my mind threatening to snap. "Devon . . . ?"

"Hey, Lex," the monstrosity said. "I thought it might be you. You still messing around with being all artsy fartsy?"

"You're . . . you're *alive*," I said, thankful that he was holding me up, as it felt like I might faint any second. When he set me down, my knees buckled but I remained standing. I backed away until I bumped into Stanis, reaching back to put my hand on his chest for support.

"Turns out there *are* some things more valuable than money," he said. "Living forever, for example." The hulking stone figure spun around in that familiar, irritating cock-of-the-walk style, but on this abomination of a figure, it was somewhere between horrifying and just plain creepy.

"*That's* living?" I asked. "Jesus, Devon, what have you gotten yourself into?"

The creature looked down over its massive, clumped body, twisting this way and that, examining itself. "Okay, so things didn't go *exactly* according to plan, no," he said, "but we're working on that."

"We?"

"My new . . . business partners, I guess you'd call them," he said.

"At the risk of repeating myself, what the hell have you gotten yourself into, Devon? How . . . *Why* are you like this?"

"Because I know how to make a deal," he said. "Making me *still* a better businessperson than you."

"Making a deal with *who*?"

"The Servants of Ruthenia," he said. "They've been looking for our family for centuries, Lexi. When they came across me, they wanted to kill me, but I traded them something in exchange for the promise of eternal life. Only I didn't expect it would be in this form."

I recalled the name from the night I met Stanis and from later discovering it as the subject of many of my great-great-grandfather's books. And here was my brother cutting deals with them. It didn't make much sense.

"Father told me that our great-great-grandfather fled from the old country," I said, "but he didn't know why."

Devon chuckled to himself. "You're going to love this," he said. "You know your hero, the famous architect and artist?" I didn't bother to respond and he continued. "Turns out Alexander Belarus was a bit of a traitorous bastard. And a murderer to boot."

"What are you talking about?" I asked. "That's insane."

"I know why our great-great-grandfather fled Kobryn," he said. "It's a story that those who become Servants commit to memory, taught by Kejetan Ruthenia himself."

"The Accursed Lord himself is *here*, in New York?" I asked.

Devon nodded. "You probably saw him in the throne room just now."

"That's shit company you're keeping, Devon," I said. "You know, considering I've had several attempts made on my life by his Servants. Whatever they're telling you are lies."

"I don't think so," he said. "For centuries these hard-core Servant dudes have lived in service to their Ruthenian lord. And if you serve Lord Kejetan well, the promise of eternal life is yours."

"What did you promise him in return for this form?"

"Hold on, hold on," he said in that petulant way of his. "Don't you want to know why our great-great-grandfather fled from them?"

I nodded.

"He was, in fact, supposed to be one of them."

"Alexander?" I asked. "Impossible. He would never serve such a cause. He fled the country, running to America with his family, fearing for their safety."

He laughed, the sound coming out like rocks in a tumbler. "Well, he certainly served Kejetan Ruthenia, at least. That's just historical fact. Although, truth be told, I don't think the men of ole Kobryn became Servants so willingly at first. I don't think they were given a choice, especially if someone had a hidden talent like, say, for things that go all David Copperfield."

"So the lord made him a slave?" I asked.

"Not *a slave*," he said, like I was suggesting the stupidest thing imaginable. "A landowner has the right to press his people into service for the greater good of the kingdom, and our great-great-grandfather was earning a reputation among the common people."

"As a Spellmason . . ." I finished.

"People believing in magic were pretty ordinary in the old country," he said. "Unlike now. Shit, I barely believed this whole other world *existed* until I saw my first stone man. Figured I was drunk or someone slipped me some little red pills. But back then, the landowners were big into it. The people of Kobryn knew that if they had a problem—like their crops wouldn't grow, if a child needed one of those mustard plaster things, or milk started turning sour overnight—they knew to go to Alexander. He had a way of handling such matters; everyone knew it. Some called it witchcraft; other more holy roller types refused to call it anything but simple good fortune."

"So word spread," I said. "To a ruler already mad with ambition."

"Kejetan didn't—*doesn't*—want to just rule. He's always

been seeking ways to extend his influence beyond one life-time, and pressed our great-great-grandfather into service to the court. Alexander, understanding that it might be problem-atic to just hand over arcane power to men of great ambition, at first said no, saying he was merely a simple stonemason. For his refusal, they killed his firstborn. Alexander did *not* refuse their second invitation, which came in the form of shackles. He lost what little land he had claimed for himself, was forced to leave his wife and remaining child behind, but Kejetan gave him everything he needed at his disposal in service of unlocking the secrets of prolonging life."

"I'd run from a life of servitude, too," I said.

Devon shook his head. "Alexander didn't run. Not then, anyway. He was afraid he might never see his family again, so he bided his time, studying what arcana was already accu-mulated and adding more to his own knowledge, even pre-tending to teach Kejetan's only son the alchemical arts. But it was all part of his master plan for escape. One night, our great-great-grandfather killed the boy and stole away in the night with the secrets of the Spellmasons. He and what remained of his family vanished from Kobryn and Lithuania, never to be seen again by Kejetan or his people. So congratu-lations, Lexi, your 'hero' is a child murderer and a thief."

"Impossible," I said, struggling to process every detail I had just heard. "Look at the legacy he left behind. Alexander was a creator, not a destroyer."

"You believe it because you've read it in books," Devon said. "*Alexander's* books, some messed-up revisionist history by a coward trying to hide his despicable past. I've talked to someone who was actually there hundreds of years ago. I know the story I believe."

"And I know the one I believe," I said.

"Your great-great-grandfather knew the lord would change his most loyal of servants to the stone that lives eternal, imper-fect though it was, and they have been looking for him since. Alexander ran, changed his last name to the one we know now, came to America, and began life anew in hiding. Kejetan has waited a long time to get his secrets back. He's had a long

time to stew on this. He's way more pissed off at our family
than I ever was."

"I don't get you," I said. "I don't think I ever have. How can
you even buy into that madman's story, for real? What reason
on earth would you have to hate on our family, outside of
maybe our father made us go to church far too often?"

Devon's face changed. If I was reading his features right,
he looked like his thoughts were off in a dark and unhappy
place, his voice confirming it as he spoke. "*You* come from a
long line of liars and betrayers, Lexi, so it's hard for you to
hear. But not me. Did you know I was adopted?"

"It's recently come up," I said. "Yes."

"Do you know what that's like?" he said, anger rising in
him. "No, of course you don't. Lexi got to do just about everything she ever wanted."

"Is that what this is about?" I asked, incredulous. "You didn't
get to slack off as much as me?"

"Don't make light, Lexi," he said, spitting the words out.
"This is important to me, living a life that was a lie. Finding
out I was adopted for the sole purpose of being the male heir
apparent to the family business? That's messed up, Lexi. I'm
sorry, but it is. You got to do whatever you wanted and my
entire life was just a contractual setup. I'm product development. I was bred for business, like cattle for the slaughter. Do
you know how that feels?"

"I can imagine," I said.

He shook his head at me. "No. I doubt you can, really. I
don't know how the Servants found me—"

"Your ring," I said, remembering the night I received the
call from the police telling me they had found only Devon's
hand. "The sigil in the stone was enchanted to conceal us
from our enemies. That magic, however, has been fading."

"Awesome," he said. "So *that's* how they found me at our
building down on Saint Mark's. They threatened my life looking for the secret knowledge stolen by my forebearer. I thought
it was all a bunch of bullshit until I later discovered some of
our great-great-grandfather's jumbled notes up in our family
library about how the sigil had been 'charmed' to offer us

protection. Still, that night their intent was clear by the knives
in their hands, but you know me. I might not have been born
of true Belarus blood, but I was still a master of the deal. They
wanted to get their secrets back and I had family library
access to all that—or so I thought—and in return for helping
them, I get the Life Eternal."

"You were always a screwup, Dev," I said, "but this time,
it's beyond the beyond. You're backing the wrong team here.
You sold your family out."

"First of all, *none* of you are my family," he said, "but I'm
not the monster I look. I didn't sell anyone out. They have no
idea where you live thanks to whatever power still obscures
the building to them. If they had an idea, you'd all be dead by
now. I could have told them, but I didn't. I figure I'd give them
the books they were looking for; they'd get what they want and
go away. I'd get what I want and everyone's happy."

I wondered *what* books he had taken from Alexander's
library. Several of my Revelation of the Soul reading threads
in Alexander's notes, mostly about finding the soul stone for
the Heart of the Home, had dead-ended because there were
a handful of books I simply hadn't been able to find yet. Now
at least I had an idea they might not even *be* in our massive
collection at all.

"I need your help," he said. "The books I brought the Servants didn't satisfy them. What they really want are Alexander's books on how to make something more refined, like your
winged friend there. I wasn't able to find any books on that."

I kept staring him in the cold, dead sockets that were his
stony eyes. I wanted there to be no indication to him that the
very book he wanted was in the pack on my back. I felt
the smallest amount of petty triumph that I at least had been
smart enough to find and unlock Alexander's master secrets
where my brother had failed. Still, among all this overwhelm-
ing knowledge, it was a small victory.

"I don't know if I can do that," I said, conflicted. "If our
great-great-grandfather moved halfway around the world to
keep these secrets from them, I'm not so sure just handing them
over is such a great idea."

Anger filled the hollow sockets where his eyes should be. "You don't understand," he growled, lifting me up by the front of my jacket. "We all want out of these crude forms. You have to help. I can't stay like this. Look at me!"

Stanis stepped forward to intervene, but Devon, using his free arm, knocked him down with surprising ease, stepping on his neck with one of his thick, malformed feet.

I struggled to free myself, anything to get back on the ground before the bind of my twisted jacket strangled me. "You're hurting me," I said, as calm as I could. "Why don't you come with me? I can help you back at home." I wasn't sure how exactly, but right now was not the time to admit that. I just wanted Stanis and me to get off the damned ship alive.

"I *can't* leave," he shouted into my face. "Not now. If I disappear, they'll come looking for the family all the quicker. There are at least a dozen of them like me." He looked down at Stanis. "You're lucky I found you first. If the big guy had found you, you might not be alive right now. I'm at least giving you a chance here."

Some chance, I thought. "What do you want me to do?"

"You've taken such an interest in our family's artist legacy," he said. "Now's your opportunity to put some of that knowledge to use. Find the secrets our great-great-grandfather stole."

"I don't think I'll find the answers you're looking for," I lied, the weight of the book on my back feeling all the heavier.

"You *will.*" He looked down at Stanis. "You hold some sway over big ugly here. That means you know something about the Spellmasons. It's only a matter of time for you to figure it out. Do you understand?"

I nodded.

"And be quick about it," he said. "I cannot keep them away forever."

Despite being a rag doll in his hands, something inside me snapped. "You . . . selfish *asshole,*" I said, pounding ineffectively against his jagged stone chest. "Do you know what you've put me through? First, there was the grieving we've done over your sorry ass. Then I was pretty much forced to put aside everything artistic that I love so I could learn the family business—"

"At least you're doing it out of *real* familial obligation and not because someone bought you from another set of parents to do it," he said.

"So kill us yourself, then!" I screamed at him, the sound echoing in the hollow chamber. Somewhere far off a commotion rose up.

"I don't wish harm on you or our 'parents,'" he said, "despite my initial anger at them. I've gotten what I wanted. Sort of. Well, soon I will have, thanks to you. So, go. Enjoy the money. Enjoy your birthright empire. Either way, these are mortal concerns now." Devon tossed me aside as if I were made of paper. I rolled across the length of the cargo hold until I hit the wall with a solid *thump*. "They no longer matter to me."

Devon took his foot off Stanis's throat and turned, walking away as the sound of others came from down the hall behind him.

"Find what I need, Lexi," he said. "Find the stolen knowledge. Now go. They're coming."

As I lay crumpled on the floor, anger had me stumbling to my feet in seconds, charging after him, but one of Stanis's stone arms grabbed me gently but firmly around my waist.

"Let us go," he said, calm. "We must go or we will die. We are outnumbered."

"I don't care," I said, trying to pull free but to no avail.

"But I do," he said, which I was surprised to discover calmed me. "And I must protect."

Whether he was simply following his programming or not, I didn't know, but I stopped struggling as he brought me up through the ship and out onto the deck as shouts of anger grew closer and closer behind us.

"Your brother has one thing I envy," Stanis said, stopping, standing stone still, unreadable.

"Which is?"

"Your brother may be forced into that unfortunate form," Stanis said, spreading his wings, "but at least he knows who he is."

"We *will* restore you," I said, more determined than ever. The wave of emotion coming off of him broke my heart, how much it would mean to him to feel complete. My anger against my possibly traitorous great-great-grandfather only made me more resolved. "You deserve to be whole, Stanis. I don't know why Alexander would be so cruel as to take away parts of you. But I will make you whole. I swear it." And if it made Stanis stronger to fight my brother and his newfound friends at the same time, well, that was just a bonus, wasn't it?

Without another word he leapt into the sky with me in his arms and we flew off to the fading sound of outraged cries down below.

Twenty-five

◖

Alexandra

My day was spent pushing back morning meetings to spend some time following reference book to reference book all over my great-great-grandfather's library, investigating one of the soul stone threads, the one called the Ruler's Chest. I crushed all my meetings into the early afternoon, throwing down contracting decisions and job-site zoning rulings like I was Donald Trump. All of this in an effort to meet Rory and Marshall at a diner on the Upper East Side around four after pleading via texts, e-mails, and voice mails for them to *please, please, please* show up. I even sweetened the deal by promising gyros, onion rings, and milk shakes all around, which I had waiting when they both sat down at the booth.

The two of them looked at the food like I had maybe poisoned it. I didn't blame them.

"Our favorites," I said. "A sort of peace offering. I think maybe I might be a bit overburdened here and emotions *might* be running a little high."

"Might?" Rory repeated, and grabbed the straw of her milk shake, diving in.

"Okay, *are*," I said. "I'm not excusing my behavior, but with work, people trying to kill me, gargoyles to train . . . I'm in over my head and I'm sorry if I've been lashing out. We good?"

Rory nodded, picking up her gyro and taking a bite big enough that I thought she was going to choke. I envied her metabolism sometimes, then remembered it came from five to eight hours of dance regimens every other day, and my little green monster died on the vine. I looked to Marshall. He still hadn't touched his food.

"Stanis and I had a talk," I said to him. "He feels horrible about what happened. This whole restoration process flooded him with memories and emotions—"

"It dials them up to eleven," he said.

"It does," I admitted. "And moving forward we need to *all* keep that in mind. Especially tonight, because I think I have a lead on a second gemstone."

Marshall, on the verge of dipping his first onion ring in his milk shake, paused. "You do?"

"Are you sitting down?" I asked, drawing looks like I was stupid. "All right, all right. Let's just get all the emotional stuff out of the way at once, I suppose. I went back to that freighter last night, with Stanis. We met someone who gave me a name. Kejetan the Accursed."

"Sounds pleasant," Marshall said.

"A real tyrant. He ruled Kobryn. It's near the Polish border, but that's not the important thing. This informant gave me that ruler's name: Kejetan, which is one of the statues in my great-great-grandfather's puzzle path of clues. The other night after we found my attacker dead in Gramercy Park, my father pointed out a statue model of him my great-great-grandfather had done. So I checked the markings on it. The inscription read, 'The soul of a ruler lies in his chest.' That's the Ruler's Chest, what the master book was pointing to as a hiding place for the next soul stone."

"So you found the stone with the statue in your great-great-grandfather's art studio?" Marshall asked.

I shook my head. "No, but a *full-sized* version of that miniature model resides in one of the historic buildings Alexander worked on in New York, so I think I have a fair idea where we might find the next stone."

"Where?" Rory asked.

I turned my head to look out the window, both of their eyes following mine. The Metropolitan Museum of Art stood occupying the city block directly across from us.

"Is this source reliable?" Rory asked.

Now came the hard part of the news I had to break to them. "Not in life, no," I said, "but in death, I believe him."

"In death?" Marshall repeated, eating another onion ring. "Who the hell is it?"

"Hurry up and eat," I said, opening up my backpack and pulling out three baseball caps. "I'll tell you on the way over."

Once I had paid for our late lunch, I told them about Devon, his not being dead, his new monstrous form, and the events on the freighter last night. Both of them had a ton of questions as we started through the museum, all of which I tried to answer, but they seemed never-ending.

"Enough!" I finally whisper-shouted. "We need to focus here."

Normally I loved visiting museums, but not at the pace we were rushing around the Metropolitan Museum of Art, especially with the added weight of Alexander's secret tome in my backpack. I couldn't take the time to appreciate the actual art within it or really take in the work my great-great-grandfather had done on the building centuries ago.

"What are we looking for exactly?" Rory asked, the brim of her hat sliding down onto her glasses every few steps as we sped through the museum. The other visitors, few that there were, were snailing their way around, but we were purposeful and driven in our movement.

"I'm not one hundred percent sure on that," I said, "but we need to find the rest of the soul gems to restore Stanis completely, give him his memories and his power back, the things that Alexander—be he good or be he bad—deprived him of.

But I've only seen the reference to the Ruler's Chest on a miniature of the statue, the real one residing somewhere here. Not only did he give them the statue, but my great-great-grandfather carved a lot on this building, so he had all his lifetime to hide something here. Still, my money's on it being embedded in Kejetan's armor."

"So we're looking for another stone that fits into the symbol carved on Stanis?" Marshall asked from under the pulled-down brim of the *Ghostbusters* hat I had given him.

"Maybe," I said, "but don't just focus on that or we may miss whatever we're looking for."

Corridors of gorgeous ancient tapestries wound around like a carpeted maze, leading from one massive room to another. I definitely had to come back here some time when my dead brother and a cultish group of Lithuanian dictator worshippers weren't forcing me to restore my gargoyle faster.

"So what *can* we focus on?" Rory asked as we moved into another room, this one full of paintings and benches.

"Alexander died in the early nineteen hundreds," I said. "I say we look for anything that predates then."

I adjusted my brother's old Yankees cap, pulling at the hair I had stuffed through the sizing loop at the back of it, then drew the brim of it down as far as it would go. I hadn't wanted to look too suspicious coming in off the streets but I had to do something to disguise us from the security cameras, so it was hats all around.

We hurried down another hallway and into the promising-sounding Lives of Our Leaders section, continuing our search.

"These statues all look so serious," Rory said, examining a group of imposing-looking men nearby. Their carved robes and armor were impressive. "Well carved, but serious."

"Nice looking," I said, moving on, "but the styles aren't Alexander's." The full-sized statue of Kejetan Ruthenia stood among several others farther into the room, and I went to it. Alexander's hand had captured a cruelty and harshness in the stone, especially in the armored lord's features, but when I checked the figure over, there was no sign of any kind of gemstone on it.

Marshall came running over to us, one of the guards at the far end of the exhibit hall shooting him a stern look.

"Did you find something?" I asked, excitement causing my stomach to clench.

"Hell yeah," he said. "They've got glaive-guisarmes here!"

Both of us gave him a blank stare, but it was Rory who asked, "What the hell is that?"

Marshall's eyes went wide while he tried to both talk and catch his breath at the same time. "It's a pole arm," he said, like we were the dumbest people in the world for not knowing what it was. "Kind of like a staff with an ax head or sword at the end of it. My warrior monk uses one."

"Gisarme," I repeated. "That sounds French."

Marshall nodded.

"Slavic," I said. "We're looking for things a bit more Eastern Europe than France. Focus."

"Sorry," he said, his excitement deflating.

Rory had finished looking over another section of well-carved, well-dressed Russian-looking minions. "Well, nothing stands out to me, but really the only art I pay attention to are those dancer statues by Degas."

I took my time going over the other statues nearby, shaking my head when I was done. "None of these other ones are half as good as Alexander's work," I said.

"I'll say," Marshall said. "They don't even come to life!"

"Shut it," Rory said. "Before I decide to take up the glaive-guisarme and make you my practice dummy."

"Watch it," he said. "Or I'll up your half of the rent."

"Stop it," I hissed out as quietly as I could in the large open space, my voice echoing. "You're drawing looks from security."

Thankfully that worked and the two of them fell silent. "Sorry," Marshall said.

Rory sighed. "Me, too," she said, forcing it out.

"You two can get back to bickering like a married couple once we find what we came here for," I said. "Promise."

"Awesome," Marshall said, sitting down on a stone bench along the wall.

"Hey!" the guard shouted from across the room. "Off the exhibit!"

Marshall didn't move. His hands were spread out on the stone he was sitting on, oblivious.

"Up! Now!" the guard said, starting over to us.

"Marsh!" Rory called out. "Get up, dumb ass."

He lifted his eyes to meet mine. They were wide, not with panic, but excitement. He started drumming his hands on the bench to draw my attention.

Only it wasn't a bench, I realized. "Get up," I said, my voice calm but dead serious. *"Now."*

Marshall stood and I turned to the guard. "Sorry," I said, quick as I could. "My friend thought it was a bench."

The guard stopped, hesitating in his tracks, then adjusted his uniform on his walk back to his spot between rooms, but kept watching us. I grabbed Marshall by the arm and pulled him farther away from the piece, which seemed to satisfy the guard enough that he turned his attention back to watching our room and the next one over.

"What was that about?" Rory asked, coming over to us.

"Look," Marshall said, pointing to the "bench."

Marshall's bench wasn't a bench at all, but an ornately carved stone chest. Most might mistake the braid work all over it as Celtic, but I knew better. "Those patterns remind me of something very particular."

"The carvings on Stanis's chest," Rory said.

"Thing is, I don't see any stones on it," Marshall said.

"Don't you see?" I asked, but continued on without waiting for an answer. "It's a puzzle box. Look at the way all those designs run through each other. They interlock. And like Alexander's notes said, it *is* a chest where we found the ruler, so whatever we're looking for is going to be inside it."

"So what the hell do we do?" Rory asked.

I cracked a smile. "We open it."

"You mean *you* open it," Marshall said. "But what do *we* do? Let me guess . . . Distract the guard."

"I can do that," Rory said. "I can be very distracting when I want to be. How long do you need?"

I shrugged. "Not sure," I said. "I've messed around with some of my great-great-grandfather's puzzle boxes in his studio, but I suppose it really depends on how puzzling it truly is."

"We'll just position ourselves between you and him, hopefully blocking his view," Rory said. "So get to it."

I nodded, then turned to the chest, walking over to it. The guard wasn't paying us much attention now, and I examined the chest by simply walking around it first to keep suspicion off us. I traced the knot work of the intricate carving. "It looks like an ornate tangle of snakes," I said. "But I think I can untangle them if you can cover me while I work out the spell." I fished the tome out of my backpack and flipped it open.

Rory and Marshall moved into position, Marshall looking like he was about to throw up. "I don't deal well with deception," he whispered. "I never played any of the Chaotics . . . not Chaotic Good, Neutral, or Evil. Definitely not Chaotic Evil."

Rory patted him on the shoulder. "This is another one of those gamer things, isn't it?"

Marshall nodded.

"I figured that was why I didn't understand it," she said, then quickly added, "Nor do I wish you to explain it to me."

The two of them seemed content to chatter away and I dropped to my knees in front of the chest, resting the book on the tiled floor in front of me. This was different from shifting broken bricks at the building collapse site. Unraveling a puzzle chest like this was going to take finesse, not brute force, but having uncoiled the hidden one in Stanis's chest twice now, I felt a tiny bit of hope for success.

I studied a section of Alexander's book that looked promising, one that showed a gentler way to coerce raw stone in motion, but it meant having to touch parts of the chest, which might draw the guard's attention. Still, Marshall and Rory were blocking his full view of me, so without another thought I slapped my hand along the front of the chest where two sections met and pressed my will into it while incanting the words from Alexander's tome. Many of them, surprisingly enough, were becoming recognizable to me, making sense now, and I felt the meeting of the two pieces of stone give way to my command, a low grinding sounding out from the chest.

Marshall gave me a worried look over his shoulder and shushed me, but I didn't let it break my string of words. They were the key to getting this puzzle unraveled and I had to be fast about it. We were the only visitors in our section now, but it was only a matter of time before we either drew the guard's attention again or other museumgoers came into this area.

The stone snakes pulsed as I unwound them from one another, small clouds of the dust of ages wafting off them.

"Hurry!" Marshall whispered, his nervous eyes darting back and forth from the guard to the chest.

I couldn't respond or I'd break the spell, but what I really wanted was to tell him to shut the hell up. Did he think I wasn't *trying* to hurry? I was going as fast as I could, but between the tangle puzzle and the sheer weight of the stone coils, it was like untying anchor chains. I pushed all other thoughts out of my head and focused on the elaborate puzzle box.

"Goddammit!" the guard's voice called out from some-where on the other side of my friends. "Didn't I tell you to keep away from that?"

"Shit," Marshall said. "Oh, shit." His nervous pacing caught the corner of my eye, but I held my focus.

"Don't worry. I told you I'd take care of this," Rory said.

Rory started off across the room toward the guard at a brisk pace, and I couldn't help but turn to watch her while my hands kept working on one of the inner knots of the chest. Rory hugged the wall to our right, then kicked her foot out at one of the weapon cases, shattering its front pane. She shot her arm into the case and toward the weapons rack inside, tugging at one of the pole arms within and breaking the restraint that held it in place.

The guard pulled a walkie-talkie from off his belt. "We've got a situation in Lives of Our Leaders," he said. Before he could say much more Rory freed the pole arm, which, by its look from Marshall's descriptions, *was* a glaive-guisarme, and ran at the man.

"Not the pointy end!" Marshall yelled out.

Rory swung the long hooked weapon around like she was Darth Maul, putting the spear end closer to her body than the guard's. She swung low, sweeping behind the guard's legs, knocking them out from under him. He flew up in the air, hanging there for a second almost cartoon-style, before his body fell back, his head hitting the tile with a solid *thunk* that could only be bone.

"Jesus Christ!" Marshall cried out.

Rory's face was full-on worried, stepping closer to stand over the man and leaning in. A look of relief washed over her face. "We're good," she said, giving me a thumbs-up. "Still breathing."

A commotion rose from farther off in the museum, the sound of others approaching.

"Make like the Flash!" Marshall called out again.

My arms were elbow deep within the darkened shadows of the chest, leaving me to work by touch alone, but I kept at it. After several moments of untangling, my fingers felt something more refined: the smooth, glassy texture of a better cut of stone. A gem—one of Stanis's.

"Got it!" I cried out as I closed my fist over it, but as I did, something wrapped around my hand. I jerked my arm out of the chest as some sort of self-preservation kicked in. Although most of the unraveled puzzle parts lay uncoiled on the floor all around me—now an inert pile of stone—my arm came free of what remained of the chest with a carved snake mouth clamped down over my wrist. As I backed away, a long, slender body of stone emerged. At about the six-foot mark, it came free and the creature began to curl its body on the floor, its weight starting to draw me down to it.

"A little help," I called out. I whispered some of the speaking-to-stone incantations I knew by heart now, but nothing seemed to help exert my will over it. "Belarus blood or not, this thing is not going to play nice."

The guard groaned from where he lay on the floor, his body stirring.

"He's waking up," Marshall said, his nerves shot. He looked at Rory. "You couldn't have knocked him out for longer?"

"I was pulling my punches," she said, and started toward me.

"Why?" Marshall asked.

"He's not *evil*, jackass," she said. "He's just doing his job! I'm not going to brutalize a guy for that. That doesn't really jive with my moral compass. A girl has got to have a code to live by."

Rory turned away from Marshall completely, picking up speed as she came for me. She tore across the floor while twirling the pole arm in her hands like she had owned one all her life. She leapt toward me on those strong, lean legs of hers and brought the blade down hard just behind the head of the snake creature. The spearhead pierced the stone, going deep before Rory twisted the blade, pulling free a thick chunk of stone it had displaced. The living piece dropped away, going inert and rolling across the floor. Cracks appeared all along the creature's head and body as the whole thing stilled and solidified.

Rory spun her weapon around. "Oh, I need to gets me one of these," she said.

I raised my trapped hand high overhead and brought it down on the edge of the puzzle chest's frame as six more guards poured into the far end of the room. The snake head shattered, flaking off my still-closed fist. When I opened it, there was the stone I had come for, this one red. I looked at Marshall in triumph, but he was busy fretting over the men closing in on us.

"I can't go to jail," he said. "They don't have Magic: The Gathering tournaments there!"

"I don't intend on us getting caught," I said. "Now, run!"

I took off without hesitating another second, getting all the way to the only other exit from the room before stopping, Marshall and Rory at my side.

"We need to go up," I said. "We need stairs."

Marshall nodded. "I know where they are."

"You do?" Rory asked, impressed.

"Guess who got stuck doing all the mapping in my gaming campaigns?" he asked without really expecting an answer. "I can't help but retain the layout of a place when I enter it now." Marshall pulled his hat down to just over his eyes and took off to our left. Rory shot off behind him, and after I took a look back at our ever-closing pursuers, I followed. Seven of them, I counted.

Marshall led us through several rooms full of armor and then statues before he pushed open a door on his right leading to a set of stairs going up. He and Rory shot through the doorway, and several seconds later I came through it myself. The two of them were already a flight or two ahead of me, and I started up the stairs after them.

By the first landing my legs were killing me. "Wait up," I called out to them.

Rory stopped, then Marshall. "Sorry," she said. "We're already good at stairs from living in a fifth-floor walk-up."

"Where are we going?" Marshall asked, looking only a little winded.

I sprinted up to the next landing where they stood. "Up," I huffed out. "As high as we can go."

"Okay," he said, and took off up the stairs once more. This time Rory stayed at my side as we went.

"This better be an awesome plan you have," she said. "Like lure them all up here, then have the entire way down through the museum free for our escape."

"Not quite what I had in mind," I said. "Now, shush; I'm trying to panic here."

"You mean *not* panic . . ."

I shook my head. "I wish," I said, "but I'm going for full-blown panic here. Now, shut it."

We went as high as we could up the stairwell, the final single set of doors opening up onto a gallery filled with animals, both stuffed and skeletal. Marshall and Rory stopped once they came onto the floor, but I didn't and rushed right past them. "Try to keep up," I said without looking back. I had to find what I was looking for.

Museum visitors got out of my way fast, looking at us like

we were crazy, which I really couldn't argue with. I mean, who really ran through a museum at breakneck speed anyway?

I passed what looked like a prehistoric sloth that stood eight feet tall, then turned, finding exactly what I was looking for—a wall of windows. Seeing them brought a sense of relief, but I fought against it as I ran for them. I needed my panic. I needed to boost my signal. I skidded to a stop when I got to the window wall, spinning around.

Marshall and Rory came sliding to a stop with me. Marshall's eyes looked around in a wild way. "It's a dead end," he said. "*This* was your great plan? What the hell?"

Rory looked at me with the same expression of confusion. "I'm kind of with Marshall on this," she said, twirling the pole arm between her hands as she turned to face our pursuers.

The guards and several staff members cornered around the sloth, boxing us in.

"This is good," I said.

Rory, who was striking a defensive posture, stood and turned to me, stamping one end of her pole arm on the ground. "Good? Good how?"

"We're cornered, right?" I said. "And that terrifies me."

"Being scared is good?" Marshall asked. "Oh, I'm doing better than good, then."

"You don't get it," I said. "If I'm terrified, that's like a broadcast signal. To *him*."

Rory looked behind us out the window. "Sun's down," she said.

I felt a sharp twinge of familiarity in my chest and it was growing. Fast.

"Now might be a good time to duck," I said, and threw myself off to the side of the wall of windows.

Rory dove to the other side, grabbing Marshall, who was too busy watching me get out of the way. Glass, brick, and wood exploded into the room as several hundred pounds of flying gargoyle swooped in from the early-evening sky. Chunks of wall and window frame hung from his wings as he landed, fluttering them until they were free of debris. He folded them to his side while the museum staff simply stared.

"What the *hell* is that?" one of the guards asked.

Stanis stepped toward them, glass crunching under his feet. The crowd moved as one away from him, but now the gargoyle stood between us and them.

"Don't hurt anyone!" I shouted, stopping Stanis in his tracks. The sensation in my chest had passed now that he was here.

The gargoyle turned to me, his face scrunched up in thought. "That is going to make it more difficult to ensure your safety," he said.

"Bluff for a minute, then," I whispered.

Stanis cocked his head at me. "Bluff?"

"Menace them, but don't hurt them. Look . . . umm . . . badass."

Stanis nodded, then turned back to the guards and museum employees, spreading his wings out to their fullest. He puffed his chest, then let out an inhuman roar I'd had no idea he even had in him. It reminded me of the Tyrannosaurus Rex at the end of *Jurassic Park* and I shuddered. Being on the receiving end of it would have sucked, but from where I stood it simply was thrilling. I looked past Stanis's sizable form. Most of the staff had backed away, but several of the guards held their ground, their eyes wide in disbelief. Two of them had guns and were going for them.

I turned to Rory and Marshall. "Okay, guys," I said. "Time to leave."

"Leave?" Marshall repeated. He held on to one of the beams by the broken window and looked out into the open air on the other side. "Leave how?"

"We're flying the friendly skies," I said with a smile. "You come to love it. Promise."

Marshall tightened his grip on the beam and craned his head down outside.

"Did you factor my fear of heights at all into this plan?" he asked.

In truth, I had forgotten, but now was not the time to get into it. "Would you rather get shot?" I asked.

He sighed, then buttoned his coat up. "Time to get over one of my fears the hard way, I guess."

Rory looked at the pole arm in her hands. "I'm going to miss you," she said to it, then kissed it before letting it drop to the tile floor.

The first shot fired, all three of us flinching at the sound of it. A fragment of stone flew off of Stanis's left shoulder, but it was enough to get the three of us moving. I stood by the hole in the window wall and the two of them joined me.

"Stanis!" I called out. "To me!"

The gargoyle spun, keeping his wings spread out to protect us, but knocking over several exhibits, including something that resembled a six-foot-tall prehistoric beaver. He crossed to the window.

I looked up at him when he stopped before me. "You *can* carry all three of us flying, can't you?"

"We will find out," he said, a grimace filling his stone face.

"Was that a joke?" I asked.

"Perhaps," he said. "I am not sure. It just . . . seemed appropriate. That first gem may have indeed restored my 'funny bone.'"

Another shot fired out, the sound of it ricocheting following.

"We need to leave," Marshall said, looking for some way to grab onto the gargoyle. "So how are we doing this?"

"Each of you grab a shoulder," I said. "Stanis, you grab them around their waists."

"That doesn't leave much room for you," Rory said, grabbing on.

"Or any," Marshall said.

"I'm riding shotgun," I said. "On his back."

"Don't get shot!" Rory exclaimed.

"That will not do," Stanis said. Stone wings folded over Marshall and Rory while Stanis pushed away from me and spun around, offering me his back. I hesitated, but another shot firing put me in motion. I threw my arms around his neck and he backed his way toward the window.

"Hold on tight," I reminded everyone. "This isn't as easy as those Superman movies make it out to be."

Stanis stepped out through the broken window and we were falling.

"Fly!" I screamed, my legs kicking wildly out into the open air.

The gargoyle struggled to right himself while bearing the three of us before spreading his wings out and away from Marshall and Rory, catching the air, and arcing up into the night sky as we left the museum behind us. My heart filled with hope.

His eyes met mine and he gave a small smile, the hint of his fangs behind it. "I had to protect our friends first," Stanis said, then turned his gaze back to the task of navigating our way among the buildings all around us.

I smiled. *Our* friends. He said *our*. That was something now, wasn't it?

Twenty-six

☾

Stanis

I flew lower across the tops of buildings than I normally did given the extra weight I was carrying. Going much higher than that did not seem possible.

I had been built for flight, but with this many mortals? I did not think that had been in Alexander's plan. As I thought of what my old friend would make of it, it warmed me.

"Look at him," the one called Aurora said, breaking my thoughts. "I think he's . . . smiling."

"He is," Alexandra confirmed.

"He can do whatever he likes," Marshall said, "as long as he stays up in the air."

"He'll stay up," Alexandra said from over my shoulder, her arms tight around my neck and her legs locked around the front of mine. "Won't you?"

I nodded, the smile remaining on my face. The connection to the maker's kin was stronger now, more so than simply being born of the maker's blood. Since the first soul gem had been reclaimed and placed, new waves of sensations had begun to fill me more and more, the simple anger of that first night having long since calmed itself.

"Maybe he's smiling *because* he's going to drop us," Marshall said, his voice filled with nerves.

"I am not going to drop you," I said, then smiled wider. "Unless that is what you wish."

Marshall gave a tentative laugh. "Now is when he finds his sense of humor? That was humor, right?"

"No offense," Aurora said, "but my skin is kind of chafing against the stone."

"We are almost home," I said, coming in just above the tree line of Gramercy Park, angling up to the top of the Belarus building. I came down harder on the terrace that led into the library than I would have liked, the two humans in my arms grunting with the impact. Alexandra slid off my back and I stepped away from the three of them.

"That—" Marshall started. "That was—"

"Cool, right?" Alexandra finished, laughing.

Marshall's face went dark. "Insane," he spat out. "I was going to go with *insane*."

"Calm down," she said, lifting her fist up, opening the palm to reveal a gem. "We did it."

I went to speak but could not for a moment until words once again came to me. "You found another piece," I said.

"'We did it'?" Marshall asked. "By *it* you mean *almost dying*, right? Yes, we almost did *that*. Dammit, Lexi!"

He was near hysterical. I had seen this in humans before. "You would not have come to harm," I said. "I would have protected you."

"Would you?" Marshall said, stepping toward me with eyes as cold and empty as my own. "Look, Stan, I don't doubt your prowess, being magical and all, but the world has changed a lot since your creation. Those men had *guns*." He walked up to me and pressed a finger to my left shoulder, where I was surprised to see a small piece was missing. "There are things out there that even stone can't withstand."

"Give him a break," Alexandra said. "Tell Marshall to calm down, Rory." She pushed Marshall's hand away from my chest, examining the spot herself, tracing her fingers over it. "Does it hurt?"

Now that the moment was past and I could focus my mind, I checked myself and nodded. "I will be fine, though," I said.

"I can fix that," Alexandra said. She turned to Aurora, who was staring at the ground now, avoiding her. "What, Rory?"

"Look, Lexi, I'm an adrenaline junkie and all, but I kind of agree with Marshall on this one."

"Are you kidding me?" Alexandra asked.

"That shit was dangerous," Aurora said.

"I didn't know how it was going to go down!" Alexandra said. "I thought that this was going to be easy, civilized. We were in a museum, after all, the home to culture! I really thought there was a ninety-eight percent chance of us walking out of there alive."

Anger filled my chest, but I did not fully understand where it was coming from. Seeing my maker's kin agitated at her friends' reactions was bringing out the same in me.

"That's still two percent too dangerous, if you ask me," Marshall said.

"Enough!" I shouted, all three of the humans jumping and turning toward me. "We cannot live in the past. This I know from experience. What is important is that we are safe."

"Easy to say for the most invulnerable guy in our little group," Marshall said.

I turned my growing anger on him, glowering, rendering him silent. No one spoke and my anger gave way to what felt like satisfaction.

Alexandra took her hand from my chest and turned to the other two.

"It's my fault," she said, her voice as soft as the whisper of wind through the dying leaves still in the trees of the park down below. "I'm sorry. I didn't mean to put us in harm's way. But like it or not, we all *have* been put there nonetheless, not by me, but by my family's long and sordid history. I did not mean to drag you two into this so deep."

Aurora walked over to her. "You *are* family to me," she said. "So I'm in it whether you want me there or not."

"I do want you here," Alexandra said, "but make no mistake there is danger. We've seen that . . . repeatedly."

Marshall sighed. "I know," he said, "only this time it wasn't something unnatural and straight out of my nightmares attacking us. This time it was people—people just trying to do their jobs. Hell, I would have shot at us, too!"

"You don't have to stay in this," Alexandra told him. "You've got no investment in it, really."

"Like hell, I don't," he said. "I don't want to see my roommate get killed. You know how hard it was to find someone who wasn't a Craigslist creepazoid in the first place? I'm in. Besides, now that I'm alive and on solid ground again, I'm kinda . . . pumped."

"Okay, then," Alexandra said, turning back to me. She raised the dark red gemstone to my chest.

I raised my own hand to meet hers, stopping it. "I would like to speak," I said.

Alexandra gave me a soft smile. "Of course, Stanis."

"Very well," I said, looking back and forth between Marshall and Aurora. "I would like to express my—" I searched my mind for the word a moment. "*Gratitude*. Yes, gratitude . . . to you *both* for your help. You owe me nothing, yet you risk everything."

Aurora stepped forward, clapping both of her hands against my chest. "You've saved Lexi more times that I can count already," she said. "It is we who owe you."

"Not so fast," Marshall said, stepping closer. He jutted his jaw forward and puffed up his cheeks. "One day I will ask you for a favor. You will not refuse me this favor."

Both of the females laughed, but I just nodded. "Very well, Marshall," I said. I cocked my head at Alexandra, who was staring at me.

"You've never seen *The Godfather*, have you?" she asked. "No."

Her eyes brightened. "God, I have so much to show you. You've never been to the movies?"

"Movies," I said, my memory striking on the word. "I believe I have seen movies, yes."

"You have?" Aurora asked, laughing. "What do they charge you for admission?"

"Charge?"

"Never mind," she said. "How have you seen them?"

"There is a park north of here where other humans gather to watch others through an enormous arcane window," I said.

"Oh, yes!" Alexandra said. "Bryant Park! They show movies outside in the summer."

"It's not magic, though," Marshall added. "It's technology."

"Then yes," I said. "I remember 'movies.'"

"Good," Alexandra said, pulling the bag off her back. "Let's see what else we can help you remember." She opened it, pulled the stone book free, then whispered to it. Its shape yielded to that of an actual book and she flipped through it before stopping on an open page and handing it to Marshall. "Hold this."

Alexandra pressed her right hand over her left and turned back to the book. First she uncoiled the knot work that lay beneath the smooth surface of my chest, revealing the one stone already set there. She placed the new one in the bottom slot, where it fit perfectly. When she spoke again, the familiar warmth quickly spread through me once again, radiating from her hand out through my whole body. At first, I welcomed the sensation, thrilled to be able to feel anything, but as it grew, the burning became more unbearable than the last time. I staggered back from her, but Alexandra kept with me, pressing her hands tight to the spot as I felt the stone shifting and wrapping itself around the gem.

Centuries had passed without having felt a pain so great, at least to my ability to recall, and I could take it no longer. I fell to my knees, wings fully extending as I cried out into the night sky. Marshall flinched, but stayed steadfast in his duty to hold the book in place for Alexandra.

"I think you're killing him, Lexi!" Aurora shouted as the wind rose up in response to the energy coursing through me.

Alexandra bent forward, keeping her hands in place. Her eyes were filled with concern, but she did not waver in her incantation. I leaned into her, also not wanting to break the cycle of what was happening to me. The pain tore through me but I would not yield to it. It had been so long since I had felt anything of such power that I almost relished it.

Alexandra shouted the final words and the wind started to settle, her hair falling back to the sides of her face. The energy dissipated as the stone coiled in my chest wound itself closed over the gems embedded there, but like the last time, fresh memories unlocked in my mind and came to me. Akin to when the first soul stone had been placed, those familiar stone walls rose up around me. I awaited the great and terrible crushing sensation that had come with it as well, but it did not occur. Instead, the walls around me were moving—no, *I* was moving through them, this time recognizing them for what they were a part of. *A castle.* I ran through corridor after corridor, the dull glow of torches lighting the way, all sensations foreign to me. My wings were gone, I realized, and something else . . . My footfalls no longer had the heavy sound I was now accustomed to. I attempted to focus my thoughts, but the crushing sensation returned and overtook me, the pain becoming unbearable until my mind's eye jumped to another memory. My maker, Alexander, stood before me as foreign and confusing emotions were fading from me, four gemstones in his hand, the coils under my chest closing over themselves. I pressed myself to work out the meaning of the ebbing emotions but my mind's eye slammed shut like a door and it rushed my thoughts back to the present.

The pain still burned in my chest, and my mind raced with confusion, pitching me forward. I was falling, and I could only hope my maker's kin would move in time. Alexandra jumped back in haste and the stone of the roof met with the stone of my skin, calming and cooling against the burning sensation in my chest.

"Stanis!" Alexandra cried, the pain radiating off of her doubling my own. Her soft hands wrapped around my left arm and shoulder. "Guys! Help me."

Aurora and Marshall's hands joined hers, ready to try to lift.

"I don't think this is going to work," Marshall said.

"Stop being so logical!" Alexandra said, her tone serious. "Now, lift!"

The three of them pulled at my inert stone form, but to no avail.

"I told you," Marshall said.

Alexandra's anger rose, bringing mine with it, but I felt compelled to stop it. I pressed the flats of my hands against the roof, pulling my wings against my body and rolling onto my side until I was able to sit.

"I am fine," I said. "It has simply been a while since I had felt such . . . pain. Or anything, really."

"That's what I feared," Alexandra said. "Each piece we find is bringing back different parts of you, including an ability to feel. In this case, pain."

"You felt it, too?" I asked her.

She nodded. "That's growing as well, whatever this connection is. But not just feelings. There was . . . a castle, too, yes?"

"Yes," I said. "I was running through it, only . . . I did not feel like myself. I felt different. Am I—*was* I human?"

Alexandra looked up in my face. "You think you were human once?" she said. "I'd always assumed you were simply a marvelous creation of my great-great-grandfather, but seeing Devon transformed . . ." She paused, sadness flashing across her face. "What I've discovered in his notes so far says very little about your past beyond the rules set upon you, but yes, I think that makes sense. That you had been human once. I don't know who, but we've seen firsthand that it's possible for humans to take some kind of stone form. For example, my brother."

I stood in silent contemplation of the thought. It struck me as beyond the beyond that I could have once been like these fragile creatures.

"Don't look so sad," Aurora said. "It's not so bad to be human."

"Humanity is overrated," Marshall added, in what I assumed was an attempt to make me feel better. He turned to Alexandra. "Although if your great-great-grandfather took this person and trapped him in this form while taking the core of his soul away, that's messed up. Maybe your brother is right. Maybe Alexander was a dick. Maybe your family has evil tendencies, after all."

Anger rolled off of Alexandra; I could feel it touch me, but I also felt her trying to calm it. "I'm going to forget you suggested that," Alexandra said, giving him a dark look. "If Alexander Belarus did something like that, he must have had a good reason."

Marshall did not say anything more and Alexandra turned back to me. "Do you remember anything new?"

I let my mind drift back through my past, looking for anything out of the ordinary. I raised my hand to my chest, which was now smoothed back over. "Since placing the first stone, I remember Alexander more and more," I said. "And now I remember when he created these soul stones."

"So what *did* he do?" Marshall asked.

"I remember nothing of my own world before that day," I said, my mouth forming into a grimace. "I do remember when he pulled these stones from me, however. He said he was taking them from me for my own safety. I asked him what he was keeping me safe from, but he would not say. The less I knew, the more he said I could live with myself."

Alexandra sighed, closing the book and slipping it back into her pack. "I don't suppose he told you where he put all four of them . . . ?"

I shook my head. "He only alluded to them, but would not tell me anything direct. Again, for my safety."

"Looks like Alexander had issues," Aurora said.

"I cannot speak on that," I said. "He did, however, have a great love of puzzles."

Alexandra laughed. "We know," she said. "You should have seen the puzzle box he left that last piece in. Have you even seen how many are in his studio? It's filled with them."

I smiled. "He used those in my education."

"Education?" she asked.

"Once he had taken those gems from me, there was much for me to learn," I said. "Or relearn, it seems. He thought thinking through solutions for his many puzzles was the perfect tool for it."

Alexandra looked to Aurora. "Looks like I'm going to have to homeschool Bricksley."

Rory shook her head and put her face down in her hands.

"Who is Bricksley?" I asked.

"You'll meet," Alexandra said. "What did Alexander allude to about the gems?"

I pressed through my newfound memories. "One thought seems to linger," I said. "It does not feel wholly mine, however. I can hear his voice, talking about something called the Eye of God. I do not recall what that is exactly."

Alexandra smiled, sliding her book back into her bag. "I think I have an idea about *that* one," she said, looking up at me. "That's one of the things Alexander mentioned in the Spellmason primer I found in the base of one of the puzzle boxes. I've been rolling it around in my head and I think I have a possible location for it that Alexander helped build." She looked up at me. "How do you feel about a night out on the town?"

Twenty-seven

☾

Alexandra

"We're going clubbing?" Rory asked as we stood in a long line of costumed people on the corner of Sixth Avenue and Twentieth Street. "On Halloween?"

For the sake of carrying Alexander's arcane tome, I had come as a modern Goth witch with a tombstone-shaped backpack, opting for thigh-high striped stockings to give it a Tim Burton-y kind of vibe.

"Not quite," I said, looking at the old stone church and bell tower that stood on the northwest corner of the intersection. "Cathedral was actually a real church before it became a hot spot. It was the last church my great-great-grandfather built before he stopped doing them. From what Stanis said about the Eye of God and what I've deciphered from Alexander's notes, we should find one of Stanis's gems here."

"Good," she said. "I'd hate to have put on a costume for nothing."

"You look cute," I said. It was true. Blue fairie wings that matched her hair peeked over her shoulders. Killer black knee-high boots and an aqua-colored Tinker Bell–cut dress completed her ensemble. "Not that you had to do much. All of that came out of your closet, except for the wings."

Rory's face went red. "Actually . . . those came from my closet, too. My ex had a thing for fantasy characters."

Marshall coughed. "TMI," he said, adjusting his bloody suit and blood-drenched lab coat. His face was made up so his eyes and cheeks looked sunken in.

Rory looked him up and down. "And what are you supposed to be?"

"I'm patient zero from the coming zombie apocalypse."

She patted him on the head. "Of *course* you are," she said.

A low grumble came from behind me. "You okay? I whispered over my shoulder before turning to Stanis.

His wings were tucked close to his body and his figure was as it always was except for several false, artistically placed joint lines I had painted on him to make his true form look more costumey. I thought about asking him what he made of my costume, but repressed the urge.

"This is . . . *unique*," he said.

"What is?"

"Being among your kind like this, being so . . . close." He turned and looked down the line. "You understand it violates one of Alexander's rules. I am supposed to remain hidden away from humanity. This is truly fascinating."

The sexy Red Riding Hood standing behind us in line looked up at him.

"Great costume," she said, the tone in her voice driving a surprising spike of jealousy into me.

Stanis looked down at her, unaffected, his face as blank as ever, allowing my flash to pass. "Thank you," he said after a long, awkward moment. His clear discomfort, I had to admit, was kind of adorable.

"How long did it take you to make?"

He paused again in thought. "Several hundred years."

She laughed. "I used to watch *Gargoyles*, too," Red Riding Hood said.

Something about her flirting got under my skin, and I stepped forward, grabbing his arm. "Come on, now, Stan, hon," I said, spinning him back around. "Line's moving."

It didn't take long before the four of us entered Cathedral.

Its interior was still reminiscent of an old church, with the addition of multilevel dance floors, a bar, platforms, and cages with dancers in them that hung from the high-vaulted arches of the old church's interior.

"Wow," Marshall said. "It's like a Goth's dream in here. Very spiritual and creepy all at the same time. First round's on me."

He headed off to the bar as we walked around the outside of the dance floor where superheroes, sexy cat ladies, and hipster zombies danced the night away. Despite my artistic attempt to hide Stanis's true form, everyone in the club gave him at least a glance or stared, but nothing that indicated that anyone thought for a second he might be an actual gargoyle. Why would they? Until a few weeks ago, I wouldn't have given it a thought that it wasn't a costume, either.

Rory looked around the club. "So we're supposed to find this gem somewhere in this throng?" she asked. "We're talking the proverbial needle in a haystack here. Of course, the only difference is that all these needles are dancing their asses off."

I pulled off my backpack, patting the book within. "That's why I brought this. My great-great-grandfather said that the gemstone is located in the Eye of God."

"The stained glass windows, maybe?" Rory asked. "Lots of angels and saints depicted up there . . . Maybe one of their eyes?"

Both sides of the massive church held long rows of what looked to be the original stained glass. They were gorgeous, backlit by lighting units hidden in boxes that protected the club from ever seeing the light of day, a Goth or vamp's paradise. I turned to Stanis.

"I don't suppose you know where it might be?" I asked. "It *is* a part of you, after all."

Stanis didn't respond, looking almost as statuesque as he had for years in the daylight on the roof of my family's building.

"Stanis, what's wrong?"

His smooth stone eyes turned to me. "Perhaps you are used to being in such a crushing sea of humanity, but I am not. I have seen the people of this city for centuries, but I have never walked among them. I find myself . . . incredibly distracted."

I nodded. "I can only imagine. But you've no sense for the location of the gemstone . . . ?"

Stanis closed his eyes in concentration for at least a minute, then opened them. "I am sorry, but no."

Marshall came back cradling four glasses in his arms, handing one to Rory, then me, and finally holding one out to Stanis.

The gargoyle looked down at it. "I do not drink," he said.

Marshall laughed. "In recovery, eh?"

Stanis cocked his head. "Recovery?"

Ah, the modern-day idiom, still lost on him. "It's what they say about alcoholics who are trying to stop drinking," I said. "That they are in recovery."

He straightened his head, nodding. "I see," he said. "Then no, I am not in recovery. What I meant to say was that I am incapable of consuming food or drink."

Marshall kept the glass out in front of him, still offering it. "At least hold it, then. You'll blend in better. Look less conspicuous."

Stanis took the glass in his large stone hand, looking rather absurd. "Thank you."

"All right," I said. "Let's take different sides of the church and check out the stained glass up close. You see anything that looks like an Eye of God, let the rest of us know—got it?"

Marshall and Rory nodded.

"Stanis," I said, heading to the right side. "You're with me."

Stained glass rose up all along the wall behind the bar, but the press of people trying to get a drink was too much to work our way through. "At this rate, it'll take half the night to push our way close enough to get a look."

"I can correct that," Stanis said, stepping past me. He cut a path through the crowd, which parted out of the way for him fast. Whether they suspected he might be a real gargoyle or not, he still cut an impressive figure and it made our going easier, allowing me to examine the stained glass as we went. Despite the glorious artistry of it all, nothing screamed out to me. We met up with Marshall and Rory at the back of the club, where they were standing outside a sitting area that had bright white couches that ringed around the circular wall of the room within.

"Any luck?" I asked.

Rory smiled and held up a handful of napkins. "I'll say. Blue Faerie got a few numbers."

I shook my head at her. "Way to stay focused."

"Well, *I* paid attention," Marshall said. "But I didn't notice anything odd. Other than the girls gyrating in the hanging cages over the dance floor."

"I do not understand this ritual," Stanis said.

I sighed. "It wouldn't make much sense if I explained it."

"So what next?" Rory asked.

I looked into the room behind her. "I saw the bell tower from the outside. I think this is where it should be. Come on."

The four of us pressed our way into the circular room, which I discovered had no ceiling as I stared up into the darkness that rose high above.

"It's like being at the bottom of a well," Rory said. "A very fashionable well, but still . . ."

"You want to find something called the Eye of God," Marshall said, pointing up, "I think you look at the place highest in a church."

"You do?" I asked.

He nodded. "Closest to Heaven, where his eye could look down on you."

"You only thought of that because of your gaming group, didn't you?" Rory asked.

Marshall's face went defensive. "Does it matter?"

Rory smiled. "Not really," she said. "I just like seeing that look on your face."

"Great," I said. "Now we just need to find the stairs!" I looked around the space, but saw nothing. I walked over to a muscle-bound guy in a Cathedral security shirt who stood by the arch between the club floor and the round room at the base of the tower.

"Excuse me, is there a way to get up to the bell tower?"

The man looked a little pissed that I was talking to him. He shook his head. "Not anymore," he said, curt.

"Really?" Rory asked. "I'd think it would be one of the draws in a place like this."

The guy simply shrugged and went back to looking out over the crowd.

"What's up with that?" Marshall asked.

The man looked at my friend the way burly guys for generations had looked on skinny nerds.

"Seriously," I said, refusing to let up on him despite his efforts to ignore us. "Why isn't it open?"

He glared at me for a moment, but when I refused to look away, he sighed and spoke.

"It used to be a VIP area, but we had some issues . . ."

"With?"

He sighed. "People jumping. It became trendy, so now no one gets up there. *No one.* You can look up and see the bell, but there's no way up there anymore since they bricked up the stairs."

We walked away before he could get any more of his stink eye on us. I took a long drink before speaking.

"This location feels right to me," I said. "I'm almost certain this is the place. We need to get up there."

Marshall shook his head. "You heard what the security guy said. There's no way up anymore."

"Yes," Stanis said, letting his wings twitch just the slightest. "There is."

Rory looked out across the sea of people on the dance floor. "You're going to do that . . . *in here*? Lexi, talk some sense into your bodyguard there, will ya?"

"I'd love to," she said, "but I can't."

Rory's face narrowed. "Why the hell not?"

"Because I'm going with him."

"You are?" Rory asked.

"Like hell," Marshall said, stepping toward us. Stanis stepped forward, stopping Marshall in his tracks. "Whoa, now, big fella. Easy. Lex, we need to teach him the big difference between someone who's an actual threat and someone who is just acting out of *concern* to try and stop you."

"Relax," I told Stanis. He didn't move, which I supposed was him acquiescing to my command. Standing stone still was as relaxed as I figured he could get. I turned to Rory. "I'm going up. You two can either help or get out of my way. Either or."

Marshall sighed, and he gave a reluctant nod. "Fine," he said. "I'll do my part, then."

"Which is . . . ?" I asked, waiting for an answer.

"I'll distract the guard watching the bell tower."

Rory laughed. "And how are you going to go about that? Ask him to play some Dungeons and Dragons?"

"Please," he said, looking insulted. "I'm far more resourceful than that."

"So, what, then?" I asked.

Marshall eyed the half-empty drink in his hands, then grabbed Stanis's full one. "Just be ready to fly." He took off without another word back toward the base of the bell tower. The closer he got, the more he stumbled like he had been drinking for hours.

"Oh, God," Rory moaned. "He's going to get himself thrown out, isn't he?"

Marshall stumbled forward, slamming into the security guy. Both drinks flew from his hands, their contents spilling all over him. The man's eyes widened and he brought his meat-hook hands down hard on Marshall's shoulders, spinning him around. He bent poor Marshall's arm behind him, pulled up on it, and started pushing his way through the crowd without any hesitation.

"Come on," I said to Stanis as we waited for the two of them to pass. "We have to act quick, while people are distracted by it."

Rory took off first, slipping through the crowd with ease. Stanis and I followed, with several people congratulating him on his awesome costume once more. When we got to the area under the bell tower, the crowd was thinner, with Rory at the center of it, looking up.

"I'm going, too," she said, looking down. The way she said it had me wondering whether she was trying to convince herself more than me.

"You don't have to," I said.

"Yes," she said," I do." She looked up into the tower again and pointed.

I looked up into the darkness above. "I don't get it."

"Give it a second," she said.

I continued staring. The darkness softened as my eyes adjusted to it, and that was when I saw it. "There's something moving up there." Tiny dark figures swirled around the central shape of the bell high above.

"I don't know what they are," Rory said, "but I'm not about to let you deal with them on your own."

"I have Stanis to protect me," I said.

"Judging from the activity up there, I'm fairly sure you two might be outnumbered."

I turned my eye to look over the dance floor. The security guard was pushing Marshall out onto the street where the bouncers would see that he didn't come back in. The guard then turned toward the dance floor and started making his way across the club to his post by us.

"We have to go," I said. "Now."

Stanis unfurled his wings from his body, drawing a round of applause from the people closest to us who no doubt thought it was just another detail to his intricate costume. I threw my arms around his neck and stepped to his left side as Rory ran in close on his right. She threw her arms around his midsection and locked her hands together.

"You sure this is safe?" she asked.

"Not at all," I said, then tapped Stanis on the shoulder. "Go."

He bent his knees before jumping up into the air, letting his wings catch their first wind as we started to rise. Several people fell back from the powerful blast of his wings flapping, but the rest were half-drunk and cheering.

"At least they'll have something to tell their friends at work on Monday about the superlative special effects at the Cathedral Halloween party!"

"Too bad I'm missing it all," Rory said, her eyes clenched shut.

My stomach sank at the speed of rise, much like it did at the top of the camelback hills on a roller coaster.

"Funny," I said. "I would have figured this would be right up your alley."

"Only my second time flying," she said, "and first time inside a very confined bell tower. Might get used to it. Might not. Answer unclear. Try again later."

A walkway and ladder leading up to the bell room was coming up fast. "Put us down on that catwalk."

Stanis slowed and came up even with the platform. I caught the railing with the backs of my knees and slid myself over it onto the wooden slats of the walkway. Rory grabbed the railing, swinging under it and landing gracefully next to me.

"Nice," I said.

She stood and grabbed onto the railing. "I'm trying to ignore how high we are and how rickety this walkway looks, but I can at least show a little style while trying not to panic."

Stanis hovered next to the walkway, his wings working in a short, quick pattern of flaps. Rory looked up. "What *are* those?"

Up close it was easier to see the creatures now. Maybe a dozen or so winged gray figures about waist high flitted back and forth around the bell overhead. They were leathery bats, but there was also something vaguely humanoid about their bodies and faces, save for the razor-sharp teeth in their mouths.

"I'm not sure," I said, pulling off my coffin from my back, "but I swear I've seen them before." I knelt down on the walkway, undoing the straps and pulling out Alexander's tome.

"I can dispatch them," Stanis offered.

"Hold on," I said, flipping frantically through the book as fast as I could. Rudely sketched drawings filled the spaces that weren't covered in the arcane scrawling in his handwriting. Dozens of horrific images passed as I searched on, but I tried not to think about any of them. My only concern for the moment was the creepy, fluttering monstrosities overhead. When a drawing of one of them caught my eye, I turned back to the page. "Aha!"

"They're in there?" Rory said, still minding the goings-on up above.

"Yup," I said. "I always assumed they were just sketches of simple Gothic statues. Now if I can just figure out some of the notes here . . ."

The words on the page made more sense to me now than ever before, although every fourth or fifth word was still a mystery. I only hoped that getting the gist would be enough.

"We *must* be at the right place," I said, "because these things are said to be drawn to the arcane. They can feel its pull and will do anything to possess it."

"Talk about bats in the belfry," Rory added.

"Alexander didn't have a name for them, but he noted how they interfered with some of his alchemical carving work. He called them . . . *stone eaters*."

"I love a man who's a literalist," Rory said. "That doesn't bode well for Stan here, though."

"My survival is of little consequence," he said.

I couldn't help but look up at him, pain tugging at me from those words. "You really mean that, don't you?"

"All that matters is protecting the family," he reminded me. He hesitated, seeming to tap into something deep inside him, and said, "Although, I would *prefer* it if I did not die, I suppose."

"Well," I said, standing up with the book in hand. "Me, too. Right now, we need to get up there and find that gem of yours."

"As you wish," he said. His wings were flapping away still, keeping him steady in place as if he were standing on the walkway with us. I wondered whether he ever tired.

"I need you to lead them away," I said.

"As you wish."

"Please," I added.

"You do not need to plead."

"I was trying to be polite," I said.

He paused, as if processing the idea. "Ah. Yes."

"We can discuss that later, too," I said, "but for now, go. Please. And be careful. He didn't call those creatures 'stone eaters' for nothing."

Without another word, Stanis folded his wings in, causing him to drop out of sight below us. I rushed to the railing and peered over, only to catch him extending his wings to their fullest and giving a mighty swoop of them, propelling himself upward past me at an astonishing speed. He tucked his wings again as he went through the opening in the walkway, up and around the bell itself. He contorted his body to avoid the large metal bell as he grabbed one of the creatures by the throat, but one of his wings still clipped it, causing it to erupt with sound. Standing directly under it meant we caught the brunt of it. The bell started swinging as the creatures flew off after Stanis.

Rory covered her ears, but I couldn't get to mine in time. My hands were stuck in the middle of slipping my backpack back on as the wall of sound hit me, harder than any bass at a concert ever had. I finished pulling the pack on and simply gestured upward without trying to shout over the tolling bell. Rory nodded and motioned for me to go up first. I gave one more look up to make sure there weren't any creatures in sight and scurried up the ladder, with Rory following close behind.

The bell was surrounded on all sides by a narrow walkway. It and the stone walls of the tower were covered in bite and claw marks. Rory came up the ladder and stopped when she saw the state of things. "Jesus," she said, which I barely heard through the ringing in my ears.

"We have to hurry," I said, and began looking around the top of the tower. Rory went around one side of the walkway and I took the other until we came together on the other side.

"I don't see anything," she said. "Maybe it's not up here."

"It's up here," I said. "I can *feel* it."

Rory gave me a skeptical look. "You can?"

"I can't explain it," I said, "but something up here *feels* like my home, the way the Belarus building exudes protection. Alexander wrote that he had warded the property, the same way he did my necklace. I think he warded this place, too."

"So even if we want to see what we're looking for, we wouldn't be able to see it because of magic?"

I shrugged. "That's the best I have," I said.

Rory smiled. "That's not bad."

I narrowed my eyes at her. "It's not?"

"Nope," she said, looking around some more.

"Why not?"

"Look at this place," she said. "It's a mess. Those *things* flying around out there have clawed and bitten this place apart trying to get to the magic, but they couldn't find it! Why? Your great-great-grandfather's mad phat warding skills."

"As I've read it, the magic pretty much repels notice, driving people away from it. Like we experimented on Marshall with when I was re-enchanting the necklace."

"Then that's what we try to look for," she said. "Even with being repelled, those creatures sensed *something*, even if they couldn't find it. If the magic drew those creatures to it, but Alexander's warding *still* kept them from it, then whatever looks different, whatever's *untouched* from what those creatures ruined up here, must be it."

I considered it for a moment before breaking into a smile. "*That's* not bad, Miss Aurora Torres."

She gave a deep bow as if she were onstage after having danced at Lincoln Center.

I looked around the space until my eyes settled on the one block that remained untouched, sitting directly above the bell at the center of the arch. "The keystone," I said.

Rory looked up. "Where?"

"There," I said, pointing at the spot.

Rory looked where I was pointing, but her eyes didn't fix on anything. "I'll take your word for it," she said.

"You don't see it?" I asked. "Seriously?"

"I'm trying to, believe me, but no."

"Maybe it's my bloodline that lets me," I said.

Rory turned away and looked out of one of the many stone archways around the tower. "Either way, we need to hurry. I can't see Stanis or any of those little things out there, but it's only a matter of time before they come back."

"Right," I said. "Help me up."

Rory ran over, interlocked her fingers, and I stepped into her hand. I reached up as she lifted, and I grabbed onto the support yoke over the bell, hauling myself up. The bell rocked with my legs dangling down against it, its clapper sounding out once again.

"Shit," I said, trying to steady the bell with my legs.

"Hurry!"

"I *am*," I yelled. I pressed my hands against the cool sides of the untouched keystone, feeling all along it. "This may take a few minutes. There's nothing on the outside. The gem has to be embedded in it."

"Do it!" she shouted over the clanging of the bell. She ran along the walkway, leaning out of each of the arches as she went. "Incoming!"

"Help me down, then."

"No," she said. "You keep doing what you need to. I'm going to let out a little aggression here."

I pushed my will into the stone, searching, letting the rituals I had studied take over as I incanted the words that were becoming increasingly familiar each and every day.

Below, one of the creatures flew into the opening of the arch where Rory was standing, but she dropped and flattened herself to the walkway with her dancer's grace. The winged stone eater slammed into the side of the bell, causing a whole new cacophony as it pushed back from it, dazed, its wings struggling to flap and keep itself afloat. Rory didn't waste the opportunity. She grabbed the creature by its wings while it was still stunned and swung it in an arc over her head, slamming it against the wooden walkway. It struggled to push up on its tiny humanoid arms, but Rory wasn't having it. With the wings still spread out in both hands, she dropped her foot onto the creature's body, letting out an aggressive scream. She bore down hard, pressing her heel into it deep, then she stood up fast, the muscles in her arms taut as she pulled. The sounds of the creature's screams as its wings tore free from its body rose over the sound of the bell. Rory dropped the wings into the open space below us and kicked the twitching, dying body of it down after.

The rage on Rory's face disappeared as she looked down at her hands, where bits of wing webbing were still stuck to her fingers. Flicking them didn't seem to help so she ran to the wall and started wiping her hands on the rough stone. "Gross, gross, gross," she said.

I was still locked in finding the gem or I would have said something, but before I could give it more thought another creature flew into the interior of the tower, shrieking and hissing at me while I continued my incantation. I turned my eyes from it, focusing myself more wholly on the keystone, trusting in Rory to deal with the monster. The sound of its rising shrieks filling my ears confirmed my trust in my friend, and, confident in her abilities, my mind was free to zero in on the gem within the stone. I whispered to the stone to give way, to open at my command, confident that it would. I was a Belarus, after all. It was in my blood.

The connection to the stone was strong and I felt the gem pulling out of it toward my now-cupped hands along the bottom of the keystone. Bits of rock crumbled away, slipping through my fingers, but the gem itself caught in my hand, its yellow hue sparkling in the dim lighting up here.

"I have it!" I shouted, turning to Rory down on the walkway. She had the legs of another of the stone eaters in one hand, hanging it upside down as it flapped its wings wildly trying to right itself.

Rory chanced a look up at me while avoiding its razor teeth, a look of triumph on her face. It lasted only seconds; then I saw her look past me.

"Lexi!" she shouted. "Look out!"

I turned. The hole that had crumbled away in the keystone was still growing. Panicking, I tried to force my will on it, but I couldn't feel the connection anymore. Cracks rippled out into the keystone, the joints from the bell's yoke giving way as the tower's dome caved in on itself, and the bell beneath me slipped off-kilter and began tumbling down. The walkway tore loose from the walls as they collapsed, and Rory came down after me, the wings of the creature in her hand doing little to slow her. I reached out in all directions to control the stone all around me, but there was no connection.

We were in free fall.

☾

Twenty-eight

Stanis

When Alexandra sent me to task against the creatures she called stone eaters, I did as she wished. I shot up through the opening just below the large church bell, spinning myself to avoid it. One of the creatures startled in front of me, and I spun again to narrowly miss it. I grabbed one of its wings as I passed, but my own clipped the side of the bell, pulling it until it rose to its fullest height, unhooked from me, and began tolling. This seemed to drive the creatures mad, but my presence had the effect I desired and they fell in behind me as I pulled my wings in to slip out of one of the many arched windows leading out into the night sky.

I looked back as I flew. All of them, nine in total, had followed me. I turned, focusing on my flight, the creature in my hand trailing behind the grip I had on its one wing. *Be careful,* Alexandra had said. I needed to thin their numbers. I steered myself to an older building made of brick. I swung my arm as I spread my wings to slow myself, catapulting the creature forward at a deadly speed. It flew from my hand, desperate to right itself and flapping like wild, but it was no use. The velocity was too much and it hit the wall with such force it died on impact. I did not wait to confirm it, and drove myself higher into the night sky.

Just below the clouds, I stopped. I did not want to fight them where I could not see them and, looking down, I saw their approach. As they got closer, they broke away from one another, spreading out to surround me. Pack hunters.

I circled around in the center of them. There was no holding back on their part. No pause to assess me, just animal instinct to attack kicking in. I could use this to my advantage. I kept my eyes on them as I spun, waiting until the last second as they closed, then shot myself straight up. Unable to stop themselves, they crashed into one another, a twist of limbs, wings, and teeth. I folded my wings in and immediately dropped on them, driving *through* them. My claws caught one in the face and it fell out of the sky. Two more plummeted, still tangled together, biting at each other in a futile attempt to free themselves but falling nonetheless.

Three of them got their wings sorted out and came for me. I brushed one away with a mighty blow of my wings, and shoved my sharpened claws into the chests of the other two. My hands came out through their backs. Before I had a chance to shake them free, the two remaining ones were coming at me. Their mouthfuls of teeth snapped and gnashed, and I shoved their dead pack members in the way to keep them from taking a chunk out of my body. I swung my arms wildly, both driving them back and using the force to get the broken bodies off my arms. They came free, plummeting to the earth below, and before the last two could close again, I flew farther from the church, leading them away. They screeched and fell in behind me, trying to keep up. This time they were close and closing every second, curse my fatigued body.

A sudden twinge rose up in my chest. This time I recognized it as the bond to the girl, but it was still enough to catch me off my guard. I grabbed two of these stone eaters by the throat, clenching my fists until the stone of my fingers came together underneath their flesh. Their wings ceased flapping, their bodies falling, and I used their added weight to flip me around, heading me back toward the tower.

Already I could see the problem—the top of the tower simply was not there, having caved in on itself. I pushed my wings as hard as I could. The first rule—*protect the family*—burned at the center of me and I would not fail. I arched my body back, propelling myself higher, before I dove down into the center of the collapsing tower, wings tucked in tight. Falling chunks of the old church blocked my way, but I pushed through them as easily as I tore through clouds, the stone no match for that of my skin.

"Stanis!" I heard Alexandra's voice cry out before I could even see her. I drove my hands down into the stones beneath me and threw them aside, revealing her figure several stories below me. The blue-haired one was close to her, one of those creatures clutched in her hand, flapping wildly. The club below was rapidly getting closer.

I pumped my wings to close the distance and grabbed for Alexandra's wrist, but stopped myself, remembering how fragile these humans could be. I worked my wings again, shooting past her, coming up from beneath, catching Alexandra under her arms. She jerked with the sudden stop, letting out a hiss of pain, but she seemed to be intact.

"Rory!" she called out to me in a state of panic. My arm flashed out and caught the other girl in the same manner. The creature in her hands slammed into my head and shoulder, momentarily dazed.

"Let go of that thing!" Alexandra screamed to her, but it was too late. I could not bat it away without dropping one of the women, and before Aurora could act, the creature bit at the stone of my upper right arm. Fire erupted in it as the blue-haired girl pulled the creature away from me. Crunched-up stone flew from its mouth. *My* stone.

It slammed into the wall of the still-standing tower and Aurora finally let go of it. I spread my wings to slow our fall as debris rained down on us, and, remembering their frail nature, I raised my wings in protection over the women before working them to make my way back up through the falling tower. The going was slow, and by the time I reached the top of what was left of the structure, the collapse had stopped altogether.

"I think I just inherited Marshall's fear of heights," Aurora said, clutching around my neck as hard as her arms could hold her.

"We need to land," Alexandra said, "before I can't hold on any longer."

"Fear not," I said. "I would catch you."

A warmth radiated from her. "I know you would," she said with a smile. "Nonetheless, I would prefer to have all three of us safely on the ground." She looked around down below. "Can you land us behind the club?"

I slipped into the shadows there, coming down slowly. Only after I landed and the women stepped away did I relax my wings, and that was when my body finally reminded me of the burning sensation on my right upper arm. As I looked it over, Alexandra and Aurora moved closer to it.

"Sorry," Aurora said.

"Does it hurt?" Alexandra asked.

"Yes," I said. "It is a sensation I am not overly familiar with except as of late. It is . . . interesting."

"I think I can do something about that back at our building," she said, "but not here."

"I will be fine," I said. "Long have I desired to feel something. If it is pain, so be it."

I followed them out of the alley onto Twentieth Street. A dusty cloud met us along with dozens of dazed and costumed humans from the club. The three of us walked with caution back onto Sixth Avenue to the entrance of Cathedral. Sixth Avenue was less filled with smoke but there were more people here, a press of them shoving their way out of the old church still. The one called Marshall spotted me and came running over to the women, hugging them both.

"I . . . I thought you were dead," he said, shaken, with tears on his face.

"We almost were," Alexandra said, "but thanks to Stanis here, we made it out alive."

Marshall turned to me. "Thank you for that," he said. "I know I've been a bit suspect about, well . . . everything with you, but I can see your heart, or whatever that coily thing in your chest is, is in the right place."

"Thank you," I said.

He turned back to the women. "Did you find what you were looking for?" Marshall asked.

"Oh, Jesus, I almost forgot!" Alexandra brought up her still-clenched fists, opening the right one. Another of the gemstones sat in the center of her hand, yellow this time, its imprint pressed into her skin.

The sound of sirens rose off in the distance. The dull flash of red and blue lights gave off large indistinct flares of color that colored the growing dust cloud all around us.

"We should go," Rory said, choking a bit.

Alexandra closed her fist over the stone and pressed her other against my chest. "You need to get out of here," she said. "Now."

I nodded.

"I'll meet you back at the building," she continued. "You should go back into the alley before you take off—"

Too late to heed her words, I was already in flight, shooting up through the dust cloud, away from all the humanity, my soul already feeling relief that I was no longer going against one of the principal rules by being among them.

Twenty-nine

◖

Alexandra

Stanis had flown off in such a hurry after the incident at Cathedral that I hadn't had time to truly assess any of the damage to him other than that one bite on his right arm. I was just happy we had gotten the damned gemstone out of there and all got out alive. Now in the comfort of my great-great-grandfather's studio, however, the nicks and dings to his form were more than evident.

"I think somebody's been putting up a brave front," I said, readying the book spread out on one of the worktables. Next to it was a pile of broken stone chips I had Bricksley gather up from various sculpting attempts around the studio. Somewhere off in the studio I could hear the little guy still rummaging around for more.

"What do you mean?" Stanis asked with his usual inquisitive head cock.

I pointed to a bunch of areas across his torn-up chest and body. "You took a lot of damage tonight," I said. "Those creatures, the tower collapse . . ." I shuddered. "Do these hurt?"

Stanis nodded. "I wish I could say they do not," he said, "but then I would be . . . What is the word . . . ? Lying?"

"I'm sorry," I said, sifting through the pile, looking for something the right size for the spot on his chest I was eyeing.

He didn't respond, which drew my eyes back to him. To my surprise, he was smiling, his fangs showing. "What?" I asked.

"All of this . . . it is a small price to pay for regaining part of my soul," he said.

His words struck something deep in me that forced me to hold back the tears I felt forming at the corners of my eyes. I turned back to searching through my pile of stone pieces in silence until I found one that seemed about the right size.

Consulting my great-great-grandfather's book, I placed the stone into the groove on Stanis's chest before I incanted the words on the page. The piece went warm beneath my fingers as it melded with Stanis, the gargoyle letting out a low, slow hiss. When I pulled my hand away, the stone of his chest was smooth and once more whole in that spot.

"I may not be the best at real estate," I said, "but *this* I seem to be getting the hang of."

Stanis looked down at the spot, then met my eyes.

"This is what you were meant for," he said. "Much like your great-great-grandfather. It was his destiny, and it is yours as well."

I gave a nervous laugh, finding it hard to look away from him. "Destiny schmestiny," I said. "Anything beats office work."

He slid his hand over mine on his chest, careful with his claws, pressing it against the cold stone. "You may tell yourself that, Alexandra, but I know better. You are a maker; it is in your very nature."

This time I didn't argue. How could I when his words fit so right, like knowing when you've found the perfect pair of boots or gloves. "Thank you," I said after realizing I hadn't said anything for several moments.

"You are welcome," he said, and strangely, I felt the sincerity in it. The foolish notion of kissing him passed through my mind for a brief moment, but the idea of scraping my lips on the stonework killed that thought. Luckily, Bricksley interrupted us, his tiny form carrying more pieces of stone over to me. I took the latest batch from his tiny arms, patting him on his "head." Without another word, I set about repairing as much of Stanis as I could, finding that with repetition I was grinding my teeth together the same way I had when first using my newfound Spellmason skills to push back all the rubble at the building collapse site. I worked until I had an aching jaw and all that was left was the yellow gemstone we had reclaimed from the old church.

"I should probably take care of this now," I said.

"Very well," Stanis said, seeming in better spirits now that much of his body had been restored.

I flipped through my great-great-grandfather's arcane tome until I found the words that I was looking for. I pressed both hands against the gargoyle's chest, focusing myself on the task at hand. Power poured out of me, causing the pattern hidden beneath his chest to snake to the surface and reveal itself. The gemstone fit perfectly into one of the two remaining spots there, and I held it in place while I used the rest of the spell to bind it there. The fitting took, the stone locking in place before disappearing as the rocky inner coils wove in on themselves until the pattern was once again hidden beneath the surface of his skin. Stanis's eyes slammed shut, and he fell to his knees, shaking the floor, which I hoped wouldn't bring my family running.

"Stan . . . ?" I asked, kneeling down in front of him. His wings spasmed out and away from his body, knocking everything from the worktable next to us, sending the book flying.

"I am all right," he said through clenched teeth. "These . . . restorations do not get easier."

My phone rang across the room on the drafting table where I had left it, vibrating toward the edge. I looked back at Stanis. "You going to be okay?"

He nodded as he attempted to settle his wings, but they remained flapping in a wave of spasms. "It will pass," he said, but the look on his face didn't seem too sure about that.

I ran and grabbed my phone seconds before it slid off the table's edge. *Unknown*, the ID read. "Hello?"

"Alexandra," the strange deep voice said, but the singsong way it came out left little doubt as to whose it was.

"Hello, Devon."

"The news was reporting a gargoyle sighting tonight near the collapse of that nightclub Cathedral," he said. "What have you and your friend been up to exactly?"

"Nothing that need concern you," I said.

"Your public antics are making the Servants very antsy, dear sister. My masters *need* the rest of those books. Kejetan has waited centuries, but now that his faithful Servants keep *dying*, he knows he's close and his patience is wearing thin. He's pressing me to give him the secrets I promised in exchange for eternal life, Lexi. The books I stole aren't enough. I'm a good negotiator and a good staller, but I can't hold them off forever. They want good old Alexander's arcane secrets."

I was livid. Since my brother had told me about the books in his possession on the ship, I had confirmed that indeed three were missing that tied into my quest for the Revelation of the Soul, specifically the threads leading to finding the Heart of the Home. For too long I had put off figuring out how I could reclaim those books, focusing instead on finding the second and third soul stones with the knowledge I already possessed, but this call from my brother was a painful reminder that I could delay no longer. I needed to get those three books back.

On top of that I couldn't help but recall the circumstances under which I had learned Devon was still alive, bringing all my anger back to the surface again like a flash of lightning. "Calling to threaten me some more?" I asked, trying to do some stalling of my own. "I haven't found them yet." Although if I found the fourth stone, somehow reclaimed the stolen books to restore Stanis, and could finally figure out enough about how he ticked, I had every intention of using those secrets myself to crush my brother and the Accursed Lord.

A noise came over the line, and it took me a moment to realize that it was my brother's heinous new form of sighing. "Listen, Lex. It's a wonder I could even dial a phone with this body of mine right now, okay? It's like trying to call you using bricks on the keypad."

I tried to imagine it but couldn't without picturing his rock-like form using one of those giant phones for old people with the massive number buttons on them. "I need more time to find them, monster," I said.

"Don't be like that, Lex," Devon said with a gravelly chuckle. "What did you want me to do at our last meeting? Give you a big hug? Besides, *you* set your gargoyle on *me*, forcing me to beat him down. You want me to apologize for protecting myself?"

"Screw you, Devon," I said. "You were a piss-poor brother in life. You sold out the family for your own purposes. The only person you're protecting is the tyrant who's behind this old blood vendetta."

"Time is running out, little Lex. We want those books."

"I'm not giving you the books, Devon."

"You don't understand," he said, his voice changing, becoming ultra serious and a whisper now. "I *need* them. They're going to kill me if you don't bring them, Alexandra. You have to either find them or else get me the hell out of here. I'm losing what little bargaining power I had when I first agreed to all this. They *will* kill me."

"Didn't they already do that to you once?" I asked.

"This is not the time to joke," he said. "They mean to destroy this body I'm in rather than let me be completed once we have those stolen arcane secrets back. Without that hidden knowledge, I think they mean to break me down so they can see how I work if they don't get them. All they want are the books."

"I'm not giving them," I said. "I'm sorry. I can't allow them to have that power."

"Then you have to help me! They won't let me leave this ship." There was a near-histrionic quality to my brother's voice that I had never heard out of him in life. The sound wore hard against my heart.

"Fine," I said, thinking up a plan on the fly, one that might both save my brother and help me find the last soul stone for the Revelation of the Soul. "I'll help you, but I'm not just going to give them what they want. And I want the books you took from our great-great-grandfather's library."

He lowered his voice to an even more hushed whisper. "Okay, okay. What are you going to do?"

"I'm coming to get you," I said. "It'll be after sundown tomorrow. Try to stay alive until then, all right? I'll bring help. Don't worry."

"I have to go, before one of the people on board find me making this call," my brother said. "But . . . thank you, Alexandra. I know I was never an easy brother to get along with."

Sincerity and my brother didn't go well together, just making me feel awkward. We'd see how he'd be after I liberated him. "You can thank me once we get you out of there," I said.

He laughed. "All right, then," he said. "Hurry! They've already got me on lockdown. I don't know how much longer until they try to dissect me."

"We'll be there," I said. "Stay strong."

I hung up. Stanis had worked himself up from his knees and stood tall once more, his wings pulled in close to his body. "Where will we be on our way to?"

"To rescue my brother," I said. "I've bought myself a day to rally Rory and Marshall, a day to plan an attack, all four of us hitting the boat this time."

"Rescue?" he asked. "We are going to save the one who tried to crush my neck in? Why would we do that?"

"Because he's my *brother*," I said. Whatever I had restored in Stanis, I found it interesting to see him asking questions about things that had personally wronged him, something indicative of having restored a greater part of his personality. "Because most importantly, he can help us once we free him. He knows the enemy, and once we get back the books he stole, I think I can restore you to your full power. And hopefully *that* will give us a way to stop them. So we're going to get him."

"Very well," he said, and fell silent.

Between nightclubs collapsing, repairing gargoyles, restoring personalities, and talking to my brother, I needed to collapse myself. There was no way I was going to plan out our rescue tomorrow without my beauty sleep.

Thirty

Alexandra

I got a solid eight in, had a big, hearty breakfast, then ignored day-job stuff the entire day as I looked for things throughout my great-great-grandfather's whole library that might prove of some use in rescuing Devon. I texted Rory and Marshall the details, stressing how ass-kickingly important this was to make sure they'd show on time, and I had just finished charming necklaces of their own when I realized the sun was going down. The charge in the talismans wouldn't last forever, but I hoped it would be enough to get us on the boat unnoticed. I heard Stanis come to life out on the terrace, and after double-checking my backpack, we were off.

The gates of the Brooklyn shipyard, locked at night, were nothing when you had a gargoyle in tow. Stanis landed us on the inside of them and we hid among the stacks of cargo containers near the main entrance while we waited for Rory and Marshall to show. Ten minutes later, a cab dropped them off a block away and they skulked down the street toward us. Their skulking was so obvious I had to laugh.

"Go get them, please," I said to Stanis, "before someone calls the cops on Mr. and Mrs. Obvious."

Stanis nodded, then leapt up into the air in flight, arcing

high above and coming down behind them. He wrapped an arm around each of them. Rory startled but remained quiet, but Marshall let out a yelp that sounded like a small dog barking. Stanis rose, gliding soundlessly back over the fence, and extended his wings fully to bring all three of them down softly. It amazed me how utterly graceful stone could be in motion.

"Thanks, Stanis," I said, as he walked over to me. Marshall and Rory were busy pulling themselves back together, Rory adjusting a strap across her chest that connected to an artist tube on her back like the one I owned. I looked up at the gargoyle. "Now I want you to position yourself on the highest point of the ship. You're our backup."

"Backup?" Marshall asked, nervous laughter escaping him. "Why don't we just send him in first? Then we can mop up after him."

"I told you what happened here last time I brought him," I said. "Even my brother was stronger than him. In a straight fight, we're screwed. That's why we need to go in stealthy and use him only as backup."

I reached into my bag, pulling out the two charms I had made earlier.

"*You* get a talisman," I said in my best Oprah voice, "and *you* get a talisman."

"Thanks," Marshall said. "Does this have Protection from Evil on it?"

"It should make you a little stealthier in there," I said. "I wouldn't test out what the line is by running out waving your arms at anyone we find on board, but it should help. Not sure how long it will last, but it's something."

Rory put hers on but her eyes were looking over at Stanis. "You sure you don't want to go gargoyle first?"

"I do not mind dying," he said, "if it would mean your safety."

My stomach clenched at the words, and I surprised myself by finding tears fighting to leave the corners of my eyes, but I held them back. "I appreciate that," I said, turning away. "But let's try our sneaky approach first, okay?

"They're expecting you to be our first line of attack, but that's not what we're giving them. We need to rescue Devon. He promised us the three books he stole from Alexander's library and we need them back to help us with finding the last soul stone and answering some of the questions I have on the Spellmasons and alchemy. Then I'll be able to build . . . more of you to defend us." I blushed a little, trying to ignore the fact I caught myself avoiding the word *companion*.

"As you wish," he said. He hesitated as if he might say more, and I secretly hoped he would, but after a moment he leapt up into the sky and was gone.

Rory undid the strap across her chest and took the artist's tube from her back, unscrewing the end of it. She pulled two short lengths of wood—one plain and one with a hooked blade at the end of it—and snapped them together where they met at a metal coupling. She slung the empty tube back across her body. The pole arm twirled through the air in front of her before she set it down, the bladed tip up.

"Holy crap," I said, pulling her into the shadows of the cargo containers so the light didn't shimmer off the blade. "You actually found a pole arm."

I turned to check the nearby boat docked there, the one I had been on with Stanis the other night and Rory a few days earlier. Other than the movement of crew members up on deck, there didn't seem to be any awareness of us.

"I had a little help," she said, jerking her thumb at Marshall, "but yeah. I told you I'd get one. You have no idea how good that one at the museum felt in my hand."

Marshall gave a small smile. "I know a guy down in Chinatown who does all the weapons for the Tuxedo Park Ren Faire. My group uses him, too, although this weapon hasn't been dulled down like the ones we use for LARPing."

"LARPing?" I asked. "Do I want to know?"

Rory waved a hand at me. "Don't get him started on live-action role playing," she said. "He'll spend an hour talking about his character and how his friends dress up and act like they walked off the set of *Lord of the Rings*."

"You said you wanted to know," he said to her, hurt.

"When we first became roommates and I asked, I was just being *polite*," she said. "I didn't think you were going to actually embark on a whole lecture series on gaming culture."

"Guys!" I said in a hushed whisper. "By all means, keep it up. Let's really lose the element of surprise here."

The two of them fell silent. Marshall joined me, checking the ship out for himself, then turned to Rory. "You're not going to use the pointy end, are you?" Marshall asked.

Rory shrugged as she looked where we were focused, her eyes shifting among the signs of movement on the boat. "Depends, really."

"Those guards," he said, pointing. "They're *human*."

"So?" she said, her eyes narrowing. "These people aren't the same as the ones at the museum. Those people were just doing their job, protecting art. But these minions here, well, they're . . . minions, in league with our enemies. If I see one of those hand tattoos or a white-handled knife, I'm not holding back on any of those Servants of Ruthenia assholes. If they get in our way, they've earned what they get."

Marshall didn't argue, and neither did I. Getting my brother out of there, grabbing the missing books, and restoring that fourth soul stone were all that mattered at this point. Then we might really get to the bottom of why they were after my family. Still, the less bloodshed, the better.

"Try to avoid using the sharp end . . . if you can," I suggested. "Ready?"

Marshall sighed. "I haven't been ready for *any* of this," he said.

I squeezed his shoulder. "You've been doing fine," I said. "You brought rope. You got us through the museum; you even found the chest . . . You, sir, are a brilliant tactician."

"Just leave the fighting to me," Rory said, tapping her pole arm on the dock. "And the gargoyle, if it comes to it."

I reached out with my mind at the mention of Stanis, feeling the pull of him nearby, but I immediately forced myself to remain focused. "Just keep an eye out for any of the books from my great-great-grandfather's library," I reminded them.

"Will do," Marshall said, seeming to snap out of it with a

strong-armed salute with his fist across his chest. "And you try not to be crushed by giant rock men."

"I will definitely try not to," I said. "Let's go."

Old abandoned docks at night were an almost perfect place for sneaking around, once I got over the sheer creep factor of it. There were plenty of shadows and hiding places among unloaded shipping containers, and Rory started for the docking tower and its gangplank, but I stopped her. The direct approach hadn't paid off so well last time. The ship itself was long enough that it was easy to find a spot along its side that was unlit, and that was where I led my two friends. Marshall dropped to his knees and rummaged through his bag, pulling out a thick coil of rope.

"Ha!" he said. "Rope, bitches! Paid off twice! And you mocked me . . ."

He stood, twirling one end of it, and after several attempts, he got it over the railing of the ship that sat about thirty feet above us. He worked the line until the other end came all the way down to us and he began knotting them together.

"You are *not* serious," Rory whispered, giving an uneasy look up the side of the ship.

"Hey, you're a dancer," he said. "You've at least got a shot at it. I failed climbing the rope at gym class, but I don't see any other way to do it."

"We could have used the gargoyle," she said.

I looked up and down the dock, but Marshall was right. Other than walking up the gangplank past the crew, we weren't getting on any other way. "We can do this," I said, feeling a rush of adrenaline hit me. "We don't need Stanis for everything. We can do this."

"You first, then," Rory said, collapsing her pole arm back down to slide it into the artist's tube.

"Fine." The sheer challenge in her words made me determined. I checked the straps on my backpack, then wrapped my arms and legs around the rope. The tension in my arms was intense, but I started up the rope while repressing the thought that I might just slip down into the ice-cold November ocean water below. My arms burned by the time I reached the railing, but I still took time to make sure the coast was clear before hefting myself up over it.

Rory came up next, having a much easier time of it, but when it came to Marshall, it quickly became evident we were going to have to help him. He clung to the line like a tensed-up yo-yo at the end of its string, and we had to pull him up. His hands clenched white-knuckled over the railing and he pulled himself up over it, landing on the deck of the ship hard. I looked around, but with all the other sounds out on the water, we hadn't drawn any attention.

We took a moment to gather up the rope and for Rory to put her pole arm back together before making our way down into the bowels of the ship. Navigating around the comings and goings of the crew was easy enough. We could hear them approaching from a mile away and there were plenty of corridors clearly meant for the passage of the large stone men that we could hide ourselves away in. My memory of what led where was still fairly fresh, just not wholly accurate, but soon enough we found ourselves back in their makeshift throne room, which I had barely taken in when it was full of stone men. Thankfully this time it was empty, at least for the moment. Several oversized tables sat in the center of the room with piles of books in a variety of languages spread out all over them.

"These have seen better days," Rory said as she ran her fingers over the gouged and scratched-up wood of the tables.

"You try flipping pages with rocks for fingers," I said, starting through one of the piles. "Let's hurry. Then we can find my brother."

The three of us tore through the books scattered across the table, Marshall and Rory pausing every now and then to show me one when they weren't sure what to make of them. After several minutes of searching, I came across a familiar title mentioned in my great-great-grandfather's notebook. "Found one!" I said, and scooped it up into my arms.

"Awesome!" Rory said, continuing her search.

"Great," Marshall said, moving to the next table. "Two to go!"

A third voice called out in a language I almost recognized, something Slavic, but I doubted it held any level of congratulations in it. Two men had appeared at the doorway we had come through and they called out into the corridor behind them.

"Shit," I said.

"Keep looking," Rory said, dropping the book in her hands and scooping up her pole arm from the edge of the table. "I'll keep them busy."

"Thanks," I said, but she was already running across the room, swinging the weapon around her in an ever-widening circle. She struck one of the men with the blunt end of the pole, knocking him over, but five more poured into the room behind him.

"Help her," I said to Marshall.

He looked up at me, stopping his search with two books in his hand. "How?!"

"Improvise," I said, and continued on, my hand landing on a promising book. I flipped the cover open to see Alexander's familiar handwriting. "That's two. One more . . ."

Marshall still looked stunned not knowing what to do, then looked at the books in both of his own hands. He hefted them, feeling their weight, then turned to the men streaming into the room. He posed like some sort of book-wielding ninja, then launched the books. One hit the wall next to one of the men uselessly, but the other caught a corner against another one's head, drawing blood and knocking him down.

"Holy cats!" he shouted, then grabbed a couple more books before charging forward. I couldn't watch anymore. I had to find the third book.

The sounds of battle raged from the far end of the room as I continued my search. It grew as I continued on, and, feeling the press of time, an idea struck me. I called out one of the lesser spells I had memorized, directing it at the table in front of me, the same one that had helped me turn my great-great-grandfather's secret tome to and from stone. As I spoke them, I searched the table for any signs of change and was rewarded when a dark blue bound book reacted, shifting into a gray slate state.

"Found it!" I shouted, pulling the heavy book free from the pile. Now that my head was no longer lost in the tables full of books, my heart wanted to pop out of my chest. Twenty or so men had come in since I had looked up last, and I found myself backing away toward the farthest wall. Rory, to her credit, was holding her own, but the odds were against her and decreasing every second, and from the sound coming down the hall, the stone men were en route.

Well, stone *man*, anyway. Stanis came through the door, popping his wings to the fullest and using them to take down several men at once. Marshall backed off from the pile of books he had been using at the end of the farthest table, turning and running toward me. Rory had to dance herself around several of the men Stanis had flung aside, but she was nimble enough it almost looked choreographed, violent poetry in motion.

"Something's not right," I said, trying to assess the situation.

"You notice something?" Marshall asked, joining me against the wall. "What is it?"

"I'm noticing lots of things," I said as I watched Stanis crumple another guard to the ground with one of his clawed hands. "Anything specific?"

"Rory!" Marshall called out. "To us!"

Two men stood between us and her. She drove the pole arm into one of them like a joust charge, toppling him onto his back. She continued forward, planting it like a pole-vaulter and gracefully launching herself feetfirst into the second man. They slammed with force into his chest and she righted herself midair, her last steps toward us a landed, stumbling jog.

"What?" she asked, winded.

"Notice anything odd about this fight?" I asked.

Rory looked around. "Yeah," she said with a smile. "We're winning. A girl could get used to this."

"That's part of it," I said, "but not all."

"Where are all the stone men?" Marshall asked, getting it. "Exactly!"

"They're not here," Rory observed, stating the obvious.

"None of them," I said. "Not my brother. Not the men he said were threatening him."

"So where are they, then?" Rory asked.

"I have no idea," Marshall said.

"I do," I said. "They're *with* my brother."

"And where is he?" he asked.

"On his way home," I said.

"What?" Rory shouted. "On Gramercy?"

I nodded, my face turning red, a combination of anger and embarrassment. "He didn't call me here to save him," I said. "He called to distract us."

Thirty-one

——— 🌙 ———

Stanis

After the maker's kin told Marshall and Aurora to hurry back to the Belarus building as quick as they could, Alexandra and I flew off across the night sky back toward Manhattan, over the river. Anger and frustration radiated from the woman like a fire as she sat cradled in my arms with one of her newly acquired books clutched to her chest. It took much of my concentration to keep her emotions from washing through and taking over my own senses, making flight more difficult, and I found myself fighting not to swerve like a leaf blowing in a storm. I pushed my heavy wings hard for a few seconds to gain more height before finally stretching them out to their full extension and steadying myself into a controlled glide.

"Alexandra," I said, looking down at her grim face. "Please. You must relax yourself. Unless you wish us both to fall into the river. Your mood is . . . distracting."

"Sorry," she said. "I'm just so pissed at myself."

"Why is that?"

"Because I fell for it," she said. "Here I was racing to help my brother, and all the while he was playing me. I'm a fool."

"You are, perhaps, being far too judgmental about your own actions," I said as I fought to keep control of my glide.

Alexandra laughed. "You mean I'm being too hard on myself."

"You are not the 'fool' you say you are," I said. "Your frustration with yourself speaks more of the good in you and the ill in him more than anything else."

"That is some small comfort," she admitted, pulling the book away from her chest, attempting to read it by the light of the moon. "Still, if they get to the building before us and my family comes to harm over Alexander's alchemy notes and books . . . I'll never be able to bear it."

I felt her trying to lessen her frustration, making my flight easier, and I pushed my speed until I was just beyond the river and heading past the bridge they called Manhattan.

"Fly over the building first, please," she said. "We'll look for signs of forced entry, then straight to Alexander's library and studio. If they're looking for his notes and books, that's where my brother would take them first."

"As you wish," I said, and angled myself toward the growing patch of green of Gramercy Park, darting down between the buildings as I came in low over it. Scanning the building showed no signs of forced entry and I landed on the terrace, Alexandra lingering in my arms before stepping down and heading through the French doors into the library.

No signs of chaos or sounds of conflict came from within, but that did not relax her. Her backpack was off and she pulled out the secret tome along with the three newly acquired books, which she spread out over one of the worktables of the art studio. Somehow she was managing to consume all of them at the same time while frantically taking notes in her own notebook. I made sure that the little one called Bricksley did not tread across the books as he tried to join her on top of the table.

A short while after, the groan of strained metal arose from outside and Alexandra looked up from her work, running back out to the terrace. Before I could reach the edge of it myself, a figure came into view coming up the fire escape. One of the malformed monstrosities from the ship.

"Do something!" Alexandra called out, peering over the edge. She held up her notebook. "If I can restore you with the last stone, you'll have the power Alexander hinted at in his books, our only chance to beat them, but I need time to find the Heart of the Home. Deal with these monstrosities. Please? There are more of them coming up!"

"As you wish."

Alexandra smiled, then looked down and flipped through the book as fast as she humanly could, continuing her search.

I turned to my foe out on the terrace. "You cannot stop us," the one coming up off the fire escape said. "We are the Servants of Ruthenia, and we are stronger."

"You are *nothing* like me," I growled, stepping up to him.

"Yes, we are," he said, confidence in his very tone.

"We are *not* alike," I said, spreading my wings wide. "For one, I have these."

The stone figure paused and laughed. "So? We are stronger."

"So *this*." I shoved at him with all my might, sending him flying straight through the railing. The creature tumbled down through the night sky, end over end, its cries ending with a shattering *crack* on the pavement below.

The broken railing pulled away from the rest of the fire escape as its mounting tore loose from the weight of the men of stone coming up from below becoming too much for it. It broke free from the building, sending the other creatures tumbling with it, save one close one who dug into the stone of my forearm. I shook my arm back and forth, but the stubborn thing refused to let go, and it quickly became clear that if he were to fall, I would end up going with him.

I dug the claws of my feet into the terrace stone and stepped back from the edge, using my wings to bring the creature up. I fell back with it toppling on top of me, but I refused to let it have the advantage. Rolling, I got the struggling creature under me, only to see Alexandra's tiny servant Bricksley get crushed under it.

"No!" Alexandra cried out, but there was nothing I could do, and given the superior strength of these abominations, I would not keep the upper hand long unless I acted.

I drove the pointed tips of my wings into its shoulders, stone digging through stone. Raising both arms, I joined my fists together and brought them down hard onto its head. Although I met solid resistance, the blow still managed to shoot chips of stone out all across the terrace.

My enemy went still for a moment, but not any longer than that. He bucked up at me, tossing my body up in the air. If it had not been for my wings settled into the stone of his shoulders, I would have gone flying, but they held fast in place. I came down hard on the creature, my body driving the fight out of him as I landed. Hands still raised, I brought them down again and again on his head. With each strike, larger chunks of stone broke away until there was little left but a pile of crumbled rocks and dust.

When I could finally take my focus away from my now-lifeless enemy, Alexandra was standing in silence, clearly shaken. Her nerves tumbled into me, and I stood. "I am sorry you had to see that," I said, then realized that while I felt her nerves, there was no fear or horror behind them. "I am sorry for your servant. As well."

"It's all right," she said. "He went down swinging. And when I watched you destroy that creature . . . I can . . . feel you now, a part of why you do what you must. That bond you've been feeling protecting me, the one formed by my restoring parts of you . . . It seems to work in reverse. There was no hate in what you did. Only duty."

She looked like she wanted to say more, but I nodded my head once, closing my eyes, then turned to look out into the night sky. "Maybe a little hate," I said. "After all, I am becoming more in touch with my humanity, but we were lucky just now. I could not have fought them all."

"Hopefully you won't have to," she said, holding up her notebook. "I think I've found what I needed out of the three books. I've written down everything I think I need to find the last gemstone for the Revelation of the Soul." She ran to the edge of the balcony and looked down.

I joined her by the remains of the fire escape.

"They're gone," she said.

"No," I said. "Not gone. Merely regrouping. They did not cross an ocean to get here to be so easily turned away. Not with what they seek out so near."

Alexandra spun, then ran into the building, going straight for her spread-out books. "If they're regrouping, then that means they're going to take the easy way in now."

"Which means—"

"They're coming in downstairs," she said, and as if to confirm it, a cacophony of sound rose from the back of the building, coming up through the shaft of the elevator.

"They're messing with the elevator," she said, grabbing up her backpack, notes, and Alexander's tome. She ran for the elevator, but I was quicker to it.

I came to the doors seconds ahead of her, pressing my claws into the thin seam in the middle of them. They did not want to give, but I made them. Dark open space met us, a series of thick wire cables running down. The sounds of metal being crushed filled the entire shaft, forcing Alexandra to cover her ears.

"They know they're going to have trouble dealing with us so they're going to hit us where we're weakest," she said, her face filling with horror. "My parents."

The first rule—*protect the family*—flared at the center of my mind. Without another thought, I grabbed Alexandra, pulled her close to me, then stepped into the empty elevator shaft.

Thirty-two

Alexandra

My stomach sank as we fell, Stanis pulling his wings around me before crashing through the roof of the elevator below. Metal crunched under Stanis's feet as we landed, and despite him slowing us with the drag of his wings before punching through the elevator's roof, my shoulders ached from where he had been gripping me.

When he unfolded the heavy stone wings from around my body, I saw we were inside the crumpled remains of the elevator car itself. The gargoyle set me down, then tore open the broken doors of the car, tossing them aside like they were made of paper. Making sure not to cut myself on anything jagged, I worked my way out of the shaft and into the main living quarters on our family floor. I pulled out the compiled notes in what I thought of as my book of arcane knowledge now, then tightened the straps on my backpack before running down the main hall in search of either my family or trouble, most likely both.

The trail of destruction along the way made it easy to follow as I stepped over broken chairs and knocked over piles of my father's hoarded newspapers and magazines. The sound of commotion rose up as I approached the dining room and kitchen at the other side of the building, and my stomach tightened. I readied one of the binding spells I had learned while creating Bricksley, one that had rendered his stone form inert when I'd wanted it to. I only hoped I had enough force of my own will to render some of these creatures the same.

I rounded the next corner, stepping into our kitchen with Stanis coming in behind me, his wings tucked close to his body so he could get around the overturned dining table in his path. My eyes sought out a target while I incanted all but the final words of my spell. Movement—figures standing in the doorway at the opposite side of the room. I let my will go as I completed the incantation, forcing my words of power in that direction.

Only it wasn't the stone men or my parents. My friends stood there—Rory with her pole arm at the ready and Marshall holding one of my great-great-grandfather's statues from the back hallway—a centaur. The figure exploded into a cloud of dust as my spell hit it and the two of them jumped.

"Christ!" Marshall cried out, counting his fingers. They were covered with a fine gray dust, but other than that, they all seemed to be accounted for. "Watch it with that stuff, will you?"

Rory ran across the kitchen and hugged me. "We got here as quick as we could," she said. "We were worried."

"I still am," I said, hugging her back just as hard. "I went through the three new books, though. There's a lot to learn, but I think I know where the fourth soul stone is. I was piecing it together when those things tried to come up the outside of the building, but Stanis here knocked them off."

"What does the Heart of the Home even mean?" Rory asked.

"I have an idea," I said.

"Your front doors were smashed in," Marshall said, joining us.

"So much for the warding on the house," I said. "Not that it would have stopped Devon from finding his way here."

Rory stopped hugging me and stepped back. "There was a smoke cloud pouring out of the elevator into the lobby so we followed a different path of destruction up the stairs past all the offices."

"We were following a path of our own from the elevators around this floor," I said, "but we didn't see anything, other than you two."

"So where are they if not here?" Stanis asked.

"There's only one other way *to* go," I said, and ran off to the back hall, the last piece of my great-great-grandfather's puzzle falling into place. "To the Heart of the Home, of course."

Thirty-three

Stanis

Alexandra, Marshall, and Rory led the way into the depths of the building.

"Where are you taking us?" I asked. "I do not feel much comfort in going into a more confined space. I cannot protect you as well."

Aurora tapped the end of her weapon on one of the stone steps. "We stand a fair chance of protecting ourselves, you know."

"If you think to take down these men of stone with a mere bladed stick, then you are in for a harsh awakening," I said. "I was hard-pressed to hold my own against Alexandra's brother."

"For the record," Marshall said back over his shoulder, "I'm okay with the gargoyle trying to keep us safe as a first line of defense."

"Shh!" Alexandra whispered from up ahead of us. "We need to stay quiet from now on. We're going to need the element of surprise if we stand any chance of getting my parents away from them."

"If they're down here," Marshall added.

"Trust me," she said. "If my parents heard intruders, they

would have run for the catacombs. Especially my father. At any time of stress, he'd prefer a place to pray, and what better place than in our own private cemetery?"

"Catacomb?" I asked. "Cemetery?"

Alexandra looked up at me in wonder. "It's where we bury those of us who have passed on," she explained. "You've never been down here, have you?"

"Actually," I said. "I have."

Alexandra stopped. "You have?"

"Yes," I said. "I do not fully understand your custom of burial, but sometimes I would come and rest here among the carvings of *grotesques*. There was a comfort in it. Other times I merely came down here to watch over you."

Alexandra smiled, the warmth of it filling me; then she turned and continued on.

The stairs continued farther, but we did not follow them lower, instead walking out among the graves on the first floor down. Voices came from farther along, Alexandra motioning for our group to slow as we approached. Up ahead I saw many of the creatures from my first visit to the freighter; among them were Alexandra's father and mother, the woman looking horror-struck, but not the father. Alexandra's brother was in the crowd, but he remained still, only watching the exchange going on between the humans and them.

"Your father does not look afraid," I said.

"Of course he doesn't," Alexandra said. "Why would he? He's been visited by an *angel*, remember? He believes in a better place. He's not afraid to die."

While most of the creatures made sure the two humans stayed where they were, there was a clear leader of the pack, a larger monstrosity whom I recognized. "Kejetan," I said.

"Hail, hail, the gang's all here," Marshall said, unenthused.

"We need to help your parents," Aurora said. "We need to strike!"

"Very well," I said, and moved to pass them, but Alexandra's hand on my arm stopped me.

"No," she said. "Not yet. We have to go."

Aurora looked at her in disbelief.

"Go? Now?" she whispered. "We have to help them, Lexi!"

"And we will," she said, looking through the new book of Alexander's she had brought down with us. "But the Heart of the Home isn't up here. I need to keep my promise to Stanis. I need to restore him . . . because it's important not just to him, but to me." She paused, almost unable to speak, as if the words were catching in her throat, tears at the corners of her eyes. She wiped at them, then turned to smile at me. "And hopefully we get the added advantage of Stanis returning to his full power."

My wings gave an involuntary flutter against my back, and I took a moment to still them. "I pray you are right," I said.

"I think I know where the final stone is," she said, then snuck her way past me back the way we had come, heading farther down the set of stairs there.

Aurora looked unsure, but nodded and followed after her friend, pole arm at the ready.

"I hope she's right," Marshall said before also heading down.

I hoped they were right as well. I did not relish the fight to come without being as whole as I could be.

When I reached the bottom of the stairs, the three of them were in conversation, waiting.

"I can be the bait," Marshall said. "I've got the skills for that. Annoying people, running away . . ."

"Maybe you should just stay out of harm's way," Aurora offered. "I don't want to look for another roommate . . . you know, if you get killed or anything."

"Touching," Marshall said, "but hear me out. We can't take these things on one by one, *but* we can outsmart them."

Aurora nodded. "Makes sense," she said. "They do have rocks for brains, after all."

"*I* have rocks for brains," I reminded her, unable to help the low, gravelly tone of my words.

Aurora rolled her eyes, then clapped me on the shoulder. "Yes, darlin', but you're refined. Not at all like those brutes. No offense meant."

"No offense taken," I said with a smile. "Thank you."

Alexandra smiled at me. "Let's get moving, Mr. Sophisticated," she said, and started off through this older section of the catacombs.

Aurora took off after her oldest friend and I did the same, Marshall running to catch up with us.

Marshall cleared his throat. "Very touching, really," he said, "but listen up. At least if you want to get through this . . . As I started to say, we don't have to match their brute force. We've got several advantages here."

"Such as . . . ?" Alexandra called back.

He stretched his arms to the side of the narrow walkway between the tombs. "We're in a confined space, which hopefully makes it harder for those big boys to fight."

"Me as well," I said, flexing my wings, which hit two of the columns near me, scraping against them.

"I'd rather we be able to slow a dozen of them down if we can," he said. "Sorry."

I looked across the space leading farther back into the catacombs. This bottom floor was different from the one above it, the construction older, the ceilings higher. I pointed up at them. "I may still be able to use this to my advantage," I said.

"Excellent," Marshall said before turning and grabbing for Aurora's pole arm, but her grip on it was strong. Unable to take it from her, he instead shook it in her hands for emphasis. "This is more than just a striking weapon. It can be used to trip them up by going for the legs, using it to throw their leverage off, to unbalance them. And when they're going down, maybe a few of them crack their skulls. I doubt the pointy end will do much good."

Aurora nodded. "Noted," she said. "Go for the legs."

"Hurry up," Alexandra called back to us from her now-considerable lead through the catacombs. "If my hunch is right, that's going to be awesome, but it still won't leave us much time."

The three of us picked up our pace as she led us deeper into the catacombs. The farther back we went, the more spaced out the tombs were until she stopped at one of them that sat along what I sensed was the back wall of the building.

"Welcome to the heart of the building," she said, and slapped her hand down on top of one of the tombs. The carving on the top of it was of a man at rest, lying with hands folded together at his waist. He wore an elaborately carved breastplate with knot work similar to that of his secret tome, and at the center of his chest was a single red gem resting above his heart. "Meet your maker."

I stood in silence, staring, expecting him to sit up, the carving so lifelike. Seeing his face next to Alexandra's, the resemblance was even stronger than my mind's eye had imagined it to be. Without opening any of the books, she laid her hand over the gem, whispered out an incantation, and the stone came free.

"Ready?" she asked. "This might be too much to bear, judging by how the other ones went."

The sounds of approach grew in my ears, but the humans registered no signs of hearing it. "They are coming," I said. "We must hurry." Alexandra turned her head to listen, but I touched her face with the smooth stone of my hand. "Now, Alexandra."

She pressed the stone in place against my chest, and without bothering to look to the notebook, she incanted the words as if she had always known them. The coil in my chest unwound one last time, her hands moving the gem quickly in place and letting the coil wind back around the last stone, something wild rising up in my body in response. The stones wove themselves into a new pattern, fresh pain filling me as the coiled stone paths within me changed. The shock of it drove me to my knees, and I dug my claws into the side of my maker's tomb to keep from falling over completely. A searing bolt rose from my chest to the center of my head, a white heat and light rising in me until I could no longer see. My sight was replaced by a flood of images at the center of my mind, rushing back in time to my earliest memories— those of my time with Alexander in old New York. The pain in my chest grew, tearing at the center of my thoughts, and a veil that lay across my memories lifted, pushing my mind further back to a time I had never recalled before, long before my time in Manhattan or even America.

Images of a green, foreign land washed over me. The trees and rolling hills were different from the ones of the city and its parks, a land of massive stone castles, lords, and servants. This, I could now recall, was Alexander Belarus's homeland, and at the thought of him, a specific memory hit me. Deep within the stone walls of a castle, my maker's face rose up before me, still wrinkled at the edges of his eyes but younger than I had ever seen before. I struggled to recall the circumstance of our meeting. So much was strange and new that I was having trouble sorting out all the differences, but before I could process all of it, the now-world forced itself back upon me, a familiar voice filling my ears.

"You ready for a rematch?" Devon, Alexandra's brother.

The voice was close, somewhere in front of me. I focused my mind past the wave of flooding memories to see his bulky stone form standing just on the other side of where Alexandra knelt before me. A rocky swarm of his fellow creatures was pouring into view every which way through the maze of tombs and columns all around us, but my eyes stayed on Devon, his rough and rocky face giving a sinister smile. "What? My first beating wasn't enough for you?"

"It is true I cannot hope to beat you on strength alone," I said, forcing myself back onto my feet through the still-burning pain of the last stone's placement in my chest. Alexandra stood as well, smart enough to step out of the way. "However, strength alone is not part of my plan."

Finding it difficult to concentrate through my fresh swirl of memories, I staggered. As I struggled to find my balance, Devon laughed. "No?"

"No," I said, then dashed toward him, spreading my wings as I went. Devon swung at my approach, but I was already rising above him. I grabbed his wrist, his arm still extended from the swing, and I pushed my wings for momentum as

I forced myself up. His feet left the ground and we rose despite his efforts to struggle free from my grip.

His free hand slammed against my shoulder, whole new levels of pain I was unfamiliar with filling me, but I pressed us higher to the top of the catacombs.

"You confuse me," I said. "You say you are Alexandra's family yet you do not act the part."

"Enough, Boy Scout," he said. "What do you know about mortals, anyway? You're just pissed that you're not unique anymore. You're not the only one who gets to live forever."

"Is that so important a thing?" I asked, truly wondering. "Living forever?"

"It is to me," he said, and drove the balled-up rock of his fist into my face.

Pain overwhelmed my senses, both that from the blow as well as more memories returning to me. *What did I know about mortals?* Fresh images of my time before the Americas came to me. My mind reeled as I realized they were *mortal* times. Human, the body of a young man, made of flesh and so fragile . . . and so broken, crushed, full of pain. The face of Alexandra's great-great-grandfather met mine in what struck me as the final moments of my days as a young mortal.

Devon brought me back into the moment at hand with another blow. My wings collapsed in around me, but I did not let go of him. Alexandra's brother and I spun in the air as we fell, the tops of the tombs below coming up fast. Despite the pain and disorientation, I forced my wings back open and took to the air before throwing his stone form up in front of me.

"If living forever at the cost of all others is your only goal, then there is no hope for you," I said, and struck into him with both of my clawed hands. His screams pierced the air as bits of stone tore away from him, the force of my blows spinning his body through the air, crashing him into one of the ornately carved columns. He collapsed against it, sliding down the side of it, but I grabbed him again, flying higher once again. "Your lack of remorse for your family makes this easier."

I tore at him with growing fury, each blow more vicious than the last, his cries of pain becoming weaker with every swipe.

Only the sensation of Alexandra's panic stopped me, her brother falling to the floor below, the bulk of his stone body snapping a large granite cross in two.

"Stanis!" she cried out. I looked down. Alexandra was fending off a circle of incoming stone monstrosities, keeping a tight ball of fallen debris flying around her defensively, bits of it flying out when an open target presented itself. Chunks of rock drove back stone men, but despite her valiant efforts, from up here it was evident that it was only a matter of time until the tide of battle turned. Numbers alone ensured that, and this fight could not be won in such a manner.

I tucked my wings in and dropped down hard with my full weight crushing one of the stone men. It sank to the floor and moved no more.

The room was full of the stone legion, and I found my two other friends in the thick of the fight with them farther out in the catacombs. Aurora was using Marshall's suggestion, toppling many of her foes with the shaft of her pole arm, piles of them clogging the aisles. Marshall himself worked his way through the maze of columns and tombs, leading his foes back to her, but there were too many on him and he was dead-ended against the back wall of the building. Rory ran to him, tripping up several of the stone men in the process, but the pole arm stuck between the legs of the last one she went for and snapped in two. I checked Alexandra again, whose own fight was waning, the circle of debris flying around her thinning out and losing some of its momentum.

I dove back into the fray, getting between her and several of the approaching stone men, their larger leader watching at the back of their group with Alexandra's parents each in one of his enormous stone hands.

"Let them go, Kejetan," she said, the name driving a spike into my overwhelmed mind.

"Give up," said the massive stone form menacing Alexandra, but she stood her ground, my pride in her strength growing.

That name and that voice . . . so familiar now. I pressed my newfound memories, going back further until Kejetan's rocky body appeared in them looking more whole than it did now—less broken, jagged, and chipped away.

The memory began to take shape—the night my mortal form had died, I realized. The night I was broken. Both this creature and Alexander Belarus had been there.

"You cannot hope to win," Kejetan continued, shaking the two human figures he held with both his arms, causing the woman to scream.

His words rang true, but the raw emotion and physical pain of my broken human form was too fresh in my memories now to simply give up. My panic, fear, confusion drove me and I threw myself back into the fight, needing to embrace the rules set upon me—*protect the family*. I grabbed the stone man to my left and threw him into one coming up on my right. Chips of rock flew from the impact of the two as they went tumbling, only to be replaced by two more.

I stepped toward Alexandra as she let her spell go, the floating debris all around her falling to the ground.

"He's right, you know," she whispered to me. "We can't win. I thought restoring your soul stones would make you more powerful."

I turned to her, feeling her own wave of raw emotion pouring off of her, mixing with mine. The familiar feel of Alexandra calmed me, helping my mind settle and sort through my new wealth of memories. "Perhaps it has," I said, surprised to discover I was already formulating a plan. "There are ways to win without physical consequences."

"Enough!" Kejetan said, walking forward, pulling the two humans along after him as they struggled to break free. "Long have I waited. Long have I sought Alexander, the betrayer who stole our most sacred secrets."

Alexandra stepped forward at the mention of him, defensiveness rolling off her. "My great-great-grandfather was a good and noble man! A Spellmason."

"He was a thief," Kejetan said. "He stole our books of secret knowledge for himself."

"Only to keep them from a mad king," I countered as my memories unfolded. "To keep them from men like you. The alchemy and spell magic in those books were far too much for those desiring power simply for power's sake. Alexander knew that." Flashes of the Spellmason filled my head—of him spending time with me as a mortal, teaching me like a son. But though Alexander had treated me as such, I was *not* his child, despite my desires. My own memories were those of a young man whose father was called the Accursed Lord. "Potent and terrible arcana you were looking to learn, all in a quest to live and rule forever. You even forced Alexander into a life of servitude, to better your hold on the land. When your only son took an interest in the alchemical arts, Alexander could have been cruel to him, but the Spellmason was stronger than that. He chose not to force the sins of the father onto the son. He laid no blame on the boy, training him and dearly loving the son as if he were his own."

"No," Kejetan said, a pained anger in his voice. "Alexander murdered my son and stole our knowledge!"

"The Spellmason did not murder your son," I said, my new memories still sorting themselves out. I pulled deeper into the events leading up to the death of my corporeal form that night at the castle. "Did you not cripple your own child by your very hand?"

"How dare—"

"You were impatient for power," I said, cutting him off. "So impatient you even made Alexander put you into that crude stone form before he had a chance to perfect the magic. Your own son begged you to wait, but you refused, further incensed by how strong a bond the boy was forming with the Spellmason. You could not control your mad greed or your jealousy and you lashed out, your son moving to protect Alexander. The strength of your blow in your new and monstrous form was enough to break him, to cripple your only son."

Kejetan became agitated, pain pouring out through his angered words. "This form was new to me," he said. "I could not yet control it."

"Your son's body was broken that night . . . by *you*," I said, feeling the agony of the past creeping over me. "Every second that followed what you did was pain for him."

"So Alexander thought to show him mercy and end that?" he asked, his anger growing. "It was not his right!"

"No," I said as my past returned to me. "He did show mercy, yes, but not by killing him. Alexander ended your son's suffering . . . by taking the boy's soul from that broken vessel, taking it away, and giving him a new life . . . in stone. He would not leave him there with as dangerous a man as you. If a lord would do that to his own son, who knows what would happen to others or even to Alexander's own family? Seeing the boy in that broken form, barely living, was unbearable for the Spellmason. He trapped the boy's soul, stole away in the night, gathered his family, and vanished from Kobryn and Lithuania for good."

"How . . . how do you know all this?" the ancient lord shouted. "Are these the sort of lies that Alexander filled his greatest creation with?"

"No. I was there, *Father*," I said, my body a mix of unfeeling stone and the pains of the past coursing through it. Was this what if felt like to be alive? I wasn't sure. There was, in fact, only one thing I *was* sure about. "I am Stanis Ruthenia, and I remember what you did to me that night."

Kejetan fell silent, unable to answer, and when he did his voice came out in a near whisper. "Stanislav?" he said, and I stared into the dark holes of his eyes. He stood silent for a long time. "It has been ages since I have thought upon that night . . ."

"I live," I said. "Thanks to Alexander."

"I spent years looking for him, for the man who betrayed me and my people," Kejetan said, his voice still quiet, lost in dark thoughts. "The one who stole our secrets."

My mind flowed with memories of the kind man who had built me, thoughts I had only glimpsed masked as strange dreams upon waking every night. "Alexander created me, taught me, was *kind* to me." I stepped away from Kejetan and moved toward my maker's tomb. "And he lies here, dust and bones, a threat to you no more. Leave these people be."

Kejetan's face turned to pain and he shook his head slowly, anger returning to his voice. "Alexander took much from me," he said, "and I *will* be repaid in blood. I will kill all of his kin for leaving me in this monstrous form for centuries."

I stepped back toward him, putting myself between him and Alexandra. "Whatever you perceive as the mistakes of Alexander are not the fault of these people," I said. I let my voice rise when I next spoke, its echo filling the tomb. "You will leave this family be."

Kejetan stood, unmoving, but shaking Alexandra's mother and father in his grip, causing them both to wince. "That is unlikely," he said. "I have searched too long for what is rightfully mine. I will not stay in this form any longer. I want our secrets back."

"You are going to leave here without harming anyone," I repeated. "Do you understand?"

"These people will die and then I will reclaim what belongs to my family. To *our* family." A sentimental madness filled his eyes.

"If you do not leave, it is at your own folly," I said, spreading my wings. "For I am bound to these people. Any move to harm them and I cannot help but defend them. You knew Alexander and what he was capable of. The binding of that Spellmason is strong. You cannot break it and I will be forced by the first rule to protect these people. I will fight until I am torn apart. It is what I am built to do. I will not be able to stop myself. With every last bit of my strength, I will die protecting them, until I crumble. Is that truly what you wish?"

I saw the conflict on my father's face as I stood there waiting, every second spread out like a century before me.

"I wish vengeance," he admitted, "but not at the price of my son. But I must have our secrets back."

The Belarus family would never be safe unless I could make him and his men of stone leave, and I could see only one way of that happening. I did something I had not known I was capable of right up until the moment I spoke.

"The secrets are in me," I lied. "Once Alexander put me in this form, he split my soul and hid it from me so I did not have to live with the constant pain of my memories, of what you did to me. In addition, he committed all of his arcane secrets to those stones as well. Now that I am restored, I will share them with you. You and your servants can be shaped and formed like me. I will leave here with you . . . *if* you leave this family alone."

The room fell silent for a long time, the only sound that of bits of crumbling architecture falling.

"Very well," he said.

Alexandra moved somewhere far behind me. "You're not going to believe that psychopath, are you?"

"We need more than just a 'very well,' " Marshall called over from where he stood with Rory.

"Your word will be your bond," I said. "Swear on it."

"I shall not seek vengeance on this house," Kejetan said.

"That will suffice," I said, and turned to Alexandra, walking back to where she stood alone. I took her hands in mine, the skin soft and soothing to me.

"You don't have my great-great-grandfather's secrets," she whispered, her eyes concerned. "Do you?"

"No," I whispered back, "but it will be some time before they figure that out. In the meantime, learn what you can. Rebuild what your namesake built for you. Prepare yourself."

"I didn't know you were capable of lying," she said.

"To tell the truth, neither did I," I said with a dark smile, "but it is still in service to the first of all rules, is it not? Protect the family."

Alexandra nodded, then pressed her forehead to the cool stone of my chest.

"There is one thing I must ask of you, however," I said, raising my voice for all to hear. "You must release me."

She looked shocked as if I had slapped her, stepping back. "I . . . I thought restoring you would have already done that," she said.

"The Servants of Ruthenia need to know that I am no longer under your control," I said. "You must release me."

She fell silent, squeezing my clawed hands. I could feel her shaking, and the connection we shared filled with sorrow.

"I don't know if I can," she said, her voice quiet, full of reluctance.

"Do it," Marshall called over. "For heaven's sake, Lexi, what's it even matter now?"

"It *matters*," she shouted, on the verge of tears. "What if I release him and then he becomes like . . . like them! What if he's got centuries of bottled-up anger out of being put into servitude by Alexander? What then?"

"I can speak for myself," I said, pushing as much calm into her as I could. "What your great-great-grandfather did for me, he did out of kindness. He could not stand what had happened to me. He instilled that kindness within me, making me this *grotesque* you see before you. That was his gift to me."

"You don't have to do this," Alexandra said, the pain radiating off her almost unbearable.

"I know," I said. "I wish to do it."

Alexandra nodded, then took a moment to compose herself. She looked into my eyes, wet with tears, and spoke. "I release you," she said.

"Louder!" Kejetan called out from behind me.

"Leave her be," I shouted, not taking my eyes from her. I went to let go of her hands, but she would not ease her hold.

"I release you," she said, louder this time, and then let her hands drop away from mine.

I smiled. "Thank you," I said, then whispered, "Prepare yourself. This does not end things."

She nodded, then wrapped her arms around me. Other than during flight, she had never done this, and I found a strange comfort in this most human of gestures. I returned it for a long moment, before letting go and turning from her.

I walked to my father, Alexandra's own father stepping in front of me. He was crying.

"I know you," he said.

"It is good to see you again," I said, and I could not help but smile. "Take care of her."

He nodded, then stepped aside.

"Let us go," I said to my own father, folding my wings in and stepping past him, not looking back. The sounds of painful groaning came from Alexandra's brother as the Servants of Ruthenia gathered him up, but I did not look back. With every step, I felt my connection to Alexandra fade, and if I gave in to my longing for it and didn't keep going now, the family would never be safe. The sounds of the silent procession behind me followed, and by the time I hit the stairs going up, I felt nothing at all.

Thirty-four

Alexandra

Free of invaders, the building felt empty, despite Rory and Marshall on either side of me on one of the couches up in the library. It felt twice as empty without feeling any connection whatsoever to Stanis, wherever he was now, probably on his way back to their floating kingdom in Brooklyn. The only small ray of sunshine in it all was discovering Bricksley still miraculously intact. The silence of the art studio would have been unbearable between the three of us without the sound of my little man's tiny feet tottering to and fro cleaning up the damage from the home invasion.

"I'm sorry," I said to my friends. "I feel like such a failure."

"On what curve exactly are you grading yourself a failure?" Marshall asked. "It's not like there's a job performance scale to judge any of this on."

Rory put her arm around me, squeezing. "At least we're alive. You did the right thing, Lexi. You freed him. You saved us—both of you did. That's no small feat. Look at me. They broke my pole arm! I was practically fighting with toothpicks there at the end."

"And they didn't get the book," Marshall added. "Stanis

saw to that. And by going with them, he bought us the one thing you *do* need—time."

Despite everything they were saying, compared to Stanis, I had barely done anything. I had restored him only to force upon him the most painful of memories, those of being the struck-down kin of a centuries-old madman. How he could bear all that sudden knowledge was a miracle. And how he could sacrifice himself still to keep me safe transcended even that. My heart felt like it would actually burst from the sheer selflessness of it all.

The sound of footsteps coming up the stairs at the back of the building had me up and off the couch, still on edge, but judging by their cadence, I needn't have worried. I simply wasn't used to the sound of my parents coming up here, especially since my father had insisted they go to church following the earlier incident in the catacombs.

"So this is where you spend all your time," my mother said, her eyes rolling over everything across the large expanse of the studio with deliberate adoration. She and my father crossed over to the three of us. "I forgot how beautiful a history this family has."

I nodded. "I didn't take up art just for the hell of it. Not sure about our beautiful history, though . . ."

My mother froze when she saw Bricksley waddle by with a giant chunk of twisted metal, adding it to a pile in the art studio. Despite his diminutive stature, my mother's eyes were filled with wariness.

"He's not one of those . . . *things*, is he?" she asked.

"Not one bit," I said, a small swell of pride rising up in me despite everything else I was feeling.

"He's one hundred percent Team Belarus," Rory said from the couch.

"Courtesy of your friendly neighborhood Spellmason," Marshall added, gesturing to me.

My father walked over to Bricksley, leaning down close to study him. "Fascinating," he said, turning to look at me with a sparkle in his eye.

I couldn't meet his and turned away. "How can you say

that?" I asked, feeling a bit of hysteria setting in. "None of this jives with your worldview. You'll tell the church, this'll get back to the Vatican, and the pope will probably set up a special secret council to contend with the seemingly demonic goings-on at stately Belarus Manor."

"We went to church seeking clarity," he said. "Relax, my little Alexandra."

I turned back, forcing myself to meet his eye. "How do you make your peace with this? With Stanis, alchemy, spell casting, what you might call witchcraft . . ."

"Because I've met your angel before," he said with a warm smile. "Long ago when he saved me, if you recall."

"You told me," I said, "how you thought God stepped in to save you from drowning under the ice in the Central Park reservoir, but that's not what happened at all. That gargoyle fished you out of the reservoir because Alexander Belarus took pity on a dying young man centuries ago, protecting him from his own crazed father and leaving him to watch over us. It's chemicals and arcana. God had nothing to do with it."

My father remained calm, which frankly surprised me. "You call it a gargoyle," he said with a shrug. "I call it an angel."

I shook my head, a little anger building in me and wanting to be clear here. "No, it's not an angel. It's a gargoyle, Dad. Trust me. A mortal man turned to stone to save his soul, given a new life by my great-great-grandfather."

My father's smile remained unchanged. He reached over and brushed my hair out of my face like I was a child again, his eyes lit up with a look I knew too well from him—he was humoring me. "Yes, yes, I know, my dear girl. But who are we to say that this is not part of God's plan?"

My mother took his arm and they headed off toward the stairs at the far end of the art studio. I didn't speak up. Why should I fight him on this? He had his faith, and nothing I could argue would change that. And I wasn't sure I wanted that, anyway. He looked happy, as if the weight of his child-hood trauma had been lifted off him with having seen his savior after so long a time. I'd easily take his happiness over my own desire to simply prove my point. In the end, who was right was ultimately immaterial.

"We will talk about finding a suitable replacement for the business side of things later," he said, stopping at the top of the stairs leading down. His words knocked the wind out of me harder than any blow I had received during the fight earlier.

"We will?" I asked, barely getting the words out.

He turned, both he and my mother smiling, a rare sight in recent years and a welcome one. "Of course," he said. "It seems the universe has more in store for you than I had planned, and clearly this is His will at work. Wouldn't I be the fool to stand in the way of it?"

"But they have Stanis," I said. "They've won."

He shook his head. "Have they? Alexandra, my dear, I do hope you've learned a little something in your time working with our holdings. The Belarus family did not get where it is by giving up in the face of adversity. Yes, I talk about the luck we've had, but it would seem with the resources at your disposal that maybe it's time you realize that sometimes we need to make our own luck when opportunity presents itself."

My fingers rose absently to touch the talisman around my neck as I watched the two of them descend back into our home proper.

I spun around, looking at Rory and Marshall. "Enough sitting around," I said.

"Considering my bone bruises and possible breaks, I'm good with sitting," Marshall said, not moving.

"Rory, help him up," I said, and didn't wait, heading instead to one of the book-covered worktables in the art studio section of the floor. By the time I had flipped open our newly recovered books and had my own notebook out, she had hobbled him over to me.

"Stanis gave himself over for our protection," I said, feeling a dash of hope in my heart. "Yes, because he was infused with rules telling him to, but in the end, he made choices based on his feelings, on his humanity. I won't let that be wasted now that I've restored it."

"But how?" Marshall asked.

"The more I learn, the more I learn there is to learn," I said, searching for a pen. "And Stanis didn't just hand himself over to save us. He said to prepare ourselves. As Marshall just said a minute ago, Stanis was both protecting the family and buying us time."

"Time for what?" Rory asked, but I was already picking my way through the books and scribbling down notes and reference numbers to the other books that were part of the grand Spellmason puzzle.

"Time for us to return the favor. To learn what I need to, to save him. To prepare for whatever Kejetan has in store. Mad men of power crave war. We need to be ready to bring him one."

Even though I no longer felt a hint of our connection, I prayed that somewhere out there he felt the hope I was feeling. Much like everything I'd learned so far, this was about the power of will, and right now, I felt like its patron saint.

About the Author

ANTON STROUT was born in the Berkshire Hills mere miles from writing heavyweights Nathaniel Hawthorne and Herman Melville. He currently lives outside New York City in the haunted corn maze that is New Jersey (where nothing paranormal ever really happens, he assures you).

His writing has appeared in several DAW anthologies—some of which feature Simon Canderous tie-in stories—including: *The Dimension Next Door*, *Spells of the City*, and *Zombie Raccoons & Killer Bunnies*.

In his scant spare time, he is an always writer, sometimes actor, sometimes musician, occasional RPGer, and the world's most casual and controller-smashing video gamer. He now works in the exciting world of publishing, and yes, it is as glamorous as it sounds.

He is currently hard at work on his next book and can be found lurking the darkened hallways of www.antonstrout.com.

Look for the latest Simon Canderous novel from
ANTON STROUT

DEAD WATERS

With Manhattan's Department of Extraordinary Affairs in disarray (forget vampires and zombies—it's the budget cuts that can kill you), Simon Canderous is still expected to stamp out any crime that adds the "para" to "normal." And his newest case is no exception . . .

A university professor has been found murdered in his apartment. His lungs show signs of death by drowning. But his skin and clothes? Bone-dry. Now Simon has to rely on his own powers plus a little help from his ghost-whispering partner and technomancer girlfriend—to solve a mystery that has the NYPD stumped and the D.E.A. shaken and stirred.

M786T1010